D1602993

FORTUNE'S SON

EMERY LEE

sourcebooks
casablanca

NOV 1 0 2011

SUPER ROMANCE

Copyright © 2011 by Emery Lee
Cover and internal design © 2011 by Sourcebooks, Inc.
Cover illustration by Aleta Rafton

Sourcebooks and the colophon are registered trademarks of
Sourcebooks, Inc.

All rights reserved. No part of this book may be reproduced in any
form or by any electronic or mechanical means including information storage and retrieval systems—except in the case of brief
quotations embodied in critical articles or reviews—without per-
mission in writing from its publisher, Sourcebooks, Inc.

The characters and events portrayed in this book are fictitious
or are used fictitiously. Any similarity to real persons, living or
dead, is purely coincidental and not intended by the author.

Published by Sourcebooks Casablanca, an imprint of Sourcebooks, Inc.
P.O. Box 4410, Naperville, Illinois 60567-4410
(630) 961-3900
FAX: (630) 961-2168
www.sourcebooks.com

Printed and bound in the United States of America
QW 10 9 8 7 6 5 4 3 2 1

To John, my first and only love

Contents

Prologue

PHILIP DRAKE, EARL OF HASTINGS, AWOKE TO THE cockerel's crow with the anguish of a thousand anvils ringing in his head. He shifted in his chair with a groan, his entire body feeling as if it had been pummeled. He blinked in confusion at the shambles of his surrounds. Broken glass covered the flagstones. His coat, cravat, and tie wig littered the floor.

When he inhaled, his stomach lurched from the pungent odor of brandy that had, since last evening, lost even the faintest appeal. He realized he'd never made it to his bed after—now regrettably—having knocked back nearly a full bottle of his favorite poison.

He shook his head to clear the cobwebs, but gasped, seizing it between tremulous hands, as the demons gleefully struck their hammers anew. Holding his body completely inert, he shut his eyes again, waiting for the reverberations to subside. The broken glass, the spilled brandy, all bore witness that it had not been

just some ghastly dream. The entire scene of the day
before replayed itself in his throbbing head.

He thoughtfully considered how little he knew of
his nemesis. Why had Roberts challenged him? Why
had he not dropped his gauntlet before another noted
turf man? March, Portmore, Hamilton, or certainly
Devonshire, could have covered such a wager with
barely a dent in their coffers. Had he been singled out?
He laughed bitterly to think a man of *his* vast experience
of the world could have been so completely gulled.

Having no answers to these questions, he resolved
to address the immediate problem of money, or,
better said, the lack thereof. He sat behind his desk
to compose two missives, the first to the mysterious
Roberts, with the hope of buying some time, and the
second to the Duke of Cumberland, who had long
coveted the Hastings's brood mares. He signed and
sanded the billets, impressing the wax seal with his
signet, and then rang for a footman to dispatch them.

By an unwritten code, a gentleman must settle
his debt of honor promptly. An obligation of this
magnitude might be granted three days' grace, but
even with such a reprieve, calamity hung like a noose
about his neck.

With a groan, he raked his hands through already
disheveled hair, racking his brain in desperation to
find some way out of this morass of... he finally
admitted... his own damned making.

෨෧

Midafternoon saw a speedy reply from the Duke of
Cumberland, with a summons to Palace House. Philip

knew it impolitic to refuse a royal invitation, though his mood was far removed from roistering with the duke and his racing cronies.

These votaries of the turf included the Dukes of Grafton, Bedford, Devonshire, and Ancaster, Lords Portmore and Chedworth, Sir John Moore, Captain Vernon, and others. The duke's cabal included some of the most powerful and influential men in the land, the horse racing, wine-tippling, debauching men-about-town who referred to themselves as the "Jockey Club."

Philip endured the hours-long bacchanal filled with ribbing over his defeat nursing his port, while bumper after bumper was tossed to the health of king and present company. After the mandatory salutes, dozens of bottles followed suit, swiftly emptied in inebriated encomiums to the swiftest horses and the fastest women.

While Lord Coventry extolled the alabaster skin of Miss Maria Gunning, the Duke of Hamilton followed with words of veneration for the statuesque figure of her sister Elizabeth. Lord Portmore marveled at the lively eyes of Mrs. George Pitt, until the toastmasters, with wigs now askew, cravats dangling, and waistcoats unbuttoned, finally degenerated into vulgar tributes to their mistresses and other "frail beauties."

"To the fair Fanny Murray," spoke Sir Richard Atkins, raising his glass in a poetic declamation. "A salute to a whore be only a farce, lest it praise milky white tits and a plump, ripe arse."

"Hear! Hear!" The room roared. Glasses clinked. Wine sloshed.

Rising in the spirit of one-upmanship, Captain Vernon followed with a lascivious leer, "To our lewd Lucy Cowper, pray she ne'er gets the pox, our purses would be fuller, but withered our cocks."

"Now there's a bloody poet for you!" The room rang with ribald guffaws.

"Alexander Pope may rest undisturbed," Philip remarked wryly to Sir John Moore, who was eager to join the debate whether Lucy Cowper, Fanny Murray, or Nancy Parsons should wear the crown as London's most coveted courtesan.

"Order! Order!" cried Sir John, rising from his seat and declaring in stentorian tones, "With such a dispute in the house, I move for a divide."

Philip's mind was far from the raucous revelry. Cumberland had purchased the mares. Although he knew he need not long await the duke's gold, it would still not be enough. Even full dispersal of the remaining racing stock might only bring half the sum he required to settle his immediate debts if his multifarious creditors were to call in his loans. His finances were already balanced as precariously as a house of cards, and one small breath of scandal over the racing wager would be enough to blow it all to hell.

Philip was pulled abruptly from his morose cogitations by the unexpected arrival of Prince Frederick. "Gentlemen, I am moved to forestall these proceedings."

"Insufferable prig," Cumberland murmured under his breath, but not quite low enough.

The prince scowled at his brother, the duke. "If you gentlemen are naming the toast of London, you overlook a most exquisite specimen of womanhood."

"Mayhap the Lady Hamilton?" someone sniggered. "He has certainly examined that specimen at close range."

Ignoring the remark, the prince took up his glass and cast a pointed look in Lord Hastings's direction. "This lady of whom I speak is a nonpareil, the epitome of ageless grace and beauty. I nominate Susannah, Lady Messingham."

Turning to Philip, Sir John remarked, "How now, Hastings? It appears word travels fast. Whilst the duke may covet only your horses, 'twould appear our worthy prince would have your mistress."

PART I

"The very dice obey him."

—William Shakespeare, *Antony and Cleopatra*

One

A ROLL OF THE DICE

The Rose of Normandy Tavern
Marylebone Pleasure Gardens, 1739

"SEVEN'S THE MAIN!" THE YOUNG GENTLEMAN CALLED
out in a voice pitched with anticipation. The vibrantly
hued flock of velvet-clad gentlemen and silk-draped
ladies surrounding the table watched with rapt eyes
glazed and breath bated as, with a long-practiced flick
of a hand, he cast the ivory cubes from the wooden
box onto the round, bevel-edged table. The dice clat-
tered to a halt, rolling up six and one.

"Damme, nicked again!" The central hazard table
resounded with the low curses and shrill cries of
dismay from its punters.

While others at surrounding tables hovered with
solemn concentration over their cards, the proprietor,
Daniel Gogh, surveyed the scene with pride and
satisfaction. Surely his *ridotto al fresco* to open the new
Marylebone Pleasure Gardens would be touted the
event of the season.

He had risked both reputation and a small fortune

to transform a venue once offering such sanguinary attractions as cockfighting, bull baiting, and bare-knuckle boxing into an elegant place of genteel dining, gaming, and musical entertainment. The varied diversions of the evening had included an organ concerto by Mr. Handel, a performance by the noted violinist Knerler, and illuminations at midnight. He had topped it all off with a late supper inside the Rose of Normandy tavern. Hours later, the gaming rooms still buzzed with activity: the resonating clink of champagne glasses, the echo of gay laughter, and cries of anguish and triumph interspersed with the spinning E-O wheel and rattling of dice boxes.

❦

At one of the tables, a young gent of no more than twenty, with all of the affectations of a town beau, remarked to his equally raffish companion, who had cast the dice, "You've the devil's own luck tonight, Drake."

"Don't I though?" his cohort replied with a wolfish grin as he raked in his winnings. "I should advise you, Bosky, that your money would be better placed on the next cast, rather than trying to set me."

"Will you never drop that infernal sobriquet? Moreover, that's the third nick in a row! What were the odds of that?" He lowered his voice and added a pointed look. "Might I warn you that I am not the first to wonder about those dice of yours?"

Philip Drake's sharp eyes narrowed, losing all trace of good humor. "What are you implying, my friend?"

"Simply to take care if you are up to any tricks. You might take particular heed of that burly fellow with the broken nose." George Selwyn slanted a warning look across the table. "He looks like a bruiser, and none too pleased that you have so singularly defied the odds this evening."

"Don't tease yourself further, Bosky. I doubt my good fortune will continue. The odds, as you so succinctly stated, are against it."

"Nevertheless, I think you're up to some mischief to which I won't be a party."

"I've heard that before, but suit yourself." Philip tossed another five guineas onto the table, doubling his stake. Thereupon, the groom-porter announced the new odds, but as he reached for the dice, a low and husky feminine voice stayed Philip's hand.

"Might I yet place my stakes, gentlemen?" she asked. "I'd like to wager with the caster. He appears an uncommonly lucky young gentleman."

"The rules permit you to wager on or against the caster, madam," answered the groom-porter.

Philip looked sharply up from the dice, meeting a pair of eyes as deep and brilliant as the emeralds she wore. Though much of her face was concealed behind a domino, her mouth was well-formed and as lush as her figure, which was generously displayed by the low-cut gown. The sum effect would cause any but a blind man to stumble.

Philip wasn't blind, but he was for a moment stunned. *Who the devil was she?*

❧

She had watched him with fascination from across the room. He was a cool one, indeed. While others at the tables cursed and shouted with every cast of the dice or unlucky turn of the card, the only trace of emotion displayed by the young man at the center of the hazard table was a slight upward tilt of his lips as the croupier paid out his winnings. His movements were always deft and self-assured, as if the dice were his to command.

After a time, she nudged Lady Hamilton to ask, "Jane, who is that young gentleman over there at the hazard table?"

Jane, Lady Hamilton, squinted. "That would be George Selwyn, an aspiring wit, but more of a sad rattle, I'm afraid. He's younger brother to Albinia, one of Princess Augusta's new Maids of Honor. You met her earlier this evening—do you remember?"

"But I do, and I am well-acquainted with the Selwyns. No, it's not George, but his companion, the one presently holding the dice box, whom I inquire after."

Jane's eyes narrowed again, raking the young gent appraisingly. He was taller than average and uncommonly well-proportioned. His complexion was dark and his features strong rather than regular, with a determined set to his jaw and a sensuous mouth, but the intensity of his dark eyes was most arresting.

"Hmm. I know him not, but he cuts quite a dashing figure. I think I now comprehend the nature of your curiosity. Surely a cut above a hot brick to warm a young widow's bed. But don't you think him a bit… fresh… for a woman of your years?"

"I'm hardly in my dotage!" the younger woman protested. "Besides, you misapprehend my interest. I only observe his uncommon skill at the tables. It appears he never loses."

"It is purely his skill you admire?" Jane's indulgent smile bespoke her utter disbelief.

⌘

Fascination supplanted Philip's initial appreciation of the mystery woman when she emptied the clattering contents of her purse nonchalantly onto the table, challenging the other players. "I believe it is fifty guineas, gentlemen, but feel free to count it, if you must."

Fifty guineas was a small fortune, and as the caster, Philip was required to match her stakes if he chose to acknowledge her wager, but even after his considerable run of luck, Philip had barely half that sum to his name.

In answer, ol' reliable George handed over his own purse with a nod of reassurance. Philip could always count on Bosky when in need. George Selwyn was generous to a fault with the last penny of his quarterly allowance—while it lasted, which wouldn't be long if Philip threw out on the next cast.

The groom-porter looked back to Philip, announcing, "The lady stakes with the caster at three to two."

Forcing his attention away from her and back to the game, Philip affected a cocky assurance, knocking the dice box on the table beside her money to acknowledge the stakes, and once again called his main at seven. His attention once more diverted back to the game, he steadfastly met the bellicose stare of Crooked-Nose as the dice rattled onto the table, turning up six and five.

"Eleven! Caster nicks again!" called the groom-porter. The beauty at Philip's side squealed her delight.

As Philip reached to take up his winnings with one hand and dice with the other, Crooked-Nose slammed a beefy paw on top of his.

"I be thinkin', jontlemen," he said, his brogue betraying his Hibernian origins, "that it be high time to have a closer look at the young sprig's dice."

Philip colored at the insult.

Perceiving his friend's flaring temper, a panic-stricken Selwyn spoke in a loud whisper, "Good God, Drake, don't answer back, lest you care to have your pretty countenance rearranged. I remember him now. His name's Knight and I swear I've seen the Irish brute best Sutton, the Gravesend pipe maker, at Hockley-in-the-Hole. You know, the one who soaks his fists in brine?"

Philip gritted his teeth and retorted back to his companion, "Nevertheless, had I not recently pawned my sword for rent money, I'd spit him like a roast pig for such an affront!"

"You forget too quickly your near-run at Blackfriars," said Selwyn. "Had you not finally thrown crabs... I begin to fear I risk my own neck just by association with you, ol' chap."

Unarmed and at a considerable disadvantage, Philip still turned to his accuser, prepared to answer the insult. Meeting the fellow nose-to-crooked-nose, Philip's eyes never left his antagonist as he coolly addressed the groom-porter, "Mr. Martingale, pray oblige the *gentleman's* request. A simple hammer should do the job to a nicety."

Martingale by this time had signaled Mr. Gogh that some bad business was afoot. Distressed that a scene of violence might blight the success of his opening night, the proprietor swiftly answered the call.

Having witnessed the exchange, the lady's eyes widened in mixed apprehension and dismay.

"Mr. Gogh!" She stepped forward and laid a staying hand on the proprietor's arm as he approached.

The gentleman sketched an answering bow, while his eyes fixed on the hazard table.

Undeterred, the lady gushed, "What a delight this evening has been, with the violins, the illuminations, and only the best of wines! Your pleasure gardens are sure to become a resounding success."

"I am overwhelmed by your encomiums, dear lady. You arrived with the Prince of Wales's party, did you not?" Gogh managed his growing impatience with obsequious civility.

"I did indeed, and well-received we have been, dear sir! I have already heard Lady Hamilton, who has the ear of the prince," she winked, "state that she vastly prefers your establishment even to the Spring Gardens at Vauxhall. I've no doubt the entire court of Leicester House will purchase season tickets."

"It has been my inestimable privilege to receive such personages of distinction, but now if you will pray excuse me…" He cast a panicked look to the lackey, who by this time had returned with the requested hammer.

"But sir," she held fast to his arm to whisper, "there is something I must say to you."

"I am honored by your confidence. What might it be, my lady?"

"Only one… element… would mar a near perfect

evening." Her eyes were wide with apprehension as she slanted a look back to the bruiser. "From a lady's perspective, you understand… such creatures make one feel ill at ease. Although I have had the best of good fortune at your tables, my pleasure is blighted with the fear of being robbed when I depart."

Mr. Gogh was now all concern. "By Mr. Knight? I admit he is a bit rough about the edges, but quite a harmless fellow outside his professional domain, I assure you. Pray dismiss any such fears."

"But this quarter has had such a reputation in the past…" she spoke with a worried frown.

Eager to avoid any blight on his opening, he answered, "If it would relieve your anxiety, my lady, I'll have the rascal removed from the premises at once." Gogh nodded grimly to the groom-porter to carry out the silent injunction.

"You are all that is sympathetic, Mr. Gogh." She beamed in triumph.

ॐ

"What the devil is that minx up to?" Philip exclaimed when two very large fellows appeared to escort his antagonist outside.

As she tripped gracefully back to the table to collect her winnings, George replied with grudging admiration, "Never underestimate the wiles of a woman, particularly a beautiful one, ol' fellow. Moreover, I'd advise avoiding *that one* in future; she appears to be particular trouble."

"Indeed she does," Philip murmured speculatively. "But still, who is she?"

"Hang me if I know."

"Come now, Bosky. You know all the courtiers. Your parents practically raised you in the king's bedchamber."

"A gross exaggeration, of course. As to her identity, I haven't a clue, but I'll be hanged if she didn't call Gogh over just to save your pretty hide," George taunted.

"My hide or her winnings?" Philip wondered aloud. "In either case, I'll hang myself before I'll stand accused of cowering behind a petticoat!"

"Is that so? Then you'd rather have had a knife embedded in your gut this fine evening? It appeared to me you were well on your way, if that were your heart's desire."

"Pox on you, George! I had it in hand."

"'Tis the size of the fight in the dog, then? I fear you are over-emboldened by drink," Selwyn mocked. "The blighter easily held a three-stone advantage, not to mention evidence of experience with his fists, and you with no weapon."

"But by her actions she dismisses me like some no-account."

"So that's the truth of it. You're pricked that she failed to distinguish the man behind the façade of callow youth, but hear me once, my friend—she has done you a favor that, thank God, you might now live to repay."

"Bugger you, Bosky."

"Your wit overwhelms me this night."

Philip answered with a scowl.

"Best forget her, anyway, Drake. She's well above your touch."

Philip caught her eye across the table. She answered back with a suggestive quirk of her lips. He turned to

George with a triumphant smirk. "Would you care to wager on it, my friend?"

&

To Philip's surprise, Mr. Gogh detained him as he sought to leave. "A word with you, young sir?"

Philip became instantly defensive. "If there is question of my gamesmanship—"

"I assure you, it is nothing of the kind. I was asked to deliver this message."

Philip opened the note written in a woman's delicate hand:

> *My Bold Young Gallant,*
>   *Fear of footpads and cutthroats has me desirous*
> *of your escort.*
>   *Lady M.*

"Above my touch, did you say?" Philip handed George the note. "I trust you can find your way safely without me?"

"Indeed, and I daresay I would be much safer without you this night," George remarked, and then read the missive with a low whistle, adding a cautionary word, "Very interesting to have attracted such notice, but I warned you about such types."

"Mayhap you are right, and she simply mocks me, but still, I am intrigued. In either case, I intend to satisfy my curiosity."

"You might be *assured* of satisfying a great deal more than curiosity, should you choose to accompany me to Tom King's rather than dallying with trouble."

"No doubt you'll find enough trouble of your own at that pox-ridden hole-in-the-wall that disguises itself as a coffee house."

"I hardly think your purse fat enough to become so nice in your tastes, Drake. Besides, if you so choose to involve yourself, mark my words, she'll cost you more dearly in the end than the best whore in Covent Garden."

Mr. Gogh cleared his throat in mild rebuke at the exchange. "The *lady* is outside in her carriage. A *gentleman* should never keep a lady waiting."

Philip answered, "I would rather say, a gentleman always awaits a lady's pleasure."

Two

LADY OF THE MASK

HER CONFIDENCE WAS NOT MISPLACED IN MERE VANITY. Susannah, Lady Messingham, was neither a young and simpering miss nor yet a world-weary jade, but at eight-and-twenty was beauty ripened to its prime.

She waited outside the Rose of Normandy much longer than she would have expected. Surely he would not refuse to come. She opened and then closed her painted fan with an exasperated huff. No man of her acquaintance would have passed up such a brazen invitation.

Of course, she told herself, she had cared only for his protection, the callow fool, but if he chose to dismiss her note… She shuddered to imagine his handsome young body bloodied and stripped naked. *Stripped naked*? Why should that vision have come to mind?

She had nearly decided to depart when the footman opened the door and the young man she had singled out at the hazard table sprang into the plush velvet interior of her coach.

He seated himself lightly at her side and brought

her hand to his lips with much exaggerated gallantry. "My lady, I present myself as your most obedient and humble servant."

"Humble? I fear the young gentleman's swaggering airs belie *that* particular attribute." She laughed, a low, ironic chuckle. "Now then, pray give my coachman your direction."

"My direction, my lady?"

"Why, to carry you home, of course." She could detect his flush even in the dimly lit coach. "Did I not say so very clearly in my missive?"

He tersely repeated her written words: "Fear of cutthroats and footpads has me desirous of your escort."

"Indeed. I had the greatest fear of cutthroats and footpads when I imagined you departing unarmed from the gaming house."

He bristled at her disdainful reply. "I shan't stand for your ridicule, madam!"

"Pray do not take such umbrage, *child*," she laughed. "How do you expect to slay such dragons as Mr. Knight with not so much as a dress sword?"

"I suspected you of mockery when I read your note. I almost didn't act upon it."

"Is that so, my young buck? Then precisely why *did* you act?"

He paused to consider the truth of it. Curiosity? Bewitchment? He answered quite differently. "I suspect it was a misplaced sense of gallantry, my Lady Disdain. But if not fear for *your* safety, why did you really send for me?"

"Forgive me, child," she paused, "but I do not yet know your name."

"I am the Honorable Philip Drake, at your service."

"Drake? I know not the family, yet you are surely a gentleman."

"As you say, by birth a gentleman, but also, sadly, an inconsequential younger son."

"Nevertheless, it is my observation that the ambition of the younger son often exceeds that of the heir."

Philip laughed. "Therein lies the rub, madam, as I am generally accounted as singularly devoid of any ambition. But now you have me at a distinct disadvantage, my Lady of the Mask."

"And so you shall remain... until we have come to some agreement," she replied.

"Agreement?" Philip wondered what she could possibly want with him.

"Or better said, mayhap, I have a proposition."

An interesting choice of words. He found himself growing more intrigued by the minute. "This, ah, *proposition* is why you invited me into your coach?"

She repeated his earlier unspoken words. "I was most curious, you see, almost bewitched. I was enthralled to know the secret of your dice."

Philip shrugged. "There is no secret. Luck was simply on my side tonight."

"I don't believe you. Besides, you owe me a debt of gratitude, you know, after having saved your magical dice from Mr. Knight and his hammer."

"You thought to have saved me?" His laugh was derisive. "I assure you, madam, the dice were fair. Mr. Knight may have split them to his heart's delight, and I would have rattled any other set of bones in my box to the same result."

"In truth? Then it is not the dice, but the box? How does it work?"

"*It* doesn't, and devil carry me away should I introduce a lady to such vice."

"Now don't prose with me. I have seen thee in thy glory at hazard, young Philip." She moved in closer now, her breasts nearly in contact with his chest, providing him a gratuitous view of her décolletage.

His nostrils flared unconsciously in response to her proximity and her scent. *Aqua Admirabilis*—he recognized the essence. This heady fusion of bergamot and womanly musk threatened to overwhelm his senses.

She took firm grasp of his lapel with one hand, and while her warm breath fanned his ear in a seductive whisper, the other snaked slowly down his chest. "Teach me your trick, Philip, and mayhap I'll reciprocate with a lesson of my own."

Philip swallowed hard, fighting the incipient stirrings of arousal.

Roaming freely, her fingers continued a steady exploratory descent.

He closed his eyes, his body rife with anticipation, but that's where it ended, as her hand darted into his pocket and snatched out the dice box.

"She-devil!" Philip cried an imprecation of disappointment and growing frustration.

She turned away with a triumphant chortle, holding the box just out of his reach. "Now I have taken your magical box and shan't return it until you reveal its secrets."

Philip glowered, considering how to turn the tables

to his advantage. "If that is your pleasure, my lady, I propose an exchange."

"Exchange?" Her eyes narrowed with suspicion. "What kind of exchange?"

"I'll reveal the trick of the dice when you reveal your face."

"No. I don't think that would be wise."

"Why not? Are you disfigured?" he goaded.

"Of course not!" her vanity cried out. "I only wish to remain incognito until I am assured I can trust you."

"Why should you have such a need for anonymity?" he asked.

"I am a widow, and a ready target for gossipmongers."

"You'll simply have to trust that your secret is safe with me."

She paused, biting her lip in indecision, considering whether the dim light of the coach would keep her sufficiently in shadow if unmasked; but if he agreed to do her bidding, it would scarcely matter. "Very well," she decided and removed the domino.

Philip peered closely at her face. Her profile was well-defined in the dim light, even if her features were indistinct. The clean lines of her forehead, nose, and chin left no doubt she was as lovely as he had imagined. First his good fortune at the tables, and now he was alone with Botticelli's Venus herself. Surely his guardian angel looked fondly on him this night! Now, if only he played his cards right...

She regarded him expectantly. "I have fulfilled my end of the bargain."

"All right. Give me your hand. You must master the proper technique." His long, slender fingers stroked her palm as he placed the cool ivory cubes upon it.

"The technique?" she repeated blankly, acutely aware of his touch on her skin.

"The outcome of the dice, of course."

"Of course," she said. "But how can it be done?"

"Retaining one die, whilst dropping only the second into the box, ensures that only one of the two should tumble. Mastering the technique allows one to better manage the number of pips that turn up, thereby significantly reducing the odds."

"So you are able to predict what will fall?"

"Not precisely. One can never know for a certainty what will turn up, but with skill, one may greatly increase the odds in one's favor. The first trick, however, is to retain one die."

He delicately placed one of the cubes between her thumb and index fingers, and then pressed the other between the joint of her thumb and palm. He took her hand in both of his and turned it over, instructing her to drop only the first into the dice box. Both dice fell.

"Oh!" she cried her dismay. "'Tis not near as simple as you make it appear."

"Practice, dear lady, practice." He took the dice back from her to demonstrate and repeated the gestures so fluidly that she could barely follow the motions. He then cast the dice from the box onto the carriage seat, rolling up six and five.

"Thusly." He waved his free hand with a flourish.

"I know what you did, but could barely follow it."

"Precisely the point of this exercise. It is an art not easily mastered, and if clumsily executed it is practiced at one's greatest peril. I dedicated my entire youth to the technique as assiduously as the most ardent scholar to his Ovid and Homer."

"So while your Eton schoolmates were reading the Greeks, you were studying to become one? A wicked confession indeed, that you so squandered a proper and genteel education."

"Harrow," he corrected with a frown. "I attended Harrow, at least until embarking on a more worldly education."

"You left school for the Grand Tour?"

Philip laughed outright at the suggestion. "My *Grand Tour* was limited to the lower gaming hells of London, interspersed with spring and autumn forays to the racetracks. I was dismissed," he explained, with more than a trace of bitterness.

"What would prompt the son of a gentleman to become an adventurer?"

"What would prompt me, madam?" His voice grew harsh. "I was induced by several most inconvenient necessities—sustenance and shelter, for example."

"How can one of your tender years have grown so cynical?" His revelation tinged with hurt behind the cynicism mysteriously moved her. She instinctively reached for his face, but he caught her palm and grazed it as smoothly as any courtier.

She regarded him, bewildered yet fascinated. One moment he was a wounded boy, and the next he would play at seduction. The sensation of his warm lips, coupled with the intensity of his dark gaze, made her wonder vaguely if she might be losing the upper hand. The confines of the carriage seemed at once too close.

"You too would be my lover, Philip? Others greater than you have vied to be my protector, and I would have none of them. And you? You can't even have reached your majority." She laughed to dismiss the notion, but wondered at her own discomfort at this burgeoning sense of intimacy.

"Let not my years belie my experience," Philip replied.

"La! How you talk, as if I am some artless tavern maid!"

Philip flushed. "I have done with your scorn, my lady. If not for want of a lover, why did you ask me alone into your carriage?"

She paused, considering just how much to reveal. "Is it not evident? I wish to learn to master the cards and the dice."

He surveyed her dress, her jewels, and the elegant carriage with an arched brow. "Why the deuce would you want to do that?"

"For diversion, of course—gaming is all the rage, and I am a woman of fashion, after all."

"Have you considered the consequences if you lose? Many a great lady has compromised her virtue to pay a debt of honor to an inveterate rake."

"La, child! As if I would be so careless with my *virtue*! Besides, you are going to teach me not to lose."

"Why in damnation would I do that?"

She leaned into him, stirring him once more with a warm, moist, lingering kiss full on his mouth. "Because I asked you to."

Three

THE COUNTRY WIFE

SUSANNAH, LADY MESSINGHAM, ARRIVED INTENTIONALLY late at the Drury Lane Theatre. With far more eyes attending the goings-on in the boxes and the pit than upon the stage, she was grossly mistaken in her belief that she could slip into the box unremarked.

Jane, Lady Hamilton, seated incongruously between her husband, Archibald, Lord Hamilton, and her lover, the Prince of Wales, beamed a warm greeting with a wave of her fan to indicate the empty seat behind her. After making her obeisance to the Prince and Princess of Wales, Susannah slipped as inconspicuously as she could contrive into her seat.

The play was Cibber's revival of William Wycherley's *The Country Wife*, a notoriously bawdy Restoration comedy, with Kitty Clive as Margery. It was a favorite production of the prince's; he was well-known for his vulgar sense of humor. Act I had already begun with the young bride, Margery, just up from the country, conversing with her new sister-in-law, Alithea, as Margery's jealous husband, Mr. Pinchwife, eavesdropped from behind the drawing-room door.

While the audience enjoyed the satire of the pretty young country girl married to the jealous and possessive older man, Lady Messingham's mirth faded with the dour reflection that the scene played out much like her own life of the past ten years.

Like Wycherley's Margery, she had been a country bride, the property of a jealous and possessive husband, and ignorant of the ways of the sophisticated world. Unlike Margery, however, *she* had also spent the past months languishing by the sickbed of a dying man.

She had longed for a normal life, one so many others took for granted, but those days were now behind her. Free at last of husbandly constraints, she was determined to live, yet the strictures of mourning made her new widowhood both blessing and curse. After six months of formal mourning, she was restless, yearning for the pleasures of town life so long denied her. Making an effort to throw off the melancholy thought, she drew her attention back to the stage.

When the curtain dropped signifying the end of Act I, the men departed to procure a drink, leaving the women alone in the privacy of the box. Lady Baltimore and Princess Augusta were engaged in a tête-à-tête, and Jane turned to Susannah for their own private conversation.

"How are you enjoying the play, my dear?" Lady Hamilton asked.

Lady Messingham affected an impish air and mimicked Margery, "La, but what proper, comely men are the actors!"

"Well done!" Jane let out a peal of laughter. "You

might do as Lavinia Fenton and take to the stage to catch yourself a duke."

"Lavinia Fenton?" Lady Messingham asked blankly.

"She was the first actress to play Polly Peachum in Gaye's *Beggar's Opera*, and was quite the star. She was for a time the most talked-of person in London, even before causing the greatest scandal of the decade."

"What was that?"

"You really were buried in the country if you never heard of her elopement with the Duke of Bolton. Lavinia was a grasping actress, and no better than she ought to be, but the poor fellow was so smitten that he scarce missed a performance. By the end of the season, he left his wife for the shameless hussy! She let the whole thing quite go to her head too, the vulgar baggage. While the duke may have kept her on the side without remark, their setting up house together was truly beyond the pale. Such outré behavior is just not to be borne."

Harsh words of denunciation, and more than a tad hypocritical, coming from a royal mistress, thought Susannah, with Lady Hamilton's ongoing liaison with the Prince of Wales such a poorly kept secret. Uncomfortable with the topic of mistresses, she deftly changed the subject.

"You truly are an angel for including me this evening, Jane. I have few acquaintances of my own age. My social circles were limited to Nigel's set for so many years that I feel rather akin to a fish out of water, but I'll be deuced if I'll be cloistered any longer."

"I understand your position far better than you think, dearest. I was little more than a schoolgirl myself when I was pledged to old Archie, thirty years my senior. And as his third wife, no less, though I really have no cause to grouse. No wife could wish for a more even-tempered and complacent husband." Jane smiled. "I certainly shan't judge you for wanting to live, Sukey. Sir Nigel died a happy man. You have no reason to feel guilty."

"To tell the truth, Jane, I have not the slightest guilt. I was his faithful nurse through it all, but now I am no longer attached to an old man crippled by gout, *living* is precisely what I intend to do. I'm done with mourning and kowtowing to the dowagers."

"I warn you to maintain discretion or they will eat you alive, my dear."

"I don't even care anymore, Jane! They never accepted me from the moment Nigel took me to wife, the jealous old cows. They have no pity, no compassion, even though I spent nearly a decade of my life married to a man who could have been my grandfather."

"You know you can always count on me," the lady smiled. Delighted with her new role of benefactress, her voice became animated with the formation of her plan. "My darling girl, I fully intend to induct you into our Leicester House set, where I've no doubt you'll soon become one with the most beautiful ladies, and a toast among our brilliant men."

"How I would love that, Jane! Nigel would never take me out amongst such fashionable people."

"No doubt for fear of the attention you would draw, as evidenced this very evening."

"What do you mean?" Susannah quirked a thinly shaped brow. She had chosen her gown with the greatest care, but without her customary lace fichu the cut revealed much more than Nigel ever would have allowed. Although pleased by the compliment, she now wondered if she might have been a bit too daring—but wearing it so was her own little rebellion.

"Come now!" Jane laughed. "You must know what a stir you have caused. Half the peers in this theatre craned their necks for a better view when you came into the box."

Including the prince himself, Lady Messingham thought ruefully. Although seated with his wife on one side and his chief mistress on the other, the heir to the throne had cast his eye upon her a number of times throughout the performance. Perhaps he'd begun to tire of Jane's constant importuning for her husband's advancement, or, more likely, was just following family tradition by adding to his collection of mistresses. In either case, the proposition of a liaison with the bug-eyed prince held no appeal to Susannah.

Leaning closer, Jane spoke behind her fluttering fan. "You know, Sukey darling, there are any number of highly placed gentlemen who could ensure you a *more than comfortable life*. You could easily take your pick of the lot, after a proper interval, of course."

"But, Jane, I haven't the slightest desire to remarry."

"Pshaw! What nonsense!" Jane said and gestured grandly to the posh theatre and its fashionable occupants. "You well know, such a life as this is not lived without considerable expense."

"I am more aware than you know, but any eligible man of my own age won't have me. After my childless marriage, 'tis no secret I'm barren. If I cannot provide the requisite heir, I have only the options of an aged bachelor or widower, and I refuse to live the rest of my life warming another old man's bones!"

Jane smirked. "Then do you intend to spend your dotage as a shriveled-up old dowager with only the company of a house full of cats?"

"Indeed not!" Sukey heartily denied the thought. "I'll not lack for company. Now that I've put off my weeds, I plan to attend the opening of every opera, dance holes in my slippers at each ball, and promenade all of London's pleasure gardens on the arm of a different dashing beau every evening."

"Do you now?" Jane's brows rose in mock censure. "Then perhaps a word of wisdom would not go astray? Though I hate to disillusion you, dearest, even the most gallant of men will expect some... tangible reward... for his service to you. But with youth and beauty yet on your side, wife or mistress would be purely your choice..."

"But Jane, you don't understand at all." Her voice was nearly choked with frustration. "After living so many years akin to an exotic pet on a chain, now that I am finally free, why should I trade one cage for another?"

"You know as well as I, Sukey, a woman in your position has but two options: a husband... or a protector."

"I won't have it, Jane. There must be another way," Susannah insisted. "I refuse to be placed under any man's dominion again. Who, now, must I truly please but myself?"

Jane's eyes only grew wider. "But without a man's

patronage, how in heaven's name do you propose to maintain your lifestyle?"

After a moment's reflection, Sukey asked, "Jane, just how do so many *men* of similar reduced circumstances go on?"

Jane scoffed in reply. "Those without a patron, you mean? Far too many of them subsist only by gaming. Cards, dice, cocking, pugilism wagering, horse races… the list of worthless pursuits goes on and on."

"Gaming?" Sukey repeated with a sudden gleam.

Jane was aghast. "My dear, you have no idea the danger you would court in contemplating such a ruinous thing!"

"But why not, Jane? If others make a living at the green tables, why shouldn't I?" She thought of the young gentleman she'd met over the hazard table the prior evening and her face lit with a winsome smile. "After all, I only lack someone to teach me…"

Four

A PROFLIGATE LIFE

ONE KISS.

Just one bloody kiss and she had awakened in him a conflagration of lust. Although Philip was no innocent, she was completely beyond his experience. The feelings she'd awakened were nothing he could explain, though he cared not to ponder too heavily upon them.

When her carriage returned him from Marylebone to his lodgings at the George and Vulture on Lombard Street, Philip sought the taproom rather than taking to his bed. Restless and more than a little disturbed, he couldn't bring himself to retire for fear of deeper reflection. A drink was what he really needed.

The tapster, having long ago made the last call, glowered when Philip slapped thruppence upon the bar. "Don't ye young bucks ever seek yer beds?"

Philip answered by adding a twin to the copper coin. "A single tankard is all I require."

"Tap's turned off for the night, and off it remains 'til a more respectable hour. Them's stays open all night begs fer nothing but trouble if'n ye ask me."

"Strange," Philip remarked. "I don't seem to recall asking."

The tapster growled something indiscernible and shoved the coins back across the bar. "I 'spect ye know very well *where to go...*"

Philip quirked a lone brow. "How unfortunate. I had so hoped to avoid that pit at this ungodly hour." Eyeing a heavy cudgel in a corner, Philip inquired of the tapster, "If I must venture out, perchance I might borrow your bludgeon? I seem to have mislaid my sword, and would quite dislike finding myself in need."

The tapster assessed him with a frown that appeared to find him wanting. "Much good 'twill do, 'less yer knows 'ow to use it."

"Fear not, my good man. After habiting this godforsaken purlieu nigh on four years, I assure you I give quite as good as I get." Indicating the money on the counter he added, "Here, you may keep it as surety."

Readily accepting the money, the tapster grinned toothlessly and tossed the club over the bar. Philip caught it one-handed and swaggered out of the tavern.

The tavern maid, who had been wiping down tables, looked wistfully after Philip's departing figure. The door had no sooner closed behind him than she'd torn off her apron and cap to follow after him. "Wait," she cried. "I–I don't suppose a fine gent like yerself would want fer some comp'ny?"

Although Philip had never been disposed to look a gift horse, or in this case a fine-looking filly, in the mouth, he was suddenly struck by Lady Messingham's earlier intimation about his predilection for tavern maids. Although it rankled, it also rang true. He turned to the girl with an uncharacteristic hesitation. "I've seen you before, haven't I? It's rare I forget such a comely lass."

She blushed. "Indeed, sir. Me name's Nell. I been working the taproom a sennight now. I saw ye the first night and 'ave hoped fer a word e'er since."

While only a night ago he would have thrown her skirts up with enthusiasm, oddly the thought of a quick tumble suddenly held little appeal. Yet he still hadn't the heart or inclination to rebuff her. Instead, he offered his arm as if she were the grandest of ladies.

"As it stands, Nell, I am indeed feeling singularly friendless this evening. How would you care to accompany me for a pint?"

"That I would indeed, milord." She beamed and gave an awkward curtsy.

"Philip," he amended. "Just Philip."

⁓

He dreamt of drums. Or was it cannon fire? Neither, Philip realized, awakening to the dull and incessant din of pounding on his chamber door. He groaned and pulled a pillow over his head to muffle the sound.

"Drake! What—are you dead?" the voice of George Selwyn shouted through the wooden barrier.

"Hang you, Selwyn! So you shall be, if you don't desist the infernal hammering. What the hell are you about, beating on my door at the crack of dawn anyway?"

"Dawn?" Selwyn cried. "It's bloody well noon, you laggard. Have you completely forgotten the

Main? They've been at it for hours, and if you don't pull your arse out of your pallet, we'll miss the entire thing. There's to be a battle royale at the end, don't you know."

"Bugger your mother," Philip mumbled, and pulled himself from his rack, drew on his breeches and boots, and raked a hand through his disheveled hair. He pulled the door open just as his companion decided to throw a shoulder against it. George Selwyn crashed to the floor, upsetting both a chair and the chamber pot.

"Piss on you, you sodding jackass!"

"More like the piss is on you! 'Twasn't my idea to break down the door. By the by, you land like a sack of shit, Bosky."

"Sod off, ye whoreson. Are you coming to the cockpits or what?" George asked, as he stood and brushed himself off.

"Since you asked so charmingly, how could I possibly refuse?"

❧

The cockpit at Grey's Inn Walk dated back to the Restoration, when the Merry Monarch seemingly made it his life's purpose to restore all of the pleasures prohibited under the former Commonwealth. It was circular in design and built for the singular sport of cocking. Laid out much in the manner of an anatomical theatre, it featured a raised platform surrounded by a railing with semicircular benches rising in tiers to accommodate a multitude of spectators.

Entering the theatre, Philip's nostrils flared in affront

at the mixed redolence of whiskey, pipe tobacco, stale sweat, chicken dung, and blood.

Unfazed by his surrounds, George pointed eagerly to the front where the next bout was set to commence. "What a stroke of luck! We haven't missed it. They say 'twill all end in a match between that blinkered claret, Sir Robin, and the bloody-heeled bantam, Billy Pitt."

"I'll wager twenty pounds on bantam Billy, for surely Sir Robin's reign is nearing its end."

"Do you now speak politics or cocking?" George asked as they elbowed through the socially mixed throng.

"Devil take me if I ever become political! I've no such leanings, I assure you."

"So you say, but what else is a younger son to do but support the elder in his political endeavors, and serve as a spare lest some mishap befall the golden one. You are no different in your family's expectations of you, Drake—placeman politics later rewarded by some comfortable sinecure."

"Is that all you aspire to, Mr. Selwyn?" Philip's tone was laced with derision. "To place yourself in the pocket of some lord? To be only a greater man's puppet in Parliament?"

"Every man has his price, you know," George answered just as cynically. "But I shan't be bought cheaply. No. My support will require a number of perquisites and emoluments. As a matter of fact, now I've reconciled with m' father after that unfortunate incident that sent me down from Oxford, my name has been put forth as a nominee for the Clerkship of the Irons and Surveyor of the Meltings." He puffed his chest visibly with the pronouncement.

"Has it indeed, George? That's quite a mouthful too. I stand duly impressed. But what the devil does the Clerk of the Irons and Surveyor of Meltings actually do?"

"Hell if I know." George grinned. "Aside from attending the weekly dinners provided at the public expense, I fully expect that any actual duties assigned to my position will be cheerfully dispatched by my clerk."

"The clerk to the clerk?"

"Indeed. All of these government positions include an underling of some sort to do the dirty work. I don't suppose you are disposed to consider such a position?" he offered cheekily.

"Your personal lackey? I'd rather be hung... by my bollocks."

George affected affront and then laughed. "So you say now, but you'll come around just like the rest of us, once you've done with your bout of rebellion."

Philip frowned. "Of *that* you are gravely mistaken, my friend. I desire nothing more than to be completely free of my family's hold. I've already told you, I've no liking for politics, nor do I adhere to my family's particular leanings."

"Jacobite sympathies, you mean?"

Philip shot his friend a warning stare.

"Now don't look so surprised, Drake. It's a poorly kept secret after all, though your brother would try to play both sides."

"I'd rather not discuss my bastard of a brother if you don't mind. Besides, you couldn't understand anyway. While your family survived the viper's nest of two courts and even thrived, mine, having never fully accepted the Hanoverian crown, has fallen completely from grace."

"But what are your aspirations, if not politics? Don't say you are bound for the church?" George gasped in mock horror.

Philip laughed at the absurdity. "You know how I despise the hypocrisy of the church, with its deans and bishops who defile on Saturday the very law they would impose upon others every Sabbath. You only need look around this very place for the evidence." Philip gestured broadly.

Surveying the crowded cockpit, George knew he couldn't argue the truth of it. "I had no notion you suffered from such idealism."

"Idealism? No such thing!" Philip replied. "I simply deem that if one chooses to sin openly and without shame or remorse, he is more virtuous than one who hides his sins behind acts of piety."

"Apostasy!" George barked with laughter, but recovered enough to ask, "Then if not the church or the House of Commons, do you look to the Inns of Court?"

"Gad no! I've neither love for the law nor talent for academia."

"So we may safely rule out any career as a barrister. Then what *are* your plans, Drake? You cannot think to continue indefinitely on your feckless adventure as the prodigal son."

"My life of independent indolence has suited me well enough these past four years, but if you really wish to pry like an old women, I expect to soon adopt the life of a respectable gentleman."

George was incredulous. "You what? Just how do you propose to manage the 'respectable' part when you make your living by frequenting gaming rooms, late-night drinking dens, and the occasional horse race? How will you come by the funds? Though you're no doubt one of the luckiest bastards I know, you've lived fairly hand to mouth since we've been acquainted. Have you begun playing deep of a sudden? Broke the bank at basset?"

"Let's just call it a long-anticipated windfall."

"Windfall? What sort of windfall?"

"I am soon to come into a very adequate competence. Not a fortune, but shrewdly invested, it should provide sufficient income for me to set up a modest establishment."

"How is this, Drake? You've never spoken a word of it."

"It is a trust left by my mother, part of her original marriage settlement. I have not mentioned it before because I shan't come into the bequest until my twenty-first year. I also did not care to advertise the fact and become prey for scoundrels."

"You may trust me to keep mum, then. But we'll surely celebrate the event, eh?"

The peal of the bell, indicating the start of a new match, diverted George's attention. "We'd best find a position on the rail. We'll see nothing of the real sport from here," George said, and began edging closer toward the stage where the setters-on were already applying the gaffs to the legs of their respective cocks.

"Nothing of sport, or just not enough blood for your fancy?" Philip asked.

George held his reply until they had threaded and wedged through the stinking throng for a better view at the center of the amphitheatre. "It's the purpose of the sport, after all."

"What *is* the purpose?"

"The blood, of course, the sight of which fires the passions of any true Englishman."

"I fear you are endowed with a much heightened lust for it, my friend," Philip said.

"Mayhap you are right, but look how much more easily *my* lust may be sated compared with yours."

"What is that supposed to mean?"

"You've been strangely abstracted since encountering a certain female at Marylebone, is all."

Philip ignored the intimation, knowing his friend right but refusing to admit it. He was glad of distraction. "Dog's bollocks! What is he doing?" Philip exclaimed upon observing the trainer's final preparations for the match.

George chuckled his reply, "I see we have at least one adherent of the Richard Seymour school of cocking."

"Is he actually licking that bird's head?"

"Both the head and the eyeballs, to be precise."

"Good gad, what for?" Philip exclaimed.

"'Tis one of the more mysterious and amusing of Seymour's famed training practices, to include bathing a wounded cock in warm urine. After battle, many suck on the bird's head to draw out blood. At least they shave the fowl's head first. Can't say I'd relish a mouthful of feathers."

They turned their attention back to the pit where the masters, having strapped on their respective warriors' sharpened spurs, handed them off to the respective "setters-to" who brought their birds, well-in-hand, to the center of the pit. Holding the birds face-to-face, they allowed the cocks to eye one another, until Bantam Billy nearly leaped from his handler's grasp to get in the first peck.

"Do they use silver or steel, I wonder?" George asked.

"The spurs? What does it matter?"

"You really know little of this sport, don't you, Drake?" George remarked impatiently.

"I've spent far more time at dice, cards, and horse races than at cocking matches," Philip said. "You are by far the greater votary of blood sport than I."

"And yet, I do not yet despair of converting you. Just look at them facing off!" George cried as the two birds, now released, began to circle around one another with feathers fanned and puffed out to intimidate. In a sudden flurry of beating wings, the combatants assailed one another, but Philip's mind was far from the spectacle.

He was distracted. Without warning, some shift had occurred in the precarious scales of his life that he couldn't quite comprehend. While he tried to occupy his mind, all of a sudden his normal diversions simply failed to amuse. *It had all begun with that one damned kiss.*

Five

DIPPED IN DEBT

THE SOFT CLICK OF THE DOOR AND MUFFLED CLATTER of metal told her that the chambermaid had arrived with breakfast. When the heavy velvet bed curtains opened to reveal the midmorning sun, Lady Messingham greeted the day with a lazy yawn and a feline stretch.

Setting the breakfast tray on a bedside table, the chambermaid poured a pot of steaming liquid into a delicate hand-painted cup of the finest bone china, which she handed to her mistress with downcast eyes.

Accepting the cup with a puzzled expression, the lady asked, "Nancy, how long have you now been in my employ?"

"Nigh on a twelvemonth, milady."

"And for the past year, what have you served me for breakfast?"

"Chocolate, milady."

"Then if you have not suffered a lapse of memory, why on earth would you decide to bring me tea? And Bohea? You know I only drink Hyson."

"Yes, milady, but Mistress Graham said we have

neither chocolate nor green tea, so Cook sent up a pot of her own brew."

Lady Messingham regarded the contents of her cup with distaste. "No doubt she intends to serve me black bread for my dinner as well? Do we not have at least cream and sugar?"

The maid answered with a flush. "Mistress Graham gave cook strict orders to save the remaining cream and sugar, along with the white bread, in case you have callers, milady. She feared you would be embarrassed…"

With the shocking realization of the dire state of her affairs, the lady hid behind a façade of annoyance. "Botheration! Allendale must be held accountable for sorting this mess out."

"Aye, madam. The servants all hope so."

The lady paused with cup to her lips, her brows rising. "Do you say they talk?"

The maid's color deepened. "Some feels it's high time to look for another position, ma'am. But I be not among 'em. You're a right kind mistress. I shan't leave ye jus' because you've fallen on some hard times."

"Is that what they say? That I've fallen on hard times? Do they speak outside this house, Nan? Pray tell me at once." Mounting alarm added an edge to her words.

"I think most of 'em's loyal, milady, but wages is wages…" She shrugged.

"Nancy, pray tell them all that I have complete confidence the accounts will be back in perfect order this very week, and all back wages will soon be paid."

"Indeed, ma'am?" The maid couldn't conceal her skepticism.

"Yes, yes," she said impatiently. "You have my pledge. Now go and tell the others before word is all over London that I'm a beggar. Go, Nan. Go! And send Mrs. Graham at once!"

"Yes, milady." The maid bobbed a hasty curtsey and flitted out the door.

The beleaguered housekeeper shortly appeared, wringing her apron.

"Mrs. Graham," the lady began calmly. "I've always held utmost confidence in your running of this household, but I cannot countenance how you've allowed us to run out of the most basic staples as cocoa and tea."

"But, milady, I placed the usual order. 'Tis no fault of mine 'twasn't delivered."

"Did you not send word to Mr. Twining about his delivery service?"

"Aye, madam, I have."

"And?" She waited expectantly.

"It would appear our credit with Twinings Tea House is on hold."

Had it already come to this?

"There is obviously some mistake," her well-modulated tone supported the lie as she digested the news.

The housekeeper expressed her growing trepidation by dropping her apron to wring her hands instead. "But the butcher as well has asked me for payment before he will supply the meat. And the staff, madam, have not got their wages for a full quarter..."

"Well then, Mrs. Graham. I thank you for bringing the matter to my attention." Lady Messingham spoke with an affected aplomb. "Pray send a dispatch to Allendale that I require an interview with him forthwith."

"Yes, milady. I will send a footman at once." The housekeeper repeated the chambermaid's diffident bob and hastily departed.

Lady Messingham left her bed for her sitting room, dumping the offending tea into the chamber pot along the way. She padded barefoot to her escritoire and unlocked the top drawer, knowing full well what she would find. There was no error on the part of Nigel's ever-pedantic factotum. He had been assiduous in his duties, forwarding every past-due account with an earnest appeal to cease all but her most vital expenditures, but like a rebellious child she had ignored the warnings.

She opened the drawer to reveal a large sheaf of papers, all past-due accounts that he had forwarded to her in exasperation: Longacre the cartwright, for refitting the velvet interior of her carriage, one hundred sixty pounds; Madame Guilane, London's most fashionable mantua maker, two hundred forty-four pounds.

Perhaps she should have selected something other than hand-painted Chinese silk for her last three gowns, let alone the imported Mechlin lace for trim and fichus, one yard of which could have bought a simple day dress. Another sixty pounds was owed to the vintner.

Her hands began to tremble as she continued to leaf through the pile. Twinings Tea House, twelve pounds eight shillings. Hodgins the butcher, eight pounds six shillings. The milliner, the glover, the haberdasher, the chandler, and on and on. She mentally tallied her mounting debt, awakening to the undeniable reality that in less than three months' time she'd already spent thirty-six months of her living allowance.

Others would have already been arrested for much less. Due to her mourning, the merchants had been uncommonly forbearing, but in short shrift she would find herself face-to-face with the magistrate at the sponging house.

She had held off her creditors as long as she could, and the servants' wages had to be paid, at least to ensure their loyalty.

A drawer full of debts and no way to pay them. Was this all she had to show after a lover's betrayal, and ten years of her youth sacrificed to a man who could have been her grandfather? Her eyes misted at these lugubrious reflections.

In frustration, she crumpled the papers in her hands. It was past time to put her plan into action. She had hoped that he would have come to her voluntarily by now, but after days of waiting she could delay no longer.

Desperate for any means out of her morass, she resolved to summon all the wiles at her command. She sat at her escritoire and wrote, *My Dearest Young Gallant*...

Six

A Dubious Code of Honor

"CHILD! I AM SO PLEASED YOU HAVE COME." LADY Messingham greeted Philip with a brilliant smile when he entered her small salon. "Have you, perchance, your dice box? I thought we might resume where we left off." Her expression was innocent, but her voice seductively husky.

He bowed over her extended hand, his eyes never leaving her face. "As *I* recall, where we left off had nothing to do with dice."

"Indeed? Then perhaps my memory falters." She artlessly tapped her fan against her lips, tauntingly invoking the memory but altogether ignoring his reference to her kiss.

Philip cleared his throat, speaking stiffly. "I have come at your summons, my lady, and I ask what you mean with me?"

Normally arrogantly self-assured, he puzzled at his sudden gaucherie. No other woman had such an effect on him, but truth be told, he was not accustomed to intimate contact with ladies of her social standing, or used to *ladies* at all, for that matter. The *females* of his close acquaintance were little more than girls, buxom and cheerfully free with their favors. Lady Messingham could not have stood in stronger contrast if she'd tried.

She laid a hand on his arm, and her expression became coy. "Did I not say in my missive? I thought I was especially clear?"

"Mayhap mine is the memory at fault. I fear I was distracted at the time."

She had the effrontery to laugh at him. "What do I want with you? Why, I want you to teach me the games, Philip. I wish to win at the tables."

"The skills you desire to learn are not so easily or rapidly acquired as you appear to believe. Besides, gaming of any sort is rarely harmless. You would do better to attend the theater or the opera, if it is diversion you seek."

"I have attended the theatre, and the opera bores me. I'd much rather attend the masquerade at Belsize House Thursday sennight."

"I can only presume that you have never been to a public masquerade."

"Why would you say such a thing?"

"Because Belsize House *by morning* is a place of genteel company and breathtaking vistas, but by night takes on quite another character altogether. It is the milieu of sharpers, harlots, scoundrels, and rogues."

"But I was invited to accompany a perfectly respectable party from Leicester House. With the prince and princess in attendance, what harm can befall me? I would like you to meet me there."

"Why?"

"To play, of course. If we arrive separately, no one will know we are together."

"You propose for us to play as confederates?" he asked in astonishment.

"Well… yes, I suppose. Did we not do so, in a manner of speaking, at Marylebone? I can provide the capital—"

"Couch stake," he corrected.

"Pardon?"

"The initial wager is the couch stake, my lady." He smiled indulgently. "Are you quite certain you wish to pursue this course with so little knowledge of gaming?"

"But that is precisely why I have you. With your extraordinary skills, how can we lose?"

"We? Now it's a partnership?"

"Precisely!" She beamed up into a glowering face.

"No. I don't think so, my lady."

"Wh-what did you say?"

"I said no."

"I heard you."

"Then why did you ask?"

"Because you said no!" She scowled in petulance. While most men of her acquaintance were effortlessly led by the nose, Philip, she realized with dismay, would not be as easily manipulated as she had thought.

"I'll be a very apt pupil," she insisted.

He answered with impatience, as if addressing a simpleton or a child. "The point isn't whether or not you can learn the skills, but your naïveté about those who habit the tables. Only years of experience and particularly keen senses allow one to identify those who would place you at a disadvantage. There are many who prey on the inexperienced, particularly upon members of the frail sex."

"But are you not one of that same society? The very ones who prey on the inexperienced and the *so-called* frail sex?"

His expression revealed his resentment at the insinuation. "It appears you grossly misapprehend my manner of play, Lady Messingham."

"I saw you at the hazard table. The punters who endeavored to set you had little chance." She moved gracefully to the silk damask sofa, where she perched and patted the seat beside her billowing skirts. She turned her face to him, attentive but dubious. "Pray explain yourself."

Philip moved to take his place beside her, feeling as ungainly as a virgin schoolboy. *What in hell was wrong with him?* Then, there it was again, her scent. His nostrils flared to take it in.

"You were saying…" she prompted expectantly.

He looked blank for an instant and then mentally shook away the descending fog. "Er… I was saying that you misunderstand me."

"In what way is that? Are you not a professional gamester?"

He looked uncomfortable and then carefully chose his words. "The question is not so easily answered. While I don't deny taking my living from the green tables, I assure you that I endeavor to maintain… certain standards… in my play."

"Do you indeed?" Her half smile accompanied by a lift of her finely shaped brows bespoke disbelief.

"First of all, I endeavor never to sit down with a lady, or even with a man who has already over-imbibed. I find no allure in taking from those so disadvantaged. These players present ready targets, pigeons for plucking for those less scrupled, but I am not of their ilk."

"I would like to know in what way you consider women *disadvantaged*?" she bristled.

"I only mean to say that ladies, suffering from an innately heightened sensibility, are predisposed to emotional play."

"So you deny that you win by cheating?"

He flushed. "'Tis such an unpalatable word, *cheating*, associated with swindlers, cutthroats, and highwaymen. By my troth, my lady, I have never marked a card or rolled weighted dice. *These are the trademarks of a cheat.*

"I would merely say that I play with enhanced skill. I do not seek out victims to dupe, nor do I play intentionally to ruin any man. If, however, one wagers foolishly and has not the sense to know when to leave the tables, he deserves what he gets."

"Are you not still a sharp, Philip?"

He paused to consider. "No. I do not say so. Not in the truest sense of the word. Besides, the term hardly encompasses the entire world of gamesters."

"You speak almost as if it were a society in itself."

"It is precisely that. Simply put, there are many types of players, varying degrees of Athenians, Captain Sharps, Amazons, blacklegs, tricksters, bamboozlers, and outright swindlers, inhabiting both the upper and the lower classes of society."

"Fascinating. I have heard of the Greeks, but I don't

understand why the brethren of our much-venerated Aristotle are so vilified."

"Ah," Philip answered, "'tis a story that goes back to the days of Louis XIV, when a certain chevalier named Apoulos, a man of Greek origin, was admitted into the court. He was astonishingly adept at play and won a veritable fortune from the princes of the blood before his true methods were revealed."

"What happened to him?"

"The king was much displeased and sentenced him to twenty years in the galleys, where he slaved until his eventual death. A true Greek tragedy," he quipped.

"Thus all players of his stamp are called Greeks?"

"Nay, only the select few. It is the name reserved for only those who play with great mastery. The Greek of the *ton* is by far the subtlest, most adroit, and the cleverest of creatures. He is accustomed to the best of company, and his deportment and manners are all that can be desired. Either he dazzles with his wit and brilliant conversation or he is one with the loftiest reserve, who in truth applies his mind wholly to his game. Even whilst engrossed in his cards, all the while he appreciates what goes on around him with veiled and furtive glances.

"He unites his profound knowledge with the most challenging conjuring feats—the partial shuffle, the false cut, the shift-pass, mucking, palming, pegging, and culling. No one surpasses his skill in drawing the ace, or breaking the cut, concealing cards or placing them. He raises the practice to an art."

By now, Lady Messingham hung in rapt attention upon his every word.

"He is a master who lives for naught but the game, playing each one with unparalleled skill and equal perfection, concealing himself as the most suave and venerable of courtiers, and playing only for others' ultimate destruction. Attempts to hide emotion from him are in vain. He discerns the least movement or contraction of the features, peering with uncanny ability into his adversary's very soul..." Philip ended with a pregnant pause.

"Lackaday!" she exclaimed, wide-eyed. "It sounds as if you describe Beelzebub himself!"

"He is not far removed!" Philip laughed. "True vice, my lady, would frighten us all if it did not wear the mask of virtue."

"But how to recognize him?"

"As he wears a perfect disguise, one does not, unless one is equal in his own talents."

"Then it is impossible to evade a fate as his victim?"

"Not at all. One can easily do so by avoiding deep play. He is a master who only delights in high stakes. Steer clear of his table, and you'll never fall victim."

"Sage advice, indeed. But I must now ask if you count yourself among those who are, as you say 'equal in his talents'?"

"Not I, madam!" Philip barked. "I'd never make such a boast." He paused with a thoughtful frown. "Though I learned at the hand of such a one. Nay, I do not endeavor to make my fortune so."

"But then why do you play as you do?"

"'Tis but a current necessity and only the means to an end. I do not *live for the play* as others do." His voice grew pensive. "I still have hope of something better."

"Do you? And what might that be?" she softly prompted.

"I am yet undecided, but suffice to say, my future will be *my choosing*."

He met her quizzical look without further elaboration and abruptly shifted back to their prior topic. "You have yet to learn of the wandering Greek—" He flashed a grin, breaking the solemn mood.

"Not to be confused with the wandering Jew?" she quipped.

He laughed. "Indeed not. Although this manner of sharper does travel from place to place. He frequents the taverns, public assemblies, and pleasure gardens, seeking out the young and unwary, but rarely working alone."

"He has an accomplice?"

"Yes, he employs a decoy, often an Amazon."

"An Amazon?"

Philip looked for a moment chagrined. "It was my misfortune to fall prey to such a one. Once. Her charm and pulchritude drew many susceptible young men into injudicious play."

"A woman?" she remarked thoughtfully. "So there *are*, after all you said, women who are successful gamesters?"

"I have never encountered one who does not act in conspiracy with a man, although she may be near as skilled as the one who employs her. Her role is more to play the siren, or, better said, the shepherdess to lure the hapless sheep to the wolf, a sharper who, not nearly as skilled as the Greek, often resorts to marked cards and high-rolling dice.

"This pair does not discriminate in their victims,

but will dupe anyone who unwarily veers into their path, whether stranger or even friend," Philip said ruefully. "I would never have known the gentler sex capable of such deception, but then again, a lesson learned painfully is not soon forgotten."

"How ruthless!"

"Yes. Yet this is not even the worst type." Philip's voice now took on a harsh, gritty quality. "The lowest sort of creature is the varlet who frequents the public gaming hells and the low drinking dens. They are naught but evil wretches, wrought out of idleness and debauchery. After plying a victim with strong drink, their 'games,' involving any manner of trick or treachery, begin."

"You speak as if you have fallen victim."

"I was very young… and a fool. I am lucky to have escaped with my life."

She stared at him, stunned even more by what his words had not said than by what he had revealed. Her heart ached at what a hell this boy-man must have lived.

"Have I now opened your eyes?" he asked softly. "Or are you still bent on this mad gaming scheme?"

"It is only harmless diversion," she lied. *"It's not as if I intend to make my living at the tables."*

Seven

PRINCELY COMPANY

UPON LADY MESSINGHAM'S FINAL FITTING IN THE French sacque gown bedecked with sprays of silver stars, Madam Guilane had fondly called her "*la Grande Dame de Minuit,*" or the Lady of Midnight. Now that she had donned the completed ensemble, ordered especially for tonight's occasion, she confessed that it was ravishing.

When the coach arrived, she descended the staircase with regal satisfaction knowing she had never looked better, but when the footman opened the door of the emblazoned carriage, her ebullient smile froze.

"Your Highness? I was not anticipating... er... I understood Lord and Lady Hamilton were to escort me this evening."

The prince assumed a wounded look that with his bulging eyes reminded her of nothing more than a Pug. "I am disconsolate, indeed cut to the quick, with your seeming dismay at my humble escort," he said.

Overcoming her distaste, she quickly recovered. "But Your Highness, I am only overset by the unexpected honor."

"Lady Messingham." He inclined his head with a smug smile. "May I avail myself of your Christian name?" He proceeded to do so without awaiting her consent. "My dear Susannah, why do you not enter the carriage, where I assure you all will be made clear."

Laying aside both reservations and jangled nerves, she stepped inside. Although the prince moved to make room for her, she assumed the opposing seat.

"Come now, my tear." The prince's occasional lapses in pronunciation betrayed his Germanic origins. "I do not bite; vell," he chuckled, "perhaps I take a nibble now and again, but only when tempted by a dish so delectable I cannot resist." The lascivious gleam in his bug-like eyes revealed precisely those intentions.

She responded nervously, hopefully. "Is the Princess Augusta to join us? Or the Hamiltons? I was under the impression…"

His lips curved in false regret. "Sadly, Lord Archibald had some business at the Admiralty that keeps him well into the night, and the princess is abed with a megrim that I assured her only her Lady of the Bedchamber could soothe. Thus it is just the two of us until we arrive."

She shifted nervously in her seat, her anticipation of the evening already blighted by the prospect of spending an entire night fending off his advances. After all, he had just made it abundantly clear that this entire solo outing was his contrivance. His mistress was keeping company with his wife, at his behest, and Lord Archibald, to whom she might have turned for aid, was occupied as well.

The prince chidingly patted the cushioned space

at his side. "Now, my tear, would you not be more comfortable by my side? It is cold in de carriage, is it not?"

She forced her lips to curve into a semblance of a smile. "You are all consideration, Your Highness, but I am quite comfortable."

"Ah, but it is precisely *your comfort* that I wish to discuss. Your circumstances, they greatly concern me." His voice oozed false sympathy. "Such a beautiful woman." His eyes swept her with unveiled appreciation. "With no husband. No protection. Moreover, no money. You haf debts, my lady." He awaited her reaction, not displeased to see her eyes widen in trepidation.

Only the artificially enhanced pallor of her cheeks disguised the draining color. *How did he know? Did the whole world know that she was dipped in debt?*

He raised a hand to silence her forthcoming protest. "There is no denying it, *liebling*, but I am moved by compassion to help you. I can arrange to pay your debts, quietly, through your man of business. Allendale, is it not?"

"Who told you? Jane!" she realized belatedly. "But why?"

"She was seeking my advice on a match for you. But now I make no secret of my own admiration, my pretty vidow, and I am a generous man." His lips curled meaningfully. "In many ways. My mistresses, they are well satisfied."

His double entendre was not lost on her. Although he boasted of his manhood, rumor held him to be an unimaginative and clumsy lover. She turned away, parting the curtain and gazing out the window as if thoughtfully deliberating the offer. If not for the desperation of her circumstances, she might have laughed.

Lady Hamilton's favors to the prince had merited her positions in the Royal Household amounting to an astounding income of nine hundred pounds per annum, as well as an offer to her husband as Lord of the Admiralty. Although a similar position in the royal household would be the end to her own problems, she could not debase herself to such a private whoredom, even to a prince. Other women would be tempted to close their eyes and endure his attentions for far less, but she was not among them.

She shuddered at the thought of another loveless, passionless coupling, remembering poor Nigel's breathless rutting before the gout had left him completely impotent. Although she'd endured it for his sake, she'd never become insensate to the distastefulness of the act.

Nevertheless, she could not afford to fall afoul of a prince. Given her dire circumstances, the heir to a throne might one day be a useful ally. She posed her response carefully to avoid hubristic injury. After all, what man with a prince's pride would mind the challenge of a rival?

"I am flattered by your interest, Your Highness, but you see… I have already taken a lover."

～

Belsize House, with its extensive park, wilderness, and garden, was once a grande dame of Elizabethan mansions, until a Welshman named Howell had purchased the private residence to transform it into a place of public amusement. In its heyday, the house was used for many a gala affair, attended by all persons of rank, with music and dancing into the wee hours, but unbeknownst to Lady Messingham it was now a mere shadow of its former self, its reputation for low gaming and intrigues having become as degenerate as its habitués.

When Philip saw her, a vision in midnight blue surrounded by a coterie of admiring swains, she looked uncomfortable and out of place amongst the coarse revelers. She was devoid of a domino on this occasion, Philip remarked, with only a filmy veil obscuring the upper half of her face. Nevertheless, even in costume, the tilt of her head, the rich chestnut of her unpowdered hair, and the lush curves of her silhouette in the form-fitting confection gave her away. Her presence also proved his earlier efforts at dissuasion had all been in vain.

She stood in the company of an openly roistering party from Leicester House, with the prince and his chief sycophant, Bubb Doddington, foremost among them. The few ladies within the mix comprising the company of gamesters might not have been called ladies at all if not for their lofty titles or dubious attachment to a man of rank.

"What the hell is *she* doing here?"

"Who?" George asked.

"The Lady Messingham, damn her."

She was fixated on the spinning E-O wheel, an object of universal fascination invented by a Frenchman in an endeavor to create a perpetual motion machine, as if determined to unravel its secrets.

Within the wheel itself were forty pockets, twenty labeled *E* for even and twenty labeled *O* for odd, and two unlabeled pockets designated for the bank. The table itself was marked all around with the two letters, offering spaces for each adventurer to place his wager before a ball set in motion around the gallery of the wheel commenced the play.

It was a simple enough game, giving the punter twenty out of forty-two chances of winning, but while others drank, laughed, and carelessly threw out their coins, Lady Messingham's expression revealed her ill luck.

Serves her bloody well right for dismissing his warnings.

"What should you care, Drake? She lacks not for company, surrounded by swains, and by the look of it, the prince himself fawns over her. Seems you've developed quite an unhealthy interest in the widow Messingham."

At first, Philip intended to leave her to her own devices, but while she contrived to humor her companions' drink-inspired vulgar jests and *bon mots*, her gaze shifted about the room as if seeking escape. Philip once more remarked the prurient looks of the prince and something vastly unpleasant churned in his gut. He unconsciously moved toward her.

"Leave her be, Drake, she's trouble," George advised, not for the first time. "There's faro and hazard to better occupy your time."

Unlike those paying particular court to the prince, who appeared quite bedeviled by drink, Philip found his head still remarkably clear. He turned back to George. "Go on without me, Bosky. I've another game in mind."

❦

In addition to his lavish and impulsive spending, Prince Frederick was best distinguished among the royal family for his preference for low company. Yet, among his numerous so-called friends, the Prince of Wales had as many enemies, as nobody was too great or too good for him to betray.

Lady Susannah's brief time in his escort lent truth to what even his own family said of him: that he was singularly loutish and insincere. When he aimed to be merry, the manner of Frederick's mirth was to genuine cheer what wet wood is to fire, damping the flame it is meant to feed. The prince desired without love, could laugh without pleasure, and weep without true grief, for which Susannah knew even his mistresses were not truly fond of him.

For what regard was it possible to have for a man who had no truth in his words, no justice in his inclinations, no integrity in his commerce, no sincerity in his professions, no stability in his attachments, no sense in his conversation, no dignity in his behavior, and no judgment in his conduct?

Nevertheless, this man, whom so many despised, was surrounded by parasites who anticipated the day he would wear the crown.

Trapped in this company of drunkards and louts, Lady Messingham wore a doleful expression that transformed the moment she remarked Philip's familiar swagger. She made little effort to disguise her gratitude at his approach.

"Your Highness." Philip swept a courtly bow to acknowledge the prince before extending his hand to the lady. "I have come to claim a partner, for there is dancing in the next chamber. Madam, would you do me the inestimable honor?"

The inebriated prince turned to Bubb Doddington. "Who is this jackanapes who would poach on royal preserves? Is there not a penalty for such a trespass?"

"Hmm…" Doddington replied thoughtfully. "The Game Law may apply. It clearly states any creature to which no man can claim ownership belongs by prerogative to the crown. Would not this same law then also apply to widows?" He observed the prince and knew the moment his mind grasped the nuance.

The prince stared and then erupted in drunken laughter. "A brilliant interpretation of the law, my good Doddington! Remind me to consider you as my lord high chancellor."

Lady Messingham's cheeks now flamed in affront.

Philip rose to her defense. "Surely Your Highness does not mean to classify the lady with the beasts of the field?"

Philip's rebuke caused the prince to regret at once his ill-chosen words. He reached for Susannah's hand with a suitably contrite expression. "My dear lady, 'twas all but a poor effort at jest and meant only to repel this interloper." He eyed Philip with haughty contempt.

She slanted a meaningful look to encompass the prince and his sycophant before taking Philip's proffered arm. "A very mean effort indeed, expressed at my expense," she answered and turned to Philip. "Come, sir, let us go and walk the minuet. I am thankful to escape such boorish company." With this retort, Lady Messingham tripped away, leaving the royal heir gaping after her.

"Just who is that contemptuous, poaching whoreson?" the prince asked.

"Hastings's stripling, I believe."

"Hastings? The Jacobite?" The prince's lips twisted on his words.

"By conjecture only, Your Highness. He was acquitted after the '15."

"You are an invaluable asset, Doddington."

Having provided the heir to the throne with countless thousands in loans, never repaid, Doddington knew the remark to be true as literally as it was figuratively.

Eight

VINGT-ET-UN

RATHER THAN ESCORTING HER TO THE BALLROOM AS she'd expected, Philip steered Lady Messingham toward the French doors leading outside.

"I thought we were dancing."

"Dancing is the least of my talents," he replied, propelling her onto the open terrace. "You looked in need of rescue and 'twas the best excuse I could muster."

"It's lovely out here." She inhaled deeply of the cool night air, taking in the cascading fountain that shimmered in moonlight enhanced by a hundred lit torches.

Oblivious to his surrounds, and in no mood for pleasantries, Philip demanded, "What are you doing here? Didn't I warn you about the company of places like this? Its habitués are nothing more than rogues and harlots."

His harsh words transformed her warm smile of gratitude into ice. "Think what you will, but the particular company I keep is only the highest. I was with the Prince of Wales, for goodness' sake! Moreover, what right have you to demand an account of my actions? I am free to do as I wish. And with whomever I please."

"Indeed, and you looked none too pleased with the choice you had made only a moment ago," Philip replied testily. "Their conduct leaves much to be desired. Prince or not, the man is a vulgar buffoon, and his preferred companions can only claim gentility by virtue of rank. You despise the lot of them as much as I do. God save us if Freddie ever does obtain the crown."

Acknowledging the truth of his claim, she dropped her defense. "I am thankful for the rescue, Philip. I admit their decorum diminished markedly with every bottle passed and every glass poured. I was, in truth, glad of escape."

Lady Messingham regarded Philip as if puzzling out a great enigma. He, who so convincingly affected the manner of a reckless ne'er-do-well, was surprisingly sober. Moreover, Philip had incurred a prince's displeasure in her defense. Even in his pique, she felt strangely protected rather than threatened by him.

"Why are you here, when I expressly advised you against it?" he asked.

Her mind worked to compose a plausible answer that was not an outright lie. "For the play," she blurted with a slight flush. "I came for the play."

"This is no place for a lady. I'll call for your carriage."

"I did not come in my own," she said.

"I see." He directed a scathing glance toward the ballroom.

"It's not what you think."

"That you encourage him one moment, and repel

him the next? I believe I understand only too well." He laughed mirthlessly, wondering if she'd only acted the damsel in distress to inspire Frederick's jealousy, using Philip as part of an intricate ploy to fix the prince's interest. Then again, hadn't she emphatically repulsed Frederick when she practically had the heir to the throne at her feet?

Her rising color said that his biting words had indeed left their mark. "Do not make presumptions. He manipulated me, Philip. I had not intended to come here with him."

"You don't belong here. Especially with *him*."

"There's the question," she remarked almost rhetorically. "I don't seem to know where I belong."

He studied the angles of her face, shadowed by moonlight. "At this moment?" His voice was low and husky in her ear. "I'd say with me."

"Is your conceit boundless?" She tilted her face and discovered their lips only inches apart.

"You deny you want me?"

She opened her mouth to do exactly that, and then closed it with a perplexed frown. His lips twitched smugly. "We've both known it since that night in the carriage. I dare you to refute me."

She couldn't, in all honesty. Something pulled deeply within, tempting her to explore it, to learn precisely what lay between them. Giving in to the urge, she leaned into him with parted lips.

Philip didn't hesitate. He claimed her mouth in a ravaging kiss that clearly bespoke his desire. She answered back instinctively, with an involuntary moan, but the sound of her own pleasure seemed to stir her back to her senses. She broke away with a gasp, regarding him with a look of mixed guilt and bewilderment. "*That* was a mistake," she said.

Philip stifled a curse and raked his hair with a groan of frustration. In that fleeting kiss he had felt her reciprocal desire. There was nothing ambivalent about it, but in the same breath she kissed him, she once more rejected him.

"I'll call you a hackney," he said tersely.

"But I don't wish to leave."

"Are you already so infected with the fever?" he asked, his black eyes deeply probing.

"It's complicated," she said.

"Complicated? Are you saying you are in want of money?"

"It's uncivil to ask such a thing."

"You didn't answer me." He pressed. "Is that why you're here?"

"If you insist on knowing, I had indeed hoped to win a few pounds. I have several new gowns on order and have shamefully overspent my allowance." She laughed lightly, as if embarrassed to have revealed such a triviality.

"How much?" he asked and reached for his purse.

"Wh-what?"

"How much do you need? I will make you a loan."

"I don't need your money. Pray put away your purse. God knows what will be said, if anyone sees you hand me money!"

"I only meant to keep you from the tables. They are a dangerous place."

"But not nearly so dangerous with you to guide

me. Please, Philip," she cajoled, "accompany me to the tables."

He conceded with a scowl of displeasure. "If there is no dissuading you, it appears I have little choice."

❧

After their brief interlude on the terrace, Philip and Lady Messingham returned inside to the clattering dice, whirring wheels, press of bodies, and peals of bawdy laughter. As they navigated the rooms, Philip positioned himself deliberately to shelter her from the undesirables, but her attention was only for the tables.

As he guided her, Philip explained the basics of the games, warning her in particular against basset and faro.

"Why?" she asked.

"These are most dangerous and ruinous games, frequented by only the deepest and most unscrupulous players."

"The Greeks of whom you spoke?"

"Ah! My prior admonitions did not fall on completely deaf ears. You just *chose* to ignore me."

She refused to take the bait. "I wished to play, but I had deplorable luck at the E-O table earlier."

"That comes as no surprise. E-O requires no skill and is little better than a lottery, and the payoff, even when one wins, is negligible."

"Then what should I play? I am determined not to depart with an empty purse."

"Every gamester's most famous last words," he chuckled.

They had approached a table where the banker

was in the process of dealing out a single card to each of four players who, in turn, examined his card and placed a wager in front of it.

"What is this solemn game?" They stopped to observe the play. "Does the punter place his stake on just one card?"

"Not quite, my lady. The game is called *vingt-et-un*. Although there is considerable luck involved, it also requires a certain skill."

"Indeed? Will you teach me?"

His nod directed her toward the table, where he silently encouraged her to observe the play.

The dealer looked at his own card without placing a stake and then dealt a second card to each player again, and finally back to himself.

He then turned to the first player on the left. "*Carte?*"

The gentleman frowned in irresolution but then replied, "*Content.*"

The dealer proceeded to the next player who nodded. "*Carte.*"

The card, a deuce, was dealt face upwards.

"*Encore,*" spoke the player, and a nine appeared. "*Crevé,*" said the punter with a grimace, throwing his remaining cards face down in the middle of the table. The croupier swiftly swept the wager to the bank.

"*Crevé?*" she looked to Philip for explanation.

"*Crevé,*" Philip translated, "is burst. The object of the game is to achieve a perfect *vingt-et-un*, or twenty-one, without going over. The player erred by anticipating a low card but overdrew and broke."

The game proceeded with the next two players holding with the cards dealt them.

"At this point the dealer will reveal his own hand and may hold or draw as he sees fit."

"I see. It appears a simple enough game."

"There is a certain strategy," Philip explained. "The banker will generally draw if he holds anything below sixteen, but in this case three players have failed to draw additional cards, leading one to surmise that each holds at least sixteen. This could motivate the dealer to play more aggressively."

The dealer tuned over his own pair of nines.

"Eighteen," she said. "The dealer will stand?"

"He must. Any sensible man would," Philip said as the remaining players each showed their hands, revealing twenty, seventeen, and eighteen respectively.

"Twenty wins, seventeen loses, and eighteen loses," Philip said.

"But the last is a tie," she exclaimed.

"Ties go to the dealer. There is nary a game that doesn't present some advantages to the house," he said. "But there are ways a savvy player may overcome his disadvantage and even increase his odds to win."

Her eyes took on an excited gleam. "How, Philip?"

"By close observation of the cards played and the number of additional cards dealt, one may deduce if there is yet a high percentage of ten-cards and aces in the remaining deck, which can be good for the player and bad for the dealer."

"How can you tell?"

"The key is to look for extremes in play. A player with a ten-card or ace will generally take a second card and forego a third. Thus, when a number of players stand on their dealt hand, it is a disadvantage to increase your wager. However, when there is a noticeable dearth of high value cards, the advantage is for the player to increase the wager. While this is no guarantee, it is playing to your best possible advantage."

∽

They spend the remainder of the night at *vingt-et-un*. With Philip a constant presence at her side, she quickly learned the strategies of the game, how to split pairs, when to receive a card, and when to rest. His hawk-like stare took in every movement, every card, and every nuance of the dealer's expression. With his subtle cues, she doubled her wagers when the odds best favored her, and began to win.

She had come with a purse of fifty pounds, and having lost more than half at the E-O wheel, sat down to the cards with only twenty. After two hours of play, her accumulated winnings now neared seventy-five pounds. Bound to leave with one hundred in her purse, she would have stayed until the table closed had not Philip intervened.

"You've lost the last three hands, my lady."

"When I next double down, I shall win it all back."

"You've grown overconfident. Recklessness follows, and ruin inevitably ensues. It is time to leave the table."

"But everyone loses a hand or two. My luck will surely come back around."

"Luck, my lady, tires just as surely as the player. It is time to quit."

"Surely. Right after this game." She signaled the dealer, but Philip stayed his hand.

"The lady no longer plays."

"What do you think you're doing?" she hissed, as he forcibly lifted her from the chair.

"Protecting you from yourself."

She glared. "Perhaps I only require protection from you!"

Philip replied with a low, ironic chuckle, "That may prove truer than you know."

❧

She was infuriated when Philip had curtailed her play by manhandling her at the gaming tables, and outraged when he bundled her unceremoniously into a hackney, but with the light of day came the remorseful acknowledgement that he had indeed protected her from her own uncontrolled impulses. Had he not intervened, she might well have continued losing.

As it stood, she'd departed Belsize House with seventy-five pounds in her pocket, half again what she had brought with her, but unfortunately not enough. At least it was sufficient to pay her servants' back wages, and more important, the evening had proven that her plan was not as outlandish as Jane had implied.

If she could win twenty-five pounds in a single night with minimal tutelage, how much more might she gain if Philip were to take her truly under his wing?

Although he had preached a very pretty sermon about the evils of the tables, she remained undeterred. On the contrary, she was more convinced that she could soon come about, if he would only cooperate.

The wrinkle, to her growing consternation, was that Philip was not so easily led.

Nine

THE PRODIGAL SON

PHILIP ROSE WELL BEFORE HIS HABITUAL NOONTIDE
with a purpose he refused to dwell upon too closely.
He set about his toilette with unusual care. For lack
of a manservant, he washed and shaved himself. He
then donned his best white lawn shirt whose former
magnificence had since dimmed, adding the mark of
gentility, cascades of French lace at his throat and cuffs
that spilled over his hands to reveal only the tips of
his fingers.

With as much tenderness as the best valet, he
dressed in his claret-colored silk breeches and brushed
the nap of his velvet coat, pausing with a frown at the
visible wear in the fabric, the fray of the silver lacing,
and the thinning of the elbows. One would hardly
note his shabby finery in the darkened gaming rooms
he frequented, but surely his less-than-prosperous state
of affairs would be remarkable under bright streaks of
morning sun.

He shrugged with resignation. If invited by his
lordship to sit, he would simply choose a place away
from any window. Philip paused at his reflection in the

tarnished looking glass, wondering if he should have powdered his hair, and although it was morning, he took a generous fortifying swig from a flask he then secreted in his pocket.

The sudden summons from the earl after a four-year silence had him more shaken than he cared to admit. Exiting his lodgings, Philip hailed a passing sedan chair to convey him via Oxford Street to King's Square.

⸎

Arriving at what was, in the last century, one of the most fashionable addresses in London, Philip alighted from the sedan chair and paid the two bearers. Surveying the locale, he noted little change during his extended absence. At the center still stood the two distinct landmarks, a half-timbered hut for the gardener of the meticulously manicured square and a statue of Charles II, carved by Danish sculptor Caius Cibber.

The square itself was originally named after the Duke of Monmouth, one of the monarch's many bastard sons, who had resided there until his rebellion against his uncle, James II. After Monmouth's subsequent execution, the address thereafter became known as simply King's Square.

The statue also was claimed by many to have actually been of Monmouth rather than of King Charles, and, confessing a certain admiration for the bastard son who would attempt to usurp the crown, Philip had always fancied the notion that it was. Feeling in many ways a kindred spirit to the king's ill-fated bastard, Philip swept a playful obeisance to the statue.

Having now stalled long enough to marshal his will for the much-dreaded interview, Philip strode purposefully up to the door of Hastings House.

∽

Grayson, the faithful retainer, answered the door. "Master Philip, what a delight to see you home."

Philip noted, with a degree of pleasure, the almost-smile that registered on the butler's stolid face. "I don't know that I ever called this place home," he said upon entering. His gaze swept the twenty-foot ceiling, Italian marble floors, and luxurious appointments, as if retrieving the entire layout from a distant memory. "Indeed, I'm not sure I was ever here but twice in my life."

"It was meant figuratively," Grayson explained. "Home is the bosom of the family from which you have been absent for far too long."

Philip grinned. "Is that a scold, Grayson?"

The butler gave a dignified sniff. "Suffice to say, you have been missed."

"Thank you. It means much, but I still wouldn't have come at all were it not for his lordship's summons. Do you have any idea what he wants?"

"I would have little notion. The earl does not confide in his servants."

"True enough." The Earl of Hastings was a man who held his cards closely and kept his own confidence at all costs. Two separate charges of treason, even though acquitted, might do that to a man, Philip decided cynically.

"He wishes to see you in his private chambers."

"Gout attack?"

"It's one of his longest episodes, I'm afraid. He refuses to follow the physician's recommendations."

"What a surprise that is. He'll no doubt be in a damnable humor."

Grayson offered only a tight-lipped smile in reply.

With the exception of their two sets of echoing footfalls, they continued in a protracted silence through the long corridor to the earl's private apartments. The foreboding starkness penetrated into Philip's very bones.

Philip was bleakly reminded of his last encounter with the earl. He'd been sixteen years old and certainly no wilder than most of his cohorts at Harrow, but less prone to feigned contrition. He'd also failed to govern his tongue, for which he'd suffered many a lashing at the master's hand, and finally expulsion.

He'd been falsely accused of leading the other boys astray, when in truth he'd learned gaming from the very schoolmates who'd peached him, once he began to clean out their pockets. After the requisite caning, he'd been expelled in disgrace with no opportunity to defend himself. When he'd faced Lord Hastings, who would believe the worst of him in any case, Philip had maintained an obdurate silence under his interrogation, resulting in a reopening of the stripes on his backside that had only begun to heal.

For a young man of sixteen to be publicly whipped by a servant, at his father's command, it was more humiliation than Philip could bear. Rather than facing the daily opprobrium of a father who despised him, Philip had obstinately struck out on his own, determined more than ever to live down to his father's expectations.

This, to his anguish and regret, had also broken his mother's heart. In the first six months, he'd written her only one letter to inform her he was well, and shortly thereafter she was gone, consumed by the wasting disease.

The guilt had nearly been his undoing. He'd taken to heavy drink and low company shortly after that, and might well have lost his life on three occasions. The experience had taught him the three rules he would come to live by: trust no one, as every man is a cheat; always follow one's instincts when in doubt; and lastly, depend upon no one, as ultimately every man will fend for himself over and above any other. These three cardinal rules had guided him well enough until now.

Grayson preceded him into the earl's chamber to announce his arrival. Philip followed more tentatively than he had hoped he would when he'd envisioned the interview, but this long-accustomed regard of mixed awe and loathing was difficult to overcome.

Lord Hastings, garbed in a Turkish-style banyan and cap, reposed in an overstuffed chair with his bestockinged and visibly swollen right foot resting atop a mound of pillows on a gout stool.

Although Philip had expected no warm familial sentiments from his estranged father, the earl wasted no breath even on the most mundane pleasantries. "Don't skulk," snapped the earl. "Come and let us have a look at you."

With a half shrug, Philip ventured forward and forced his bow of obeisance.

"You've the look of your mother," the earl accused.

After a prolonged scrutiny, he raised his index finger vertically and made a loop in the air.

Philip's brows pulled together.

"Turn around," the earl demanded.

Philip performed a slow revolution with arms akimbo to the earl's appraising nod. "You've grown tall in stature. That's to a man's advantage. I daresay you surpass Edmund."

"Four plus years are bound to have wrought many changes," Philip remarked with insouciance.

"Yet your insolence persists."

Philip met the intimidating stare without faltering. Eager to hasten the interview and end the unpleasantness with all dispatch, he said, "I'm at a loss why you've sent for me after all this time."

"Willoughby informs me that you're soon to come of age."

"In scarce more than a fortnight." Philip consoled himself that a mere seventeen days separated him from the respectable competence that would allow him to plot some viable and rewarding course for his future.

"It is high time you accept your responsibilities."

"My responsibilities? And what might those entail?" As if ignorant of the diatribe that would inevitably ensue, he had intentionally baited the earl.

"You know damned well what is expected! You've run amok, disgracing your family nigh long enough. It's time you come to heel."

An eminently revealing turn of phrase, as if he, like some well-trained hound, would suddenly accept his father's dominion at the snap of his fingers.

"Just what would you suggest?" Philip continued his affected air of artlessness.

"I *suggest* nothing. I *demand* your deference to duty."

"Ah, back to that, are we? Just what is *duty* to a wastrel, my lord?" Philip spoke the last with a sardonic curl of his lip and sprawled lazily in a chair, intentionally fueling the earl's simmering temper.

"Then let me make my expectations of my youngest son absolutely clear. Upon attaining your majority, you will immediately cease this dissolute lifestyle and prepare to assume a seat in the House of Commons."

"I will do what?" Philip affected astonishment.

"There will be a general election in a twelvemonth in which several Sussex MPs, in Bramber, East Grinstead, and Seaford, will become vulnerable for replacement."

"Bramber has representation? The village can't have but thirty residents."

"Nevertheless, the borough has two representative MPs and twenty registered voters."

"Then it's nothing more than a rotten borough that rests in the pocket of the major landholder."

"Which would be me." Lord Hastings's lips curved into a shameless smirk.

"But Edmund already serves your interests in the Lower House—why would you want me?"

"Winds of change are blowing. Walpole's losing his grip on the ministry and his power is steadily slipping. With this shift, our time of vindication may be coming at long last."

"Vindication or usurpation?" Philip asked. "I have no taste for politics, *my lord*, and even less stomach for Jacobite intrigues."

"You would refuse an offer of position and future influence to continue in your reprehensible, shiftless, and ignominious existence?"

"You would deem treachery and intrigue a nobler calling?"

The earl's face went rubicund and his eyes bulged. "I'll cut you off without a groat, you ungrateful whelp."

"That's quite a threat when I've not drawn a bloody farthing from your hallowed coffers in over four years."

"And you live hand to mouth for your obstinacy. Although in time you'd inevitably have come begging, I'm disinclined to further humor your conduct."

"You thought I'd come groveling?" Philip laughed. "You are hardly in a position to know my state of affairs."

"I have my sources when information is needed. I know exactly your state of affairs, you insolent whoreson!" The earl attempted to rise and cursed in pain.

Refusing to be cowed, Philip stepped closer to the earl, speaking lowly but clearly. "You seem to have forgotten the matter of a certain trust, *my lord*."

"It is out of your grasp until you attain your majority."

"Precisely."

Silence reigned while realization dawned. "It is but a pittance that won't last you a six-month. I'm prepared to offer you a substantial quarterly stipend."

"A bribe to toe the line?"

"An inducement," the earl said. "Two hundred fifty pounds per quarter."

Philip blinked. *One thousand pounds per annum.*

It was an enormous sum. His pride moved him to dismiss the offer, but his common sense gave him pause. "In return for what?"

"Your loyalty and support of Edmund's advancement."

"That toad-eating, detestable prig?"

Lord Hastings returned a black look. "He is your brother, and heir to this earldom."

"Half brother," Philip corrected. "And how precisely am I to pledge support to one whose own loyalties shift with the tide? Stuart Pretender one day and the Hanoverian-born Prince of Wales the next. Above all, Edmund would hedge his bets."

"Your naïveté astounds me."

"As I stated, politics does not suit my nature; thus I must regretfully decline your offer."

"You what?"

"I decline, my lord."

"You'll come to regret this, Philip, and sooner rather than later!"

"Mayhap you're right. Shall I call Grayson to bring you a restorative? You appear rather flushed."

"You may go to the devil!"

"I may very well yet, but it'll be in my own way, *my lord.*"

Ten

CUPID'S GARDENS

My Own Dear Gallant,
I'm about to expire of a widow's ennui.
Meet me at 1:00 at the stairs of Cuper's Garden
where we might walk and take tea.

Lady M.

HOW POETICAL, PHILIP REFLECTED DRYLY BEFORE
re-pocketing the foolscap. He was yet unsure how
he felt about this somewhat clandestine meeting. He
didn't trust Lady Messingham. His instinct told him
not to. It warned she was intent on a far deeper game
than she let on, but part of him, the reckless part,
didn't care. She'd singled him out amongst many men
who would gladly share her company, heady stuff unto
itself. Moreover, rather than seeing him as a ne'er-do-
well as did so many others, she openly admired his
dubious skills and even looked to him as a mentor. He
couldn't make sense of it, but there it was.

Philip had tried to heed George's advice and forget
her, yet he found himself unable to dismiss Lady
Messingham from his mind. He just couldn't seem

to move beyond that night at Marylebone, or the
interlude on the terrace at Belsize House. His attraction had become a powerful force that battered against
his common sense and against his will, and although
his gut said to stay away he just couldn't get enough
of her.

Nevertheless, while his masculine pride rejected
the idea of dangling after a woman, this same pride
drove him to pursuit. She was so unlike any other
he had known, but was this hold, just as George had
suggested, simply because she was above his touch?
Philip couldn't deny that was part of the appeal. Her
occasional displays of aloofness and patronizing disdain
simply made the conquest more challenging.

Until now, the fair sex had never presented the
slightest resistance. Most of the females with whom
he dallied would have lifted their skirts for a good
tupping in exchange for a mere wink and a smile, but
she was quite another kind. Even now, her damned
haunting kisses lingered, as if branded on his lips as
well as his brain.

࿇

Cuper's Gardens, or more frequently called Cupid's
Gardens, with its myriad arbors and walks, was an
ideal location for a lovers' tryst. Located at what once
had been just a narrow strip of meadow surrounded
by watercourses on the south side of the Thames,
there were two approaches to the gardens, one
through St. George's Fields (best traversed in daylight)
and the other by boat with the waterman tying up at
Cuper's Stairs.

Philip had come by way of the fields. By her stated rendezvous point, he knew she would arrive by water, but at a quarter past the appointed hour, she was nowhere in sight. The only passengers disembarking at the stairs were an elderly woman with her companion, a few married couples of the middling class, and a young woman in the dress of an upscale shopkeeper.

He looked impatiently upriver for another vessel, saw none, and consulted his timepiece with a frown. Piqued that she had played him for a fool, he turned to depart, but a husky feminine voice arrested him.

"Child! Do you not recognize me?" She had concealed her identity with a plain cotton gown and a chip bonnet, which might have passed for a better servant's garb. She was devoid of powder or paint, and her hair simply coiffed. The effect, subtracting a decade from her age, was remarkably fresh and equally charming.

He endeavored to kiss her hand, but she demurred with a cheeky grin that displayed a previously elusive dimple. "I am incognito, don't you know?" She executed a flirtatious curtsy for the benefit of passersby.

"Indeed you appear quite the pert lady's maid." He grinned. "But I fail to understand the subterfuge."

"Do you not? I am already dubbed the Merry Widow Messingham by the *Tatler*, that cheap broadsheet, all because I attended that rout at Marylebone. How I was identified behind my domino, I'll never know. I have been ever so careful, but I still risk complete social ostracism for engaging in any social activity. The less I am known in public, the better."

"Hence the disguise."

"Indeed! I couldn't stand another moment trapped in a cage without any diversion. I've lived thusly for far too long, Philip. You have no idea what it's like, and as a man, you likely never will. I envy you your liberty, you know." The note of wistfulness in her voice was impossible to miss, as was the razor edge to his reply.

"My liberty? I think you harbor misapprehensions about my mode of life, madam. I live under a yoke as surely as you do. I have neither rank nor fortune, for which sin I am consigned to live on the outer fringe of *good* society."

"But does that not afford you even greater independence? You are not forever under their watchful eyes. You may come and go wherever you choose, whenever it suits you, and with whatever company pleases you. You do not call that freedom?"

He paused to consider it. "In all truth, I have never viewed it in such a positive light, but rather have seen myself living in a kind of perdition between two worlds."

"How do you mean, Philip?" She took his arm and they began to walk.

"Regardless of my sometimes diminished circumstances, I was raised the son of an earl and educated, at least for a time," he injected wryly, "at one of England's finest schools with the scions of peers. Even a younger son is afforded some advantages in coming from such a station, but now I have left that life entirely behind me."

She digested his revelation with a frown. "You mentioned being a younger son the night we met, and

I knew immediately by your speech and bearing that you were the son of a gentleman, mayhap a knight or baronet. But an earl's son? I don't understand…"

"Why I turned my back? It is a long and no doubt tedious tale. I would not presume to bore you with it." Philip attempted to close the line of discussion.

She turned to face him with a searching look. "I would not find it dull in the least. I realize now just how little we know of one another. I would truly like to know why you reject a privileged life, one so many only dream of. I am at a loss to understand it."

"That makes two of us!" Philip laughed, still wondering what devil had possessed him to inflame the earl's passions and reject a comfortable future out of hand.

"You have regrets?"

"Daily, my lady. I have no possessions to speak of but what I win at the tables, and when fortune favors me after my brief periods of privation, I have a most unfortunate tendency to spend like the prodigal. Yet I love what I hate. It is a vicious cycle of feast and famine, leading me to extravagant binges followed perforce, more frequently than not, in seeking out the pawnbrokers on the Strand."

"Forgive my ignorance, but what is a pawnbroker?"

"A vile creature who makes his living at the expense of desperate wretches."

She frowned, dissatisfied with his explanation.

"A pawnbroker, if you *must* know, is a type of money lender, but rather than loaning solely at interest, he accepts an item of value as surety, and loans a fraction of its true worth, with the promise of repayment at an unconscionable rate of interest within a predetermined time. If the loan is repaid as agreed, the item is reclaimed by its owner."

"And if not?"

"If not, it is permanently retained by the pawnbroker."

"And this transaction is legal?"

"Perfectly. Pawnbrokers are brigands under the full protection of the law," he said sardonically.

"You have had many dealings with such creatures?"

"Unfortunately so." He spoke with contrition.

"If you have no possessions of value, what would you pawn?"

"The spoils of the gaming tables. Gold rings, silver watches, bejeweled snuff boxes. You would be surprised what men will wager when the fever is running high. I've even wagered the clothes off my back a time or two," he confessed ruefully.

"You'll get little pity from me, Philip. It is at least your choice to live as you do."

"Do you not see the difficulty of such an existence?" he asked. "I was bred for a world in which I now have not the resources to sustain myself, but having become accustomed to the finer things, I can never be satisfied with less."

She stared. It was as if he had spoken her own mind.

Oblivious to her reaction, Philip continued, "Until I obtain financial security, my life will never be truly my own. Yet my only way of achieving such security is to abandon my free will and pledge myself to follow another."

The veracity of his words resonated loudly in her brain. "I identify with your plight more fully than you know, but you do have the choice. You could always swallow your pride and go back."

"God no! I'd never give the ol' bastard the satisfaction." His vehemence took her aback.

She turned to face him. "But you just said you harbor regrets. What was the cause of such an irremediable rift with your family? Do you not at least continue relations with your siblings?"

"Sibling," he corrected. "Only a half one at that," he added with contempt. "To answer the second part of the question, I do not. Edmund and I grew up little more than strangers. We are separated by over a decade in age. He was already at school when I was born. What little rapport we might have developed was destroyed by his jealousy."

"Jealousy of what?"

"I think it was my relationship with my mother, though I'll never understand why. His own died shortly after giving birth to him. My mother was a warm and loving woman who tried her best to nurture him, but he hated her. He hated us both."

"How very sad. Where is he now, your brother?"

"Edmund, Lord Uxeter, was in London last I knew, though we thankfully run in distinctly separate circles."

"Lord Uxeter? I believe I have met him at Leicester House! He was among the most unctuous of Prince Frederick's entire troupe of toad-eaters."

"Madam, you have most aptly described my elder brother." He laughed. "He would curry the prince's favor. He maintains only a seat in the House of Commons for a rotten borough in Sussex, but has boundless ambition for advancement, whereas I have not the slightest interest."

"Is this the core of it, then? Your desire to go your own way?"

"In part. Suffice to say my bridges are now naught but smoking embers. It's a complicated morass, but enough of me." He abruptly turned the subject. "You sneak away from your house in disguise. Is that not also rebellion against those who would rule you?"

Deciding not to press him further, she answered with an unconscious jut of her chin, "I suppose one might perceive it so, but I promised myself upon my return to London to explore all of its delights. I intend to do exactly that."

"So you, like me, would thumb your nose at the lot of them." He grinned roguishly.

"I'll be discreet. 'Tis why we meet here, where the company is comprised of merchant cits, young attorney's clerks, and Fleet Street sempstresses, rather than at the more fashionable Vauxhall. I have little risk of recognition here, and I trust you with my secret."

His eyes glittered in a way she had not remarked before. "Perhaps your trust is misplaced."

"Oh, I think not," she said breezily.

"Then you do me too much honor."

"And you may soon weary of that *honor*!" She tilted her head back with an impish grin that both charmed and disarmed him. "But for now, pray let us pay our shilling and walk the gardens."

The acres of park comprising Cuper's Gardens were once part of a notable resort that had fallen into disrepair until Boyd Cuper transformed the whole into a well-frequented and picturesque public pleasure garden. The walks also included some very good bowling greens. It was at one of these that the strolling couple stopped for a time to observe a group of boisterous youths playing at bowls. When Philip taunted the lads for throwing into the ditch, she goaded him into trying his own hand at the game. He eagerly doffed his coat while she looked on, chortling with delight.

Philip was newly enchanted, having never seen this side of her, so lighthearted and carefree. They passed a lazy afternoon in complete amity perambulating the secluded walks and impeccably manicured arbors. Their promenade ended along the river at the Feathers Tavern where they partook of tea and Mrs. Evans's famed almond cheesecake *al fresco* at a table near the orchestra stage.

The Welshman Jones, the famed blind harper, played selections from Corelli and Handel.

While they sat in silent appreciation of the music, Lady Messingham studied him in mixed fascination and befuddlement.

No doubt, he cut a handsome figure with his deep-set, penetrating eyes, and strong, almost exotic-looking features, not to mention those sensuous lips, but it was more than a physical attraction she felt. Philip Drake was a fascinating man-child, with an experience of the world beyond his years coupled with an easy boyish charm. His physical appeal was impossible to deny, but it was becoming much more than that. It seemed with every hour they shared company the pull became stronger.

What was this hold he had suddenly taken on her? He was twenty years old, a mere youth for heaven's sake. While she had first singled him out from amongst the Marylebone gamesters, believing his youth would make him easy to manipulate, to control, he had proven otherwise. She had yet to sway him fully to her purpose.

Only that morning she had reviewed her accounts with Allendale. Even after taking steps to economize, her debts continued to accrue. She still needed money, and Philip was in a unique position to help her—if he chose to do so. Perhaps it was time to try a more honest tack? This moment, following their frank discussion, seemed as good as any.

"Philip," she began, "although I've immensely enjoyed our time together, I confess to have asked you here by design."

"Indeed?" Instinctively, his inner guard came up.

"I need your help," she said simply.

"Anything short of murder, my lady," Philip answered.

She dismissed the remark with a laugh. "If only it were so easy. But it is nothing quite so ominous."

"Then I am yours, body and soul, to command."

She answered, matching his flirtatious banter, "Come now, what use would I have for your soul when your body should more than suffice?"

"Would it indeed?"

She felt a strong pull in the pit of her stomach. Perhaps she had encouraged this flirtation too far? It had been much too long since she had known a lover.

"Nothing so lurid," she answered, deflecting the conversation away from the quicksand. "I only want you to teach me about gaming. I want to learn which games to play and how to play them. I want to win money."

"Good God," he exclaimed. "You left Belsize House only a few nights ago with over seventy pounds in your purse, enough to feed, clothe, and house an average family for a year! Have you spent it all so quickly? Has the fever taken to your blood?"

"You don't understand."

"I've lived this life for nearly five years, my lady; I understand only too well the danger you court."

She flashed her most beguiling smile. "But with you by my side, someone I trust for protection, what possible harm can beset me?"

"I am confounded how I have inspired your faith," he answered sardonically.

"Mayhap it is not so much what you have done as who you are," she softly replied.

"What? A gamester? A scapegrace? A feckless ne'er-do-well?" He laughed mirthlessly. "Just *who*, or *what*, do you think I am?"

His retort took her aback. Though he carried a jaded, world-weary demeanor beyond his years, his youthful vulnerability surfaced at the most unpredictable times. While Philip guarded himself closely, in those brief moments of candor they'd shared when his defenses were down, she'd glimpsed pieces of the real man, or the one he secretly wanted to be.

"Not who you pretend to be, and far too much like another for whom I once cared deeply." Her words were out before she realized and were not to be taken back.

It was the last thing Philip had expected to hear,

but there was more. It shone in her eyes, and though evanescent, he had seen it. "An erstwhile lover?"

His black eyes probed too deeply for comfort. She ignored the question, instead turning her attention to the harper, who plucked the opening strands of a popular old ballad.

"Do you know this one?" she asked, anxious to break the mounting tension. "It's an old favorite of mine." In a dulcet contralto, she sang the first verse:

> "'Twas down in Cupid's Garden
> For pleasure did I go,
> To see the fairest flowers
> That in that garden grow.
> The first was the Jessamine,
> The lily, pink and rose."

Surprisingly, Philip broke in to finish the stanza.

> "And surely she's the fairest flower
> That in that garden grows."

"La, child! You do take the role of troubadour to heart!" Disconcerted, she plied levity as her weapon.

His hand moved to possess the hand that lightly rested on his arm. Once captured, he replied lowly, "The verse was apropos."

Her bemused smile faded with the last notes of the harp. Her bantering tone sobered under his searching stare. "Between lovers, perhaps."

He answered by drawing her hand to his lips and upturned her palm. The lingering kiss he planted there made her pulse throb acutely. She attempted to extract her hand, but he held it firm. His eyes never broke contact with hers as his lips traced a path to her wrist.

With a hammering heart, she followed his motions, mesmerized by the sensation of his warm mouth on her cool skin. When at last she broke the lengthy silence, her voice was husky. "I seek only gaiety, Philip. Not a lover."

"Do you not? Then why are you here with me? What do you *really* want from me?"

She fixed her eyes above his left shoulder. "I told you. I desired the diversion of gaming and needed someone to teach me."

"I think you deny what you truly desire." He met her indignant stare with a look that sent tremors of desire to her very core.

Shocked by her own reaction, she pulled abruptly away. "You now *presume* to know my mind?"

He answered with a laugh. "What need have I to read your mind when it's written all over your face?"

She visibly started. She had told herself she'd made that afternoon assignation to persuade him to accompany her to a gaming house, but deep down he was right. She longed to feel a lover's caress, the passion of a lover's kiss, and betrayed by this truth, she made to mask it with a lie. "I think you make far more of our time together than what it is. You are a charming and diverting companion. That is all."

Philip's mouth twitched. There it was again. Every time she allowed him closer, she would just as suddenly repel him away. He was devilish tired of this game she played. "Very well," he replied, rising stiffly.

"If those are your sentiments, our idyll is indeed at an end."

They proceeded back toward the stairs with a perfunctory civility alien to them until then. She slanted a glance at his face, but his expression was inscrutable, and with every moment of the strained silence, she regretted more deeply the hostile ending of what had earlier been for her a blessed escape.

Her remorse grew as they ventured nearer the waterman. Turning to speak, to make amends, she found herself swept into a fervid embrace. He silenced her protest with his mouth.

Philip's lips melded with hers, dragging over them in a possessive kiss. She willed herself not to answer him in kind, schooling herself to passivity, but all the while her body, quivering with outrage and suppressed passion in equal measure, begged to respond.

He paused for a breath, only to claim her again, but with a kiss nothing like the first. *This* kiss threatened to sweep away all of her resistance and lies. Tenderly he cupped her face, probing her lips with his tongue. With a moan, she parted for him and he entered her mouth, exploring her more deeply, transforming what had begun as almost an assault into a warm, languorous question. She responded fervently, each tangled stroke stripping away layers of her defenses, crumbling her walls. She clung to him now, powerless to demur.

Just as suddenly as it had begun, Philip broke the embrace.

Leaving her breathless.

Whirling.

Wanting.

He removed the trembling hands that clutched his lapel. "I thought perhaps you needed something to ponder." Without a backward glance, he turned toward St. George's Fields.

Dazed and unsettled, she realized the truth: all the while she had lied to him, she really only deceived herself.

Eleven

A GAMING PEDAGOGUE

PHILIP TRIED TO STAY AWAY, TO OCCUPY HIMSELF otherwise, but after only a few days he was drawn back, as ore to a lodestone. Although she yet refused to acknowledge the growing magnetism between them, Philip knew she was as uncomfortably aware of it as he was. Yet when he called upon her, it was as if their honest, candid, and unmasked moments had never transpired.

"You've had a change of heart? You will teach me after all?" she asked hopefully.

"I will teach you the basics, my lady." He had yet to discover her true game, but somehow she'd engendered in him a desire to protect her, if only from herself.

"I am delighted!" she exclaimed, giving him a fleeting glimpse of the damsel in distress from Belsize House and the pert maid of Cuper's Garden. Just as quickly however, she transformed back to the Merry Widow Messingham, hiding behind her firmly fixed society façade. "Shall we begin with the cards, or do you prefer the dice?" she asked, indicating a chair at the green baize-covered table.

"Cards," he said. "No dice. The game is too fast and the stakes run too high. I'll teach you whist, loo, and perhaps piquet, the more genteel games you would be expected to know. The ones most frequently played at any assembly, dinner party, musicale, or rout."

He had conceded, against his better judgment, to teach her a few games. When he joined her at the table, it was with reluctance, but he decided with a glimpse of her milky breasts as she leaned forward for the cards that it was not such an onerous charge after all.

"What game shall it be? I would much like to learn piquet." Lady Messingham knew many people wagered high on the game.

"You must first learn how to shuffle."

"But I already know how to shuffle," she protested. "I wish to learn your tricks with the cards."

Philip laughed. "So innocent of the arts, and yet the lady would aspire to the society of the Greeks? Pray allow me." He purposely brushed her hand as he retrieved the deck from her fingers.

Taking the cards in his right hand, Philip used his middle finger to cut the deck into two perfectly even stacks. Then, with the expertise of a professional conjurer, he spread the cards fanlike onto the table and then flipped them to ripple over one another like a row of dominos. The effect was as if they were suddenly animated. Smoothly sweeping them back up, Philip then performed a precise and rapid series of softly clicking riffles and flawless bridges. He completed the act by fanning them once again, face upward, onto the table.

Lady Messingham's eyes grew wider and rounder

as she followed the deft movements of his hands, but gaped outright upon discovering the cards once more in perfect order. "Amazing!" she gasped. "And I thought your talent limited to dice! How do you do it?"

"Simply the product of my misspent youth," he remarked dryly.

"You will teach me this?"

"God no! Even if we had the time, do you wish to announce yourself an Athenian to the world? 'Twas but a conjuring trick I used only to achieve that priceless look of awe on your lovely face. My little performance was sheer vanity, my lady, nothing more. There are three cardinal rules to live by at the tables. Rule the first: one succeeds best at the tables by appearing an errant novice."

"Is that so?" she asked, her interest completely engaged. "What is rule the second?

"Ah, rule the second is of paramount importance." He gave her a meaningful look. "Know when to quit the table."

"But how can one know? The luck can always reverse in one's favor again."

"An absolute fallacy. Luck tires as surely as the mind, and once fortune turns, it rarely reverses. I tried to tell you as much at Belsize House."

She had the sense to look shamed. "I'm sorry I didn't heed you, Philip. I was so caught up in the game, you see."

"This segues right into the third rule. If you choose to follow no other rule, hearken to this one: never engage to play with a troubled mind or excited emotions. Lucidity of the mind is crucial and once one's emotions become engaged in the play, all is lost."

"But isn't the emotional charge the attraction? The thrill of winning?"

"More than balanced by the anguish of loss."

"I have seen you at dice, Philip. Though you hide it well, I refuse to believe you maintain such a cool detachment from the game."

"I don't deny the temptation. The table to a gamester is as powerful as the lure of cheap gin to a drunkard, but in both cases those who cannot exercise control are surely doomed to hell. I have come to know my limits in gaming, and if you endeavor to play, I entreat you to learn the same."

"Oh, fear not for me," she said. "I intend to play with care."

"I pray that is true. Women who play deep risk far more than *financial* ruin."

"La! How you go on. As if I would be so careless with my *virtue*! Besides, I told you I intend to win." Her confidence didn't waver. "Now, be pleased to show me how."

While she still exuded feminine charm, he now detected a steeliness he had never before remarked.

"As you wish." He gave a resigned shrug. "We'll begin with a very clumsy shuffle, and then proceed to deal the cards to your advantage."

"Is that possible? How can one control the place-ment of the cards when the entire purpose of shuffling is to randomize them?"

"'Tis child's play, my lady. Let us say that we have just completed a rubber of... a simple game... let's call it five-card loo. The player to your right has just played Pam—"

"The knave of clubs," she volunteered.

He nodded and then fanned the deck in search of this card, adding, "Otherwise known as Pamphilus, the ultimate trump card. You have taken note of Pam's position on the table and are next to deal. While collecting up the cards you place Pam on the bottom of the pack." Showing her the card, he places it under the stack in his hand.

"You divide the cards into two slightly uneven stacks with Pam on the bottom of the larger. You then commence by first riffling the bottom card of the larger stack, whereby Pam remains on the bottom. You split the cards in like fashion, and in repeating the maneuver, Pam will ever remain 'civil' in his place." He finished the demonstration with a flourish. "You then bottom deal the ultimate trump card to yourself. You try now." He handed her the pack.

After a few clumsy attempts, she squealed with glee at her success. "But it is so simple!"

He answered with a vulpine grin, "The best tricks usually are."

Twelve

DESPERATE MEASURES

LADY MESSINGHAM SAT AT HER DRESSING TABLE IN *dishabille*, garbed only in her stockings, shift, and stays, as her lady's maid put the finishing touches on her coiffeur. The lady regarded her reflection in the glass with a slight moue. Though Sarah was a competent enough dresser, she lacked the flair of Monsieur Brissard. The unfortunate dismissal of her personal *friseur* was but the first of what already appeared vain attempts to economize.

Sarah applied a light dusting of powder to her mistress's face, and foregoing the proffered black silk patch, the lady rose to be dressed for her morning call to Lady Hamilton, currently in residence with the Princess Augusta at Leicester House.

Sarah had already pressed her best dove-colored mourning gown for the occasion, but Lady Messingham turned up her nose. "I have done with mourning, Sarah. I care not what anyone says. If I am to go to Leicester House today, it will be in the height of style."

After selecting a modish new mantua of Spitalfields silk, Sarah assisted with panniers and petticoat, then pinned onto the gorgeous confection of rust and ochre hues an ornate stomacher worked in a complex pattern of silk and gold lace. It was one of Susannah's dearest gowns and suited her coloring to perfection, but also the last she would order from Madame Guilane, she thought with a touch of melancholy.

"What shall it be, my lady?" Sarah proffered the jewel box.

"The emeralds, don't you think? I am going to the court of the Princess Augusta, after all." Lady Messingham donned eardrops and matching pendant, pausing to admire the effect of the milky stone surrounded by diamond baguettes that lay shimmering against the creamy white expanse of her bosom.

"Aye, my lady. Those jewels be fit for royalty."

Her mistress's lips curved with the consolation that though she must economize, no one had finer jewels.

❦

She had already descended the stairs and called for her chairmen, when the footman announced the arrival of Mr. Allendale. She swept into the library where he awaited with a worried frown. "Sir, you are unexpected and come at a most inconvenient time."

"A thousand pardons, my lady, but there is never a convenient time for such pressing matters. The state of your accounts—"

She silenced him with an admonishing look and swiftly moved to close the library door. "Your discretion leaves much to be desired."

"I beg your pardon, madam, but I fear I am a bit overwrought these days." The gentleman pulled a handkerchief from his pocket to mop his bushy brow. "I genuinely fear for you, Lady Messingham. If you had only heeded my advice to take up residence in the country, all this may have been avoided. But now... I'd never have guessed that matters would come to such a pass."

"What are you saying, sir?" she asked with mounting alarm.

"My dear lady, I know not how to break the news gently."

"Then just out with it!" she exclaimed, her face already ghostly pale.

"I am in receipt of a summons for you to appear before Colonel Sir Thomas de Veil, the Westminster magistrate. Unless you are immediately prepared to settle your accounts, there is little I can do."

"When, Allendale?" she asked with rising panic. "How much time do I have?"

"Tomorrow at half eleven, you are expected to present yourself at number four Bow Street."

He pulled the parchment from his pocket and presented the summons into her trembling hands. She grasped the back of a nearby chair with the fear she might soon collapse.

"I am sorry, my lady. I will see myself out." She watched in silence as Allendale stiffly departed, leaving in much greater haste than she would have expected, but then again, he evidenced obvious relief in having dispatched his duty and was no doubt pleased to have washed his hands of her.

She tried to focus on the document in her hands, desperate for a loophole or some way to forestall the proceedings, but her welling tears blurred the words. She collapsed into the chair. "Good God! What am I to do now?"

She briefly considered asking Lady Hamilton for a loan, but dismissed the notion as quickly. Little good ever came from borrowing from a friend. Besides, the sum was too great and she had no true assurance of repayment.

Reflexively, her hand went to her throat where her fingers met the cool stones, and the answer was upon her like a bolt from the blue.

She paused to consider the prudence of it, but perceiving no other viable course she scrawled a hasty note of regret to Lady Hamilton, claiming a severe megrim. Then, feigning the same, she instructed her servants not to disturb her for the balance of the afternoon. Sarah helped her to undress and returned to her with the jewel case, which Lady Messingham accepted before dismissing the servant.

With a determined but heavy heart, she removed her emerald necklace and eardrops. She lifted them reverently, holding them up to the light. A perfect match for her eyes, the emeralds had always been her favorite. No. These she could not bring herself to sacrifice. Instead, she laid them aside to her right.

She lovingly caressed the carved mahogany lid before raising it to reveal her full treasure trove. The first item to catch her eye was a triple strand of pearls with a diamond and ruby clasp. Taking them into both hands, she raised the pearls to her lips and passed them lightly over her front teeth. She closed her eyes to appreciate the slightly gritty sensation she might never know again.

With regret, she laid them on the dressing table to the left. She continued through the box delicately examining, mentally appraising, and sorting the contents into two distinct piles before replacing those few items she had reserved back into the box. The rest she swept, along with her diamond wedding ring, into a silk-lined purse.

She dressed herself once more in her plainest gown and slid her bundle into the pocket beneath her petticoat. Covertly, she moved through the house and down the servants' stairs to exit facing the mews. Stepping through the garden gate, she pulled her cloak closely about her, and with her hand protectively over her hidden treasure, made her way briskly down Bedford Street toward the Strand.

From this bustling intersection, it was little trouble to hail a passing sedan chair. "Where to, missus?" one of the burly fellows asked.

Her response was tremulous but resolute. "To Fleet Street. I seek a pawnbroker."

Thirteen

THE SOCIETY OF GREEKS

AFTER ONLY A FEW LESSONS, LADY MESSINGHAM HAD proven a quick study with nimble fingers. She could competently perform the false cut and had nearly mastered the simpler variations of the partial shuffle. Yet after teaching her the finer points of various games, Philip found her little beyond an indifferent player. What she lacked was instinct, an intangible trait inbred rather than acquired.

While he held little reservation about her risking a few shillings at whist or loo at the more genteel gaming tables, he harbored serious misgivings if she ventured to the venues of any true gamester.

But where to safely test the waters? They had played once together at Belsize House, but he was avowed not to allow her to return. Renowned after hours as a place of illicit assignations for married ladies and a haven for more disreputable gamesters and blacklegs, many of whom he knew only too well, it was entirely unsuitable for a lady.

George Selwyn inadvertently provided the answer to Philip's dilemma when he grumbled of having to

attend a fete in his brother Charles's honor. While
Philip frequently jested that George had been raised
in the royal bedchamber, it was in truth little exaggerated. His father, Colonel John Selwyn, was close
to the Prime Minister and held a position among the
king's Gentlemen of the Bedchamber. His mother
and his brother Charles had also been part of the royal
household, with respective posts as Woman of the
Bedchamber and equerry to the departed Queen Caroline.

"Since Charles lost his post as equerry, my mother
has determined, in her boundless ambition for her eldest,
that he should now embark on his political career,"
George said. "She's holding what will surely be a mind-
numbingly dull dinner this evening for the purpose of
inducting him into the inner political sanctum."

"With your mother in charge, I daresay Charles
will soon find himself well-launched and quite at sea,"
Philip said with a laugh.

Although Colonel John Selwyn's connection to
the court dated back to the Marlborough wars, it
was actually Mrs. Mary Selwyn who had the truest
insights, having closely attended Queen Caroline.
Until her death two years prior, the real power
behind George II had been universally acknowledged and much satirized:

> You may strut, dapper George, but
>   'twill all be in vain,
> We all know 'tis Queen Caroline,
>   not you, that reign.
> You govern no more than Don
>   Philip of Spain.

> Then if you would have us fall
>   down and adore you,
> Lock up your fat wife, as your Dad
>   did before you.

Mrs. Selwyn's soiree would undoubtedly include a few low-stakes rubbers of whist, whereby Philip could partner Lady Messingham. Such a venue would ideally suit his purpose.

"Bosky, ol' friend, I seek a boon…"

✍

When Lady Messingham returned from her morning call to Lady Hamilton, a gilt-edged invitation to dine with the Selwyns awaited her. She absently tapped the invitation to her lips. It was a private dinner party. Though the Selwyns themselves were not noble, they were notoriously well-connected, and where two or more aristocrats gathered, play inevitably followed.

She had already paid enough of her debt with her pawned jewels to keep her temporarily out of the magistrate's clutches, but she still needed to get them back, before word leaked out about her circumstances. She had to find a way to come about quickly.

Surprisingly, Philip had come through for her after all. He had not only taught her the necessary skills, but had now provided the opportunity to ply them, and as a friend of George, Philip would be unremarkably present to oversee her play.

With a sigh, she smoothed the furrow of worry from her brow.

◄◇►

"Lady Messingham." Mrs. Selwyn stiffly greeted her guest, who had arrived fashionably late. "What a surprise to be honored with your presence *so soon* after your husband's demise."

"I only honor Nigel's wish that I not go into deep mourning and isolate myself completely from society. Besides, what harm can there be in attending a quiet dinner party?"

Mrs. Selwyn affected a mocking sympathy. "How painful to your sensibilities to bind you to such a promise... or should I say... how convenient to be compelled by said promise to blatantly defy all social convention."

Lady Messingham's eyes flashed, but she schooled herself to reply civilly. "Nevertheless, I was pleased to have received your invitation, Mrs. Selwyn."

"Let us not be coy, Lady Messingham, as we both know it was only George's singular insistence that compelled me to issue the invitation. Since you appear such a *particular acquaintance* of young George, I ask you pointedly, *madam*, precisely what is your association with my son?"

"A particular acquaintance?" The younger woman's lips quirked at the insinuation. "I assure you, Mrs. Selwyn, you suffer under some misapprehension. I am only recently introduced to young George through a mutual friend."

"Really? Given your recent conduct, one might be led to presume—"

"Presume what, madam?" Lady Messingham's eyes glittered dangerously. "That I have designs on your

son? A young man ten years my junior with little
fortune and few prospects?"

Involuntarily, her mind conjured a completely
different young man with similar fortune and prospects. She shook away this vision to lean into Mrs.
Selwyn in a dangerous whisper. "Or perhaps you
imagine that I use poor, hapless George to get to his
elder brother, the heir?"

Mrs. Selwyn cast a panicked look across the room
at her eldest son, Charles.

Lady Messingham chuckled aloud at the absurdity. "I
think you have been far too long among the intriguers
at court, madam. Fear not for your sons. Had I any
such designs, I would surely look to a more... mature
gentleman." She suddenly flashed a beatific smile that
stopped said lady's approaching husband dead in his tracks.

"My dear Colonel Selwyn!" Lady Messingham purred.

The elder gentleman unconsciously adjusted his
corset before bowing over her extended hand. "Lovely
to see you again, my Lady Messingham." He beamed,
oblivious to his wife's jealous glare.

"I was just telling Mrs. Selwyn how pleased I was to
accept your invitation. After I disclosed to George my
grande passion, he assured me I would find satisfaction
within your company."

Mrs. Selwyn's pupils narrowed to a pinpoint at
the boldness of the remark while the colonel shifted
uncomfortably. "Your grande passion? Satisfaction?
I assure you I am at a loss as to your meaning." He
glanced nervously at his wife.

"Why, I speak of whist, of course! Did I not say as
much?" Lady Messingham replied artlessly.

"Whist?" the colonel repeated blankly.

"Indeed, whist. I have recently learned the game and am eager to try my skill. I had spoken of spending an evening in one of the more genteel gaming venues, but my gallant Mr. Selwyn would hear of no such thing. He feared my inexperience would be taken advantage of by those disreputables who inhabit even the best public houses these days. Young George assured me that your company would be comprised of only the finest, most honorable scions of society."

"Quite right, my dear." The colonel relaxed his spine and his shoulders dropped in relief. "You have no cause to fear any amongst our august circle." He gestured grandly to encompass his assembled guests.

Scanning the room for the man she sought, Susannah passed over the portly, near-slovenly form of Minister Walpole, accompanied by two ladies, one presumably his wife. Beside them stood his sister and brother-in-law Lord Townsend, and Lady Yarmouth, mistress to the king. Farther down the room, clustered the martial figures of Lord Stair and General Wade, with whom Nigel Messingham and Colonel Selwyn had served under Marlborough in the late wars.

"August company indeed," Lady Messingham agreed. "Who is that young solemn-looking gentleman talking with your son Charles?" Lady Messingham asked.

"Ah, that would be the Honorable Mr. Pitt."

"Mr. Pitt?"

"A young MP whom Sir Robert has long wished to muzzle. It appears he is well on his way to becoming the most formidable force in the House of Commons, and a perpetual thorn in Sir Robert's side." The colonel chuckled.

She continued to search the far end of the room and her vision finally lit upon Philip Drake lost in conversation with George and a coterie of young aristocratic bucks. As if he felt her presence, he looked up straight into her face, and with a slight nod excused himself from his company.

"My Lady Messingham." His bow was very formal and correct, as if they were newly acquainted. "Dare I request the honor of escorting you to dinner?"

Mrs. Selwyn looked from one to the other and interceded before Colonel Selwyn could open his mouth to protest. "What an excellent idea! I'll have the place cards changed at once. Now John, let us leave the young people to their discourse."

The colonel barely had time to bow before Mrs. Selwyn pulled him safely away while murmuring under her breath, "I daresay *that* pair deserves one another! I hear his father cut him off long ago. Quite penniless he is. And *she* is unquestionably fast! Imagine flouting polite society as she does."

"But the Drake family name goes back to the Conqueror," the colonel protested.

"Nevertheless, the association with either of them can surely do George no good at all. I will speak to him at once." She slanted the couple a backward glance. "I shall place them together at the foot of the table with the other… less desirables."

Then with a smile she made her way to pay homage to the Prime Minister.

❦

To Philip, dinner proceeded much as George had lamented it would. He and Lady Messingham were neatly exiled from their host and hostess, relegated to the far end of the table with Mr. Pitt.

Their position allowed them to hear only snippets of conversation at the upper end, causing Philip little dismay. Dinner progressed with dull discussions of next year's elections, who would control which rotten borough, and which MP would place himself in which lord's pocket. To Philip, it was both familiar and contemptible ground.

Bored to distraction, he wondered what had possessed him to petition George for the invitation. Philip suppressed a yawn and felt a jab from Lady Messingham's slippered foot against his shin. But even boredom was better than the stab of jealousy he felt in observing her flirt with Mr. Pitt.

"With the Selwyns' close ties to Sir Robert, I am most surprised to see you at this gathering, sir. I hear you are accounted the most vocal member of the Opposition."

"The Selwyns, seasoned as they are to politics and intrigue, know which way the political winds doth blow," Mr. Pitt said with a hint of irony. "No doubt they seek to align their progeny to whichever faction might prevail. Besides," he grinned, "our illustrious minister likes to keep close watch over his adversaries."

Her eyes widened. "Then have you made yourself his enemy? I would think Sir Robert a very dangerous man to cross."

Mr. Pitt answered with a sly curve of his lips. "Outwardly Sir Robert may regard me and my colleagues with contempt, but inwardly he knows his grip on the ministry has been slipping since the death of Queen Caroline. The king himself bucks Walpole's policy of pacifism."

Sensing Philip's resentment, she turned to bring him into the conversation, but the introduction of the Spanish War at the table's head abruptly diverted Mr. Pitt's attention.

"Sir Robert," a gentleman MP asked, "what have you to say about this latest bungled business with Spain? Our superior navy should have brought her to her knees by now, but Vernon's incompetence has allowed France to send her own fleet to the West Indies. The merchant mariners cry louder than ever for justice in the name of Captain Jenkins, and I fear losing my constituency if their cries are not answered."

Sir Robert turned from his tête-à-tête with Lady Yarmouth to respond with apathy. "Jenkins again? It has been six years. Does the infamous captain yet carry his severed ear about in a wad of cotton?" the minister asked with a laugh. Though Sir Robert thought to have dismissed the issue with his cavalier remark, Mr. Pitt took up the drum.

"To a nation of commerce such as ours, Sir Robert, we must defend our trade or perish! And while you dismiss them with contempt, patriots such as Captain Jenkins daily risk their lives to provide the very snuff you take and the wine you drink."

Pausing with snuffbox in one hand and his glass of

claret in the other, Sir Robert smiled at his political nemesis. "Patriots, you say? Patriots seem to be springing up like mushrooms! I daresay I could grow fifty of them in a night simply by refusing to gratify any of their unreasonable demands."

Many of the company laughed and clinked glasses, but Pitt remained undeterred and challenging. "My good sir, for six years our ministry has failed with tooth- less negotiations that have left the question of unlawful Spanish search and seizure of our vessels unanswered. Where is the ninety-five thousand pounds the Spanish government was bound by *your treaty* to pay us in recompense? Not only do they fail to pay, but add the audacity of demanding a counter-settlement from our South Sea Company.

"Like her cousin France, Spain seeks aggrandizement by continued infringement upon our North American borders; while *we* sit back *growing fat and complacent.*" His fiery gaze raked over the paunchy minister.

"So brashly spoken is our *boy* patriot," Sir Robert answered with a patronizing laugh. "He and his callow cohorts would beat the drum with no thought to the repercussions. Any act of aggression with Spain would surely bring France into the conflict. We would then see war on two fronts. Should this occur, our so-called patriots who ring the bells of war would soon be wringing their hands instead."

"Hear, hear!" cried Walpole's supporters with glasses raised.

Undeterred, Pitt added, "Yet the king himself advocates steps to contain the hegemony."

A protracted silence reigned, in which Lord Stair,

General Wade, and Colonel Selwyn exchanged
mysterious and knowing looks. Mrs. Selwyn's expression took on a look of desperation, Mrs. Walpole
appeared offended for her husband, and the Countess
of Yarmouth simply looked bored.

Taking this all in, and sensing the mounting tension
over the dinner table, Lady Messingham seized the
moment to introduce a new topic of conversation.
"Mr. Pitt," she began in a voice clear enough to be
heard by all, "I hear you are the MP for Old Sarum.
I am also from Wiltshire, and wonder if you are
perchance related to our legendary 'Diamond' Pitt."

"Given the multitude of his famous misdeeds and
exploits, my grandfather would surely be perturbed
to know he is best remembered for a stone." The
gentleman laughed, but his attention remained acutely
aware of remarks at the far end of the table.

"Only a stone, you say? The diamond will be
written in the annals of posterity."

"Indeed, my lady. 'Twas more than a mere stone.
Uncut, it was recorded at 410 carats."

"Lackaday, sir!" Lady Messingham exclaimed and
the countess nearly choked on her wine.

Recovering, Lady Yarmouth was keenly interested.
"A diamond of 410 carats? Pray enlighten us, sir. I
must hear this story."

"Anything to please my lady," he replied gallantly.
"As many of you know, my grandfather Thomas Pitt
was for many years a merchant in India."

"An interloper and an adventurer, little better than
a pirate," Sir Robert added in an undertone.

Overhearing the remark, Pitt turned to the minister.

"My grandfather was an independent sea merchant, a man of strong character, but not a criminal. 'Tis true he operated outside the bounds of the East India Company, but he was opposed to the monopoly."

"It was a government-sanctioned monopoly, and there were multiple writs for his arrest."

"Bah!" cried the countess. "What difference does it make? I wish to hear of this diamond!"

"Of course, your ladyship," Pitt said to the countess and continued his tale. "After he was finally *detained*, the same government which fined him forty thousand pounds for his supposed illegal trading activities appointed him governor of Madras." Pitt's expression bespoke vindication. "At the end of his five-year tenure as governor, he came by an enormous diamond. A slave is said to have smuggled it out of a Golkonda mine by hiding it within a gaping wound on his leg."

"How horrid!" cried the countess.

"Even more shocking when the slave was murdered for it."

"Murdered?" she gasped.

"Shamefully, by an English sea captain who sold the stone to an Indian merchant in Madras, who in turn sold the uncut stone to my grandfather for twenty thousand pounds. He sent it back to England with my father who for safekeeping, hid it in the heel of his shoe. Upon arrival home, he hire a London jeweler named Harris to cut it. The labor took two entire years, resulting in a hewed 141-carat cushion brilliant."

"Did you ever see it?" the countess asked, by this time fondling her own brilliant teardrop necklace.

"Sadly, no, but my father did. He accompanied my

grandfather to Calais where John Law, the Scottish financier, brokered its sale to Philippe II, Duke of Orléans. The primary stone is now part of the crown jewels of France."

"How much did he pay, dis Duc?" asked the countess, her personal avarice overriding the English taboo of discussing money.

"The largest of the three diamonds sold for one hundred thirty-five thousand pounds."

"Three diamonds?" she exclaimed. "Where are de others?"

"Did I not mention? Forgive my lapse, my lady. There were two smaller, but flawless, stones also fashioned from the same cut. These were purchased by Czar Peter of Russia."

"How I would love to have seen such diamonds," Lady Messingham remarked.

"Bah! How I would love to wear them!" interjected the Countess of Yarmouth, already bedecked with sparking jewels.

"Indeed, Countess," agreed Mr. Pitt. Catching Lady Messingham's eye, he raised his glass, adding for her ears alone, "But only the worthiest of women deserve such gems."

Fourteen

WHIST CONFEDERATES

AS THE LADIES WITHDREW TO LEAVE THE GENTLEMEN to take port, Colonel Selwyn took Lady Messingham aside. "I would be remiss if I failed to commend your adroit diversion of young Mr. Pitt earlier."

"It was nothing, sir. I was intrigued to know the story."

"Nevertheless, the shift served to diffuse mounting hostilities and may have saved the evening. I thank you, my dear." He then prompted Mrs. Selwyn with a meaningful look.

"You mentioned a penchant for whist, Lady Messingham," Mrs. Selwyn interjected. "We have need of a fourth. You may partner Lady Walpole, if you care to join us."

Susannah followed Mrs. Selwyn with more than a little skepticism of her suddenly solicitous manner. The hostess performed introductions by precedence, beginning with the Countess of Yarmouth.

Lady Messingham curtsied in deep obeisance to the king's Hanoverian mistress. After a grave assessment from head to toe, the countess's lips slightly curling upwards indicated she had passed muster.

"I belief we haf met before, *ja*? But you were den with your husband. I think such a *Gemahl Greis* for such a *Mädchen Schön*. He is now passed away, your husband?"

"Several months ago, my lady. I am flattered you remember me."

"And Lady Walpole?" Mrs. Selwyn indicated the minister's former mistress Maria Skerritt, now his wife, who nodded serenely.

"So pleased to meet you." Lady Messingham repeated her curtsy and then took the proffered chair at the card table.

Mrs. Selwyn called for cards. The footman presented the pack to the countess who began her nimble shuffling sequence of riffles and bridges. "A short rubber of five games?" she asked. The others nodded agreement and she began dealing the first of the thirteen tricks.

"But what of the stakes?" Lady Messingham asked.

"Stakes?" Lady Walpole exclaimed. "Are you not aware that parliament's Gaming Act has prohibited wagering at cards and dice except at the royal residences? With so many MPs present, dare we flout the law by wagering?"

"*Mein* dears, surely there can be no harm to venture a few coins on the game," said Lady Yarmouth.

"Others do so with impunity," argued Mrs. Selwyn. "You need look no further than our own Baroness Mordington for example."

"That may be so, but she is not married to our First Lord of the Treasury," Lady Walpole gently protested.

"Ach!" the countess cried in dismay. "It is of little consequence. It appears I haf forgotten *mein* purse."

Noting Lady Messingham's emerald eardrops with rapt interest, she asked Lady Walpole, "Dis new gaming law of which you speak, it does not preclude play for a prize?"

"A prize is deemed perfectly legal," the lady agreed.

"Den what woman needs money when we haf our jewels?" The Countess removed a golden bracelet from her pale fleshy arm, and placed it on the table. She looked expectantly to Lady Messingham, exclaiming, "What exquisite gems you wear in your ears, *mein* dear."

Perceiving no tactful way to refuse, Lady Messingham removed them with great reluctance, knowing their value to be treble that of the bracelet. The countess smiled with satisfaction at Mrs. Selwyn, who then turned to Lady Walpole. They removed a ruby ring and a pearl choker respectively, also setting them on the baize-covered table.

After eyeing the baubles with a covetous gleam, Lady Yarmouth proceeded to deal each player thirteen cards, turning up the last card dealt to determine the trump suit for the first game.

༺ঌ

When the gentlemen entered the salon, the rubber was still in progress, with Mrs. Selwyn dealing the third hand of five to be played.

Philip approached the frowning Lady Messingham and murmured, "How goes it, my Lady Fortune?"

"Feebly," she replied in a low voice. "Lady Walpole and I are at love, and it appears I am about to lose some of my most prized jewels."

"Are you indeed?" He peered at her cards discreetly over her shoulder and then struck a languid pose to observe casually the last two hands. Feigning only moderate interest in the game, he grinned and flirted with the countess, while with hooded eyes he tracked every card, every gesture of the play.

Lady Yarmouth ended the rubber, laying down her final trump card with a triumphant slap. Aglow with glee, she and her partner Mrs. Selwyn divided the booty. The countess then removed her own earrings, replacing them in her ears with the emeralds, while Mrs. Selwyn caressingly admired her own prize, Lady Walpole's milky strand of pearls.

"Another rubber after tea, ladies?" Mrs. Selwyn suggested as the footman arrived with the cart.

"I shan't play," Lady Walpole replied with chagrin. "I fear I am proven a most inadequate partner. So sorry, my dear," she addressed Lady Messingham. "I have enough to explain to Sir Robert as it stands. The pearls were his gift," she said remorsefully.

"Ach, you English lack *de Geist*... de spirit!" The countess snapped her fan shut in emphasis. "Are you also so fainthearted, my Lady Messingham? Surely we can find you another partner. Mayhap de young gentleman?" The countess grazed Philip's well-built form in obvious appreciation.

Philip stepped forward readily, bowing over her hand. "I am, as always, your obedient servant, my Lady Yarmouth."

"My servant, you say? But there are many types of servants, *ja*? Some offer humble compliance, others begrudging obedience, but very few are truly *eager* to please." Her pause was fraught with meaning. "Of which variety are you, *mein liebling*?"

"Undoubtedly one most eager to please," he answered fluently. "Do you prefer long or short play, countess?"

"Ach! What a question you ask! I find *long play* so much more rewarding. Do you not agree, *mein* dear?"

Philip responded to the innuendo with a charming flash of white, secretly pleased to see Lady Messingham's brows pull together ever so slightly at their outrageous banter. Philip answered the look. "Perhaps my partner would care for refreshment or a turn about the room before the next rubber?"

"Indeed I think I would," Lady Messingham replied and took hold of his sleeve. Once out of earshot she said, "I don't understand it, Philip. Although I culled a few cards to deal Lady Walpole and myself several honors, even given this advantage we failed to take the majority of tricks. In the last hand, ne'er a one! My partner was surely not such a poor player. 'Twas as if our opponents read one another's very minds."

"Hardly, my dear. Reading one another's signals is more the case."

"What do you mean, Philip? Do you say they cheated?"

"With a system as well-developed as any common sharper."

She looked aghast at the revelation.

"During the play, I observed significant gestures they used to cue one another on which suit to lead. When the countess fingered her necklace, it was a signal to lead diamonds. When Mrs. Selwyn sipped her claret, it was to indicate hearts as her strong suit. Finger-tapping on the table indicated clubs."

"And spades?"

"Use of the ubiquitous fan."

"I would never have guessed it! How perceptive you are!"

"I have a natural gift of observation, and necessity has led me to hone it."

"Then we'll now ply it to *our* advantage."

"Indeed we shall. As we have seen, these two ladies are old hands at play. Court circles are notorious for cultivating cheats, especially amongst the fair gender who love to play but are so very reluctant to pay."

"How shocking!" she replied.

"'Tis why I endeavor never to engage in play with women."

"So why do you now make exception?"

He paused as if asking himself the very same question, and slowly answered, "Perhaps I've a guilty conscience for leading you down this perilous path."

"But you did not lead. If you recall, I gave you little choice."

Her green gaze met his intently, suddenly igniting the memory of her lingering kiss that first night in the carriage. *Little choice indeed.* He shook himself from this brief fantasy, painfully struck with the awareness that there was little he would not do for her, to have her.

"Regardless of how I got into this," she continued, "I'd dearly love to have my emeralds back." In truth, she was devastated by the loss, considering the jewels she had already sacrificed.

"Then you've need of a strategy which was sadly lacking in your prior game with Lady Walpole."

"What do you mean? If not brilliantly, I thought we played quite competently."

"I beg to differ. On more than one occasion you failed to lead your longest suit."

"But is it not best to lead a singleton?"

"Only when you know you will trump in that suit, and when you are reasonably assured that your partner is able to continue the suit led."

"How do you know so much of this game? I thought your forte was the dice."

"Hazard is always my preference, as I have learned to minimize the randomness of chance, but I have no short acquaintance of the cards. I neglected my classical studies by spending more hours examining Charles Cotton's *Compleat Gamester* than applying myself to Homer."

"And this *definitive guide* has made you an expert on whist?"

"Not exactly, but I consider myself more than proficient. At Harrow, I was quite the master of ruff and honors, from which the principles of whist are derived. To the uninitiated, whist appears a rather simple game, but it has tremendous potential for scientific play."

"But how can even science help while our opponents cheat?" she asked with a pout.

"It is not near as difficult as you think, now they have revealed themselves. We'll simply employ some signals of our own."

"What kind of signals?"

"Just watch my discards. If our opponents are drawing trumps, I'll indicate my preference of play by throwing a low card of my strongest suit."

"And what of the honors?"

"Fear not, my lady. Upon my deal, you will be endowed with many honors." He winked.

"How very generous of you." She beamed. "How shall I best play them?"

"I suggest in the first hand, when I ensure you hold both king and ace, you should lead the king, but in the second hand, it is ofttimes preferred to play lower, and even to split honors."

Intent upon every word, she pursed her lips in keen concentration of his instructions.

So close to his own, Philip's concentration began to waver in meditation of her ripe lips, with that damned scent of hers further distracting his thoughts. One deep inspiration and he'd be lost in her very essence.

"I'm not sure I understand. What is splitting honors?" she asked, snapping him out of his brief reverie.

Now what the devil had he been saying? Ah yes, honors. "The honors are the face cards of the trump suit. You should ordinarily play your lower face cards to protect the higher. For example, play the knave or ten while holding the queen, or the queen when holding the ace. This manner of finessing can prove advantageous. But now I fear we are being beckoned back to the table." He remarked Lady Yarmouth's frown at his extended private discourse with the younger and more beautiful Lady Messingham. "Are you ready?" he asked.

"I believe I now have a firmer grasp of the game. But Philip, what have you to wager?" she asked, suddenly noting the lack of adornment in his dress and the slightly worn condition of his clothes.

He reassured her with a grin and pulled a bejeweled snuffbox from his pocket. "Surely this item should entice the king's mistress. She may recognize it as once belonging to Bubb Doddington, one of the wealthiest men in England and close friend to the Prince of Wales. He was quite distressed by his loss."

She looked her question.

"The hazard table at Blackfriars. One should never wager what one is unprepared to lose."

"But what if *you* lose?"

He answered matter-of-factly, "The box means nothing to me. Besides, I play to win. If you follow my lead, I daresay we'll not only retrieve your emeralds by the end of the evening, but also add a diamond necklace to boot."

Giddy with the notion of replacing what she had lost, she rewarded him with a smile so dazzling his breath caught. "You know, Philip, I've always been so very partial to diamonds."

Fifteen

FIT FOR A QUEEN

RETURNING TO THE TABLE, PHILIP HANDED A NEW PACK of cards to the countess. "A rubber of nine, my lady?"

"Did I not say I prefer long play, *mein liefer*?" she replied suggestively, and proceeded to shuffle the cards. In offering them back to Philip to cut, she leaned into him much closer than necessary, brushing his arm with ample breasts that threatened to spill from her gown.

"Do we play with or without honors?" Philip asked with an appreciative smile as he cut and then handed the cards back to her.

She languidly stroked a finger along his arm before starting the deal. "But of course, *mein liebling*. While there is *always* honor in holding the king, I find myself very pleased in receiving knaves as well."

"Shall we commence now?" Susannah interjected with a tight smile, turning over the first card before the countess could answer.

Lady Messingham's high queen determined she would proceed, and as play progressed, so did Philip's hyperawareness of her every look and gesture. He felt her growing sensitivity to him, even in their play. The tension was as palpable as a pulse. When their light banter ended in seconds of locked gazes, she would avert her face, or dismiss the moment with a laugh. Yet, more than once, he had caught her regarding him with a peculiar expression speaking more than simple speculation. No. He was not mistaken. Lady Messingham was neither the worldly jade she pretended to be nor as unaffected as she wanted him to believe.

The evening ended in triumph. Accurately interpreting every signal passed between their opponents, and applying Philip's strategy supplemented by his subtle cues, they played brilliantly. They had taken the vast majority of tricks, and due to Philip's skill at the deal more than their rightful share of honors.

Lady Messingham suppressed her outright jubilation until settling in the privacy of her carriage when Philip joined her under the pretense of escorting her home. Once inside, he closed the door and signaled the driver. She turned to face him, utterly basking in their victory.

She regarded him, breathless with delight, her unadulterated joy setting her aglow. "Did you see Lady Yarmouth's expression when we took the final trick? It was absolutely priceless!"

Her skin flushed and her eyes shone with excitement, much as he imagined she would appear in the throes of passion. Ensconced completely alone with her in such close quarters, Philip was barely able to think. Their earlier play had only intensified his ache, so in tune had he become to her every signal, word, and nuance in their exchanges. The experience had taken complete hold of him and he wanted her beyond his understanding.

Philip reached inside his coat pocket, remembering the prize they had won. The necklace was magnificent, three rows of shimmering stones with a brilliant teardrop diamond at its center. He held it before her eyes and she gasped at its splendor, evident even in the dimly lit interior of the carriage.

"Jewels fit for a queen... or at least for a king's mistress," he said with a laugh. "May I?" he asked softly.

"Yes, indeed," she answered. Breathy with anticipation, she turned sideways to grant him easier access. Philip placed the gems against her throat, stroking a few stray tendrils of hair from her nape before closing the clasp.

The feel of his warm breath caressing her nape as he closed the clasp shook her with a frisson she had long forgotten. The touch of his fingers against her skin sent her pulse skittering. He didn't release her, but moved his fingers gingerly from the clasp and bent his head to brush his lips against the sensitive flesh joining her neck and shoulder.

She closed her eyes, heightening the sensation, as his tongue began to trace her pulse and his mouth moved over her skin, tasting inch by inch, while his hands began a gentle exploration, tracing the path of the necklace to the diamond teardrop lying just above the cleft of her breasts.

She moaned softly as a thick cloud of desire descended, enshrouding her. "Priceless indeed," he murmured against her skin. She had almost resigned herself to surrender, his gentle touch having torn down her defenses bit-by-bit, but the intimation of his words penetrated the thick fog of her desire.

Her eyes snapped open. "Pray remove the necklace, Philip."

He abruptly ceased the caress.

"Remove the necklace," she repeated icily.

"Why?" he asked, confounded.

"You helped me to win back my emeralds, for which I am grateful. The necklace is rightfully yours. *I, however, am not.*"

"I don't want the damned necklace!" His voice was hoarse and frustrated by unslaked lust. "Consider it a gift."

"A gift?" she repeated. "You think to buy me, then? Like a whore?"

"I would hardly compare the jewels of the king's mistress with the trinkets of a whore." He smirked, but his attempt at humor fell short of its goal.

"Well, I shan't be bought with shiny trinkets... or even with priceless ones." She grasped the necklace and jerked it defiantly from her neck, breaking the delicate clasp.

"I suppose you would have accepted it readily enough from *him*," Philip accused.

"From whom?" she demanded.

"From Pitt, of course. He spent the entire evening alternating between making sheep's eyes at you and endeavoring to impress you with his speeches."

"How dare you make such an accusation after the way you conducted yourself with Lady Yarmouth!"

"Don't be ridiculous! You know that was all part of the game."

"I do wonder about that, Philip, after the way she fondled you."

"Fondled, is it?" He barked with laughter. "Now who's jealous?"

"I'm not jealous! Nor do I want the necklace. I've told you before, I won't be beholden to *any* man."

"You know that's not what I intended."

"No? Then precisely what did you intend?"

Lacking a better answer, he growled back, "I don't bloody well know! But I've come to doubt if you are worth the aggravation of finding out!"

"Then you needn't trouble yourself further. I have learned enough from our lessons to acquit myself sufficiently at the tables—without your help."

"The hell you will! A bleating sheep to the wolves is what you will be if you are so ill-advised as to sit at any real gaming table without me."

"Oh, I beg to gainsay you on that, *my young buck*! I've managed my life perfectly fine before your arrival and no doubt will survive your departure just as well."

Her remarks only added fuel to his simmering fire of frustration. He dangled the necklace before her eyes and stuffed it back into his pocket. He then signaled the driver with a sharp rap of his sword hilt on the carriage roof.

"Just what are you doing?" she demanded, as the carriage came to a clattering halt.

Philip replied with stiff control, "You've done with my tutelage, and I've long since wearied of *your games*." He opened the door. "I go to find more *rewarding* company."

His meaning was not lost on her as he leaped out of the carriage. "You are insufferable!"

"And you, *my lady*, are nothing more than a bloody cock-tease."

She gasped.

He growled.

They both signaled the driver, and the carriage door slammed shut.

Sixteen

AN UNQUENCHABLE THIRST

PHILIP PAID TUPPENCE TO A LINKBOY TO LIGHT HIS way through the streets encased in blackness. With his right hand ready on his sword, he set his direction for the George and Vulture, absently reaching into his left pocket and fingering the necklace, wondering what price it might bring. He deliberated offering it first to Lady Yarmouth. Surely she would rather buy it back than suffer the king's wrath once the news was made known to him of her loss.

Although George II doted on his Hanoverian mistress, he was reputed as the most parsimonious of monarchs and the countess would wish to avoid an embarrassing explanation. Philip decided that after appraising his prize, he would send George Selwyn as his emissary to negotiate a price with the countess, not daring to meet with her himself after the way she had devoured him over the card table.

Still seething from the way this evening had ended, he detoured from his original destination in favor of Tom King's establishment, bent now on quenching his fever as well as his thirst at the only available venue for such late-night debauchery. Although the watering hole was notoriously dark and dank, it was, strangely, one of the few places in London where one might as easily encounter a duke as a fishmonger among the late-night frequenters. While its proprietor, Tom, tended the tap, his common-law wife, Moll, acted as procuress. The pair only managed to evade the law against running a disorderly house by the establishment's conspicuous lack of beds.

"Ye be looking fer Nell, I s'pose?" Moll King asked rhetorically when Philip entered the one-room tap.

"Is she previously… engaged?" He surveyed the room, squinting at the shadowy forms of groping couples. Although he had come for much the same purpose, tonight he was struck with a sudden distaste for the writhing and groaning in the back of the tavern. One did tend to avoid the darker corners at Tom's unless engaged in company, but the arrangement had never before seemed more than mildly incongruous.

Moll eyed Philip with something near contempt. "Nay, though she passed over several o' yer betters hopin' ye'd appear. Don't understand why the chit dangles after the likes of you when she could turn a pretty coin."

Unlike most of the women working the tavern, Nell was employed as a barmaid, having left the George and Vulture for lusher and more lucrative pastures. Philip knew in time she would succumb to the life, but as yet she had refrained from doling out her favors. He had little doubt she'd yield easily enough to him without even turning on the full brunt of his charm.

"Tell her she need not wait any longer." Philip

grinned and located a table in one of the better-lit sections of the taproom.

"So, ye finally showed yer pretty face," Nell said saucily, setting his tankard down with a slosh.

He placated her with a caress to her rump. "Surely it's not been so very long, Nell."

She answered with a pout. "Nigh on a sennight I been waitin' on ye, though Lord knows why I does. There be gents aplenty every night what offers me pretty trinkets."

"So dear Nell truly languishes for my company?" He pulled her unceremoniously onto his lap, her plump bosom close enough to his mouth to render his next words nearly unintelligible. Nell pulled away with a giggle and yanked up her bodice, mollified by his enthusiastic display.

"Enough o' that, or all the gents will be thinkin' me one o' them lightskirts. Hearken now," she whispered, "I gets off in an hour. If ye bribe Betsy, what shares me pallet, we can have it all to ourselves."

"But one would hate to deprive poor Betsy of her bed." Philip's lips curled into a raffish grin. "I've a better notion. Why not invite her to join us?"

"A randy one you surely be this night!" She snatched herself away with another peal that strangely grated his nerves. Curiously, the same artlessness he once found charming had lost all of its appeal. In his mind, a low, throaty chuckle beckoned him as a siren's song.

Annoyed with himself, he shook off the fancy and turned back to Nell. "An hour then, my dove?"

But after a number of tankards and before the clock

chimed the hour, rather than throwing the giggling Nell's skirts over her head and filling his hands and mouth with Betsy's bounty, Philip left the tavern just as he had arrived… restless and empty.

Seventeen

WHORES, ALL OF US

"My dear, the whole town is raving about your card game at the Selwyns's! Frau Walmoden was simply beside herself that you got not only what she intended as a delicious new cicisbeo, but her treasured diamonds as well!" Jane was breathless and her eyes alight for the latest *on-dit*.

"They say she absolutely trembles at the thought of telling the king. He's such a volatile little man, you know. Freddie says that in a true fit of pique he snatches off his peruke and kicks it about the room!"

"Can you envision it, Jane? The king in such an infantile tantrum?" Susannah laughed hollowly and Jane perceived the forced effort at mirth.

"What is it, Sukey? You appear blue-deviled when I'd have thought you'd be looking like the cat that got the canary after such a night. You must show me this necklace! I'm told the diamonds are of the first water."

"Oh, but they are! Or were," Susannah lamented.

"What do you mean... were?" Jane's expression was horrified. "Don't say you've lost them!"

"No such thing. They were never truly mine to begin with."

"But I heard it straight from Albinia Selwyn. Her mother has been mourning her loss for days, and need I warn you, you've no friend in *that* quarter, my dear."

"Mrs. Selwyn? What do I care about that malicious woman? She set me up, you know. She and the countess were confederates to gain my emeralds. If it were not for Philip—"

"Philip, eh? It seems you are on quite intimate terms now. I suspected as much." Jane smiled slyly.

"It is *not* what you think, Jane!"

"The lady doth protest much!" Jane chuckled. "I shan't judge you. As long as you both maintain discretion, who is to know?"

"As I said—it's not what you think and besides, it's unlikely I'll ever see him again."

"You don't say he stole the necklace!"

"Lud, how you do jump to conclusions! No. He offered it to me and I refused it. The necklace is in his hands because he rightly won it."

Jane pressed a hand to her friend's forehead. "Are you febrile? Or is your mind disordered of a sudden? Why on earth would you refuse a diamond necklace?"

"Mayhap my mind *is* disordered. I certainly haven't the lucidity of thought I had a month ago."

"It's him, isn't it? You do want the young rogue."

Yes. She did, she thought deprecatingly. Here she could have almost any man in the peerage, including the prince himself, and she pined over a penniless adventurer. "He hasn't a farthing, Jane," she said, "and besides, I won't be beholden to a man. The necklace would have bound me to him."

"Twaddle! Many women accept gifts from men without a second thought."

Sukey retorted without thinking, "Indeed. And what does that make them?"

Jane's expression lost all humor. She wished at once she could take back the words.

"You think me equal to a common whore, Sukey?"

"Jane, you know that's not what I meant!"

"No, it's precisely what you meant, just not what you meant *to say*."

"I never meant to imply..." Susannah raised her hands helplessly.

"That since I accept gifts I'm a whore, Susannah?" she replied caustically. "I have done what I deemed necessary to provide comfort for my family and still move in the highest circles. I am one of Princess Augusta's closest confidantes and *she* will one day be queen.

"And look at the prince who will one day be king—he lives rapaciously out of the hand of Bubb Doddington and his ilk, repaying his cronies with political appointments and sinecures. Whores. The House of Commons has half its members on the Lord Treasurer's pay, or in some lord's pocket.

"Just look around you! Have you lived among us for so long, inured to the reality that we are all no better than whores? Our fathers and their lawyers are no better than pimps in arranging our marriages. God knows Hogarth rightly lampoons the practice. Need I say more?"

"Jane—" she implored.

Jane's lips formed a rigid line. "Think of me what you will, Sukey, but I am not ashamed. Just remember, my dear, when you place yourself on such a pedestal, someone may be tempted to kick it from under you. Now, good day to you, *Lady Messingham*."

Lady Jane Hamilton swept defiantly out of the room, leaving Susannah feeling more alone than she had ever felt in her life.

Eighteen

A DEN OF INIQUITY

ALTHOUGH PHILIP FAILED TO SHOW THE NEXT DAY FOR Lady Messingham's gaming lesson, she occupied far more of his thoughts than he would have liked. His attempt to conceal it was in vain, the cause of his black mood obvious to George, who joined him for a tankard.

"What you need is diversion, old man," said George. "You missed a capital hanging at Tyburn yesterday. You should go with me next month. The rabble are deuced entertaining. They hardly wait until the jig is done before they start jockeying for the cadavers for the medical students. There was one burly fellow pulled so hard on a carcass he took the head clean off."

"Good God!" Philip shuddered. "You find that entertaining?"

"I am in good company, dear boy. Half of London town turned out for it."

"De gustibus non est disputandum."

"You know I hate when you quote Latin."

"To each his own," Philip translated.

"I'm sorry to offend your delicate sensibilities, but you should do something to celebrate your good fortune. Instead here you are in the devil's own humor."

"I'm not out of sorts, Bosky. I'm just… preoccupied."

"Preoccupied? I won't ask by what, but by *whom*?"

Philip's answering glare should have burned a hole through him, but George continued unfazed. "I warned you that first night at the Rose of Normandy she would be nothing but trouble. Her type always is."

"Just what would you know of *her type*?"

"You know what I mean. The so-called beauties of the *ton*, they always place unreasonable demands upon a man."

"And you speak from personal experience?" Philip mocked.

"Well, no," George replied. "I've avoided the snare, but I have seen enough poor sots completely unmanned by such women, and *you*, my dear chap, were well on your way. Leave her be, I say. There are too many merry wenches who won't complicate a man's life to bother with the Susannah Messinghams of the world." He emphasized his point with a great frothy gulp of ale.

Philip raised his own tankard as if in agreement, but even in his state of deep resentment over the hold she had upon him, he could not seem to dismiss her and move on.

"I have it!" George interrupted Philip's ruminations. "Just the cure for your condition!"

"My condition? What do you blather on about now, Bosky?"

"You know exactly what I mean. You're boorish

company of late, all because you're besotted with a woman you can't have. I can't fathom it with any number of ready whores at Tom's—"

"I think I'm done with whores. These days, one can scarce risk the cure."

"You hardly have the means to adopt such fastidiousness. At any rate, I daresay you'll have no peace until you've had *a piece*." George chuckled. "You know, Drake, there's nothing like a good bacchanal to put a man to rights. I think Dashwood's gathering might be precisely the thing."

"Dashwood? You mean Sir Francis?"

"The same," said George. "He and his cronies used ofttimes to gather in this very place." He gestured to the taproom. "I had near forgotten the... er... club... is now meeting at an altogether new venue. Do you know of Medmenham Abbey?"

"Medmenham? Isn't it naught but ruins?"

"It was, until Sir Francis leased it and began its restoration to create a more private place to host his... er... entertainments."

"A private retreat for what?" Philip's interest was piqued despite himself. "By all accounts, Dashwood's a complete libertine."

"Some might consider him so." George grinned. "A few self-righteous prigs have frowned upon his amusements during his continental travels."

"What kind of amusements?"

"He is said to have terrorized some poor pilgrims at the Vatican."

"He did what?"

"Don't look so shocked, ol' fellow, 'twas but a

lark!" George needed no further encouragement to relate the full tale.

"It was Good Friday, when hundreds, mayhap thousands, of penitents come to scourge themselves at the Sistine Chapel. Sir Francis enters among them, but hides a horsewhip under his greatcoat and waits for the priest to extinguish all but three of the candles. Then, under cover of near-darkness, Dashwood proceeds to flog the penitents from one end of the chapel to the other. The congregated were shrieking in terror, '*Il Diavolo!*' believing the devil incarnate come upon them!" George burst into a fit of mirth until tears streamed from his eyes. "And even *that* story is nothing compared to his exploits in Russia when he impersonated the King of Sweden to seduce the Tsarina."

"Is the man mad?" Philip asked, incredulous.

"Not mad, but a damn-them-all roistering devil for certain. His wine cellar is deep and the bottles flow freely. Best of all, the company of the self-proclaimed Abbot of St. Francis is mixed, and the women liberal with their favors. Dashwood's precisely the man to provide the diversion you need."

"He is indeed, Bosky. Wine, women, and unfettered debauchery?" Philip stood and emptied his tankard in a last great swallow. "What are we waiting for?"

❧

The two young men threw together some traveling clothes and set out from London on horseback for the ancient Cistercian monastery in Buckinghamshire. Abutting the Thames, the great heap of rubble that was formerly Medmenham Abbey certainly offered seclusion.

Philip's initial assessment was that the so-called restoration had progressed little beyond the incipient stage, but upon closer inspection he realized that this was precisely the impression that Dashwood intended to give. A cloister and tower, laid out in a peculiar mix of Gothic and neoclassical styles, lay partially hidden behind a crumbling wall, but the fresh mortar belied the structure's true age.

"Who the deuce are they?" Philip asked upon their approach, indicating two imposing statues, one male and one female, standing sentinel at the stone entrance.

"This couple, my ignorant friend, is the Egyptian god and goddess of silence, Harpocrates and his consort, Angerona. They remind all who enter to uphold the secrecy of the rites within. Now Drake, before we proceed further, you must swear by all you hold holy that you will speak nothing of this place once we leave."

"Sacred rites? Swearing secrecy? Good God, Bosky, this seems a bit over the top. What manner of place is this?"

"One whose mysteries shall soon be revealed." George's expression was enigmatic. "Now do you swear?"

"Yes, yes," Philip snapped. "I swear on my dear mother's grave. Are you now satisfied?"

"I brought you as my guest. You could at least *try* to enter into the spirit of the game," George retorted churlishly.

"Very well, George, I assure you my lips are sealed. Now may we proceed?"

They progressed through the gate into the cloister leading to the half-crumbled stone tower, where carved over the entrance were the words *Fais ce que voudra*.

Philip enunciated the phrase as a question, while searching his memory. "'Do what thou wilt'? Rabelais, isn't it? If memory serves, 'twas the motto of the Abbey of Thélème in the tale of *Gargantua and Pantagruel*."

"Precisely so, gentlemen," came a deep voice from behind. "The monks lived only by their free will and pleasure. 'Tis the adopted dictum of the Knights of St. Francis." The hidden voice materialized into an elegantly clad gentleman, who stepped forward to rap thrice upon the tower door.

He then turned to face the younger men and made a perfunctory bow. "Sandwich, at your service," he said. "Ah! Mr. Selwyn," he exclaimed in sudden recognition. "It has been some time since we have met."

"Indeed, my lord," Selwyn agreed, "likely not since the Knights of St. Francis last convened at the George and Vulture. I thought it high time to see for myself all the to-do about Medmenham Abbey. Now pray let me make known to you my comrade in dissipation, Philip Drake."

"Drake? Hastings's feckless younger son?" The Earl of Sandwich laughed at Philip's scowl. "Now don't take umbrage simply because your reputation precedes you."

"I daresay my reputation is grossly exaggerated."

"Then you deny expulsion from Harrow for leading the underaged scions of the noblest houses to the vices of gaming and gin? Or that your name has become the blight of every hazard table from Blackfriars to Covent Garden?"

"Surely my repute is not so wide-spread." Philip suppressed a smirk.

"Surely not." Sandwich winked in understanding. "Nevertheless, I bid you welcome to Sir Francis Dashwood's new Utopia, where such men as we may be free of the so-called moral subjections and constraints that keep us down, and where for a time we may shake off and break those bonds of servitude wherein we are so tyrannously enslaved."

"You are the humanist, George, not I. What the deuce does he natter on about?"

"Mostly whores and booze," George replied with a grin.

Sandwich continued, while rapping once more upon the door, "Man is led into vice only when he is denied, my friends; for it is his nature to long after things forbidden and to desire most fervently what is denied."

"Another translation?" Philip asked.

"Whores and booze… in boundless supply." George added under his breath, "All the better at Dashwood's expense."

"Ah," Philip said, "I stand in renewed appreciation of the philosophers."

They were interrupted by the sound of shuffling feet before the great oak door swung open. The answering servant wore the coarse brown woolen cowl of a Franciscan monk. He maintained silence, indicating by his upheld lantern that they should follow him down the dim stone-paved hallway.

As they walked, the lamplight revealed a long and graphic fresco depicting explicit sexual gratification.

Another mural displayed Dionysus and Aphrodite entangled in coitus, leading to the final figure of Priapus in all of his eternally erect splendor under the caption "*Peni tento non penitenti.*"

Philip's brows shot upward at the translation. "A tense penis, not penitence?" He looked to George. "And you described Dashwood as *a bit of a libertine*? I'd liefer call him a veritable Rochester."

"You have no idea, Drake." George laughed.

"You must wait here," croaked the voice from within the cowl. "None may enter without first paying homage."

At this Sandwich knelt and genuflected. "I hereby profess my faith and hereafter swear my eternal devotion to Venus and to Bacchus." He followed with a great draught of wine from a bejeweled chalice.

Philip eyed George once more with overt skepticism. "You still ascribe to this heretical nonsense, Bosky? Weren't you sent down from Cambridge for performing some such sacrilege?"

"Give o'er, Drake. 'Twas just some high jinks, same as this. Just play along with it, for form's sake," George urged in a low whisper. With a sigh of resignation, Philip followed his companion through the motions and drank from the ceremonial cup.

"And now you may enter the temple of Venus," spoke the keeper of the chalice before the twelve-foot oak doors swung free on their hinges.

Nineteen

A KNAVE IN SHINING ARMOR

PHILIP HAD NO CLUE WHAT HE HAD EXPECTED TO FIND inside, but the outer trappings of a crumbling monastery had not prepared him for the scene of decadent opulence within.

The room was ablaze with a thousand tapers revealing what decency should have concealed in the dark. The walls were festooned with tapestries and every conceivable pornographic work. Oil paintings depicted nymphs and satyrs *in flagrante delicto*, while the walls bore placards bearing libertine maxims and sexually explicit witticisms.

Oriental rugs were scattered about a room decked out lavishly with Turkish divans and couches of silk and velvet, upon which sprawled numerous couples already engaged in the earlier stages of copulation.

Philip took a long draught from the glass of Madeira offered by one of the flock of wooden-faced servants who stood at the ready with flasks and chalices.

George had already emptied his own, and nudged his companion in the ribs. "A man could quickly accustom himself to this, eh Drake?" He then beckoned the footman for a refill.

Philip's attention was drawn to the entrance of a man robed in crimson ceremonial garb topped with a cap trimmed in rabbit fur. The presumed master of ceremonies approached the raised platform with a smile for his guests. With the slightest inclination of his head, the doors were then closed and bolted from the inside.

With a signal to the cowled figure, a giant brass gong sounded, the resonance echoing throughout the chamber, shaking the crystal chandeliers and putting an abrupt halt to all the aforementioned activities.

"Now the fun begins," George whispered with a gleam in his eyes.

"My dear brothers and honored guests," the self-proclaimed Abbot of St. Francis began. "We gather in this holy of holies, the place of voluptuary worship for the professed profligate, to dedicate our newly erected Temple of Venus. And in this vein we do now offer up our first and our best sacrifice." He raised his hands and cried, "Enter Persephone!"

A side door opened to a parade of women who sashayed into the chamber, clad in diaphanous robes exposing the left breast in the style of Venus Genetrix. At the rear guard, Philip recognized the notorious bawd "Mother" Elizabeth Ward dressed as Demeter. The earlier cowled figure revealed himself as Dashwood's amanuensis, former poet and satirist Paul Whitehead. Between them, they dragged a bound and struggling young woman toward the sacrificial altar.

Dashwood addressed Mother Ward at their approach. "Do you, Demeter, freely and without constraint offer up your daughter Persephone as a pure and virgin sacrifice to the mother god Venus?"

"If I don't, you shan't find another in the entire of London. She likely be the only virgin left!" The retort set the whores cackling and the room rumbled in raucous, drunken laughter, but Dashwood frowned at the levity.

"Perhaps you should just repeat after me. I, Demeter, offer my virgin daughter, Persephone, to the mother god Venus."

The sacrificial "virgin," clearly not long out of girl-hood, stood frozen before the altar with ashen face and quivering lips. "Mayhap Demeter offers her up, but Persephone appears none too eager to be sacrificed," Philip murmured low to George.

"She's indeed a fine performer!" George applauded. "Dashwood'll surely pay her treble her normal take for *this* night's work."

"I fear you are mistaken, Bosky. Note how she trembles. No actress of Covent Garden is that good. I question if it's an act at all." Philip's disquiet increased when the bawd tore the robe completely off the girl and pulled her, naked, screaming, and thrashing, onto the altar. As the trio proceeded to spread the girl's legs and lash them into place, Philip asked George with rapidly escalating apprehension, "Precisely what does this *sacrifice* entail?"

Lord Sandwich spoke up from behind. "If it's the shedding of blood you dread, fear not, ol' man. The only blood sacrificed will be that of her maidenhead… if virgin she really be," he spoke with a knowing wink.

"Surely an impressive actress, that one. No doubt I have seen her on the Drury Lane stage," Selwyn remarked appreciatively while Sandwich ventured a more philosophical reply.

"'Tis really no matter whether she's virgin or not. He's likely too soused to know the difference if she isn't, and if she is, by night's end she'll be well broken in... at least by the time you get your turn." Sandwich signaled for more wine and then moved to the fore to obtain a better view.

"Can't say I fancy another's dirty leavings," Philip murmured with no attempt to mask his contempt.

"Since when have you become so exacting in your requirements, Drake? Many a time we've shared a whore betwixt us."

"And she was ever willing to be shared. I don't countenance the same of this one." Philip nodded toward the girl, having by this time ceased her struggles.

She lay across the raised platform, exposed for all to see. Her voice, hoarse from screaming, was now a mere whimper. Her breath came in short frantic pants. In desperation, she turned her head away from her captors. She frantically searched the room until her terror-stricken face was fully revealed.

"What in the devil's name?" Philip exclaimed upon recognizing Nell, the barmaid from Tom King's, and in that moment knowing for a certainty. "This is not a game, Bosky. The girl is not a willing party to this."

"Good gad, Drake! What's come over you? Suddenly you've become a bloody killjoy. I question why I brought you here!"

Philip posed his response deliberately. "While I enjoy a good *romp* as well as any man, I'll not be a party to *rape*."

"Rape? Is your mind disordered of a sudden?"

"By what other name would you call it, George?" Philip gestured to the dais, closely surrounded by leering men openly fondling themselves in anticipation of the show.

George's visage suddenly flashed something akin to fear. "Pox on you, Drake, I haven't a word for it! Nevertheless, you've no business to interfere." George's next words came out almost menacing. "See there—the Prince of Wales, and over there, the Secretary of the Admiralty. The room is filled with peers of the realm and members of Parliament. The Knights of St. Francis are twelve of the most powerful men in England and they'll ruin you without a thought—if they don't kill you first. If you mean to do anything foolhardy, I can't stand beside you."

"Then you may as well stand behind me and watch my back, as I can't allow this madness to progress any further." With a baffling sense of purpose and flagrant disregard of the repercussions, Philip drew his dress sword and elbowed through the throng to leap upon the stone dais.

"What the hell do you think you are doing? Who is this man!" Dashwood cried out to no one in particular.

"I am come to make my own offering to Venus." Philip said, drawing the blade of his sword swiftly across his left hand and squeezing a steady trickle onto the altar.

Dashwood stood dumbfounded as Philip sliced through the restraints binding the girl. Realizing what Philip was about, Dashwood grabbed for Nell. Now freed, she evaded by scrambling on hands and knees to cower behind her protector. Philip extended his sword in warning. "I remind you, the requisite blood sacrifice is already made."

"The hell it is!" Dashwood forced through clenched teeth. "*Your* blood is unacceptable. The rites of Venus require a *virgin*. Now give me the girl, you sodding sack of shit, before I'm moved to spill *all* of your blood on my altar."

Philip met the threat without a flinch, but the terrorized Nell skittered further back to crouch, quavering and clutching at Philip's coattails. Philip calmly reiterated, "If Venus requires virgin blood, my sacrifice *will* stand."

He cast Philip a malevolent glare. "You name yourself a virgin?"

"I'll fix that for ye, dearie," one of the whores called out.

"Surely you do not gainsay me, Sir Francis." Philip quirked an implicating brow. "Unless you claim to have been present upon the occasion…"

The remark caused a cacophony of teeters and snickers.

Dashwood's reply was low and menacing. "There is but one answer to your insinuation."

"But what a quandary for any *gentleman* to decide which accusation to defend—Blasphemy? Sodomy? Or attempted rape?"

Dashwood's eyes bulged with murderous intent.

"When you decide, Sir Francis, pray direct your seconds to the George and Vulture." Philip snatched the girl by the arm and headed straight to the side door from whence the harlots had entered, justly fearing that the hounds of hell would soon be hot on his heels.

"You've surely done it now, ol' chap," said George as he passed.

✧

They navigated the passageway in complete darkness, not knowing where it would lead. Philip blessed Providence that they emerged just outside the stables. "Can you ride, Nell?" he asked the girl.

"N-no," she answered.

He cursed aloud. "Why should you know to ride after all else that's transpired this night?" He had spoken more to himself but she cringed in fear. "Damn it, girl. Do you think I would strike you when I've just risked my idiotic neck to remove you from that den of iniquity?"

He wasn't sure if her teeth chattered more from fear or exposure to the cold night air, but in the midst of this contemplation it began to rain.

"Bugger it all!" he stripped off his coat and helped her into it. Perceiving the dim lantern light of the stables, Philip led her to crouch behind the adjacent hedgerow. "Just wait here and don't make a sound."

She clutched his sleeve frantically. "Yer not leavin' me?"

"Don't be daft! Even I am not so brazen to ride through the town with a half-naked girl behind me. I must go and find you something apart from my coat to cover yourself."

"Y-you'll come back?"

"Yes. Yes," he snapped. "Do you think it likely I would now lay waste to an entire night's heroics?" He heaved a sigh and turned for the stables.

After locating his horse and pilfering one of the rough monk's robes for the girl, Philip took her up behind him for the three-hour ride back to London. The ride gave him ample time to reconsider his foolhardy impulsiveness. He felt like a wanted man, and suspected that he might very well soon find himself at Dashwood's sword point.

What had come over him? He seemed now to be making a career out of misguided acts of chivalry. At least, aside from the incessant chatter of her teeth, Nell had the wisdom to remain silent. But what to do with her now?

He turned in the saddle to ask, "Why, Nell, after all this time did you decide to leave honest labor?"

"B-but I am still an honest girl," she insisted with an injured sniff.

"Are you indeed? If that is true, how did you come to Medmenham Abbey?" he demanded with overt cynicism.

"'Twas by the conniving of Mistress Ward," she said. "Like a grand lady, she comes by and offers me an apprenticeship at her milliner's shop. At a shilling a day, mind ye. A far cry from me wages at the tavern, and a chance for a respectable trade to boot. But I wasn't there a sennight afore I sees 'twas not a respectable establishment at all, but a house of wickedness she runs!

"When I tries to leave she locks me in the garret for three days wi' only stale bread and water. It was so dark and the mistress says if I do what she tells me she won't feed me to the rats! That's when we goes in the carriage to the abbey."

"Dashwood undoubtedly paid a good price for you too, if you were truly presented as a… maiden."

She dipped her head in guilt. "I *was* saving myself, but when ye up and left t'other night…"

Philip felt a momentary flash of guilt that she would have waited for him, but knowing she'd have succumbed to another soon enough. "What the devil am I to do with you now?" he asked.

"Many fine gents keep a girl." She ran one hand provocatively down his torso. He released one of his own from the reins to return hers to its place at his waist.

"Nell, please understand that I don't have the means to keep a mistress… even if I was so inclined."

"Y-you won't try to sell me to another, will you?"

"God no! I'm no whoremonger, though I durst not cast the first stone," he added deprecatingly. "Mother Ward and Francis Dashwood will go to the devil in their way and I in mine. Now, if you don't wish to return to Tom King's—"

"Lor' no!" she cried.

"Then I am at a complete loss what to do with you. Where's your family?"

"In Cheapside, but me Mum had so many mouths to feed. She's a God-fearin' woman, me Mum. She won't want me back when she hears where I've been," she sobbed.

"Good God, Nell! Don't start weeping! Surely you have some other skill that will lend to gainful service in a respectable household."

"B-but who would take me wi'out even me proper clothes?" she wailed.

"I'll find you some bloody clothes. Now cease the whimpering while I figure this out." She sniffed again, and he felt her wipe her streaming nose on the back of his coat.

"Devil take me this night!" he swore in exasperation.

Twenty

A FRIEND IN NEED

LADY MESSINGHAM SLEPT FITFULLY, HUNGRILY, WITH A thousand thoughts and images playing though her mind. Philip, with his mesmerizing, sometimes brooding dark eyes was foremost among them—Philip teaching her the dice in the carriage, flaunting his conjuring tricks, and sharing his dubious gaming philosophies.

His kisses, a lover's kisses, had ignited a flame she thought extinguished over a decade ago. It had been so very long, she'd almost forgotten how a kiss like that could bestir one's entire being. She did want him, she confessed, with an urgency she had failed to repress.

The simplest solution, provided she could trust his discretion, would be to take Philip to her bed. Was she not a free woman and able to do as she pleased? Then again, was this merely physical attraction or was it more? The same feelings that thrilled her now filled her with panic.

Only one other man had ever affected her so. Recklessly, she'd abandoned herself completely to her passion, and the repercussions had been harsh. She'd barely survived with her life, and an empty one it had been, following a broken heart and shattered dreams. Yet Philip had resurrected those powerful and long-suppressed yearnings that kept her from repose, leaving her restless, dissatisfied, and yearning.

She had vowed never again. The risk was far too great, to love and be cast aside, yet she felt connected with him at so many levels. He, like she, rebelled against another having control of his life. In her case, it had been a jealous and possessive husband; in his case, an overbearing and ambitious father who would try to mold Philip to fit his own design.

She and Philip both struggled on the outer fringe of a society they secretly despised, but while she did her utmost to maintain her position in their eyes with a false façade, Philip seemed to go out of his way to cultivate a wastrel's reputation. Yet she had seen beneath the feckless exterior. Philip Drake was so much more than he would have the world believe.

After close to four hours riding in a downpour, Philip and his misbegotten passenger reached the outskirts of London. He was by now thoroughly drenched, haggard, and still confounded about what to do with his newly acquired baggage. Moreover he was uncomfortably aware that the longer she remained in his keeping the more responsible he would become, a thoroughly unsettling thought.

It would have been easiest to take her back to Moll King, but having risked his neck to rescue the unwary chit from one bawd, how could he in good conscience deliver her unto another?

With a groan of defeat, and with great reluctance, Philip redirected his horse toward Westminster, to seek out the only person he believed might render assistance in his time of need.

Pulling around to the mews, Philip dismounted and then assisted the limp and shivering girl to the ground, catching her in his arms as her legs, cramped from the ride and numb from the cold, gave way beneath her. He cursed the want of a groom, but the hour was far too advanced, or rather, he thought wryly, far too early for any to be stirring.

By no means assured of a warm reception, Philip tied the horse under the sloped shelter, and beckoning the girl to follow advanced to the servants' entrance of the house at 10 Bedford Street.

∽

Having failed to sleep, Lady Messingham rose at the first tentative scratch upon her door. By the shadows yet looming in the room, she guessed it just before daybreak. Following the ways of fashion, she rarely rose betimes. She marked the rising sun a certain novelty, albeit not the most welcome one at the moment.

"Yes. Yes. Come in, Nancy," the lady mumbled, sitting up in bed and reaching for the tinderbox to light the lamp.

Tentatively, the maid peeked through the doorway.

"Enter for goodness' sake. I shan't bite off your head!"

The maid approached, wringing her hands.

"What is it, Nan?" her mistress demanded, perplexed.

"There be someone at the door to see ye, my lady." She winced apprehensively.

"What! Who on earth would make morning calls when 'tis not even daybreak?"

"'Tis a young gent and a…" The servant frowned seeking the right word. "…a female creature," was the best she could do.

"A creature, you say? What on earth do you mean?" She rose from bed and pulled on her wrapper. "Have you a calling card? Or at least a name?"

The servant's distress grew by the moment. "I can't rightly say, ma'am." She hastened to add, "I would not ha' woke ye, but the gent, he was most persistent like. And being he's an acquaintance of yours, I durst not send him away, not wi'out your knowledge of it, my lady."

"So I know this young gent, you say? What does he look like?" The image of Philip was already forming in her mind.

"Most like a drowned rat at the moment, yer ladyship." The maid stifled a giggle.

"Does he indeed? You did well enough to wake me, Nan."

The maid's shoulders visibly relaxed.

"I suppose I'll just take a look for myself. Where are my damp guests at the moment?"

"In the kitchen, ma'am. At least they had the decency to come by the servants' door."

"Then pray light a fire in the small salon and heat a kettle for tea. I shan't have anyone catch his or her death at my door. Let them know I'll be down anon."

"Yes, yer ladyship." The maid smiled faintly and bobbed.

❦

Divested of his wet coat, Philip shivered in his shirt-sleeves as he paced before the newly rekindled fire, thinking the wait interminable. At least she hadn't yet thrown him out on his arse, if that was any sign of good-will, but perhaps the maid had not mentioned the girl.

Knowing Nell completely out of her element, and she herself being an element that would only complicate matters with Lady Messingham, Philip had instructed Nell to take her tea in the kitchen with the servants rather than joining him in the small parlor. Although the maid had openly viewed the pair askance, she had the kindness to provide the dripping girl with a blanket.

Once assured that his reluctant charge had been seen to, Philip followed the servant to the room where he now waited. And paced.

Philip clawed an exasperated hand through his wet and tangled hair, still at a loss for a rational explanation. Whores, idolatry, debauchery, even attempted rape. The entire episode was nothing short of scandalous, and no tale fit for a gentlewoman's ears.

How much could he tell her? Would she believe a word of it? Moreover, could he trust her to help? He hadn't time to ponder the answers before the chamber door quietly opened.

"You," she said. She ventured toward him with only a blink of her eyes betraying her surprise. "What in God's name has brought you to my house at such an hour? And in this… this condition?"

She regarded him intently, fully taking in his appearance. His clothes and boots were sodden and bemired from hours on the mucky roads. His shirt was

translucently plastered to his torso, and his breeches
clung to his thighs like a second skin, revealing the
lean, hard musculature of a man in his prime.

Philip performed a sopping bow he knew would
appear almost mocking under the circumstances. Still
at a loss where to begin, he offered a sheepish apology.
"A thousand pardons, my lady, for both the state
of my appearance and for the ill-fated affair which
brought me to your door."

"Indeed?" She looked about the room. "But what
of your companion? I was apprised that you had
arrived with a... female... in tow."

"There is indeed a young woman with me."

Her eyes flashed daggers. "What game is this,
Philip? I fail to comprehend why you would think it
amusing to bring your strumpet to my home."

Philip stepped toward her with hands raised in
supplication. "Amusing? This is anything but, and pray
disavow the notion that she's a whore."

The arch of a singular brow marked her disbelief.
"Then who, or what, is she?"

Philip scrambled for explanation. "She's a tavern maid."

The brow was joined by its twin in a dubious scowl.

"Well... I suppose one might presume... but there
were extenuating circumstances."

"That would bring her to *my door*?" she asked,
incredulous. "What precisely is she... to you?"

Philip remarked her resentment, but there was
something more. Was it a twinge of jealousy? "I don't
wish to burden you with a long and tedious explanation," he dissembled through chattering teeth. Even
positioned by the fire, he visibly shivered with cold.

"Tedious? This tale is anything but that!" Remarking the blue tinge to his lips, she was reluctantly moved by compassion. "Mayhap my inquisition can wait until you've at least dried." She then departed, returning promptly with a towel and blanket.

Philip gratefully accepted the former and began to pat his face dry.

"You'll need to remove your wet clothing before you catch the ague," she said. "By the look of you, you're half there already." She set the blanket on a chair and moved to assist. "Now, out of those wet clothes."

She spoke matter-of-factly and Philip responded with a stare of disbelief. "Here? Now?"

"Oh, come now!" She forced a laugh and a tone of nonchalance. "No need to be missish about it. I am a widow, for heaven's sake, and not easily affected by male nudity," she lied through her teeth. She was very affected at the thought of him unclothed. "Besides, you'll need help," she added. "Your shirt and breeches are nigh plastered to your skin." She moved once again to assist.

Philip warily took a step back. The thought of her undressing him had him completely discomposed. Had she no idea? "Haven't you a manservant? A footman or coachman even?" he asked.

"There's food enough for scandal without waking my entire household. Besides, I have blankets to cover you."

He was frozen to the bone and knew he'd never recover while wet. With a sigh of resignation, he reached for the placket of his breeches to untuck his shirt, and she smartly went to work on the buttons.

Her trembling hands belied her feigned dispassion. In truth, it had been a very long time since she last undressed a man, and when she peeled the wet cloth from his body she realized Nigel's paunchy stomach and hairy back and buttocks had done nothing to prepare her for the cleanly sculpted muscles of this young, strong, and incredibly virile-looking body. Her throat suddenly went dry. She experienced a shiver of her own, but certainly not from cold.

Briskly, she took up the blanket and shook it out vigorously to put breathing space between them. With a jerk of her head, she indicated his breeches. "Now, your smallclothes."

Philip's mouth twitched. "There is one problem."

She raised the blanket between them, speaking in a decidedly primmer tone than she had previously adopted. "I'll simply hold this as a curtain betwixt us while you finish. You may then wrap it about you until your garments have properly dried."

"That's not the problem I meant. Mayhap you have not undressed so many men after all."

She looked perplexed.

Philip pointed down. "The boots, my lady. I require assistance to remove them before I'll be able to take off my breeches. Have you perchance a boot jack?"

"I fear not," she said.

"If you are bound not to disturb a footman, shall we call your maid to assist?"

"I've sent her for more blankets."

He glanced down at the sodden, muddy leather. "Boots are difficult to remove in the best of circumstances. Wet boots are nigh impossible."

"I'll help with your boots," she spoke impatiently. "Just tell me what to do."

"It's no task for a lady."

"Botheration!" she cried. "Just sit!"

Shrugging, Philip covered the silk damask chair with the blanket before he sat upon it. Facing him, Lady Messingham bent to grasp his heel.

"No. Not like that."

"Why ever not?"

"Because you'll pull with all your might to loosen the accursed thing, and when the boot gives, you'll fall backwards arse over teakettle."

"Oh." She blinked. "I had no idea it was so difficult. Then how am I to pull them off?"

"If you don't wish to become unbalanced, you needs must turn your back to me and place my boot between your legs for leverage to pull it off."

He watched her dubious expression as she digested these instructions. Although it sounded sensible, she just didn't know whether to believe him.

"You wish me to hold your leg betwixt my thighs, with my nether end practically in your face?"

He grinned raffishly. "That is precisely the idea, although the deed is customarily performed by a valet," he added by way of explanation. "Are you quite sure you don't wish to awaken your footman?"

"I... Of course not. I trust Nan's discretion, but dare not place the same faith in the others." Truth be told, she'd dismissed the footman just the day prior as part of her new economy. With an exasperated huff, she turned and hiked her skirts above her knees, providing him a gratuitous flash of shapely calves, before taking his extended leg between her naked thighs.

When she bent over to pull, with the perfectly

formed globes of her backside clearly defined against the thin fabric of her gown, Philip wished he had cut the damned things off.

He was nearing the end of endurance and contemplating the dangers of pulling that lovely round bottom onto his lap when the boot finally gave. She held it up with a triumphant cry.

"There's one. Now, give me the other."

God no. I can't bear it again. I'll ravish her on the carpet.

"What are you waiting for?" she demanded.

Philip shifted in the chair to relieve the discomfort his thoughts had wrought.

"Oh," she replied, raising a finely arched brow.

"I'm glad you find it amusing."

"But you still have one boot on."

"I'll keep it on, thank you."

"But then how can you dry yourself?"

"I'll sit by the fire."

"No, *child*, I insist." Her lips curled upward.

She was actually enjoying this. "Bloody hell!" he groaned. "Just take the damned thing!"

They repeated the performance. Philip forced his eyes to the ceiling with the awareness that paradise was but an arm's length away. He mentally conjugated Latin verbs to no avail, becoming so hard it outright pained him.

The door opened abruptly just as the boot came free. The maid, carrying more linen, started and then blushed crimson at what she suspected she had interrupted. She hurriedly laid down her burden and then turned to busy herself with the fire.

"Thank you, Nan. That will be all," her mistress

said as if it were nothing out of the ordinary for her to play valet to a half-naked man. The shocked servant promptly withdrew without having spoken a word.

"There now, I am sure you can manage well enough alone at this juncture." Lady Messingham turned back to find Philip already shedding his breeches, and her breath seized. She couldn't help herself. She stared. He was magnificent, every accursed inch of him.

"The blanket, my lady?" he prompted.

"Of course," she said hurriedly, averting her eyes but making no effort to move.

He took the blanket from her hands and found them once more trembling. "Now look who's being missish. Only a moment ago you declared yourself quite unmoved by a naked male." His voice was low and provocative.

Her heart thrummed erratically in her chest, sending an echo drumming in her ears. She looked up into his taunting face. He reached out to her but she pulled away, closing her eyes, suddenly seeing herself teetering on the brink of an abyss that destroyed women.

"You do fancy yourself quite the cockalorum, don't you, Philip? You have the brass bollocks to attempt seduction whilst another woman awaits you in my very kitchen?"

Philip snatched the blanket about his waist. "I told you—it's not what you think. She's *nothing* to me."

"Nothing to you? Not what I think? Then tell me at last what I *am* to think."

As she'd prayed, *the moment* had shattered.

With the blanket secured around his waist, and looking to herd his hormone-enraged thoughts back to coherency, Philip took up a towel and began rubbing his dripping hair. At length he said, "All right, I'll tell you the truth, in all of its depravity. What do you know of Sir Francis Dashwood?"

"Dashwood? What does he have to do with any of this?"

"More than you would ever suspect."

"What I hear *from ladies* of my acquaintance is that Sir Francis is charming, splendidly wealthy, well-traveled, and a magnificent catch." She paused to regard Philip circumspectly before continuing. "I also overheard *from gentlemen* that he's one of the most debauched rakes of London and is rumored to have bedded nearly every woman in the *ton*. Based on personal experience, I would call the claim highly exaggerated."

"You are surprisingly frank."

"You asked a question. I gave you a direct answer. I don't hedge, Philip."

"Then I have little fear of shocking you," he said with obvious relief.

"No. I am not easily overset, nor prone to swooning fits."

"Have you heard of the Knights of St. Francis?"

"Only whispers. They say Dashwood and his Knights couple an insatiable appetite for physical congress coupled with a certain apostasy. Don't tell me you are one of his number?"

"Gad no!" Philip exclaimed. "Ridiculous they are, playing at paganism and virgin sacrifice."

She gaped. "What did you say? *Virgin sacrifice?*"

"Indeed, and the intended victim sits in yon kitchen safely sipping tea with your servants."

"Good God, Philip!" She collapsed in the chair. "How can civilized beings think to do such things?"

"Dashwood and his cronies are the most powerful men in the land. They can do whatever the hell they wish with impunity, but they didn't plan to sacrifice her life," Philip hastily explained. "Just her…" His voice trailed off.

"Her maidenhead?" Her voice was skeptical. "Come now, if she were truly an innocent, what would she be doing in such a place and in such company to begin with?"

He shrugged. "I make no claims as to the state of her chastity, however, 'twas eminently clear she wanted no part in the blasphemous ceremony. Had I not intervened…" His fatal expression told the rest.

"You mean to say you rescued her?" She looked incredulous.

"Leaping onto the altar and quixotically brandishing my sword," he replied with self-effacement.

"I suppose one might even admire your misplaced gallantry, *Sir Galahad*. Others surely would have used and discarded her without a qualm. I've no doubt the girl in my kitchen would happily *repay* you." She scrutinized his reaction.

"I have not the least interest in the girl, or any other of her ilk. I seem to have lost my appetite for tarts. Spoiled it, you might say, in craving other things."

She looked away. "We can't always have what we desire, can we, Philip? You must accustom yourself to occasional disappointment. Now, more to the point—why did you bring her *here*?"

A flash of helplessness crossed his face and his words

came in a sudden gush, "Because I had nowhere else to turn. I needed someone I could trust... I needed a friend."

Twenty-One

THE MOMENT OF TRUTH

HIS WORDS COMPLETELY DISARMED HER. SHE HAD never felt *needed* by anyone. Her cool reserve faltered as, stoically, Philip awaited her response.

"Very well," she answered slowly, warily. "What have you in mind?"

"I am a rogue to put upon you like this—"

"You are indeed."

"I had hoped you might place her in service."

Her reaction was incredulity. "You mean for me to provide her with employment?"

"Mayhap as a chamber maid, or some such?" he suggested sheepishly, while she mentally calculated the expense of adding another member to her household.

"You don't think she would rob me blind?"

"Quite possibly," he replied with a sigh. "My apologies for not thinking this through, but I could hardly dump her on the streets."

"No. I expect not," she replied thoughtfully, weighing the benefits of his indebtedness to her against the strain of taking on another servant. "Perhaps we might consider the kitchen? I have a temperamental cook who has relieved my household of a number of scullery maids."

It was also the humblest position in the house with the lowest wage. Perhaps she could dispense with her chairmen? But Longacre had already repossessed her carriage and she'd sold the horses... *No. It was impossible.* She could barely keep even her nose above water at this point, but he had asked for her help. How could she explain?

She had deeply regretted their earlier spat, compounding her harsh words with Jane. She had never felt more alone and isolated. The burden, the pretense, the deception, it was all suddenly too heavy to bear alone.

"Philip, please know that I want to help you, but I cannot employ her."

"I don't understand. Why not?"

She opened her mouth to speak and closed it again.

"What is it you're not telling me?" he asked. "I've sensed it since the night we met." She stared at him in silence. He waited, watching every passing emotion on her face—anger, frustration, and apprehension— while she waged her internal battle.

"It would appear your game is finally up. What are you hiding?" he prompted.

She looked up into his face, her expression uncertain and wary. "The truth?" she asked in a whisper.

"It is infinitely preferable to a lie," he answered with only a hint of a smile.

"Quite," she answered ruefully and averted her face from his view. "The truth is..." Her voice cracked. She took a deep breath and began again. "The truth is… I have debts. Enormous debts. Debts I cannot possibly pay."

Philip was stunned. "But this house…" He gestured to the elegant appointments.

"Leased. And I am three months behind. I daily fear threat of eviction."

"By all reports, you were married to a wealthy man, my lady. Do you mean to say your husband left you penniless?"

"Not quite, but close enough, given my living standards. I have only my personal possessions and a modest jointure of two hundred pounds per annum."

"Two hundred pounds?" Philip's brows arched in surprise. "'Tis certainly enough to subsist on, just not in the style to which you are accustomed."

"Don't misunderstand me. My circumstances are not the fault of any lack of generosity. Nigel was exceedingly doting and generous to a fault. One might say that I alone am to blame for my present sorry state of affairs. He could never say no to me about anything, and in ignorance I allowed him to squander his fortune."

"You say nothing remains?"

"Only the properties and those all passed on to Nigel's heir. Now, if I had given him a son, perhaps my lot would have been different," she spoke wistfully.

"Then sell your jewels."

"Any of worth I've already pawned."

"But you wore emeralds only the other evening."

"The real ones are now gone, all replaced with paste." She began to pace, refusing to meet his eye. "I've no longer a horse or carriage. My household is reduced to a skeleton staff. I owe the butcher, the baker, and the candlestick maker," she finished in a sudden gush of hopeless mirth.

"You could return to the country, just disappear for a time."

"I can't," she replied in a pained whisper.

"Why not? Don't you have any family? Is there no one in Wiltshire with whom you could take refuge?"

"My father disowned me in disgrace. There is nothing left for me there but horrid memories." She choked through a haze of misting tears. "I am at the end of my rope, and you were my last desperate hope."

"You are in need and turned to me? That's almost comical. I'm the last one *I would turn to* for deliverance. I am nobody, with nothing. Why in blazes would you pin any hope of recovery on me when you have powerful friends—courtiers, and princes?"

"Because of what every last one of *them* would demand in return. Because you can help me. Because you already have and did not importune me as the others would have. Remember the night at Belsize? The seventy-five pounds you helped me win paid my servants' wages and kept my creditors at bay. You are precisely who I need."

"A lowly gamester over a prince?" he scoffed.

"Lowly? I think not. You far surpass what you care to reveal of yourself. I know this. Why did you think I sought you out?"

"I had little notion why. At first I was flattered, thinking you spoiled, neglected, or bored, and wanting…" He finished with a shrug.

"Wanting what?" she asked.

He answered with a sardonic twist. "Let's say it was not precisely what I'd hoped, though for a while you led me blindly down the primrose path."

"Indeed? That may be so, the lovely path that leads to one's destruction."

"That's not what I meant."

"Perhaps you should go now," she said, snatching up his wet clothes.

He stayed her by the arm. "I think not. We have yet resolved nothing between us."

"I have told you the truth. I sought you out to manipulate and use you. What more is left to say?"

"Much, now that the proverbial cards are on the table. I still ask you, *why me*?"

She looked askance. "Because I had the absurd notion that you would be malleable, that I could entrance and control you." She looked back at him with a wretched smile. "I was wrong."

"No," he said. "God only knows, you were right. There's not been a day that's passed since Marylebone that I haven't thought of you and wanted you."

"And now that you know how I sought to use you? What do you think of me now, Philip?" Her tone was corrosive, cutting, taunting, as if she wished to drive him away rather than have him walk out on his own.

He took her by the chin, meeting her fixedly with his probing stare. "What do I think? I think that a man is only used if he allows himself to be; and that having been in much similar straits myself, I understand you far more fully than you realize."

Her amazement was such that she forgot to breathe, and even more than his incredible answer, his ensuing kiss completely overcame her. She sank into him with a gasp when his arms engulfed her. The levee that had held her emotions at bay, now having burst, she pulled him to her, frantically, clutching his hair, as if she were drowning and he, her lifeline. Abandoning all of her defenses, she gave herself with a desperate passion she'd held in check for far too long.

~∾~

Philip awoke with a shiver. The coals in the hearth that had warmed them after their own heat had dissipated in a sated torpor were long reduced to dusty ash. He drew her body, still warmed by his own, closer still and cocooned the blanket more tightly about them and reflected on all the night had revealed.

Although he was no innocent, this woman in his arms had shown him just how ignorant he'd been beyond the very basics of physical congress. Last night with her had brought him to the very humbling conclusion that he'd known little of a woman's pleasure at all. Last night had changed everything.

When he and Susannah joined the first time, he was more than ready. He'd been randier than a billy goat since she took off his boots, but his eagerness for her, to be inside her, after so much unsated wanting, had unmanned him far too soon to give her any pleasure. She'd gasped at his sudden climax, and then her tears had flowed, tears of frustration and passion unfulfilled.

The prior females with whom he'd consorted, a jolly accommodating lot, had cared only for a hot and hard entry, more often than not, against the wall of a back room. This had suited him admirably at the time, but then he'd never experienced the deep and profound desire to please a woman, to bestir her to madness as Susannah did him.

Desperate to fulfill this need, he'd kissed her face, her eyes, her sodden cheeks, and soon his mouth and tongue began laving away the spilled tears. He tenderly ministered hot open kisses to her neck and her beautiful white breasts. He'd taken them into his mouth, one at a time, ravenously suckling, biting, teasing, until she'd frantically clutched his head, groaning urgent supplication hot in his ear. With youth and virility on his side, her grinding and whispered moans hardened him again in an instant, but she demurred when he'd moved to take her.

Instead, she'd guided him.

This was when Philip's lessons of physical love truly began.

At her urging, and with an eagerness hitherto unknown, he roamed and explored every inch of her. With his hands and with his mouth, he filled her with whimpers and pleasured cries until discovering the very essence of her need. In this place, he worshipped at leisure, and when she broke with a shrill cry, muffled by her own hand, he knew he'd proven no slacker.

She stirred with a groan. Her eyes opened and lit on his face in bewilderment. She parted her lips as if to speak, but Philip silenced her with a lingering kiss and rolled her beneath him.

"No. We mustn't. The servants." She pressed a hand against his chest, looking to the door in panicked protest.

"The door is locked, my lady."

"Even worse," she replied, before adding ruefully, "By the bye, Philip, I think last night places us well beyond formalities. My intimates call me Sukey."

"I dare hope none are quite this intimate." He grinned and ran his hand up her inner thigh. "Sukey," he repeated her name. It glided over his tongue as smoothly as warm brandy. He moved to kiss her again.

She pushed him away with a frown. "Please, you must dress. You must go. Now," she said more urgently.

"No," he replied flatly, his expression uncompromising.

"No? What do you mean, no?"

He smirked. "The opposite of yes, I believe."

"Look, what's done cannot be undone, but I am not about to compound one mistake with another."

He flinched as if she'd hit him full in the face. "Is that all this was to you? A mistake?"

Regretting her word choice, she vigorously shook her head. "Philip, I don't know what to think. But surely no good can come of this."

"I don't see it that way."

"Then I shall make you see! The reputation of a single woman is a precarious thing. Any hint of scandal could banish me from good society. Having barely weathered one such storm, I cannot afford to risk it again."

"Come now. You can think of a better excuse than that. London is full of ladies, even married ones, who carry on discrete liaisons without a whisper of defamation. Only a generation ago, intrigues were considered requisite to ladies of fashion."

"Why can't you understand? I've told you I will be no man's mistress! That way lies only tragedy and despair. Such women are only passed from one man to another until all beauty is wasted and they are left ruined, destitute, and wanted by no one."

"Is that what you fear, my love?"

"Yes. No. I don't know!"

"What if freedom could remain yours?" he asked in a heated whisper on her skin.

"I'm not sure I understand you." Growing more befuddled by the minute, she tried unsuccessfully to shrug off his attentions, but he maintained her trapped beneath him. She could feel him hard and pulsing.

Sensing her imminent capitulation, Philip drew his lips over her bare neck and shoulders in a slow, sensuous torture. "What if the choice remained completely yours?"

"What choice?" she asked, closing her eyes to the impulse to grind against him.

"To cast *me* off whenever you please?" He paused to pay particular homage to her breasts. "Though I hope to please you sufficiently and frequently enough to avoid that fate."

She was growing breathless with a desire she could no longer suppress. "What are you suggesting?"

"I don't seek a mistress, Sukey," he answered huskily, his dark eyes dilated. "I'm suggesting I might be your lover, instead."

PART II

"Lo! next, to my prophetic eye there starts,
A beauteous gamestress in the Queen of Hearts...
So tender there, if debts crowd fast upon her,
She'll pawn her 'virtue' to preserve her 'honour...'"

—George Coleman the Elder, *The Oxonian in Town*

Twenty-Two

A Secret Legacy

PHILIP HAD ANTICIPATED THE DAY, FOR OVER FOUR years, when he would actually have the means to live out his life independent of his accursed compassionless, controlling father.

Affecting all the airs of his forthcoming prosperity, he arrived at the offices of Phineas Willoughby, Esquire, administrator of his trust, proudly garbed in new, modish dress purchased from one of London's finest tailors.

Only a few scratches of the quill stood between him and two thousand pounds. Though it was a modest fortune, it would nonetheless transform him into a man of independence, allowing him to remain in comfort and exist in a manner more befitting his birth. Perhaps he would start by seeking better apartments, mayhap something at St. James Square?

He was lost in the happy reverie when the lawyer entered. "My felicitations on your coming of age, Master Drake, 'tis a milestone indeed." The aged solicitor offered his hand with an avuncular smile. "Of course you are here to claim your inheritance."

"Indeed I am." Philip returned a broad grin. "I've looked forward to this day."

"I am sure you have, but you may not be aware of another matter reserved for this occasion."

Philip looked his question.

"There is an item of a more personal nature that I was asked to hold in safekeeping for you until this day."

"A personal item from my mother? I have never heard of this."

The lawyer unlocked a drawer and retrieved a box that he set gingerly atop his desk.

"What is it?" Philip asked, his heartbeat accelerating with anticipation.

Willoughby opened the box and removed a small jewel case and a sealed letter written in his mother's delicate hand. Philip took the letter, breaking the seal with a look of agitated bewilderment. It was dated a month before her death from consumption.

> *To my most precious Son,*
>
> *I most earnestly wish that I might have seen this day that you became a man in your own right, and that I might have spoken these things I am now compelled to write. What I am about to reveal, I was sworn to withhold from you from the time of your birth, but now that you have reached your age of accountability, and I rest peacefully in my grave, I no longer feel bound to that vow.*
>
> *This ring, my dearest one, belonged to my mother, and her mother before that. It is a symbol of your maternal heritage that I bequeath to you, in hope it*

*might finally provide answers to the questions which
have long caused you heartache and distress.*

*I pray that this revelation, though perhaps at
first shocking, will explain the otherwise unex-
plainable—why a father would so reject his own
son, his own blood.*

*Please accept this ring with my fondest wishes for
health, peace, prosperity, and love.*

*Your Most,
Affectionate and Devoted
Mother*

Philip opened the case to discover a simple band for
a woman's hand, crafted in gold, unremarkable but for
the unusual symbols engraved upon it. He examined
it with the utmost reverence, as if any amount of
pressure might break it. He rolled it slowly between
thumb and index finger, puzzling over the characters
with a frown.

"Do you know what this means, Mr. Willoughby?
Is it a code of some sort? I've never seen anything like
it." Philip handed him the ring.

The solicitor accepted it, studied it, and shook his
head. "I am a scholar of Greek and Latin; I have no
knowledge of Hebrew."

"Hebrew?" Philip repeated, stunned.

Willoughby flushed at what he had inadvertently
revealed.

"My mother was an Englishwoman, born in
Middlesex and raised in London proper. She was
baptized in the Anglican church. Why would she own
such an item?"

"Your mother was indeed an Englishwoman, but also the daughter of a Dutch merchant who immigrated during the days of William of Orange. The Dutch, as you may know, received many Jews into their midst in the last century, who over time intermarried widely within the merchant classes. Your maternal grandfather married such a Jewess."

"A Jewess? My grandmother was a Jew?" Philip stared blankly at the solicitor. "Why was I never told?"

"As you are undoubtedly aware, the match between your parents was purely a business arrangement. Your maternal grandfather desired the social status and business connections an alliance with a peer of the realm could bring, and your father, after suffering crippling losses in the South Sea Bubble, was in need of the dowry to support his estate. Your mother was simply the means to their mutual ends, and was forsworn by the earl never to speak of her heritage."

"I see." Philip said nothing more, but sat stoically silent as full understanding dawned and the world, as he knew it, crumbled about his ears.

From his very birth, Philip's father had treated him with scorn and derision, almost as if he regarded him a bastard. Suddenly he understood. Although he was the earl's legitimate son, he was tainted by the very blood he carried in his veins. He was a one-quarter Jew.

"Rest assured I'll speak of it to no one," Willoughby said apologetically as he handed back the ring. "As to the inscription, if you truly wish to explore this, not that I advise you to," he hastily amended, "there is a man you might seek whose discretion you can assuredly trust. His name is David Nieto, and though a Jew, is considered by many a brilliant man of parts: philosopher, physician, poet, mathematician, astronomer, and theologian. He leads the Sephardic house of worship at Bevis Marks in Stepney."

"I'll take it under advisement," Philip replied vaguely, only half hearing the rest.

"Come to think of it, that brings to mind another matter. There is a gentleman of the same order by the name of Samson Gideon who might advise you well on the investment of your windfall," counseled Willoughby. "The man's a veritable oracle of the 'Change. You are bound to find him among the stock-jobbers at Jonathan's Coffee House in Exchange Alley."

"Thank you, Willoughby," Philip said and slid the ring onto the little finger of his right hand.

❦

Aside from one slightly disturbing revelation, Philip departed Willoughby's office feeling in every sense a free man.

Willoughby had counseled Philip to invest his capital in legitimate enterprise. Perhaps the East India Company, Jamaican sugar, or colonial tobacco. Many Scottish and Quaker merchants had garnered tremendous riches from Oronoco. Yet others continued to make their fortunes from the slave trade that supported the sugar and tobacco plantations. Philip reflected on the last only briefly before dismissing the notion with distaste. Let others profit by bondage.

Two thousand pounds wisely invested was enough

to keep a single gentleman in superior lodgings with a gentleman's accoutrements for years. But what of Sukey's debts? He hadn't pressed her for figures and wondered how much would be required to settle them. He speculated how long the money might sustain them both.

She appeared to require immediate assistance. If he took on her burden, he would have no assurance of security. Sukey had the same love of fine things as he, and no greater self-restraint. Although she claimed to have made some efforts to economize of late, he'd be ill advised to think it lasting.

His steps grew heavier and his brow furrowed as Philip struggled with the dilemma of how best to help her without jeopardizing his own future. Certainly a few good nights at the tables might enlarge the largesse, but dare he risk it?

Deciding to put aside these weightier thoughts for another time, Philip chose instead to bask in his all around good fortune. Aside from one rather rattling disclosure that he continued to digest, he felt like a new man. With the commemoration of his twenty-first year, he had come into a great deal of money. Adding to that fortuity was a beautiful woman in whose arms he could lose himself to the point of oblivion.

The knowledge of having transported her to a state of unbridled rapture drove him half mad and imbued him with a deeper satisfaction than he'd ever known. The feel of her, the look on her face, and her sounds as she reached completion occupied his thoughts until he could only think of loving her again, and again, pushing her over the brink until she cried his name aloud.

Philip felt empowered with a newfound sense of self-possession that had begun in his lover's arms. He'd soon be the envy of every man of his acquaintance. Who would have ever thought it?

His face split into a self-satisfied grin at the utter irony.

Philip's pleasing ruminations added an air of self-conceit to his usual swagger as he ventured down the Strand. It surely was a day for commemoration and he fully intended to celebrate, once he reclaimed his possessions from pawn.

He entered the dingy shop on the Strand to repay the pledge for his silver-hilted dress sword, but passing by the fine jewelry case his eye caught the milky glimmer of emeralds, a very familiar set of emeralds.

"Might I have a closer look at these?" Philip asked the greasy black-toothed fellow.

"Aye. A finer set you'll not find in Lon'on," said the man, removing the gems for Philip's inspection and adding with a wink, "'Twould get ye right quick a'tween any high-flyin' ladybird's thighs."

Philip forced a smile to encourage the talker. "Can you tell me anything of their history?"

"A lady brung 'em in. Dressed like a maid she was, but didn't bamboozle me. Knew she was the quality the minute she opens her mouf. Lots of folks what pawn come in disguised-like."

"When did you say you acquired these?"

"The emeralds and the ring, jes' yesterday, though she pledged some other gems the week afore. If'n ye'd like to see those, I've no doubt she'll not be claimin' 'em."

The man produced a strand of pearls with a ruby

clasp and a diamond ring that Philip examined with interest. The pearls he had never seen, but the ring? Was it her wedding ring? Philip made a mental note to observe if she still wore one.

"When will the items be available? I'm acquainted with a lady who might be particularly pleased to have them."

"Loan's short term. If she don't pay the interest, as I expect she won't, ye can come for 'em in a for'night."

"I'll strongly consider it," Philip said, producing a contract. "For now I only wish to reclaim my sword."

He was deeply disconcerted by the depth of Sukey's troubles, but still determined to find a way to sort it all out. He paused once more to ruminate over the ring in the jeweler's case, and, catching himself with a peculiar thought, shook it off immediately as a fatuous, passing fancy.

Twenty-Three

SPORTING MEN

SEEKING COMPANY WITH WHOM TO REVEL OVER HIS change in circumstances, Philip set out to locate and make amends with George. Although he was certain to be surly after what transpired at Medmenham, affable ol' Bosky was of a forgiving temperament, especially to whoever was buying the drinks.

Not finding George at home, Philip made inquiries at the unusually vacant Will's Coffeehouse.

"They all be gone to the mill," the proprietor said.

"The mill?" Philip asked.

"Aye. There's to be some gratuitous head-breaking. Had your own up yer arse the past sennight?" he asked cheekily.

"I've been otherwise occupied," Philip said.

"Well, the entire of Lon'on's gone to see it. Lord Peterborough challenged Figg to find a man to beat the outlander, a giant Venetian brute he is. He's said to down a man with a single blow."

"And Figg, of course, took up the gauntlet," Philip said.

"Never known Figg to back down, though I hear the odds was favorin' the foreigner four to one."

"Thanks for the tip," Philip said, and left the coffee-house to metaphorically kill two birds with a single stone. Knowing George for a most ardent votary of blood sport, Philip knew just where to find him, and with his pocket full of coin decided he may as well wager a few guineas as well.

The claim that all of London attended the match was little exaggerated. Philip had to wedge through the spitting, cursing, gin-tippling crowd forming around the wooden stage that served as the boxing ring at Oxford Circus. After a time, he located George Selwyn within the throng.

"You're in luck, Drake!" George exclaimed. "There's about to commence some gratuitous head breaking!"

"Cudgels?"

"Fisticuffs," George corrected. "Seems an Italian noble with a Goliath Venetian gondolier has been flaunting his personal jaw-breaker as unbeatable in every capital of Europe. He offered a substantial wager to Lord Peterborough to find any man in England to best his champion."

"And?" Philip prompted.

"Seems the fellow's indeed broken the jaw of most every opponent who's matched him, but Figg pledged to Peterborough, who's dropped a hefty sum on the match, to pit a man against the Italian who won't be broke with a sledgehammer."

By this time the swarthy giant had appeared. Beaming with bravado, the Venetian commenced to strip to the waist, revealing massive shoulders, long brawny arms, and a torso hard as burnished bronze.

Awestruck by the Hercules before them, an awful

silence prevailed amongst the spectators as he flexed his muscles and strutted the stage.

"What a brute!" George exclaimed.

"Who the devil might his lucky opponent be?" Philip asked, eying the foreigner with appreciative speculation.

"Bob Whitaker's the appointed one," interjected a gentleman standing at George's elbow. "Godfrey. John Godfrey." He introduced himself to George and Philip.

"Captain Godfrey of the *Sporting News*?" George asked.

"The same," he nodded. "And here's our man of the hour, Bob Whitaker, to take the brute's measure."

"By any stick, I'd say Whitaker comes up short," Philip quipped to the captain.

Godfrey chuckled. "Looks often deceive, my good man. Besides, after hearing the waterman boast that he'd take the shine out of any Englishman, Figg himself swore to come out of retirement and enter the ring if Whitaker knocks under. Heard him say myself he'd give the gondolier 'a Figg to chaw that he'll have trouble swallowing' long before he'd let an outlandish waterman rule the roost."

George remained skeptical. "I've seen Whitaker a time or two. The clumsy oaf half-throws himself at his opponents."

"He's not known for his agility or grace, but none can deny Bob's true English bottom. Fists of iron, he has, and tough as elephant hide to boot. His secret is soaking his hands an hour a day in brine," Godfrey remarked.

"But the odds are still four to one against 'im," George said. "Though I'm loathe to wager against my own countryman…" He looked to the Venetian with a defeatist shrug.

"I've known Figg a very long time," the captain returned. "If he feels Whitaker's up to the mark, my money's on our man."

At these words, the bullish Whitaker appeared on the platform. Cool and steady as a rock, he approached his challenger who stood nearly a full head above him. Undaunted, Whitaker rose onto the balls of his feet, meeting the Venetian breast-to-breast and eyeball-to-eyeball, all to a chorus of English cheers and huzzahs. Encouraged by his compatriots, Bob tore off his waistcoat and shirt, tossing them heedlessly into the crowd.

"I grant him a fine pair of fine English bollocks, anyway," George said with lessening skepticism.

Without ado, the men set to, much as fighting cocks in the pit. Coming together in a sudden flurry of blows, the Venetian struck such a hit to Whitaker's head as to catapult him over the stage and into the onlookers.

"Look! The man's already finished!" George exclaimed in dismay, having just placed a modest sum on the Englishman. Another frantic round of betting ensued with the odds now laying even thicker against Whitaker at six to one.

Though few believed Whitaker would come about, the unfazed English gamecock brushed himself off and with a grin, propelled himself over the rail, back onto the stage. Amid a second round of huzzahs and frenzied betting, Whitaker re-faced his opponent.

"I'll be hanged," Philip remarked with admiration.

"He's got grit, I'll grant 'im that, but the Venetian's a longer arm. He'll never overcome that reach!" George remarked.

"Don't be too quick to count Bob out," the captain said. "What he may lack in finesse, I assure you, he compensates in wiliness and vigor."

Without further ceremony, and as if choreographed on the captain's cue, Bob crouched low, and with the ferocious roar of a raging bull rammed a solid English peg to the Venetian's gut, driving him gasping and careening to the floor.

"Now that's a devil's leveler!" George exclaimed with pure glee. "Bob's bellyful knocked him clean onto his Venetian arse!"

The crowd went wild with raucous guffaws and deafening cheers while the dazed and winded gondolier tried in vain to recover his feet, but Whitaker's hammer was relentless. Suddenly the odds shifted again to favor the English pugilist, whereby Philip and George were both eager to get in on the action.

Whitaker fell upon the bewildered Venetian, continuing his brutal, unrelenting assault while his beleaguered opponent, thus besieged, barely managed to find his feet against the firestorm of blows, eventually losing his guard altogether.

The match continued but within just a few rounds, the tenacious English bulldog, completely and indisputably, humbled his opponent to the point of fleeing the ring in mortification and disgrace.

Captain Godfrey's tongue-in-cheek report in the next day's *Sporting News* would describe the defeat:

"The Venetian, after much vainglorious boasting, received a blow to the stomach with more rudeness than he could bear, and finding himself so unmannerly used, scorned to have any further doings with the slovenly English fist."

✁

Within minutes of the bout, the majority of spectators dispersed to their favorite taverns to celebrate or commiserate, depending on the results of their wagers. Philip and George, happily amongst the former group, accompanied Captain Godfrey to collect their respective winnings.

"Care to share a bowl of arrack punch, George? I've cause for celebration," Philip said.

Having won nearly treble his stakes, George was in a perfectly conciliatory frame of mind. "Indeed a happy outcome, though one might mourn the short duration of it. Damnably feeble fighter the foreign fellow turned out to be. But still worth a toast to our man of the hour, Whitaker."

"I don't just speak of the wager. Remember that windfall I spoke of?"

"I do recall," said George. "Is it all you expected?"

"My change in circumstances has certainly come about," Philip grinned.

"So you mean to set yourself up now?"

"I've the means to be comfortable, if that's what you ask."

"Mayhap 'twould be better advised to maintain a low profile for a time, Drake. That debacle with Dashwood won't soon blow over, you know."

"Surely you know I could not have done any differently."

"Even so, you seem to be adopting a habit of late of poaching women and brandishing your sword at anything that moves. Not actions to endear yourself to the peerage, if you glean my meaning."

"I fear you grossly overstate the events."

"Do I? Have you already forgotten your little incident with the Prince of Wales? He's none too pleased you pinched his intended mistress, and now of course there's Dashwood. Though I daresay he won't meet you *this time*, he vowed to make you answer for the episode if he ever lays eyes on you again. Sandwich will surely second him. You've made no friend of him either."

"Surely you don't expect me to go into hiding," Philip said.

"Don't you think it would be wise to play least in sight for a while?"

"If Dashwood feels the need to defend his dubious honor, so be it, George," Philip said, with perhaps more bravado than he really felt.

"You'd best hope he remembered nothing of the incident when he sobered. The man did threaten to *kill you*."

Philip flushed rubicund. "Nevertheless, Bosky, should I meet Dashwood, or anyone else, I assure you I would acquit myself creditably enough to avoid *that* fate."

"You would not expect to shed blood?"

"It would not be my plan to do so."

"Very droll, Drake. And precisely how many duels have you fought?"

"I'm no stranger to breaking bones, George. I've not survived the past four years in the company I keep without encountering blade and cudgel a time or two."

"A duel is a far cry from a tavern tussle, you know. Have you any formal training with the smallsword?"

"Some, though I don't boast of any great expertise."

"And you wouldn't expect to get pinked? How would you propose to avoid it, my cocky friend?"

"It is my understanding that one is most successful by avoiding the *pointy* end of the blade." Philip grinned.

"Well, you can expect to be called upon to use that shiny stick of yours if you continue in this current vein."

"Then I must count on my luck, superior reflexes, and hope my opponent's the worse for drink."

George paused, massaging his chin in thought. "You know, Drake, it's no laughing matter. If you truly aspire to adopt a gentleman's life, mayhap it's time to acquire more of a gentleman's accomplishments."

Philip replied, "It's a bit late for that, don't you think?"

"Not at all, and it would not be unreasonable to put some of your so-called windfall to good use," George replied, producing a card from his pocket. Embossed in the characteristic style of William Hogarth, it read:

JAMES FIGG: MASTER OF THE NOBLE
SCIENCE OF DEFENSE,

OXFORD ROAD NEAR ADAM AND EVE COURT.

"TEACHING GENTLEMEN THE USE OF
THE SWORD AND QUARTERSTAFF."

George handed it to Philip and said, "Now how about that arrack punch…"

Twenty-Four

A PEERESS'S PRIVILEGE

COVENT GARDEN, AN INNOCUOUS FRUIT AND VEGETABLE market by day, became the crown jewel of the voluptuary by night. On one side of the square stood the theatre, a convenient stone's throw from the brothels and bagnios offering ample supplemental income to the actresses and dancers.

Opposite, on Russell Street in the Little Piazza, stood the Rose and the Shakespeare's Head Taverns, fierce competitors who offered superior food, fine wines, and most important, rooms for private pursuits. Although patronized by a more exclusive clientele, the taverns were nonetheless public places which did not discriminate as long as the patron could foot his one-shilling cover. Taken as a whole, the district held potential to become a gaming mecca if one could somehow offer a haven from the scoundrels and sharps who frequented the public taverns and gaming hells.

The dowagers Baroness Mordington and Lady Casellis had just such a vision when they began hosting a series of private gaming parties. These exclusive gatherings were designed to attract the uppermost echelon and the very deepest players. Sparing no expense to outdo the upscale Rose and Shakespeare's Head taverns across the square, the entrepreneurial ladies issued gilt-edged invitations to "a private assembly where all persons of credit are at liberty to frequent and play at assorted diversions."

While the other gaming houses of Covent Garden suffered fines and penalties for their trespasses, these women openly flouted the gaming laws under the auspices of noble privilege and paid off the local magistrates; in sum, they thumbed their noses at Parliament. In short time, the gaming-mad aristocracy flocked to their gates.

꒳꒷

By ten o'clock the crested coaches and private sedan chairs, two and three abreast, lined the square in front of the leased three-story mansion in the Great Piazza. Due to the exclusivity of the company, Sukey had insisted upon Lady Mordington's so-called assembly as the perfect venue for her real gaming debut.

When Sukey waived the gilt invitation in his face, Philip had conceded, albeit with some misgivings about her readiness for those who would surely habit the tables. In truth, he was becoming utterly power-less to resist her. It was anticipation of spending the ensuing night in her arms that had induced him. With an evocative look here and a seductive smile there, she had completely bewitched him.

His passion for Sukey was anything but tempered. She was his first true lover, one who made him feel a man in every sense, and he couldn't seem to get enough of her. The cheeky tavern wenches, dimpled dairymaids, and pert shop girls of his past had already receded to a far distant corner of his memory. Yet even in their most intense moments of intimacy, she seemed to hold some little piece of herself in reserve, frustrating him with what he couldn't seem to reach.

As they awaited their turn to alight from the vehicle, Philip sat restlessly in his seat, thinking the confinement would have been unbearable if not for the chance to study her at close quarters. When she pulled the curtain aside to discern their position in the long queue, he slanted a slow heated gaze over her, desiring to drink her in with all of his senses.

His roving eye followed the graceful curve of her neck revealed by unpowdered and upswept chestnut hair. Her gown of old gold satin was cut scandalously low, nearly revealing the dusky ring of her nipples. He had instructed her to dress to distract attention from the cards, and God help him now, she had taken him at his word.

When she turned back to him, he tore his eyes guiltily away, shifting in growing discomfort and fidgeting with his lace-edged cravat.

"It appears we've arrived at last. Philip, are you unwell?" she asked coyly, noting his flushed face and overbright eyes.

"I'm near suffocating in this infernal neckcloth, and confounded peruke," he replied irritably. "Can't fathom how you induced me to crop my own mane to wear a horse's instead."

Her lips turned up in amusement. "But it is the latest mode from France, and just look at you, my darling, the absolute pink of fashion."

"*Pink!* The tailor called it salmon, declaring it the rave of the season. I'll surely *pink* anyone who dares call it otherwise."

"Oh, my!" She laughed outright. "Then *salmon* it must be!"

When the hired footman let down the coach steps, Philip and Sukey alighted in front of a magnificent neo-Palladian mansion built in the original style of Colin Campbell. With her hand resting lightly on his sleeve, they navigated the silk and velvet-bedecked crowd ascending the marble stairway to the grand covered entryway of the mansion.

Philip swiftly assessed his surroundings, the dancing flames of a hundred Venetian crystal chandeliers, the expanses of pink-veined marble, and the gilt-framed mirrors adorning richly colored, silk-papered walls. He eventually lit upon the hostess of the evening, the powdered and patched queen of her domain, Lady Mordington, who stood in her grand entry greeting each of her guests as they arrived.

She flicked him a curious glance and then raised a brow upon recognition of his companion. She moved toward them in a rustle of silk.

"My dear, dear Lady Messingham! What a delight to see you have sacrificed your period of mourning to join us," the dowager gushed.

"Old cat!" she hissed in Philip's ear before returning the greeting with an air buss to a papery, rouged, and cerused cheek.

"I am indeed back about in society, Lady Mordington, and your assembly has received such encomiums."

"You are all too kind, my dear. Lady Casellis and I

do our poor best to provide worthy entertainment," she answered with false modesty and then looked greedily at Philip. "Now I must know. Who is your *delicious* young escort?"

Philip suppressed a shudder of revulsion, thinking her look conveyed that she really would like to taste him.

"Baroness, I present to you the Honorable Philip Drake."

Philip bowed over his hostess's extended hand. "Baroness."

"So you are Hastings's disreputable scamp?" The old baroness cackled with a flirtatious tap of her fan. "How delightful to have both father and son under my humble roof!"

"The honor is all mine," Philip replied, stifling a grimace at the mention of his father.

"Of course you will wish to pay your respects to Lord Hastings at once. He was last seen playing at piquet, I believe. Shall I have a footman conduct you to him?"

"You needn't trouble yourself, madam, when you have so many new arrivals. I am sure we can manage to navigate the rooms without assistance. My lady?"

He inclined his head to Lady Susannah, clearly indicating his desire to move on. Taking his cue, she curtsied to the baroness and took hold of his sleeve.

"Ah, Your Grace," Lady Mordington gushed to the Duke of Grafton, having now moved on to her more important guests.

"How long has it been?" Sukey asked as they began a slow perambulation.

"How long has what been?" He smiled benignly as he began tracking the room.

"Since you've spoken with your father?"

"Not as long as I would wish," he replied vaguely.

"Have you no hope of reconciliation?" she asked.

"Not the slightest," he said with disinterest and nodded acknowledgement to George Selwyn who was looking pathetically doleful, anchored to his mother's side across the room.

"But there is always hope, child."

"You have no idea of what you speak," Philip snapped, more irked by her continued condescending address than by the topic of discussion. He thought she would have desisted by now. After all, he'd proven himself no naïve schoolboy. If he had her alone for a moment, he would certainly remind her. The very thought of taking her against a wall somewhere seemed to mollify his irritable temper.

"Then tell me of it," she persisted. "We've known each other for weeks. My secrets are revealed, yet you've disclosed so little in turn. Surely if you really desired, the earl would forgive your youthful misdeeds. You are, after all, his son."

"But not his heir."

"But his flesh and blood. Blood is blood, as they say."

"I would rather not speak of my family, if you don't mind." *Blood indeed.* Absently, Philip's thumb turned the ring on his little finger, as had become his habit, recalling the initial shock in learning of his own tainted blood, but was abruptly recalled to his surroundings when *still she persisted.*

"Since the earl is present, you might at least pay your respects, Philip. Your father is a wealthy man, is he not? Your unhappiness and your troubles might end just like that." She snapped. "If you would only make amends…"

"Devil take you, Sukey!" he growled. "I don't need his money and won't submit to that black-hearted bastard even for you! Now, may we please turn the subject?"

She stared at him at the slight, and then answered back, "Why, certainly we may! Since you are so ill-tempered and overcome by brooding, I'll do one better and relieve you of the burden of my company." She abruptly released his arm.

"Where do you think you're going?"

"Why, to seek out more scintillating conversation."

"Then if that is your wish, *my lady*, I suggest you restrict *your conversation* to the dowagers playing in the blue salon. Do not take it into your head to engage in any play in the gold room."

"And why ever should I not?"

"Because you'll be bloody well in too deep if you do!"

She responded with a pointed glare. "You have no right to direct me at all, Philip. I am my own woman, free to do as I please. That includes choosing my own diversions… as well as my own companions."

With that parting remark, she broke away, exclaiming, "Ah, there is Prince Frederick's party!"

Affecting a winsome smile, she tripped purposefully toward the royal entourage, making her obeisance and gushing, "My Lady Baltimore, how lovely is your gown! You must tell me, who is your mantua maker? And Jane dear, how do you fare?"

Pretending not to notice her, Lady Hamilton turned away in an undisguised snub. Lady Messingham's face fell in dismay, but she soon had to contend with the prince who appeared by her side. "Don't mind her, *liebling*, I believe her to be jealous of your superior charms." In speaking, his eyes never rose above the exposed portions of her breasts.

She wished heartily she had not eschewed her lace fichu.

"My dear, it has been too long since our last meeting, for which I still owe you my most humble apologies..."

"There is no need, Your Highness." She managed to greet the Prince of Wales with her most dazzling smile posed with gritted teeth, all while slanting a side-long glance at Philip. She offered the prince her hand, "I would be a shrew indeed if I took lasting offense to such a triviality. The best of men surely suffer an occasional lapse under the influence of wine."

"Oh, but you are a gracious angel, my lady. Others would not be so generous of spirit. Now I pray you will accompany us to the gold room. I hear they play at basset."

"I would be delighted to join you *in the gold room*, Your Highness..." She looked over her shoulder with triumph, hoping she had spoken clearly enough for Philip's ears, but he was already engaged in conversation with George. Drat him.

The moment he looked up, she laughed merrily at something the prince said and with this bit of satisfaction, they moved out of Philip's earshot.

❧

Knowing she had played that hand purely to spite him and inspire jealousy, Philip refused to pursue her, shrugging the matter off in favor of seeking his fortune at hazard.

George Selwyn had by now broken away from his mother's side to join him. He nodded in the direction of the gold room. "Basset's the word tonight, Drake, and they're playing dangerously deep."

"Basset? They outlawed the game in France, you know, after it threatened to beggar half the princes of the blood. Now it will beggar our nobility instead."

"But the odds are more in favor of the punter than many other games," George protested. "Name me any other game where one can win over sixty times his stakes in one sitting?"

"Name *me* anyone who ever has," Philip rejoined.

"Well, it's not beyond the realm of possibility," George protested.

"No, just probability," Philip replied cynically. "The chances of the punters winning are truly no better than winning the national lottery, yet the fever takes these dupes with the contagion of the pox." Philip indicated the crowds pressing into the next room.

"Then you would deem it another French pox?" George laughed.

"Nay, at least the French pox can be eradicated with mercury pills. For basset there is no known cure but ruin, and then it comes too late."

"Such opprobrium from a seasoned gamester?"

"I speak no hypocrisy, George. I simply choose to lay my money where my chances are, let us say, subject to more favorable conditions. The odds might improve with a fair deal, of course, but I daresay an honest *tallière* doesn't exist. Who holds the bank tonight anyway?"

"The Marquess of Weston," George replied.

"Weston?" Philip frowned at the vaguely familiar name. "Do you know him?"

"Only by repute," answered George. "He's recently returned from extended Continental travels. It's rumored he was sent out of the country by his family years ago after affecting some scandal. I daresay it's true, as he's garnered quite a reputation for gaming, dueling, and debauching other men's wives, *not necessarily in that order*. As the accursed Fates would have it, such a rogue has now claimed a title and family fortune to boot."

"And now such as he funds the bank at basset? I'd avoid his table if I were you, George. Now, do you still yearn to feed the bank at basset? Or do you care to join me at hazard?"

George looked wistfully toward the gold room. "I daresay my chances are better even with the lottery than any play with you."

"Come now, Bosky. It's been some time since I've been plagued with a full evening of your company."

"You've been otherwise engaged," George answered with a hint of peevishness. "Besides, you know as well as I it can never be the same."

"What are you talking about, Bosky? What can never be the same?"

"Our association. Since the incident at Medmenham... As much as it pains me to say so, I am advised that your friendship is... a liability," he finished in a rush.

"A liability, eh?" Only the twitch of Philip's jaw betrayed any emotion. "Your mother doesn't like me much, does she?"

"So sorry, ol' chap. We've kicked up some jolly good larks, but you understand how it is."

"Suit yourself," Philip said with a careless shrug. "But if you are dead set on the gold room, I beg you do me one final favor."

"And what might that be?"

"Keep an eye on her."

"Her?"

"Lady Messingham. She is, by far, too single-minded and stubborn for her own good."

"And so the pot called the kettle burnt-arse," George jibed.

"Bugger yourself, Bosky." With that parting remark, Philip turned toward the sound of clattering dice.

Twenty-Five

QUEEN OF HEARTS

How dare he! Sukey seethed but realized too late with the prince's lascivious stare down her décolletage, that without Philip by her side she would once again spend the evening warding off Frederick's persistent advances. Her only possible escape would be at the tables. The devil or the deep blue sea, she considered wryly and wafted away from the prince at the first opportunity.

She had come prepared to play. After pawning her jewels to pay her most pressing debts, she had two hundred pounds with which to wager and was determined to leave at the end of the night with at least five hundred in her pocket. Philip was to have overseen her at *vingt-et-un* and loo, later partnering her again at whist, all games in which she could now acquit herself creditably even without Philip's aid. At least that had been her plan until Philip and she had once again quarreled.

He'd been so edgy and irritable, even in the carriage, but she should have known better than to provoke him. She was well aware of his sensitivity regarding family matters but had pressed on heedlessly. Had she done so deliberately because he had come too close for comfort? She wondered now if she had cut off her very nose to spite her face.

With this unsettling thought, she wended through the crowd pressing toward the principal event. Bassett was the core of the action tonight, with peers and peeresses alike surrounding the table, eyes glazed in anticipation.

She wedged into the group, scanning in befuddlement the baize surface littered with multitudinous dog-eared cards, covered with gold and silver coins. Bassett was unfamiliar ground. Philip had reproved it in a most disdainful and high-handed manner, likening the game to a lottery, with as little chance of winning. But the crowd at the table, rapt, nearly rabid in their fervor, seemed to belie his warnings.

"Do you play, madame?" The voice of the *tallière*, smooth, refined, and slightly Continental, addressed her from behind an enormous mound of gold guineas.

That voice! It couldn't be, after all these years!

Susannah's heart pummeled mercilessly against her breastbone. Slowly, tremulously, she raised her face, half-expecting her ears to have betrayed her, but her ears no more lied than her eyes, for all he was changed.

He would be just past thirty now, but dissipation had already taken its toll, prematurely aging and blurring once finely hewn aristocratic features. One would expect as much, given his family's resources and his own prodigal habits. His years touring the princely courts of Europe had apparently educated him in both style and in vice, and his dress and demeanor bespoke wealth superior to any ordinary gentleman's means. His immaculately tailored suit was of heather-colored velvet accompanied by a peacock silk waistcoat, and snowy linen dripping with the finest wrought lace. An enormous diamond cravat pin completed the picture that was over-refined, nearing effete. Even so, he was yet a striking man.

Upon first recognition of the once all-too-familiar face, the shock was nearly enough to send her into a swoon, a frivolous affectation she heartily despised and thought never to emulate, but she had come dangerously close. Her hands clutched the table, as if her swelling emotions would sweep her out to sea. When at last she marshaled enough resolve to look directly into his gaze, certain he would react as vehemently as she had, he regarded her with the fashionably blank façade of a stranger.

"Madame?" he repeated. "Do you play?"

He doesn't even know me! He had destroyed her life without a second thought, and now the scoundrel didn't even remember her? She had almost fled the table, so shaken was she, but then the anger came. It arrived in rivulets that infused her blood and then flooded her being as a roaring, raging river. It was the force of her fury that sustained her, that gave her the strength to remain at the table.

She knew the years had changed her dramatically, not just in the lush swell of her once gangly body, but also in her overall bearing. Any trace of girlish innocence vanished when that chapter of her life had closed. Though now quaking, she reminded herself that she now faced him as a woman. She was mature, sophisticated, and seasoned by the knowledge that beauty and self-possession could be powerful weapons when skillfully wielded.

She surveyed the table with uncertainty, but her answer was confidently voiced with a poised smile of dazzling white as she waved her fan languorously before her well-displayed bosom. "Yes. I do believe I'll play."

His hooded gaze lost any hint of indolence, boring into her as if removing her clothing layer by silken layer, but still it held not the least hint of recognition. His lip twitched in a way that said she had fixed his interest, and with deft and nimble fingers he dealt her thirteen cards.

All hearts.

She examined them with consternation; racking her brain to remember what little Philip had told her about this ruinous game, while those around her frantically laid one, two, or several of their cards on the table, covering them with mounds of silver shillings and gold guineas. For a fleeting moment, she considered abandoning the table to seek her fortune at *vingt-et-un* instead, but the memory of Philip's high-handed arrogance rooted her to the floor.

She followed suit with the other punters, delving into her purse with some trepidation. Initially choosing caution as her rule, she placed twenty guineas atop the queen of hearts and anxiously regarded those around her.

When the flurry of wagering activity ceased, the *tallière* picked up a newly shuffled pack, flipping it over to reveal the bottom card. He laid it on the table, announcing, "Queen wins."

Upon this declaration, the croupier swept the table

of all silver and gold, save the couch stakes ventured on the queens.

"I have won?" She looked up, gaping in amazement.

The *tallière* answered, "The lady appears as lucky as she is lovely."

"Fortune is with us both tonight, my lady," George Selwyn said, placing himself at her elbow, and indicating his queen of spades with a grin.

"Mr. Selwyn? I am sincerely glad for your appearance. I confess I am a bit at sea here," she said with a welcome that suddenly altered into an accusation. "Philip has not sent you to spy on me?"

"Pay or *paroli*, my lady?" the *tallière* interrupted.

Susannah's suspicion was lost with meditation of her cards. She worried her lower lip in indecision.

Glad to avoid an answer to her question, George explained. "You may now choose to accept half of your couch stakes from the bank, or indicate *paroli*."

"*Paroli?*" she repeated blankly.

"Your couch stakes and winnings together remain on your card and you go to *sept-et-le-va*."

Her expression remained vacant.

The surrounding punters murmured their impatience while George softly expounded. "The first card played is called the *fasse*, and always favors the bank, but as play continues, every odd card favors the punter, and every even card, the bank. Thus, should a queen appear again upon the player's turn, you stand to gain seven times your current stakes. *Quinze-et-le-va* would be fifteen times, etcetera, etcetera," he explained with exaggerated patience. He demonstrated by crooking the right upper corner of her card.

"With thirty ventured, why that would be over two hundred guineas!" she exclaimed.

"*Paroli* then, madame?" The *tallière* tilted his head toward her tabbed card.

"It appears you have answered for me," she spoke dryly to Selwyn. "Seven times you say?"

"Indeed, but 'tis just the beginning... if luck is with you." George's eyes took on an excited gleam, "There is potential to gain a veritable fortune in just one sitting at this table."

She had staked only twenty guineas and already had thirty. Her breathing quickened in anticipation of the next turn of the cards. The *tallière* flipped the next two in quick succession, the three of spades and the four of hearts. "Three wins, four loses."

She exhaled in relief.

He dealt again. "Queen wins. Knave loses."

"You have won again, my lady!" George cried.

"But it was so easy!" Susannah gasped in delight, receiving resentful looks from anguished punters groaning as the croupier swept to the bank any coins resting with a knave.

"You are exceeding lucky, *my lady of hearts*. Do you wish pay or *paroli*?" asked the *tallière* once more.

Her breath hitched at the decision. She turned to George. "Did you not say that with *quinze-et-le-va*, the payout is a full fifteen times my stakes?"

"Indeed so, but now with only two queens remaining in the deck, the odds do not favor you."

"Nevertheless, Mr. Selwyn, being a creature of caprice, I am resolved to follow my fancy." Heedlessly brushing aside all her reservations and every warning

Philip had ever spoken, Susannah wagered several
more gold coins and crooked the second corner of
her card.

❧

With a controlled flick of the wrist, Philip cast for the
final time. The rolling cubes came to rest at deuce and
ace. Crabs.

"Finally, the young rascal throws out!" cried one
gent in jubilation, while another punter, who had
wagered with the cast, bemoaned his fifty guinea loss.

Feigning dismay at his loss, Philip passed the dice to
the next caster, knowing that he parted with far more
than what he had lost on the final roll.

A gold watch and an exquisitely enameled Sèvres
snuffbox now occupied the same pocket with Lady
Yarmouth's diamond necklace. Philip had earlier
taken the jewels to be appraised, intent on selling the
individual stones, in lieu of negotiating the sale back to
the king's mistress. Eight hundred pounds, the jeweler
had assured him the diamonds would bring.

He calculated his additional winnings at nearly five
hundred guineas, more than he had ever won in a
sitting. Overall, a decent take. Surely enough with the
necklace to more than clear his lover's debts. He saw it
all as a propitious sign for his new beginning.

It would have been a superlative night, indeed, if
it weren't for that spat, but she had a way of setting
his back up like no one else... well, no one but his
family. As to that, thank heaven, he had not come
across his father's path this evening. His emotions
were yet raw and volatile, and he was unsure how to

deal with his newfound knowledge. He should have explained as much to her. They might have then avoided all the unpleasantness.

Philip considered how much he yet had to learn of women, but his lessons at Sukey's hand had proven, thus far, less than disagreeable. He grinned at the thought.

～

"You've bollocks of brass, my lady!" George exclaimed, too lost in the moment to guard his speech.

Susannah paid him no heed; his voice had long since become little more than a buzz in her ears. She'd stayed with her lucky queen and the impulse had paid off with seven hundred guineas now on the table divided between her queen and ace. Her mind was a flurry of calculations. If her good fortune continued, she might garner enough to live out her entire life, not just a woman of independent means but one of substantial wealth.

She held her breath, and her hands clenched the table's edge as the *tallière* turned over the next two cards, the ace of spades and the three of diamonds.

"Ace wins, three loses."

"Good God!" Selwyn slapped the table. "You've done it again! You've the devil's own luck tonight!"

With her pulse drumming a deafening tattoo in her ears, Susannah dumped the remains of her purse onto the table, splitting it between the queen and the ace, the sum of her two wagers now totaling nearly a thousand guineas.

Recalling his promise to Philip, George was

reluctantly moved to intervene with a staying hand. "Mayhap you should consider the payout. I've yet to see anyone surpass *trente-et-le-va*."

With her eyes glimmering and her voice breathless, she answered, "Did you not study Virgil, Mr. Selwyn?"

He looked chagrined. "I'm afraid I left my studies at Cambridge a bit precipitately."

"Fortune favors the bold," she quipped overbrightly. She bent her card just as Philip's ominous warning came unbeckoned into her head.

And luck tires as surely as the player.

Twenty-Six

VIRTUE FOR HONOR

PHILIP ELBOWED HIS WAY THROUGH THE HAZARD ROOM with a mind to locate the object of his obsession and make whatever amends he could for his earlier surly behavior. If she had exercised good sense and deigned to take his advice, he would find her with the dowagers playing at whist or loo.

Giving her the benefit of doubt, Philip meandered into the blue salon, where those not whispering the latest *on-dits* hidden behind ornately painted fans frowned in concentration over their cards. He surveyed the chamber filled with vibrant silks and the white powdered wigs adorning old beaux and grande dames, cerused and patched in the prevailing fashion. Finding no sign of the woman he sought, he groaned in vexed frustration and doggedly went forth to the nefarious gold room.

❧

With hands clenched and breath bated, Sukey awaited the next flip of the cards.

"Four wins, seven loses."

"King wins, six loses."

The *tallière* continued in an almost soothing monotone, but with every call of the cards, Sukey's pulse rose and abated like an incoming tide.

"King wins, ace loses."

Disbelieving her ears, Lady Messingham stood mutely, as if stunned. The croupier swept away the five hundred guineas she'd wagered on the ace, half her winnings lost in one fell swoop!

"So very unfortunate how your luck turned, *madame*," the *tallière*'s voice oozed false sympathy. "But should you wish to recoup your loss, a simple request of credit is all that would be required."

"But I have lost five hundred guineas," she said. "To win it back would require doubling my current wager."

"Then you wish for an advance of a thousand?" The *tallière* presented the marker as benignly as an offer of refreshment.

The compulsion to reclaim the fortune that had slipped elusively through her fingers was overpowering. Her hammering heart filled her ears, but dismay at her loss overcame any remaining good sense. Her attention was so engaged that she failed to notice Philip's appearance as she scribbled her initials.

His expression bespoke a gathering storm. "Just what the devil do you think you are doing?" he demanded, but didn't await her reply. "Take your payout and leave the table now, my lady."

"How can you ask it of her, Drake?" George protested. "She's had but one bad card the whole night. Even you have never had such a run of luck."

With eyes blazing, Philip spun around to deliver a

lambasting to her failed guardian. "I expressly asked you to look after her, George, not bloody encourage her! Surely *you* know better than most that luck is easily *manipulated* for the unwise and unwary."

George glared. "And what is that remark supposed to mean!"

Ignoring him, Philip's attention shifted between the dealer's resentful glare and his lover's pale-cast visage with an uneasiness he couldn't explain. His initial, rapid assessment had cast the *tallière* as just another mincing popinjay, and probably a sodomite to boot, an unbidden thought that made his anal sphincter reflexively tighten. But the banker had looked upon Sukey with a lingering and predatory interest that couldn't be denied. *Definitely not a sod.*

His senses pricked. Philip turned to George in an agitated undertone. "Who is he, Bosky?"

"Who is *who*?"

"The banker, you lackwit!"

"Look, Drake, I've had about as much abuse from you—"

"Just answer the damn question!"

"He's Weston, the fellow we spoke of earlier," George answered with growing resentment.

"Devil take it, *him*?" Philip cursed under his breath and turned to the croupier. "The lady will accept her winnings *now*."

"Just what do you think you're about?" she protested.

"Saving you from the repercussions of your damnable, reckless folly."

"You dare call me reckless when you make your living from these same tables?"

"Yes. Bloody damned reckless! Though I take chances and have experienced my fair share of ill luck, I have never chanced losing over a thousand in a sitting!"

Philip turned back to the *croupier*. "You heard me. The lady will take her pay. Now."

She turned back to the croupier. "The lady will do no such thing." *Damn his arrogance! Now we are lovers, he thinks he owns me!*

Philip seized her arm, twisting her around to face him. "Don't be a fool, Sukey. I warned you about playing deep. You are in well over your head and in jeopardy of drowning."

Her eyes narrowed in rebellion and she jerked out of his grasp. "Fool, am I? I'll have you know that even after one loss I have parlayed my couch stakes into seven hundred guineas."

"A handsome sum that would keep you in silks, private coaches, and the comfort of a queen for at least a six-month. Now, for the last time, collect your winnings and leave this table."

"*Paroli*," she answered with a defiant glare and bent her queen.

"Devil take you!" Philip cried, his frustration burgeoning to fury at his inability to rein her in.

Her pupils were already dilated as if with fever and her voice pitched higher than normal. "I go *trent-et-le-va*. With so few cards and one queen yet remaining, I have an even chance that she will appear on *my* draw."

Philip's brows contracted in ferocious admonition as his gaze flickered again from punter to dealer. "The odds are *not* even. The game always, *without exception*, ends in favor of the bank."

"Wh-what do you mean?" She blanched.

"The final card always goes to the *tallière*. He collects if you lose, but pays nothing if you win. If your queen does not appear *before the last draw*, you've lost. Do you understand?"

Now the color drained even from her lips.

Philip swung around to grasp George Selwyn by the cravat. "Damn your eyes, Selwyn! How could you let her play without having even the most rudimentary understanding of the game?"

"Hell, I've never endured to the end," George replied with a helpless shrug. "How was I to know the last card went to the bank?"

Having chanced *trente-et-le-va* and unable to turn back, Sukey shut her eyes in an attempt to channel her energy into one thought, as if she could actually *will* the queen to appear. With hands clenched and breath bated, she awaited the next flip of the cards.

"Four wins, seven loses."

"King wins, six loses."

The *tallière* continued in an almost soothing monotone, but with every call of the cards, Sukey's pulse rose and abated like an incoming tide.

"Nine wins, five loses."

Unable to help herself, she peeked through a slit in her lids to fix upon the long white manicured fingers methodically turning over the cards by twos.

"Eight wins, six loses."

Her heart slammed against her chest and her nails clawed at the thick baize as the deck continued to dwindle with the queen yet to appear.

With only three cards remaining, panic pervaded her.

The *tallière* curled his lips ever so subtly, calling the final cards without even glancing down. "Four wins... Queen loses."

"Damme, but what a rousing run!" George exclaimed in the drama of the moment. At Philip's death glare, he mumbled his excuses and disappeared into the crowd.

Susannah stared blindly, but when the scales dropped from her eyes the agonizing truth was revealed... the banker had controlled the game all along.

With this comprehension, Sukey's mind whirled like a top. It was gone. *All of it. Gone.* The words resounded in her brain like a clanging cymbal. Her stomach roiled and her world came crashing down.

Her widow's jointure was insufficient even to maintain her home and servants. Her carriage was sold and jewels pawned. Now nothing remained. She clutched the table's edge for fear her legs would no longer sustain her. *Oh dear Lord, what have I done?*

Although Sukey knew the banker could not sue her over a gaming debt, Parliament having long ago taken steps to purge the bowels of jurisprudence with such civil suits, the reigning social order had its own irrefutable laws. Should she fail to make good on a "debt of honor," social ostracism awaited.

Designing to stall, she appealed to Weston with wide plaintive eyes. "I may require a bit of time, you understand."

"But of course, madame." Although his manner was solicitous, the banker's slate eyes glittered beneath hooded lids as if she were a piece of ripened fruit he was hungry to devour. "Perhaps we might repair to a more private venue to negotiate some... acceptable terms."

She swallowed convulsively, knowing exactly what his terms would be. Overcome with shame, she cursed herself a thousand times over her lack of self-restraint. Although standing in the periphery of her vision, just over her shoulder, Sukey dared not even cast her head in Philip's direction for fear of the recrimination she would find reflected in his eyes.

By sheer recklessness, she had played right into Weston's hand, achieving precisely what she had meant to avoid, her complete and utter ruin... and worse, by the same man who had ruined her once before.

Twenty-Seven

REPERCUSSIONS AND RECRIMINATIONS

DAMN HER FOR PUTTING ME IN THIS IMPOSSIBLE POSITION!
Philip's blood boiled at Sukey's obstinate refusal to heed his counsel, for George's failure to watch over her, and for his own failure to protect her from a man he recognized as a Greek of the highest order. Lastly, he cursed himself for ever having become involved with her.

She had thoughtlessly brought this travesty upon herself and now threatened to suck him into the vortex. His intuition warned him to escape, but he simply couldn't bring himself to walk away.

"My lady," Philip spoke lowly, "might I suggest *we* avail ourselves of the gentleman's invitation to privacy?"

The banker lifted a brow in distinctly aristocratic hauteur. "I do not believe we are acquainted…"

Refusing to affect any air of servility, Philip's bow was shallow enough only to mock. "Philip Drake," he said in introduction, "and the lady is with me."

Having made his decision to stand by her, Philip placed a hand on the small of Sukey's back. He could

feel her tremor even through multiple layers of petticoat, stays, and silk.

A baleful stare pierced Philip at the well-understood
gesture of possession. "So you say?" Weston's tone
held a subtle edge of threat. "She was quite unattended
when I found her, the poor little bird. Perhaps you
should not be so negligent in future." He reached out
his beautiful bejeweled hand to Sukey. "Come now,
my dove, and let us speak… in private."

Sukey unconsciously recoiled, whereby Philip
interposed himself between them. "Perhaps I wasn't
clear, my Lord Weston. Any matters concerning the
lady, you may settle *with me*."

"Hastings's ignoble wastrel?" Weston laughed
outright. "What have *you* to say to anything? Indeed,
I begin to think your sire remiss in teaching you
manners, a matter I would surely delight in addressing
had I not more pressing business with the lady."

The tension between the two men was palpable and
escalating by the second.

Sukey's anxious gaze flitted again between the
two men: to Jack, who'd once betrayed and abandoned her, and to Philip, friend, lover, and reluctant
defender. Her trepidation increasing, Sukey laid a
warning hand on Philip's arm. Philip covered her hand
with his own. Her fingers dug through the fabric of
his coat and nearly into his flesh, but his pointed look
squelched any verbal protest.

Philip turned back to Weston. "As the lady's
protector, I have every right to speak on her behalf and
am quite prepared to assume liability for her losses."
He carefully detached her fingers, one by one, raising

them to his lips with an indulgent smirk. "Tsk, tsk, my dear. What a very bad night you've had."

"You? Her protector?" Lord Weston's nostrils pinched and pupils flared. "The whelp's presumption knows no bounds!" The marquess looked at Sukey with a smile that made her blood chill. "My patience is waning," he sighed when she still hesitated. "I had thought to spare you, but if you insist on playing this out as a public melodrama…"

He looked meaningfully to the gossipmongers who, scenting blood, had drawn in to circle the trio as vultures over their carrion. Lord Weston elevated his voice only enough to be heard over their low hum.

"*Sukey*, my dove," he drew her name out in long, sibilant syllables, "for want of a proper *man* in my extended absence, have you now developed a penchant for impudent, posturing jackanapes?"

The blood that had earlier inflamed Sukey's face drained completely. She blanched paler than white. "You knew me all the time… you… you loathsome cad!"

Weston smirked. "You should be flattered, my dear, to be such an unforgettable morsel."

Philip looked from Weston to Sukey with momentary incomprehension.

They had history? Weston was her lover?

Philip turned to Sukey, desperate for a rebuttal that did not come. Pale and wide-eyed, her mouth opened and closed with no sound emerging much like a landed fish gasping its last. His brittle control was slipping fast. The shock of the revelation threatened to be his undoing.

While the marquess had aimed to cut him down,

to metaphorically pink a would-be rival, the figurative blade he wielded had penetrated straight to Philip's vital organs. It was a mortal blow, twisting like a dagger in his gut.

He struggled to block the invading visions of *his* Sukey, entangled naked and panting *in Weston's arms*, and his vision blurred. A conflagration of emotion overcame him in a furious wave—shock, jealousy, pain, and then pure fury.

Masking it was a superhuman exertion, but he managed to signal a porter and hand him a guinea with the command to escort Sukey to her carriage. When she would have protested, he squelched her with a black look. "Good night, *my lady*." He spoke stiffly and his manner was chilling.

She bristled at his imperiousness but thought better of flouting him further. With a backward glare of indignation, she accompanied the porter.

When she was out of earshot, Philip turned back to deal with Weston, speaking matter-of-factly. "As I see it, my lord, there are now *two matters* to settle between us. Shall we continue this *discussion* at Tothill Fields?"

Philip's meaning was not lost. The marquess's lips curved in satisfaction. "With pistol or smallsword?"

"Smallsword."

"You may send your seconds to Wimbledon Park."

Philip signaled acknowledgement with a silent inclination of his head.

As if an afterthought, the marquess added the mortal threat, "By the bye, Drake, you might forego the added expense of a physician. Assuredly, you'll have no need of one."

Philip turned away, flinging carelessly over his shoulder, "I'm sure you are right, my lord... but perhaps *you may*."

❧

Lady Susannah Messingham nodded abstractedly to her acquaintances as she wended through the remaining late night revelers. She awaited her hired carriage seething with words yet unspoken.

"Just what is he to you?" Philip demanded, startling her from behind.

"Nothing!" she snapped. "He is nothing to me."

"Then why in God's name would you habit his table?"

"I had no idea at first, and then upon realizing who he was, I was so overcome by shock that I hardly knew where I was, let alone what I was doing. I was overset, confused, not thinking clearly."

"Overset? Confused? Not thinking clearly? When you have placed a thousand at stake? Good God! I credited you with more intelligence! Yet when I arrived you still had a chance to walk away, but you thumbed your nose at me!"

"I had been winning!" she protested.

"And you didn't walk away. Do you still not understand? It is all part of the game. They let you win to draw you in deeper. I warned you of it, time and again!"

"I did not intend to go so deep."

"Yet you didn't leave," he accused.

Failing to summon any words to defend untenable actions, she choked back tears of bewilderment and fury.

They simmered in a protracted silence before Philip asked more calmly, as if speaking to a particularly dull child, "After all I taught you, didn't you even suspect he palmed that last queen?"

She gasped. "If you knew him for a cheat, why did you not warn me?"

"Good God, I tried!" he cried, throwing his hands up in frustration. "You don't listen!"

"What can you expect when you're so infernally high-handed! You could have taken a different approach."

"Un-bloody-believable! You are trying to cast the blame on me?"

"But you knew he cheated, and you let me fall victim! For one who claims to be my *protector*, you evince little instinct to protect! Why did you not even call him on it?" she persisted.

"*Call him out*, do you mean?"

"Yes!" she cried. "It's the least a proper *gentleman* would have done!"

"Ah, so now you impugn both my honor and my valor?"

"If the boot fits!"

"So sorry to disappoint, my dear, but I don't recall ever presuming to be a *gentleman*. Moreover, I refuse to shed my blood over your fatuous notions. If you hadn't broken every rule and thoughtlessly discounted every lesson I tried to teach you…"

She looked guiltily away.

"I warned you about deep play, Sukey, and you heeded *nothing* I said. *Nothing!*" he continued, growing more enraged. "Instead, I find you deeply embroiled with one of the most notorious gamesters and rakes in London."

When the vehicle arrived, mutely Philip handed

her up into it. She moved stiffly aside to make room
for him, but he ignored the gesture and slammed
the door.

"But where are you going? We have yet to
discuss this."

"Tomorrow," he said with a warning look. "We will
not speak any more of it until emotions have quieted."

"I am perfectly composed," she snapped.

"Tomorrow, Sukey." He silenced her with a darkling look and signaled the driver.

❧

Philip watched the coach depart in a clatter across
the cobbles. What the hell had transpired this night?
It was almost a blur. They'd arrived in a companion-
able enough frame of mind, if not precisely in perfect
harmony. They'd mapped out a plan whereby Philip
would set the punters at hazard. Meanwhile, she
would set up the dowagers, frequently the wealthiest
and most careless players, by losing a hand or two at
loo, a game she played passably well, and follow by
winning many more hands.

Philip would later join her at whist, a game in
which they were now nearly as in tune as they had
become in bed. It was a perfect plan, but not half an
hour had passed after their arrival that she'd blown it
all to hell.

He stole a deep breath before taking stock of the
calamity the evening had become.

He had entered the gold room, well-pleased with
his own success, but then he'd sighted her. Admittedly,
he'd botched his handling of the matter, but damn her

tenfold, she'd broken every cardinal rule he lived by. She had played a game she knew nothing about, and one he'd particularly cautioned her against.

She'd wagered more than she could afford to lose and had lost any self-restraint. She then defied him and resisted his attempts to extricate her from the web in which she appeared intent on entrapping herself. The sum she'd lost was more than he could fathom, and impossible for her to pay.

The worst of it was he'd now committed himself to an actual duel over her. *Bloody hell.*

What had he been thinking? Or rather, his lips curled sardonically, *with what* had he been thinking?

George had warned him about her that very first night and ol' Bosky had proven a veritable sage. She'd given him so many reasons. Why in the devil's name had he not just walked away?

It seemed she'd become his addiction, akin to laudanum, which temporarily soothes the wounded, easing away pain until one eventually overindulges—when contrary to medicinal, it becomes a poison.

She was his poison.

Twenty-Eight

THE SWORDMASTER

"YOU CAN'T BE SERIOUS," SAID GEORGE.

"A thousand guineas and a lady's honor is no jesting matter," Philip answered.

"But a challenge? By my troth, I can't fathom why you would have done such a thing. What the devil transpired after I left?"

"It all seems a bad dream and rather a blur now, but that swiving whoreson Weston was hell-bent on getting her alone. When she would have withstood his importuning he publicly defamed her, and rendered me unpardonable insult when I objected. There were a number of witnesses, which means I now have two accounts to settle with the sodding bastard."

"At least you have the advantage as the injured party to choose time, place, and weapon."

"As to that, the meeting is already set. Tothill Fields, the day after the morrow. Half six. Smallswords."

"Smallswords, Drake? He's a known expert. Studied for years abroad under a French master and is more than eager to ply his sword. According to rumor of his prior escapades, you may take that in both senses of the word. The injudicious use of the one necessitating the plying of the other, I suppose." George laughed.

"Nevertheless, I'm prepared to meet him."

"Don't be an ass. This matter is hardly worth risking your life over. God knows why you, of all my acquaintance, have become so embroiled. I say 'tis past time to rid yourself of the baggage."

"It's too late," Philip said.

"Look, ol' chap, I've already been warned to distance myself from you after the incident with Dashwood. And now you've antagonized Weston to the point of an actual meeting? Do you plan to disaffect yourself from the peerage one member at a time? What devil has possessed you?"

"I'm as confounded as you, Bosky, that these ridiculously quixotic tendencies have surfaced, but there you have it. Now, pray act as my second, and we'll make a party of it at Tothill Fields."

"I told you, Drake, I want none of this affair."

"And I am *in want* of a second."

"It shan't be me. I've a political future to think of."

"Your Clerkship of the Meltings?"

"That was *Clerkship of the Irons and Surveyor of the Meltings*, if you please."

"A thousand pardons, your eminence."

"I won't be mocked." George scowled. "These things can turn very nasty, you know. Remember the infamous duel between the fourth Duke of Hamilton and Lord Mohun?"

"Can't say I recall any of the particulars."

"It all began with a dispute over the estate of the Earl of Macclesfield when he passed away without issue. Hamilton and Mohun both laid claim to the estate, and after years of litigation without resolution Mohun called Hamilton out. According to eyewitnesses, Hamilton mortally wounded Mohun but was himself killed by Mohun's second, George MacCartney. Both seconds were subsequently charged with murder, but escaped to the Continent. You see? Two deaths and two murder charges. In all, a very ugly business!"

"Honor, above all, must be satisfied, George. Without it, how can a man look himself in the mirror?"

"Damn it all! If there's no dissuading you, at least go see Figg. Though you're an abominable friend, I'd still hate to see you dead."

"Such mawkish sentiments, Bosky! I'd no idea."

"Hang yourself, Drake."

～

Until his retirement a decade prior, James Figg was the indisputable English champion in all matters martial. Only once defeated in barefisted pugilism, he was also an expert in the cudgel, quarterstaff, and the English smallsword.

A brawny man at nearly fourteen stone, and standing over six feet, he had begun his career challenging prizefighters at local fairs until catching the eye of Lord Peterborough. An avid sportsman and gambler, Peterborough offered Figg his patronship and moved the fighter to London, and in his decade-long career that followed, Figg suffered only one defeat in over two hundred fifty recorded matches. Figg had bowed out gracefully at the peak of this illustrious fighting career to focus on more lucrative and less lethal aspects of his chosen vocation, promotion of sporting events and lessons to the aristocracy in the gentlemanly art of self-defense.

While Philip had already received some instruction in French smallsword, he knew he was little prepared to face any true swordsman experienced in the *duello*. He was also lacking the requisite seconds. Although George still refused to fill the role, he was not in the least opposed to accompanying him to Figg's Amphitheatre, where he assured Philip of finding a more suitable recruit. They arrived to find Captain Godfrey just finishing his own session with the master.

"Misters Selwyn and Drake, isn't it?" Godfrey greeted the younger gents with enthusiasm. "Haven't seen either of you since Whitaker routed the Venetian. A capital match, that. Eh, Figg?"

"Didn't I say we'd teach the Italians humility?" the master interjected. "I hope you gents had the wisdom to place your stakes on my man Whitaker."

"Indeed," George replied. "How could I ever oppose my countryman, particularly a protégé of the great Figg? Turned a nice penny on it too, though nothing like his Lordship of Peterborough. He's said to have won over a thousand on the match."

Figg's answering smile neither confirmed nor denied the rumor. "So, Mr. Selwyn, have you finally decided to take up the sport?"

"Not I, sir!" George exclaimed. "Although I'm quite the aficionado of the art, I'd as lief remain outside the ring. It is actually for my friend here that we are come."

Captain Godfrey remarked, "If you are in want of instruction, you have surely come to the right place. Figg here is a matchless master of the arts martial. I've purchased my own knowledge with many a broken head and bruised body by his hand." The captain laughed.

Figg appraised Philip's trim but athletic form, concluding at last, "You've not the muscle, but I daresay you'd be quick enough on your feet."

"Actually, 'tis your swordsmanship expertise I seek. I have a sudden need to sharpen my skills."

"Backsword or smallsword?" Figg asked.

"Smallsword."

"What do you know of the smallsword?" Figg asked, appraising the silver-hilted weapon at Philip's side with a disparaging grunt.

"I've little formal training," Philip answered, flushing under the master's obvious scrutiny.

"Who is your opponent?" Figg demanded.

"He is reputed a master of both the Italian rapier and French smallsword, but for obvious reasons must remain nameless," Philip replied.

Knowing Philip risked arrest as an antagonist in a duel, Figg nodded understanding at his reticence to say more. "When is this... meeting?" he asked.

"On the morrow."

"On the morrow?" Figg laughed outright. "Mayhap you'd do better to swallow your pride and live to see the next day."

Philip protested, "You don't understand. My reputation and my honor are at stake."

Figg remarked, "And honor has put many men in the grave. Now lad, while willing enough to take your coin, I'd hate to hasten such a young sprig to his maker. What the devil can you possibly hope to achieve in a single day?"

Philip replied, "In truth? I would hope to learn how to best avoid his blade."

Figg nodded with satisfaction. "Spoken rightly enough. If you'd said you sought to best your opponent, I'd have sent your cocky arse packing. But if 'tis truly defense to preserve your person and your precious honor—*that* we might can achieve."

The master turned to the captain. "Godfrey, I would see now if the pup knows the pommel from the point."

"My body and blade are at your service." The captain grinned and the trio followed Figg into his *salle*.

&⁂

Although fencing had been a part of Philip's early education, over the past few years he'd had little use for the gentlemanly art when his typical antagonist more often wielded a knife or cudgel. In those instances, his instincts and reflexes had served him well to disarm or disable as the situation necessitated, but a duel was a matter outside of his experience.

When two men came together in a face-off with blades, the rules of conduct were stringent. Choreographed by masters of the art over the centuries, the gracefully macabre dance *duello* was comprised of prescribed moves and countermoves, each *guarde* met and matched, each parry alternately interspersed with well-rehearsed ripostes, lunges, and thrusts.

Upon entering the *salle*, Philip doffed coat and

cravat, wrapping the latter around his left hand for protection in a parry. He then unsheathed his blade to face his opponent.

Selwyn and Godfrey, acting as seconds, marked the positions of the would-be combatants, leaving a two-foot distance between their respective weapons.

Philip faced the large, shaved-headed, fiery-eyed master with trepidation. In classical textbook fashion, Philip extended his sword hand in *tierce carte*, the point slightly higher than the hilt, directed toward his opponent's face. His left arm arced in a semicircle behind his head to balance and parry.

With a nod from Godfrey, the opponents acknowledged their readiness by raising swords in a silent salute. "*Allez*," the captain spoke the command.

Locking his eyes on his opponent's, Philip was first to engage. Shifting his balance warily onto the ball of his extended right foot, he made a tentative advance to test his steel against Figg's.

Without a blink, the master smoothly circled Philip's blade in a long scrape of metal and in the same motion thrust at the ready target. Instantly perceiving his vulnerability, Philip beat back Figg's blade in a rapid retreat and disengaged.

"Good instincts." Figg grunted approval.

"And fast reflexes," Godfrey added with an encouraging smile.

The contenders resumed their *guarde* and Godfrey signaled again.

This time Figg went on the offense. His blade connected with Philip's in a lightning-fast flash of steel. Philip moved to meet the master, fort to foible, in a parry, but having engaged him on the inside Figg lowered his point over and across, to bind and command Philip's steel, following with a clean thrust to the flank, a mortal strike had it been made in earnest.

The actions were fast, smooth, clean, and elegant, and Philip had not stood a chance. "*Flaconnade*," he explained at Philip's bewildered and mortified expression. With his left hand still on Philip's blade, Figg lowered the point toward the ground. "You stand no chance at all if you meet any skilled opponent in such a textbook fashion."

Philip answered, "While there are any number of moves I might have employed, Mr. Figg, I daresay a head butt, an eye gouge, or kick to the bollocks would hardly be counted gentlemanly."

"The lad's after my own heart." Figg laughed. "'Tis what I loved about my years in the ring: there were no such restrictions. Honor be damned as long as you won. Nevertheless, if you wish to engage with swords you must adopt another technique to better your advantage. Are you familiar with the works of Sir William Hope?"

"Aye, sir. Who has not heard of the Scotsman? My earlier study included *The Fencing Master's Advice to his Scholar*."

"'Tis the French method, taught in every traditional *salle*, but I refer to Hope's lesser known system of defense."

"*The New Method?*" Godfrey suggested.

"Aye," Figg answered. "While not so elegant as our French-inspired ways, it is yon friend's best hope of befuddling a classically trained swordsman." Figg explained to Philip. "In defense, Hope said to leave style and grace for the classroom; instead he devised a technique whose elegance is found only in its security of a man's protection. Hope's *New Method* provides such a system designed for a gentleman with no great expertise."

Figg continued. "There are only a small number of parries and thrusts, easy enough to learn, but they never caught on due to their perceived inelegance. But there's no disputing their practicality. 'Tis precisely the technique you must adopt. Godfrey, would you care to demonstrate the hanging guard *en seconde* to our eager pedagogue?"

Happy to oblige, Godfrey assumed an awkward-looking stance, with his blade directed toward Philip's thigh. The downward position of the blade, Figg explained, allowed optimal protection of the gut, the primary target for penetrating weapons.

"The greatest advantage of this hanging guard is that a man's adversary can only attack two ways, either without and below his sword, or without and above it." Figg elaborated. "A man's protection is in the cross his weapon makes upon his adversary's and the more exact and dexterous he is, the more firm and certain will his defense prove. These guards and parades are few and simple, meant to block any manner of thrust or riposte.

"If your opponent should thrust without and above your sword, you must turn him off by moving your sword arm a little upwards and to your left. This also allows you to gain the foible, the weakest part of his sword, and prevent him forcing home."

By example, Godfrey struck.

Philip deflected the point with a parry left.

"Good lad!" Figg said. "Now you have parried, you may attack from your parade with a riposte as you please."

Over the next few hours, Philip laid aside almost everything he'd ever learned of swordplay. Under Figg's guidance, his body shifted from aft to fore, with his right leg bearing more weight for a solid defense. With single-minded application to Figg's instruction, Philip perfected what was at first an ungainly series of parries and thrusts, but once adapted to it, his superior reflexes prevailed. He gained confidence with each parry and deflection of Captain Godfrey's sword. While he had no false notion of defeating Weston, Philip left Figg's *salle* feeling much less *ill-prepared*.

Now, having rashly put his life in jeopardy, Philip was determined to know why. He vowed to gain answers from Sukey… even if he had to choke them out of her.

Twenty-Nine

A RELUCTANT SAVIOR

PHILIP NEVER GAVE THE ANSWERING SERVANT THE opportunity to turn him away. Instead, he'd barged right past and taken the stairs leading to Sukey's bedchamber by twos.

She was drawn and pale, with dark circles ringing her eyes, evidence of a deeply restless night. "It's time to finish what we began last evening. You will tell me what's between you and Weston," he demanded, willing more control to his tone than he felt.

"You had no right to intervene. It was not your place to do so."

"You would rather I'd done nothing and left you to his devices?"

"Surely he would have been reasonable and given me some time…"

Philip silenced what she knew was a bold-faced lie with a darkling look. "Time for what, Sukey? You're at the end of your rope now, and we both know it. No. Weston would not have given an inch. He's a rake of the first order, a man completely devoid of principle and moved only by what he wants. *That*, it seems, *is you*."

She quivered with affront. "Let me understand you, Philip. Instead of allowing me to at least *try* to talk privately with him, you thought to better my cause by publicly defaming me as *your mistress?*"

"Am I to assume by that you'd rather be claimed as *his?*" Philip demanded.

"Don't put words in my mouth!" Her tone rose in pitch until it threatened to crack.

Philip softened his interrogation. "Don't you comprehend? There was no other way I could assume your debt of honor."

"And a fine mess that puts us both in now! You are no more equipped to pay him than I am!"

"The money is the least of my concerns at the moment."

"How can you say that?"

"I mean to know who and what is he to you, Sukey?" He waited, his uncompromising stare pinning her to the spot. She averted her face without answer.

"He claimed to be your lover last night and you didn't refute him," Philip pressed. "What hold does he have on you? I have a right to know."

"My history is my own, Philip. You do *not* have privilege to it."

"How can you say that?" he asked with a twisted grimace. "Damn it, Sukey, who is he to you!"

He stared her down.

A muscle in his jaw twitched.

Still, Philip waited.

෴

She'd thought it all long buried, that she'd never have

to resurrect the pain, anguish, and shame, but her past had suddenly reclaimed her with a vengeance. She walked to the window, peering outside at the misting rain, but seeing instead the chalk hills and wide verdant valleys of Wiltshire. The thatched parish cottage she'd once called home.

"I thought I loved him. Once," she whispered. "It has been nearly twelve years. The so-called *Honorable* John Messingham was a favorite nephew of Sir Nigel. Although Jack was a third son and bound by his family for the church, he was the one Nigel chose as his heir.

"In learning of his good fortune, Jack had come to the country for an extended stay. As the rural dean of Wiltshire and close friend of Sir Nigel, my father took Jack under his wing, but Jack was never suited to be a man of the cloth." Her laugh was low and ironic.

She briefly looked over her shoulder at Philip. "He was once much like you, you know. He had the heart of an adventurer, not a shepherd. *Unlike you*, Jack succumbed to his family's dictates for his future. They had designs on gaining him a bishopric, though it was the last thing Jack would have chosen for himself.

"Handsome, charming, and witty, he all too easily turned the head of a simple vicar's daughter."

"He seduced you," Philip accused.

"No, Philip. I could never accuse him of that. I was completely willing, eagerly enthusiastic even. What I gave, I gave out of love, however misplaced it turned out to be." She paused, absently pulling loose threads from the fabric of the drapes as she recalled the weeks they stole away in private, to the orchard, the stables, or the lakeside folly, where they tore at one another's clothes and made love in eager abandon.

His whispers of endearment had settled on her innocent ears like morning mist on rose petals. He'd pledged his heart, his soul, his eternal devotion, declaring who better than a vicar's daughter for a clergyman's bride? Naïvely she'd believed him, and hopelessly infatuated she'd given herself.

"It was all just an illusion." Her voice caught. "But I learned too late."

"He got you with child."

She nodded with a choking sound.

He muffled a curse.

"I was a fool."

"You were an innocent. He was bound to you by honor. Why didn't the family intervene?"

"Oh, the family intervened, all right. They believed I had set out to entrap him and sent Jack abroad to keep us apart until his true intended, the daughter of Lady Weston's best friend, came of age to marry."

"What of your father?" He stood behind her shoulder now. His voice had lost its hostile edge.

"Enraged. Ashamed. Devastated. I was his only child. He used to call me his treasure, and then I disgraced him. After that he spoke to me no more." She stifled a sob. "I am dead to him now."

"I don't understand how you came to be Lady Messingham."

"Sir Nigel, informed by his servants, had already come to suspect the trysts. He'd even tried to warn Jack away from me, thinking he could avert disaster, not knowing it was too late.

"With calamity and scandal on his hands, dear sweet Nigel did the only thing he could to mitigate the wrong. He stepped in to marry me himself, but in the end he might have been saved all the trouble. Within weeks of our nuptials, I miscarried and nearly hemorrhaged to death. I was six months recovering, and the physician said I would never conceive again." Her voice had broken. She nervously plucked at the drapes, marshalling the courage to go on.

"Though I could never give him a son of his own, Nigel was a doting husband, but he lived in constant fear that I would cuckold him. His jealousy kept me under his thumb until his recent death."

The assorted pieces of her tale were falling rapidly into place, but some holes remained. "And what of this Jack?" Philip asked, already suspecting the answer.

"Have you not yet made the connection?"

"Jack is now the Marquess of Weston."

Her silence was affirmation. He'd call the filthy sodding whoreson out, if he hadn't already done so.

"You said he was a third son. By what freak did he come into the title?"

"Two years after he went abroad, his eldest brother broke his neck in a hunting accident; four years after that, his surviving brother succumbed to smallpox. Unexpectedly, Jack became the marquess."

"You knew of his return?"

"And of his subsequent marriage. How could I not? He is my nephew, after all." Her laugh was bitter with irony. "But I have not laid eyes on him these ten years."

She brushed the drapes aside and spun to face him, her expression imploring. "I swear to you, Philip, I was not myself when I saw him at the table. I hardly knew who I was, let alone what I was doing, and then he addressed me so cavalierly, after destroying my life! It was all as if I were an actor in some horrible, tragic play."

Her eyes were misted and her lips trembled.

His thumb gently traced her cheek. "One can only imagine, my love. I now more fully understand your antipathy at being presented as my mistress."

She stared at him dumbly at his unexpected display of empathy. Her lips quivered. And then her tears came as a sudden cloudburst, and once begun, the full tempest broke loose.

Philip held her close as her body racked with sobs. He gently stroked her hair until the storm abated from a cascade of tears to intermittent sniffling, using the time to master his own raw emotions and herd his scattered thoughts into cohesion.

"The way I see it, there remain only two solutions."

"Wh-what are those?" she hiccupped.

"I could eliminate your obligation by killing the vile sodomite, or I could legally assume your debts."

"How," she asked warily.

Philip paused as if searching for the right words. He finally said, "As there is nothing else to answer, I'll just have to marry you."

She choked on her disbelief. "What did you say?"

"I'm willing to marry you, Sukey."

"Simply so you can pay my debts?" She looked incredulous.

"It *is* the only solution short of murder, as I see it." He gave a halfhearted chuckle.

"You're serious," she said, searching his face for any emotional clues.

Misreading her expression, Philip said, "I suppose you expect a ring." He removed the gold band from his finger to slide it over hers. "It was my mother's, but I warn you not to expect more jewels from me. While I had already reclaimed your emeralds from pawn thinking to return them to you, now they'll likely be sold with the diamonds to satisfy Weston."

"And what then?" she asked.

He replied, "I should have enough to settle your debts and to provide us a modest living... for a time."

"And after that is gone?"

"I am loathe to think it should come to pass, but if need be, Lord Hastings once offered a comfortable living in exchange for a small accommodation from me."

"You would appeal to your father?"

"If I must," he said, adding peevishly, "But we need not linger on the notion, do we?"

She turned her hand over, sadly gazing upon the exotic symbols etched in the gold. "I can only bring you ruin, you know."

He gave a sardonic laugh. "By all evidence, that's true, but having skirted the edge of ruin most of my life, why should I change tack at this late date? Now, let us make haste to Fleet Street and be done with it."

"No, Philip."

"What do you mean, no?"

"You haven't even asked me."

"Asked you?" He looked blank. "Asked you what?"

"To marry you."

"Good God, Sukey! Do you expect me to kneel at your feet?"

"Not at all, but I would expect the courtesy of actually posing the question!"

He took her hand in both of his and responded in a tight-lipped reply, "If it would please you, my dearest Lady Messingham, will you do me the inestimable honor of becoming my wife?"

"Why, Philip?" she asked, quietly studying him.

He scrubbed his face in exasperation. "I hadn't expected a bloody inquest, Sukey, and thought I'd already explained it rather clearly—I'll take care of your immediate debts and you will learn to live within our somewhat limited means. In return for your devotion, I pledge to provide for you. You'll not be destitute."

"Why are you so concerned with my welfare?"

While her heart had initially raced at the notion of becoming Philip's wife, his cavalier response failed to satisfy her deep-seated fear.

"Mayhap because you have no one else," he said flippantly. "Come. Let us go. Now."

His impatience was coupled with a vague agitation, as if he would lose his nerve if they delayed another moment.

"But do you love me, Philip?" She awaited his response with mounting disquietude as a tense silence stretched between them. The bluntly posed question had clearly taken him off guard.

Philip looked vastly uncomfortable, as if she had forced him to ponder motives he hadn't cared to probe all that closely. "Damn it all, Sukey, what more do you want from me?"

Obviously more than he cared to give.

His response left her barren. Bereft. But it was all the answer she needed.

Thirty

AN UNCONSCIONABLE ULTIMATUM

IT WAS LATE AFTERNOON WHEN NANCY TAPPED
tentatively on her mistress's bedchamber door.

"What is it, Nan?" The lady spoke in a hoarse
whisper, her throat completely raw from a night spent
in anguish, frustration, and rage. "I expressly said that
I wished not to be disturbed."

"But my lady, the footman was quite insistent that
his lordship speak with you."

"Who would speak with me, Nan?" she snapped at
the hapless maid. "I gave strict instructions that I am
not at home… to anyone."

"May I enter, my lady?" Nan asked through the door.

"Well? What is it?" Susannah flung the door open
to the startled maid, who found her normally impec-
cable mistress dressed in her wrapper with her hair a
tangled mess and her lids puffy from spent tears.

Her heart wrung in compassion. "Oh, my lady,
what has brought you to such a pass?"

"I don't wish to discuss it, Nan," she said tersely.
"Now pray tell me what is this urgent business, and
then leave me in peace."

"Yes, ma'am," she complied meekly. "Two liveried footmen come to the door on behalf of a great lord who awaits outside in his carriage."

The image of Jack Messingham came ominously to mind. Could he not at least have given her a day before importuning her for payment? Desperate to stall, she replied, "I am unfit to receive at the moment. Pray convey to the Marquess of Weston that he must conduct himself with greater circumspection and pay his calls at a more appropriate hour."

"Lord Weston?" the maid repeated blankly. "You are mistaken, madam. 'Tis not the name the footman gave." The maid produced a gold-embossed calling card. "'Tis the Earl of Hastings what insistents on speaking with you."

"The Earl of Hastings? What could Lord Hastings want with me?" She immediately wondered if something had happened to Philip.

"I haven't a notion, my lady. The footman, a lovely chap in the finest velvet, was mum about it too, though I did me best to find out." Nan smiled coyly. "For you, ma'am," she amended hastily.

"Of course, Nan," the lady replied with a knowing look. "Then if he won't be turned away, you must help me to dress."

Lady Messingham donned her most demure gray half-mourning gown and strategically confined her tangled locks under a simple lace cap. To disguise her blotched and wretched complexion, she made use of a generous amount of powder, forgoing any rouge.

When she had calmed her nerves enough to

proceed, she descended the steps of her house, followed by her lady's maid.

"If you will but accompany me, my lady." The footman led the way to the unmarked carriage standing a short distance from her house. "His lordship is a man of utmost discretion," the servant explained. "He would not wish to draw undue attention."

"By calling at my door like a gentleman? How curious," the lady said archly, determined not to show her unease. When he opened the door to the carriage, Susannah gestured to her maid to follow, but the footman interposed himself.

"No, my lady. His lordship would speak privily."

She regarded him with a slight frown, but complied when the servant moved to hand her up. When the door closed, she turned to face a pair of ice blue eyes.

❧

"My Lord Hastings, I must say I am surprised by the unconventionality of this meeting."

"Madam." He inclined his head stiffly. "The circumstances required it be so."

"Indeed?"

"You are Sir Nigel Messingham's bride, are you not? I was acquainted with your husband."

"I *was*. My husband is deceased nearly six months."

He ignored the correction. "I think Sir Nigel a vain and addled man to have taken such as you to wife." Her eyes grew wide in affront but he stilled her with a chilling look. "What had you to bring to the marriage?" he asked. "No dowry. No property, and most important, not even the ability to breed an heir."

"I take exception to this conversation, my lord." She moved toward the door, but gasped when he struck out to block her with his silver-handled cane.

"I am not finished," he said.

"Then finish what you have to say and let me go."

"We have some business to settle between us."

"What business? What do you want with me?"

"The nature of this interview is your relationship with my youngest son."

"He is a grown man. What concern is it of yours whether *or not* I am involved with Philip?"

"I am greatly concerned that a woman of loose moral fiber has served only to lead him further astray."

"You have gone beyond the pale. I won't suffer your insults a moment longer."

Still blocked by the cane, she kicked at the door, but Lord Hastings had already thumped on the roof to signal the driver. The vehicle jolted forward at a brisk pace.

"Shall it be a turn in the park, then?"

She gaped at his audacity. "This is no less than abduction!"

"It is indeed." He smiled.

"You will stop this carriage at once!" Her voice was calm and commanding but her heart raced with apprehension.

"I'll do no such thing, and you'll keep your mouth shut until I'm finished with you."

She stared at him aghast.

"Right, then, where were we? Ah yes, your loose morality. It is no secret how you attempted to entrap Sir Nigel's heir, and having failed, persuaded the dotard to sacrifice himself and his entire fortune to you instead. And what now to show for it? The money is gone, the properties mortgaged, and not even an heir of his own to carry his name. All in all, you are a very bad bargain, my Lady Messingham."

"H-how do you know all this? Nigel would never have spoken of it. He was an honorable man who pledged his word, and I dedicated ten years of my life to return his kindness."

"I gave you credit for more intelligence. How sad to be mistaken. Shall I explain, since you haven't the wherewithal to figure it out? Who else was privy to this dirty little secret?"

"Jack," she whispered and began to tremble almost convulsively.

"Ah," Lord Hastings exclaimed. "I see you are not so slow-witted after all."

"Why? Why do you wish to inflict torment upon me? What have I done to deserve your cruelty?"

"Oh my dear, nothing. *Yet.*" He waited patiently while his meaning penetrated.

"What can you possibly fear from me?" she asked, bewildered.

"It is for you to fear, my lady. I simply manage that which would endeavor to overset me."

She regarded him with a horrified stare.

"As I said, Philip appears to have fixed himself on you and I have no intention of allowing your designs to interfere with my plans."

"Designs?"

"Don't play coy, Lady Messingham. I know you for a shameless jade. Do you deny seducing my son so he would pay your gaming debts?"

"It wasn't like that!"

"Why else would he have come begging a loan of one thousand pounds, if not to pay off Weston?"

"I don't believe it! He would never have groveled as you say."

"You see what you have reduced him to already? What kind of woman would wish a man to debase himself by rebelling against his own principles? Sadly, I had to deny the request. So now here you are, once more without the means to pay your debts and without even the funds to support yourself. Even at this moment a summons is being issued by the Westminster Magistrate for your arrest. What do you know of debtors' prison, my lady?"

"My God! You are a minion of the devil!"

"No, my dear, simply an earl." The cruel curve of his lips sent a shudder down her spine. "But one who will see his house in order before he leaves this earth. That includes the younger son as well as the heir."

"But what have I to do with any of this?"

"You are a distraction that must be eliminated to bring Philip to heel. I have use for Philip once his wayward nonsense comes to its inevitable conclusion. He will assume his place with his peers and in good time will be pledged to some virtuous young woman of unexceptional breeding and superior fortune. Be his mistress *then*, if you must, but be damned if you think to infiltrate this family."

"Why do you believe I wish to marry Philip?"

"You deny it?"

"Of course I deny it!" Her hands plucked nervously at her skirts. She looked down, willing them to be still, realizing in the same moment that it came to the earl's notice—she still wore Philip's ring.

"Then where did you get that? You lying baggage!" Without warning, the back of his hand struck her cleanly across the face. "You wear his filthy symbol of taint! The deed is already done, is it? Well, what is done can be just as easily *undone*. At least we know no bastard offspring can result from this inglorious union."

"You are mistaken," she cried out. "Philip gave me the ring only as a pledge. There is no marriage. Nor will there be."

"So you say? Then he does have such intentions, regardless of your prior protest. You, however, will refuse him."

"Why should I refuse?" she taunted, if only to serve him back his own sauce.

"Why? I'll give you a thousand reasons as inducement, but if you cross me you may not live to regret it." His meaning was clear and the menace in Lord Hastings's eyes made her tremble in earnest.

She had already refused Philip, knowing he wasn't ready for such a step and that only crisis had prompted the proposal. Although he'd made an honorable offer, he did not reciprocate her feelings. Thus, she'd declined. Her heart couldn't bear to do otherwise.

Now, out of the blue, Lord Hastings threatened her. He'd described the desperation of her circumstances without exaggeration, but then unexpectedly offered her a way out—if she only played her cards right this one and final time. It was a gamble she determined to take.

She swallowed hard, marshaling her will to meet

the earl's eye, answering in a voice that was dispassionate and controlled. "One thousand pounds is scarcely sufficient to meet my needs. Make it five thousand, my lord."

"Rapacious whore!" he thundered. "Two thousand."

She stood her ground stolidly under his piercing stare and countered. "Three."

"Three it is! And be damned to hell!"

Thirty-One

THE DUELISTS

SITTING IN HIS DARKENED ROOM, PHILIP TOOK ANOTHER swig from the flask. Except for his missing coat and cravat, he was still fully clothed, having never gone to his bed. He hadn't wished to sleep, being preoccupied with the morbid thought that shortly after sunrise he might find eternal rest skewered on Weston's deadly blade. It wasn't that Philip was fearful of death, but rather regretful of the life he would have wasted. He'd lived for years eagerly anticipating his trust and mapping out a plan for his future, but overnight *she'd* dashed it all to pieces. He had pledged himself to pay debts he did not owe and defend honor other than his own. He'd spent the bulk of his modest fortune to save her and would now risk his very life for her. If she wanted his blood, it appeared she would soon have that too.

He'd never regarded himself as a man to suffer either melancholy or buffoons, but he now felt a great mixture of both. How had he come to such a pass? And all for what? It was unfathomable what an ass she'd made of him, but the worst of it was when the jade had refused him! Philip swallowed more of the cheap gin, enjoying the caustic burn as it flowed down his throat.

He had only thought to protect her when he made the offer of marriage and expected a modicum of gratitude for his sacrifice, but she'd thrown his proposal in his face, bloody well spurning him. Hell, he should have been relieved, but instead he'd felt rejected, mortified, and infuriated. Was he now becoming deranged? Perhaps he was a madman, after all.

He glanced to the window, now espying the pink and gold fingers slicing through the blackness, hailing the nascent dawn.

Taking another great swig, he tossed away the flask with a curse, strapped on his sword, donned his coat, and stuffed the crumpled cravat into his pocket. Tucking his tricorne resolutely under his arm, he departed his quarters.

Having imbibed a bit more than was wise, and wishing to clear his head, Philip set out by foot for the Cock and Tabard on the north side of Tothill Street. The timeworn single cock on the placard of the tavern had just come into sight when a voice hailed him.

"Ah, Drake!"

"Captain Godfrey? What are you doing here?" Philip asked in surprise.

"I understood you lacked for a second." Godfrey frowned at Philip's dishevelment. "Though I am glad to see you arrived, you are looking the worse for wear."

"Though my appearance may be wanting, I assure you my nerves are more than steady."

"Bolstered, no doubt, by drink?" the captain chided.

Philip scowled.

"Don't take umbrage, lad! Many a trooper in Marlborough's army relied on a good shot of Dutch courage. Let us just pray your wits and reflexes don't suffer the effects. And if you've any inclination to cast up your accounts, I advise you to avail yourself of the alley *before* Weston's arrival."

"I am far from soused, Godfrey."

"Glad to hear it, lad, but for God's sake, put yourself in order."

Churlishly, Philip buttoned his waistcoat and straightened his hat.

Godfrey plucked the cravat from Philip's pocket and handed it to him. "I also took the liberty of inviting an acquaintance who, though I hope to the contrary, might be called upon to render you some small service. May I make known to you John Pringle."

A black-clothed gentleman in a bagwig stepped forward with a bow.

"Mr. Pringle?" Philip inclined his head. "Might I ask precisely *what manner* of service my friend the captain believes I may need?"

"It is Dr. Pringle," the gentleman corrected. "I am a physician and Professor of Moral Philosophy at Edinburgh University."

"Then how do you come to be here?" Philip asked, looking to the Captain.

Godfrey explained with a grin. "Our dear Doctor Pringle lost a goodly sum to me at piquet last eve."

"Otherwise, I assure you, I should be resting in my bed at this ungodly hour," the doctor added.

"Then I am indebted to you both," Philip said.

"I also have in my possession a smallsword of the finest German tempered steel, sent with the master's compliments. A finer weapon cannot be had." Godfrey handed the sheathed sword to Philip.

"I am honored," Philip said, drawing it reverently from its scabbard and balancing it in his hand.

"It's a shame you didn't have more time to prepare," Godfrey said. "Figg remarked you show great promise and is regretful you had so little time under his tutelage."

"He still believes me ill-prepared?" Philip asked.

"Let us say you lack the experience of your ill-famed opponent."

"What do you know of Weston, Godfrey?"

"He is accounted a man of considerable, if dubious, accomplishments. He's fought and won a number of duels. He is cold-blooded, Drake, and be warned he is not likely to be satisfied with a mere pinking."

"Hence, Pringle." Drake tossed his head toward the doctor with a contemplative half smile.

Godfrey replied with a wordless shrug.

"Then I'll take the greatest care," Philip said.

Noting the arrival of two emblazoned sedan chairs borne by liveried footmen, Godfrey said, "It appears the hour is nigh."

The Marquess of Weston issued forth from the first chair, joined anon by his second, John Spencer, grandson of the Duchess of Marlborough and a gentleman of equally dissolute repute. The morbid party of five paid their respective addresses in a most solemn and perversely civilized manner and set out across Tothill Street.

❧

Tothill Fields was once part of a large marshy tract lying between Millbank and Westminster Abbey, spreading out to the Chelsea Road, beyond which lay the Five Fields extending to Knightsbridge.

With its swatches of open spaces, cloistered here and again by mazes of trees, it had made its name as a celebrated dueling-ground from the time that a Mr. Richard Thornhill fought and killed the Kentish gentleman, Sir Cholmley Dering. The infamous duel was reportedly fought with pistols so near that the muzzles touched, and the subsequent notoriety made the setting near-ideal for such appointments of honor.

Adding to its cachet was its history of being the place where the judges once sat to observe trials by combat, a bygone form of justice in which two disputants battled it out, with the loser judged as the guilty party. Aptly, it was now the site of the Westminster Bridewell prison.

For some minutes, the seconds scouted and paced the grounds, their disembodied voices penetrating through the fog-enshrouded fields, before settling on a partially obscured plot deemed suitable for the impending encounter.

Returning to the combatants, the seconds inspected and measured both blades while the antagonists dispensed with coats and waistcoats and, according to code, opened their shirts to lay bare their breasts. Satisfied that neither wore defense, Philip and Lord Weston received their weapons from their respective seconds.

As Philip rolled up his right shirtsleeve, Godfrey

said in an undertone, "The blades are of a size, but the marquess has some inches on you which will give him an advantage of reach. If you wish to thrust, I advise you come to half sword and meet him as he advances."

Philip nodded understanding as Godfrey handed him his sword and fell back with Spencer and Pringle to a comfortable distance.

Weapon in hand, Philip faced Lord Weston, who remarked conversationally, "I wonder at your eagerness to shed your blood over such a piece. Though I savored plucking her cherry so many years ago, after last evening I find her repertoire a bit bland for my taste."

Philip's eyes blazed with loathing.

Weston's lips curled into a provocative smile as he added thoughtfully, "Though I've procured a magnificent French whore who might teach her some new tricks…"

"What are you saying, you filthy whoreson?"

"Tsk. Tsk. Such language ill-becomes a gentleman. Have you a death wish, Drake?"

"My apologies for my lapse, my lord. I had intended to say filthy *sodding* whoreson."

"Wish granted," the marquess replied fatally, and at a signal from the seconds, the antagonists saluted and faced off. While Weston assumed the guard in *tierce-carte*, blade pointed at Philip's face, Philip took up Hope's hanging guard *en seconde*.

Weston regarded Philip's hulking forward stance and gave out a derisive laugh. "What is this maladroit?" His tone and expression were contemptuously bemused. "You challenge me to swords and don't even know how to hold the blasted thing? Have you no study of the weapon you wield? I thought to have at least a moment of fun before killing you."

"I believe my skills sufficient to the task at hand," Philip replied. "Shall we?" he prompted.

"All too soon proven to the contrary." Weston snorted his disdain and once more took up his position.

Remembering Figg had counseled attention to the blade, Philip warily tested his weight on the ball of his right foot, directing his full concentration on the deadly tip of Weston's sword.

The dance began with Weston at first toying with him in a cat and mouse fashion. But lithe as a cat himself, Philip evaded, springing, blocking, and countering his adversary's every move while the seconds watched in fascination.

Although the marquess's superior skill was evident in the elegance and finesse of his every action, he was counterbalanced by Philip's superior reflexes that thwarted each attempt the marquess made to get under, around, or otherwise through Philip's guard.

The marquess pressed on, repeatedly testing and taunting Philip, who resolved to retain his defensive posture. Philip met and crossed blades with each advance, successfully parrying with little expended effort.

Growing impatient, Weston advanced in a flash of metal, once more meeting Philip's vertical parry. Several more rapid passes ensued, each foiled by the grating sound of Philip's connecting steel.

The combatants waged on, performing the elegant figures of the deadly dance. Advance. Lunge. Thrust. Parry. Retreat. The marquess circled as a wolf evaluating its prey, seeking any opening, any exposure or vulnerability to exploit and impale his blade into his foe's flesh.

For Philip, whose every muscle was tensed in expectancy, the minutes dragged as hours. His sword arm grew heavier with every move, his calves threatened to cramp, and the sweat dampened his brow and stung his eyes... until the fatal moment he blinked.

In that crucial millisecond when perspiration blurred his vision, the marquess struck. With a beat and feint to Philip's left, he cut around and beneath Philip's blade in a circular counter-parry, and with lightning speed and the greatest dexterity, followed through with a thrust to Philip's vulnerable outside.

Aware of his blunder, Philip spun left to deflect the thrust, but reacting too late, the point penetrated his right side below the elbow. As the blade speared his lower rib cage, Philip imagined that he heard the crunch of bone before actually feeling the explosion of agony.

Weston's malevolent smirk invaded his pain-clouded vision, as he made to follow through with full penetration of the thrust. With his clear intent to bury his blade to the hilt in Philip's body, Philip moved to preserve himself with the desperation that precedes impending death.

Grasping the blade with his left hand, he wrenched his body to the right just as Weston moved to complete the thrust. With a great anguished groan he succeeded to dis-impale himself, but the excruciating effort brought him, depleted and copiously hemorrhaging, to his knees.

Panting from his own exertions, Weston loomed over Philip with a leer. "While your mistress has already endeavored to oblige me, I have yet to exact redress for your insolence."

"Burn in hell, you lying, poxy bastard," Philip grunted, spasms racking his body with every breath. He attempted to raise himself, but only managed semi-upright by leaning heavily on his sword.

When Weston failed to back down, Captain Godfrey stepped forward in protest. "You go too far, my lord. Honor is satisfied when a man is incapacitated." He looked to Philip's blood-soaked shirt and ashen countenance. "Nothing further need be demanded of the lad; I would call this affair quite finished."

"It is finished when I say it is, Godfrey. Any further objections may be voiced with your own blade!"

Godfrey signaled Pringle and Spencer to intervene and Weston turned malevolently back to Philip. Pointing his crimson-coated blade to his sternum, Weston looked down at Philip's kneeling figure with a prurient smirk. "Of course, if apology is not to your inclination, you are in the perfect posture to offer me satisfaction of quite another kind... I find the *duello* brings on a tremendous cockstand."

In a burst borne of unadulterated rage, Philip struck out with his left hand in a parry, while blindly thrusting with his sword. Having caught his foe off guard, Philip felt the pleasure of his point penetrating flesh, just before falling insensible to the ground.

❧

Philip awoke to a low murmur of voices. Disoriented,

he blinked several times to clear his vision. He was damnably cold, lying on sweat-soaked sheets, and his teeth chattered uncontrollably, though a fire blazed in the small, unfamiliar room.

"Back to the living, are you now, Drake?" asked an annoyingly familiar voice.

"Bosky." Philip turned his head. "Where am I? And what are you doing here? I thought you'd forsworn all the merrymaking."

"One question at a time, eh? You're at the Cock and Tabard, where Godfrey and I have taken turns as nursemaid while you've lazed abed for nigh on three days, you no-account laggard."

"Is Godfrey here then? I've yet to thank him."

"No thanks needed," the captain said. "I am honored to have been of service."

"How bad is it?" Philip asked with a groan. "I feel as if I were pierced straight through."

"Nearly," Godfrey answered. "Pringle pronounced it miraculous that your vitals were unpenetrated. He most feared intestinal injury, but with your fever breaking, one would assume you're out of any imminent danger."

"So I live to fight another day, eh?" Philip's wan grin took more effort than he would care to admit.

George answered soberly, "You're damned lucky to be alive, you know."

"So you say. I don't feel so damnably lucky at the moment. Too bad you missed all the revelry, George."

"Indeed. I'm devilish sorry to have missed it, given how it ended."

"You would be," Philip said with a weak laugh. "As such a votary of blood sport, I think the affair should have satisfied your sanguinary cravings for some time. The sod was intent on killing me, you know. The last I recall, the buggering bastard's blade was poised at my breast." Philip paused with a puzzled frown. "Oddly, all that follows is a blank."

"You don't know, then?"

"Know what?"

"About Weston."

"What of that sodding shitpot?" Philip snapped.

"He may have drawn first blood, but you, my friend, will go down in infamy."

Philip frowned. "What in blazes are you saying?"

"That you've nigh unmanned him; that he might well be a eunuch."

"What!" Philip choked.

"According to Pringle, who witnessed the whole drama, when you made that blind thrust you skewered the man's scrotum."

Philip laughed. "Surely you jest!"

"By my troth, I do not! A man's jewels are no joking matter, Drake. It's said the left testicle's a complete loss and the right is questionable."

Philip grinned. "Poetic justice, is it not?" He tried to sit up, but fell back in exhaustion.

"You might try to conserve what little strength you have, ol' man. Nor would I be making any travel plans for a while. You bled like a stuck pig even before the surgeon took his measure, and you've not eaten in over three days."

"What of *her*, Bosky?" Philip couldn't help asking.

"Good God, Drake! Why do you care? She got you into this bloody mess. You should be glad she's gone."

"Gone? What do you mean, gone?"

"The wicked jade's up and disappeared from London, though they say her creditors are satisfied."

"Are they indeed?" The news came as a knife to his gut. So Weston hadn't lied after all. Philip wondered what her favors to Weston would cost her in the end. "Then I wish the accursed baggage joy of her marquess."

"That reminds me. She sent this for you, though I've no idea why. A curious item, to be sure." George retrieved Philip's ring from his pocket.

Philip turned it over in stony silence before finally placing it back on the little finger of his right hand. And, having offered her all he had to give, Philip avowed from that day forward to think of her no more.

Thirty-Two

FORTUNE'S SOLDIER

PHILIP WOULD HAVE DONE ALL IN HIS POWER TO KEEP any word of the duel with the Marquess of Weston from reaching his father's ears, but the notoriety of the outcome guaranteed front-page coverage in London's cheap broadsheets.

Lord Hastings's cronies were more than eager to share the *Tatler* report that the M_ of W_ was unmanned, in the most literal sense, by the youngest son of the E_ of H_, purportedly in a duel of honor for the favor of a certain Lady M_.

Philip had barely risen from his sickbed when the ominous thump of Lord Hastings's cane against the door heralded his arrival.

"It wasn't enough to embroil yourself with that disreputable baggage," the earl began without ado, "but now you besmirch your family name in the scandal sheets? Weston, of all people! Have you no idea of his connections?"

"I daresay I didn't think to take his politics into account when he defamed a lady and rendered me an unpardonable insult," Philip said.

"By your thoughtless actions you would destroy all I endeavor to build by antagonizing and alienating half the peerage."

"Have I indeed, my lord? Do you think they'll revoke my membership to White's Chocolate House?"

"Have you no care for the honor of your family?" Lord Hastings demanded.

Philip considered the question and answered with an ironic twist to the words. "Has my family any honor to care for?"

The earl's eyes were blazing even before he looked down and noticed the ring. "You thankless whelp! While I've kept your ignominious secret for twenty-one years, you would defy me to flaunt that... that... symbol of taint?"

Philip raised his right hand as if to admire its adornment. "I am told it was my mother's, and her family heirloom. I wear it without shame."

"You should hang your head in shame! Your misbegotten birth has brought nothing but disgrace to a long and pure English line."

Philip laughed outright. "Knowing my ancestry, I would call *that* statement highly debatable."

The cavalier remark pushed the incensed earl over the edge. He raised his silver-handled cane and would have struck if not for the entrance of Captain Godfrey.

"How now, my lord?" Godfrey seized the cane with a manner that was civil but with a grip made of iron. "Assuredly the lad should have time to recover from his wounds before inflicting new ones."

"Unhand it at once!" Lord Hastings snarled.

Philip braced himself on the chair arm during this

brief altercation and rose gingerly to his feet. Ashen-faced with the exertion, he nevertheless laid a staying hand on his friend's shoulder. "I appreciate your concern, Godfrey, but as you can see I'm quite able to handle my own affairs."

Looking dubious, Godfrey released the cane and with a wince of pain, Philip squared his shoulders to face his father. "You were saying, *my lord*?"

"I had come here thinking to give you one last opportunity, but you have proven a shameless recalcitrant. You are useless to me and from this moment, dead. Cut off forever."

The earl grazed them both with the full hauteur of his aristocratic stare, before he and his trailing footmen departed.

"While I would be the last man to condone such a browbeating, are you sure it was wise to incite him so?" Godfrey asked. "By all indications, you've just been disinherited."

"What have I lost? I haven't drawn a groat from his sacred coffers since I left school and have managed to keep body and soul intact thus far. Edmund's the heir, not I. It is he who must make his obeisance at his lordship's every whim. I decided long ago I shan't be led by a ring through the nose—even by a golden one."

"Ah, now it all becomes clear, the basis of his lordship's wrath. But you—a placeman politician?" Godfrey chuckled. "No, indeed. The pragmatist is the mold for the politician. You, my lad, are cut from entirely different cloth."

"So you say? What cloth might that be, Godfrey?"

"You, dear boy, are an incorrigible idealist."

"You mock me!" Philip accused.

"By no means! You are undoubtedly an idealist, though I had thought the species near extinct." Godfrey chuckled anew. "You are due many disappointments. I fear you will soon learn that principles do little to line a man's pocket."

"'Tis precisely why I have no desire for politics."

"I agree. That would never do for you. Idealists, Drake, are men of action made to inspire those around them to attempt impossible things, like leading men to their deaths in a hailstorm of musketfire or advancing into a field of exploding cannons. You, lad, were born to be a soldier."

For a beat, Philip gaped. "Why would you think such a thing?"

"I only state the obvious. You come from a titled family. You are young, fit, and intelligent. You do not want for spirit, but are still able to keep a cool head under duress. Lastly, you've shown superlative talent given your limited instruction in swordplay. I might ask if you ride?"

"I've held my own on the Rowley Mile."

"All the requisites of a fine junior officer. Action on the Continent is an inevitability. We're already waging a naval war with Spain and France is rattling her own sabre. Should King Louis honor the *Pacte de Famille* and join forces with his Bourbon uncle, you can be certain our martial monarch will be raising British troops to join his Hanoverian mercenaries."

"You are suggesting I buy a commission?"

"A lieutenancy in the First Foot or a cornetcy in the King's Horse may be had for under a thousand pounds. Though the pay is contemptible and the conditions in the field execrable, an officer's life does have its perquisites." The captain grinned.

"Am I to take your own life of sporting events and gaming tables as a model?"

"You forget the women, Drake. I have found a well-turned-out uniform is a powerful aphrodisiac."

❦

With the formal declaration of war, an invasion of British shores by a combined French and Spanish force became a real and tangible threat.

Having long reflected on Godfrey's words, Philip was among the first to purchase a commission, paid with a portion of his maternal inheritance. As Godfrey had predicted, his natural abilities and cool head proved him an excellent officer, yet a dearth of funds impeded his advancement from the lowly office of cornet.

Disillusioned after months of tedious and fruitless patrols of the southern coast (the French having opted to maintain neutrality) Cornet Drake and company arrived back in London for their first furlough. While the less-discerning sought out the seedier brothels on Covent Garden Square, Philip met his former mentor at the Rose Tavern, where applying himself to hazard, the jealous Lady Fortune generously bestowed her favors. By the end of a full evening Philip had gained not only a considerable sum in gold but a captaincy to boot.

"I would not wish to be a fly on the wall when the *former* Captain Simpson gives his account to his father, the duke!" Godfrey remarked.

Philip chuckled. "Nor would I, but one should never wager what one is ill-prepared to lose, eh? The night is yet young, Godfrey, and I am flush in the pocket. What would you suggest?"

"If you truly care to revel in your good fortune and are not averse to parting with all the gold in your pockets, I have just the place," Godfrey said.

"Indeed?" Philip was intrigued. "Where might that be?"

"The King's Head, a true sensual mecca, and regardless of price a place every man must visit at least once."

❧

Upon entering the gold-painted doors opening into a large marbled foyer, Philip was awestruck by the sheer voluptuous opulence. The soaring, fresco-ceilinged entry, leading into an immense gilt-furnished drawing room, was lit by exquisite Venetian chandeliers illuminating the gilt-framed old masters hung on silk-paper walls.

The footmen in crimson and gold velvet livery offered flutes of champagne before escorting them to a large, lavishly appointed chamber comfortably arranged to accommodate the two dozen or so gentlemen who either lounged or assembled around the green baize tables. Glancing about, Philip recognized the faces of several high ranking officers playing at cards with their fellow peers of the realm.

Godfrey, however, lost no time in surveying the room for their hostess. "Ah! She now arrives." Godfrey inclined his head toward the woman poet John Gaye had once described as "the incomparable courtesan."

Now, as procuress rather than a courtesan, Jane Douglas promised, for an exorbitant price, the highest quality merchandise. Her handpicked girls were equally as celebrated for their beauty, elegance, and genteel manners as for their sexual expertise.

The voluptuous painted hostess addressed her guests with a low curtsy meant to display the full measure of her legendary charms. Having made her dramatic entrance into the receiving chamber, she rose with a welcoming smile that encompassed the room.

"My lords and gentlemen, pray enjoy a glass of port whilst you consider a selection of delectables assured to satisfy the most discriminating palate."

This speech was received with hearty toasts and salacious salutes as the bevy of beauties followed, all gowned and bejeweled in scandalous French fashion.

The soiled doves ranged in age from a questionable eighteen to five and thirty, and in type varied from the mahogany skin and sultry eyes of a Negress to the flaxen hair and China-doll complexion of a would-be school miss.

Beaming with the knowledge that she'd provided a girl for every taste, Mother Douglas worked the room. She smiled, flirted, and cooed, while with deference to rank she paired each gentleman with the girl of his fancy and then dispatched each couple to their respective venues of pleasure.

Philip and Captain Godfrey had been among the last to leave the receiving chamber. Godfrey had slung his arm about the waist of a plump, titian-haired siren with a wink, and Philip had selected an opera dancer named Lisette.

When they reached their assigned chamber, Lisette paused outside the door. "It is locked, *monsieur*." She licked her index finger and ran it leisurely down her neck and between the cleft in her breasts. "You must retrieve the key."

Determined to enter into the spirit of the game, Philip made to follow the trail of her hand with his mouth, but rather than breathing in the subtle essences of bergamot and woman, his senses were overpowered with stale sex and cheap perfume.

"You must go much deeper than that." Lisette giggled, a shrill titter he found grating.

The green-eyed, chestnut-haired temptress had at first reminded him of another emerald-eyed beauty, but upon closer inspection he found her appeal purely a creation of artifice. He closed his eyes to overcome these thoughts, but only evoked images of *her*.

Damn it all! He had needs! Why couldn't he just put Sukey out of his mind? He clawed a hand through his hair in frustration. Drink had already failed to evict her memory, and it seemed even the best whore could do no better.

Philip hesitated for a beat, wondering if *two* skilled courtesans might have the power to finally banish the memory of Sukey's touch, but was mortified to discover he had no real enthusiasm to find out.

He offered Suzette his coin purse with a brief smile tinged with regret. "You are too generous, mademoiselle, but another time perhaps?"

Philip departed The King's Head with the secret fear that even a hundred women would never be enough to banish his craving for a particular one.

Thirty-Three

REFLECTION AND REGRET

WHEN SHE REFUSED PHILIP'S OFFER OF MARRIAGE AND accepted the bribe from the earl, Lady Susannah Messingham had fled London in fear and desperation. Although wanting to send a word of explanation to Philip, she knew she couldn't. He would never understand nor forgive her for what he would surely consider a betrayal of the highest order.

Except for the unintentional pain she had inflicted upon him, she really couldn't regret her actions. Having lived so long without love, without passion, even in retrospect she would not have done differently. She had loved Philip, truly loved for the first time, but believing herself more emotionally invested in their relationship than he, she had opted for a clean break. When opportunity presented, she had left, regardless of the personal cost, consoling herself frequently with the reminder that a relationship begun in deceit was doomed to failure.

Avowing to start fresh and leave her old life behind, she departed London leaving no forwarding address. After clearing all of her debts with Lord

Hastings's bank draught, she had wisely invested the remainder, knowing the supplement to her jointure would be enough to sustain her in modest comfort. With every intention of quietly living out her days, she retired to the anonymity of a simple thatched cottage in rural Cambridgeshire with only her few servants as company.

For the first few months, she spent the bulk of her time in self-imposed isolation. Her routine consisted of intermittent bouts of melancholia, characterized by lonely walks on the chalk downs, and other periods dedicated to intellectual improvement, with long hours immersed in the works of Dean Swift, Alexander Pope, and Daniel Defoe, thinking wryly she had much in common with Defoe's Crusoe.

She might have joined a cloister for the lonely life she'd chosen, but her extended periods of introspection and reflection on her many mistakes in life taught her wisdom, and over time afforded her a sense of peace and contentment previously unknown.

As to Philip, although she thought of him more often, and more wistfully, than she wished, it was three years before she learned of his fate. He, like she, had renounced a life of gaming, vice, false friends, and decadent indulgence; she, by retiring to the country, and he, by joining the King's Horse. She pictured him cutting a dashing figure in full dress uniform astride a magnificent charger.

She wondered if he had found fulfillment, wondered with a stab of jealousy if he had found another. She thought of him often with such wistfulness, but the deep-rooted ache dulled with time.

It was only in returning to London years later that she learned the full scope of the salacious old scandal and her own notoriety as the object of the duel which purportedly unmanned the Marquess of Weston.

She was at first shocked, but then with the full knowledge of events came the reopening of old wounds and the full pangs of remorse. Only now did she understand that Philip's pride had kept him from declaring his feelings, but his actions had spoken louder than any words.

The loss of him was her own doing, she realized with stark and bitter dismay. She had loved him and lost him because fear of rejection and heartbreak had held her back. If only she had known, she would have done differently.

Now, unable to make amends, guilt gnawed at her conscience and ate pieces from her heart. Cursing herself for a fool, she grieved his loss more deeply than she ever could have imagined.

PART III

"If there is one gambler who lives by his play,
There are thousands who, famished,
see hope fade away."

—Jean Eugène Robert-Houdin, *Card
Sharpers: Their Tricks Exposed*

Thirty-Four

An Act of Retribution

Newmarket, April 1751

Arriving at the starting post, Shakespeare danced in edgy irritation. His rider struggled to hold him back, but the stallion snorted his impatience, touting his eagerness to put down the pretentious usurper.

Shakespeare's owner, Philip, Earl of Hastings, cast an appreciative gaze over his sleek and elegant chestnut that embodied the quintessential English thoroughbred. This race would be nothing short of a mockery. However, given his financial straits, how could he have passed up such a wager?

Most of his acquaintance, the most avid turf men in the kingdom, would have accepted the challenge purely for the sport, but his reasons were far more pecuniary. Twenty thousand pounds could change everything. He might at last reclaim his estate from the moneylenders, as well as salvaging his self-respect.

In his efforts to redeem his place in aristocratic society and relieve his ancestral home from decades of neglect, Philip Drake had dug himself into a financial pit from which, he had begun to fear, there was no escape. That was, until the rash colonial Daniel Roberts had proposed this outrageous racing wager.

His contender, from the colony of Virginia, stood barely fourteen-and-a-half hands. With hindquarters half-again as densely muscled as the lean chestnut, he more closely resembled a cart pony than a reputed racing champion.

Yes. This victory would allow him to repay the thousands in loans he had needed to repair the roofs of his tenants and fertilize thousands of acres of fallow fields. His estate was worthless until it could once more provide grazing lands for cattle and grow something besides the turnips upon which his near-starving tenant-farmers subsisted. The starter's signal abruptly ended Lord Hastings's introspection.

Upon the signal, the two horses exploded from the post like water from a bursting dam. Shakespeare surged forth, his long legs slicing the air, but the English champion hadn't a prayer against the explosive breaking force of his adversary, who had launched as though from a catapult in a blur of kinetic power. Setting a lightning stride in his own frenetic style, the roan, aptly named Retribution, dropped his nose, dug in, and tore up the track. By the first furlong, he had already gained three lengths.

The Earl of Hastings rose from his seat in unbridled horror. "His jockey's a fool! The horse cannot possibly sustain that pace. He'll be used up by the first mile." He spoke as if to convince himself, his heart already pounding so hard in his throat it threatened to choke him.

Shakespeare feverishly scrambled, his rider flattened to the withers, urgently cajoling, wildly spurring, and flailing the whip as stride by stride Retribution ate up yards of turf.

Lord Hastings's jockey pushed, drove, and pleaded. The game chestnut gave his all in response, but in the end it just wasn't... enough.

The Earl of Hastings stood frozen on the dais and vainly blinked, as if to dispel the vision before his disbelieving eyes. It was impossible. Shakespeare had lost the bloody race! The champion of the Hastings's racing stud was completely annihilated on his own turf by an unknown, half-breed pony from Virginia.

In his supreme confidence, or better-said extreme arrogance, Philip had broken every rule that he'd lived by in all his years of gaming. He had recklessly wagered twenty thousand pounds without even the first thought of defeat.

Now, in a single day Philip, the fourth Earl of Hastings, had accomplished what no prior supercilious and self-indulgent ancestor had ever achieved in a lifetime: the total and complete ruination of an earldom.

The surrounding voices roared in his ears, yet he was deaf to the words. He nodded dumbly to those around him. Smile, Philip. They are all watching you. The result was more a grimace. Outwardly, he struggled to concede defeat with grace, but inside he reeled.

Regaining a modicum of control over his impaired faculties, Philip employed all of his strength to compel his body away from the throng. He wove mechanically through the crowd until, reaching the relative

privacy of his own stable block, he entered the first
empty stall, clutched the wall, and heaved.

~

After his agonizing defeat, Lord Hastings had spent the
evening and well into the morning hours wallowing
in self-disgust and drinking himself senseless. At age
two-and-thirty, he had already put behind him a ten-
year military career, brilliantly begun but ingloriously
ended. His estates were heavily leveraged, his prospects
of recovery dismal. In sum, he had not a bloody thing
to show for his life but the racing stables—Charlotte's
racing stables.

He had long ago begun drinking to excess, simply
to obliterate the reality that he was half a man living
half a life. He had a title without the fortune, a wife
that was no lover, and a lover, the only light in his
darkened existence, who could never be his wife; thus,
he drank.

He had been an arrogant sot when he'd accepted
the racing challenge from a man and horse he'd
known nothing about, but drink and despair had made
him reckless and rash. Sunk in self-denigration, the
cycle began anew.

The truth rankled beyond endurance. Outside
of his military career, now forever marred by the
infamy of Culloden, he had achieved little. When he
had sold his commission to take up the mantle of an
earldom, he had forsworn the cards and dice that had
sustained him during his troubled youth and early
military career.

Over the ensuing half dozen years, he had busted

his arse to right his estate and gain the respect of his peers, but to his lasting chagrin the racing stables were Lord Hastings's only profitable venture. The truth of the matter was almost too painful to admit. Lady Hastings was the reason for its success; and her achievements, not his, had paid the interest on the loans that kept them afloat—a fact that damnably stung his pride. Now he'd gambled all, and he'd lost.

Beyond his wife's hysterical tirade and a smashed bottle of his finest brandy, he had little recollection. At least the harridan had then left him in peace. Regardless of her entreaties, he had no choice but to sell what he could. If she weren't so bloody high-minded and obstinate, he would long have been cock of the dung heap, sitting on a fortune of fifty thousand with no reason to take such a gamble.

If only he could access the bloody trust! The untouchable fortune was his only means of meeting his obligations, and though the money was rightfully his, his father's will barred him from drawing a single groat until he produced an heir. This now brought the matter of the wager and the stud full circle.

If the stud were now lost, it was her own bloody doing, he reflected in mounting resentment. He would liquidate it all without compunction to save his name and his estate, but even complete dispersal would not be enough! Not only was he indebted to Roberts for the sum of twenty thousand, once word of his racing debacle reached his other creditors' ears they would descend upon him like a pack of ravaging hyenas.

He was once more gripped by the full repercussions of his recklessness. In a sodden stupor, he had accepted

the wager that had broken every cardinal rule he'd
endeavored to live by. Now, in one fell swoop, his
entire future was gone, every blessed farthing, and all
he had hoped for.

Though reaching for oblivion, he had only achieved
piss-faced when Lady Hastings had arrived after the
race. The inevitable row had ensued, and then the
world had retracted into blessed blackness.

Midafternoon saw a summons to Palace House, a
speedy reply to Lord Hastings's earlier missive to the
Duke of Cumberland.

"Hastings!" the duke exclaimed upon Philip's
arrival, his face already aflush with port.

"Your Grace." Lord Hastings sketched his bow to
the Duke of Cumberland.

"What do I hear of you losing this wager with
the colonial?"

Careful to maintain a dispassionate demeanor,
Philip answered in measure tones, "'Twas a most
unanticipated and equally unfortunate outcome."

"Unfortunate! Understated indeed! Your jockey
should be whipped at the cart's tail! I dare say you've
already sacked him for the disgrace. But then again,
I perceive from your dispatch that your loss on the
Rowley Mile might very well be my gain. Madeira or
claret?" the duke asked. An almost imperceptible wave
of his fingers brought a footman scurrying to the earl's
side with both bottles.

"Claret will serve," Hastings answered with little
enthusiasm at the thought of drink.

"Now what is this about the mares?" Cumberland inquired succinctly, his eyes gleaming with uncon-cealed avarice.

"You waste no time, your grace," Philip remarked, knowing he would fare far better by offering a private treaty to the duke than suffering the indignity of a public auction. His Grace, the Duke of Cumberland, would jump at the chance to add the entire lot of mares to his burgeoning stud and without begrudging a farthing of the premium.

"As you know, Hastings, I am not a man to shilly-shally," the duke said. "Many a golden opportunity is lost in vacillation. Thus, I come directly to the point. What do you want for the mares? Name your price."

Philip considered his answer carefully. Cumberland had long coveted the Hastings's broodmares, all descended from the three kings of the desert, or from the royal mares of Charles II. He knew they were arguably the finest equine harem in the land.

"Two thousand guineas."

"Two thousand?" the duke echoed flatly. "Indeed a princely sum."

"For twenty blood mares by the finest sires that ever ran, and who have never failed to produce a runner amongst them? I would call it a veritable bargain."

Philip waited. The duke knew full well their worth, and as he customarily ventured thousands of guineas on the races, he would have arrived at Newmarket with the full purchase price already lining his pockets.

Cumberland thoughtfully swirled the ruby liquid, then raised his glass to plump, wine-stained lips. He

emptied the remainder in one draught, and then set
his glass down decisively.

"Done."

Thirty-Five

WHEN PIGS TAKE FLIGHT

"THE COUNTESS OF HASTINGS TO SEE YOU, MY LADY." The maid bobbed to her mistress.

"Lady Hastings, you say? How extraordinary." Sukey's brows pulled together at the unexpectedness of her quondam friend's arrival. "Pray show her in."

Although once close, she and Charlotte had over the past few years done little more than nod to one another in passing, their respective relationships to the Earl of Hastings presenting an insurmountable social barrier.

The servant returned, escorting a woman who, though nearing thirty, maintained the figure and fresh appearance of youth. She was dressed simply in a light wool traveling gown, styled much akin to the riding habits she had adopted years ago as her trademark. Though frequently remarked upon for her self-possession, the countess approached tentatively, as if unsure of her welcome. "Sukey?"

Without hesitation, Lady Messingham rushed to enfold the younger woman in her arms. "Charlotte, dearest. You are in good health? All is well, I trust?"

"I don't remember when I have been better."
The countess's eyes sparkled with excitement and she
spoke with a breathless quality.

Sukey breathed her relief. "I am so very glad.
I had the worst premonition when you arrived. I
feared... Philip..."

"No. No. Nothing like that." Lady Hastings
emphatically shook her head. She answered cynically,
"When I saw him last, he was assuredly the worse for
drink, but otherwise robust. It is actually on Philip's
account that I have come. Might I entrust a letter to
you? It is of particular import that he receives it."

"But of course," Sukey replied. Noting the countess's
traveling clothes, she asked, "Are you going somewhere?"

Charlotte, Lady Hastings, answered in a distracted
manner. "I am indeed! As soon as I have settled some
important matters, I'm leaving... for the seaside. This
letter was among my most pressing concerns." She
handed Sukey the sealed missive. "I am pleased you
relieve me of the burden of seeking him out."

Susannah knew that the estranged Earl and Countess
of Hastings barely spoke to one another and only
appeared together for the spring and autumn races.
Their marriage, like many others in their class, had
been forged by arrangement, or in their case perhaps
better said by coercion. Neither would ever have
entertained the union otherwise.

Philip had wed Charlotte solely for financial gain,
and Charlotte, whose antipathy for her husband was
only surpassed by that for her Machiavellian uncle,
had conceded only to get out from under that guardian's thumb.

On their very wedding day, with his departure for the Flanders campaign imminent, Philip had delivered his young bride to Sukey's door, initially passing Charlotte off as his ward. While deeply shaken by his reappearance in her life after years of silence, Sukey experienced a pang of hope that in time old wounds might heal. As a favor to him, and with the secret hope of reconciliation, she had taken the girl under her wing and a fast friendship had formed between the two women.

Philip, however, continued to maintain a cool and distant reserve from her, hardened by bitterness and jealousy from the continued illusion she had sacrificed his love for a life of comfort as Weston's mistress.

When she finally learned Charlotte was in truth Philip's wife, her heart had wrenched at the painful irony: When Philip would have once had her, she would not be had; and then, when she would have fallen willingly and unconditionally into his arms, the arms held another—who didn't want *him*!

The turning point in the seeming *ménage à trois* had come following Philip's return from war and his unexpected ascent to the earldom of Hastings. Although he desired to fulfill his responsibilities and needed an heir to claim his full patrimony, Charlotte had remained intractable in her refusal to fulfill her conjugal duty. Desolate and disconsolate, Philip had sought succor from his former lover.

Although six years had passed, that fateful night was still vividly etched in her memory.

❧

September 1745
10 Bedford Street, Westminster

Sukey hadn't known if it was late night or early morning when the terrified maid had awoken her from her bed.

"There be someone pounding on the kitchen door, ma'am."

In irritation, Sukey had snatched on her dressing gown and grabbed the dagger she kept in the drawer of the bedside table. She had then accompanied the trembling maid downstairs. "Philip! What are you about at this hour? Are you inebriated?" she asked, rattled to recognize the source of the tumult.

"Foxed quite to the gills, actually, but you needn't fret. I have come by the servants' entrance. None should see me."

"Mayhap not see you, but few have not heard your incessant hammering!"

Philip's voice was low and surprisingly sober. "I need you, Sukey. Let me in."

I need you. She'd only hesitated a moment before opening the door.

Leading him to the salon, she'd patiently watched his progression as he broodingly paced, waiting for him to express whatever he was so loath to put into words.

"It appears I am to become the Earl of Hastings," he stated emptily. "Though I never have wished it. The earl and Edmund are both dead, and the title is now mine by default. I suppose I should be elated, jubilant even, but instead I have this void... this emptiness."

With a pained look, he thumped his chest. "Why

do I feel this way, Sukey, when I have achieved an earldom and presumably have the world at my feet?"

It was not a rhetorical question. He had come seeking succor to a pain he'd never before acknowledged. Her own heart lurched at the angst he had been trying to bury for the past decade.

"Philip, my love," she began softly, the endearment slipping thoughtlessly over her tongue, "you have yet to truly know yourself. Though you claimed no love for your family, you feel this way because you never had the love and acceptance that should have been your due. And now, any possibility has died with them."

He stood at the window, staring silently into the blackness, digesting her words. When he spoke again, his voice was hoarse with emotion. "Why did *you* refuse me?"

The question came so unexpectedly she had no breath to respond. She was glad he still faced away, for her expression in that moment would have given away every secret of her heart.

"You dismissed me out of hand," he said. "I vowed to completely eradicate you from my mind, but here I am drawn back again—like the proverbial moth to the flame."

"Like the moth to the flame?" She laughed bitterly. "You don't trouble yourself with even a pretension of sensibility for my feelings in dredging up the past."

"No, I have no particular sensitivity for your feelings... if you indeed have any."

"You really want to know why I refused you? Six years ago, I was a woman of nine-and-twenty and you had yet to grow fully into manhood. You were living by your wits and estranged from your family. On top of that, I was your first real lover and knew I would not be your last. Moreover, I was deeply in debt. I would have done neither of us a favor by accepting your proposal. But even after I drove you away, I have never loved another. The greater jest is that now you have become exactly the man I once envisaged, you are callous and indifferent to me."

He turned to face her with burning eyes. "You believe me callous and indifferent, Sukey?"

"When you have rebuffed me at every turn, and even brought a young woman to my home who is legally your wife? You do not consider these actions cruel and callous?"

"You have hardly languished for want of me."

She had initially prickled at the barb. "No, Philip. I have no respect for martyrs… though I have never loved but you." Her look of entreaty reached far deeper inside, endeavoring with all her heart to answer his need.

He stared at her a long moment, his incredulous expression revealing that her confession, so long in coming, had touched a raw, vulnerable place, appeasing some of his bitterness and hurt. When he came to her at last, he engulfed her in a crushing embrace that selfishly demanded all she could give, and for the first time in their relationship she had given all without reservation.

❧

Sukey studied Charlotte with mixed emotions. Out of love and respect for the younger woman, Sukey had endeavored to maintain the utmost discretion in her liaison with Philip, even forgoing his escort in any public setting lest scandal be spoken against Charlotte. This, in part, assuaged her guilt and was the condition upon which she had agreed to become his mistress, yet by consequence their friendship had ended. There was still so much she wanted to say, but it had been years since she and Charlotte had actually spoken; six years in fact since she had become Philip's mistress.

While she fully understood the source of Charlotte's hostility toward Philip, she nevertheless wished Charlotte could let go of the past and forgive the wrongs that could never be righted but only pardoned.

"I have known Philip intimately for a very long time, Charlotte. He's a complicated man, comprised of many shades of gray, and not always what he seems. I wish you could see he is not half the villain you think him."

"On that account, you and I will forever differ. Philip has been a fiend of the worst kind. He knowingly destroyed the man I loved, and in so doing crushed any chance I might have for happiness."

"But people change, dearest. You don't know how wretched and miserable he was after all that transpired. If given the chance, he would undoubtedly act differently."

"But he is still responsible. Time does not change that, don't you see? He was the one to rob us of any chance when we were so close. So very, very close..." Her voice dropped off as if lost in the reverie.

"Then you would allow one incident of poor judgment to define a man for life?"

"It was more than one incident, Sukey. He showed himself a betrayer of trust, a self-promoting opportunist, and a scoundrel of the vilest kind."

"Be fair, Charlotte. He has tried to make amends. How many husbands would have allowed you the freedom to go your own way as he has?"

"He acts out of guilt, as rightly he should!"

"Mayhap that's part of it, but he has never demanded of you what every husband has a right to claim from his wife. Instead, he has held you with an open hand and protected you with his name. Despite your animosity, he has not only provided for you but has even given you the means to pursue your dreams."

Charlotte had the good grace to look away.

She'd knowingly given him every justification to divorce her, even going out of her way to provoke and needle, yet he had failed to do so. Even when Philip had unexpectedly gained the title and estates and needed an heir to claim his full patrimony, she'd remained intractable in her refusal to allow him into her bed. Certain he would then put her aside as most any other man would have done, she was confounded when he did not.

Whether out of guilt, pride, or a misplaced sense of honor, Philip had let her go her own way, but Charlotte remained staunch in her condemnation.

"Allowing me the run of the racing stud has been to *his* advantage. He would never have permitted it otherwise."

"I don't believe that's completely true. Nor deep down do you truly believe it either. Yes, you have achieved success with the Hastings stud by the sweat of your brow, but horse racing is a man's domain. How far do you think you would have gotten without *his* name and *his* credibility attached to the stud?"

"Philip always has and always will think only of Philip."

"That's not true!" Sukey cried. "I have known him to be self-sacrificing. There is so much more to him than what you care to see."

"My dear, dear Sukey, I fear your eyes are completely blind to his defective character."

"Mayhap you are right and I am a besotted fool, but I love him despite his flaws, or mayhap because of them, and even more desperately for the man he so earnestly *wants to be*. If you would only soften your heart just a little, the two of you might find peace. It wrenches my heart that you have it within your power to give him what I can't."

"I'm very sorry for that, Sukey. You are too good for him, you know."

After a silent moment, she offered up an enigmatic smile. "I promise to forgive Philip Drake when my lost love returns from the dead."

Sukey sighed with a fatal gesture. "Then there's naught more to say. As to your missive, I expect his return soon and will be sure he receives it directly."

"Thank you, Sukey." Charlotte paused. "Though I would wish your affections placed with another, with a better man, I'm glad for Philip that he has you."

They clasped hands for a brief moment, exchanged a look of wistful regret, and Lady Hastings departed.

Thirty-Six

MISTRESS-IN-WAITING

WHEN PHILIP ENTERED THE DRESSING ROOM, HE WAS arrested by a remarkably impassioned display.

In the midst of her levee, Susannah, Lady Messingham, sat at a table littered with glass bottles in various shapes and sizes, tins of tinted powders, and a silver patch box. As her maid removed curling papers from her hair, a foppish young gentleman flung himself prostrate at her feet, waxing in rhapsodic verse:

> "Your face for conquest was designed;
> your every motion charms my mind;
> Angels, when you, your silence break,
> forget their hymns, to hear you speak;
> However, when at once they hear and view,
> are loath to mount and long to stay with you.
> Love's my petition, All my ambition;
> if e'er you discover more faithful a lover,
> So real a flame, I'll die, I'll die—"

He clutched his breast with his final declamation. "So give up my game."

"Philip!" Lady Susannah exclaimed with pleasure, forgetting at once the existence of her lovelorn swain in catching his reflection in the glass. "I thought you in Newmarket for the sennight, and had not even hoped to see you for some days yet."

"Obviously not," he remarked, directing a scathing eye at the would-be poet scrambling guiltily to his feet.

Sukey chuckled and said, by way of introduction, "May I make known to you Mr. Samuel Derrick."

"Derrick, you say? Then I must have my poets confused. I could have sworn the verse was Dryden," Philip said.

The young man flushed to his ears and stammered, "My work has been much compared with the great John Dryden."

"You've a remarkably similar style. One might say to a word."

With red splotches flushing his powdered cheeks, the poet turned back to the object of his panegyric. "Perhaps I should be going now, my lady? I have yet to compose the promised ode to your eyes."

"You needn't hasten on my account," Philip said, handing the gentleman-poet his hat, cane, and gloves. Taking the not-so-subtle hint, Mr. Derrick made a sweeping bow to the lady, glared indignantly at his rival, and departed.

"Posturing, plagiarizing popinjay!" Philip mumbled before the door had even closed.

"You needn't have been so rude, my love," she reprimanded with a twinkle of humor. "I fear you have quite driven him away, when he was avowed to immortalize my pulchritude in verse."

"What, him? He's no more poet than I am. I'd call him nothing more than a rhapsodizing cicisbeo."

"Don't be cruel, Philip. Jealousy ill becomes you."

"You think me jealous? I'm not jealous. I just have a strong aversion to bad verse."

"But every lady of fashion has one these days."

"A poem or a cicisbeo?"

"Why, either or both," she declared. "Besides, he's completely harmless."

"I've been absent too long if you allow such a poor specimen to make violent love to you."

"You fear usurpation?" she teased.

He caught and held her gaze and brushed the backs of his fingers down her arm. "I fear no such thing."

The confident reply, as much as the accompanying touch, made her shiver in excited anticipation.

"My arrival is not a disagreeable surprise, I trust?" he asked.

"Only as I am positively unfit to receive you," she replied as the maid hustled to remove the last of the curling papers from her hair.

Philip cast an appreciative gaze over her state of dishabille. Only one of her long, shapely legs wore a silk stocking; the other stocking, along with her beribboned garters, hung suggestively over the footstool. His gaze lingered at the low neckline of her lace chemise where her stays revealed milky white shoulders and the generous curve of softly rounded breasts.

"On the contrary, my delightfully disheveled lady, I think you very fit to *receive me*."

The maid blushed crimson, but the lady responded to his double entendre with a well-pleased, throaty chuckle. Heedless of the scandalized servant, Philip moved to brush his lips to his lover's cheek, but she turned her face and offered her mouth instead.

Philip eagerly accepted the invitation and released her reluctantly after their long lingering kiss.

Her mouth curved with meaning. "You see, I am truly bliss-filled to see you, but shan't flatter myself that you returned early just for want of my company."

"Never doubt my desire to fill you with bliss, Sukey."

He traced a lone finger slowly along her décolletage, causing her womb to clench at the sensation. "But unfortunately, I must forgo that exquisite experience until a later time. I need to speak with you." He slanted a glance at the servant. "Privately."

Few others would have sensed the note of disquiet in his indolent tone, but Sukey dismissed her protesting servant with an imperious wave.

"But madam! The rout and the playhouse!"

"I doubt I'll be attending either after all, Sarah. Prithee fetch my cap and dressing gown, and then you may go. I'll write my regrets to her ladyship anon."

The servant returned promptly with the requested garments, sniffing with little disguised affront when Philip took them from her hands. A warning look from her mistress sent her out the door. The sharp click followed by a derisive snort announced the maid's withdrawal.

Sukey looked bemused when Philip held the robe to help her into it.

"I've removed your clothes often enough, I think I can manage creditably to dress you." His boyish smirk didn't linger but his lips did, as they played intimately upon the skin of her shoulder before finally covering it with the silk dressing gown.

With a provocative look, she entwined her arms about his neck and would have kissed him had he not held her gently at a distance.

"What is it, Philip? You had a racing engagement of some consequence, did you not?" She frowned at the shadows shading his dark eyes and the deep grooves accentuating the grim line of his mouth.

"I did," he said, affecting carelessness, but the tautness of his bearing put her in mind of a caged tiger.

"Then pray tell me what has you so bedeviled, my love?"

"It went very badly. Appallingly so."

"I have never known you to wager indiscriminately. Surely it cannot be so dreadful," she said.

His speaking look revealed the depth of his worry.

"Is it so? Then pray let us not talk of it now."

She drew him to her and reached on her toes to press fleeting kisses to his jaw while she loosened his cravat. When he laid his hand over hers to arrest her progress, she ignored him and continued her loving ministrations. Between sultry kisses and caresses, she divested him of all but smallclothes and led him to the nearby Turkish divan that appointed her dressing chamber.

With no words passing between them, she knelt between his knees, according to her pleasure. When she moved to the buttons of his breeches, she pressed a finger to his lips, silencing his protest with a reproachful look.

"Not now," she gently chided, checking his

reticence with a gaze that set him aflame. "Indulge me, dearest. Anon will be time enough to talk."

Giving himself up to her, and stroking her hair, Philip groaned in surrender. "God only knows how I need you, Sukey."

&

Satisfied she had temporarily abated his cares, Sukey lay cradled in Philip's well-sated embrace.

"How much was it, my love?"

"Far more than I care to say," he answered.

She was almost afraid to voice the words when she asked, "You don't mean to say you are ruined?"

His laugh was humorless. "Ruined? Beyond belief. Beyond any hope of recovery."

"And Charlotte? Have you told her?"

"At the expense of my best brandy."

"I don't understand."

"'Tis inconsequential, my dearest."

"No, Philip. I truly don't understand! Charlotte came to see me, you see. Just last evening, in fact, as I was dressing for the theatre. She was attired in a traveling robe, and never have I seen her so radiant. Positively ebullient, even. Given your news, it makes no sense. No sense at all."

"Charlotte was here? And dressed to travel? Perhaps she seeks to flee the bailiff ahead of me. As my wife, she shares liability in the debts."

"The letter!" Sukey gasped, nearly shooting from the divan. "I nigh forgot. She entrusted me with a letter for you." She swiftly retrieved it from atop her escritoire.

"Perhaps she has absconded with the mysterious

Roberts!" Philip laughed. "Such a finishing touch to my utter humiliation would surely explain her glee."

"How ridiculous you sound. After seven years of marriage, she can't possibly abhor you to that degree."

He regarded her dubiously as she handed him the letter.

"We both know the depth of her loathing, but why she should be so pleased about this is beyond my ken." Philip murmured something indistinguishable as his hands fumbled with the wax seal and tore it open with an oath.

Philip stared dumbfounded at the foolscap. As he struggled to digest the contents, first confusion followed in rapid succession by astonishment, fury, and then something indefinable registered on his face.

"Devington? My God, it's true! She really has absconded with the devil."

"Devington? Robert Devington? But he is dead," she said.

"Not so dead after all, it seems. It was Devington all along."

"My God!" she cried. "*That's* what she meant by it!"

"By what?"

"She made the most enigmatic remark about forgiving you when her love returned from the dead. I interpreted it as meaning 'when pigs fly' but apparently she really meant it!"

"Then after all this time, when I least would have seen it coming, the pair conspired against me!" Overcome by the magnificence of it all, Philip threw back his head and let out a cachinnatory roar.

His financial devastation and complete ruin had come by the hands of his erstwhile friend, his wife's one-time love, whose life he had ruined eight years ago. It was true, unadulterated vengeance in all its glory.

"You can't mean it!" Sukey cried, snatching the letter from his hands while tears of ironical mirth streamed down his face.

Her brows drew together as she scanned the letter.

"But 'tis a farce worthy of the Drury Lane stage!" Philip wiped his eyes. "I ruined his life, thus he bides his time until he can ruin mine. We have surely come full circle now, have we not?"

"But, Philip, don't you understand?" she said. "This letter is your reprieve. You've been given time to meet your obligations." She continued reading and her face clouded. "But wh… what is this about a son?"

Although resigned to sharing the man she loved with his wife, the thought of him with any other was almost more than she could bear.

"What of the boy?" Sukey repeated.

"*What of* the boy?" Philip echoed.

"Will you seek him out?"

"Sukey, my dearest, dearest love." He encircled her in his arms. "I know nothing of any bastard. There has been none other than you these past six years. Only you."

"Then why would Charlotte imply such a thing?"

"Purely to further my torment?" he suggested. "Besides, what good would it do to pursue the issue? Don't you think in this instance it would be preferable to all parties to just let sleeping dogs lie?"

"But a son, Philip!"

"Correction—a bastard. Legally, there will ever be a distinction between the two."

"How can you be so callous?"

"What, pray, would you have me do?"

"Find the boy and acknowledge him!"

"To what possible advantage, my love? There is none."

"But we are speaking of your blood!"

Philip gritted his teeth in an effort to modulate his tone. "The boy, *if he even exists*, has a home already. You would have me claim him to what possible end?"

Sukey turned to face him with misting eyes. "To ensure he is fed, clothed, kept safe from harm, and to educate him befitting his rightful station. In sum, to fulfill a father's obligation to his son."

"For a bastard born of another woman, Sukey?" he asked softly, bracing his hands on her quivering shoulders. "You would have me put him daily before your eyes? How could I ever do that to you?"

Her inability to bear a child would always be a painful specter between them. When she and Philip had reunited after their lengthy estrangement, he had again proposed marriage, offering to put Charlotte quietly aside, but Sukey had once more refused the man she so desperately loved. Knowing she could never bear him an heir, she had relegated herself to the position of mistress rather than risk losing him again.

She closed her eyes in an attempt to tamp down the pain Philip's words inflicted, but he saw through her efforts and wrapped her in his arms. "If it means so much to you, dearest, I will make some inquiries."

"Thank you," she said with a weak smile. "You know, Philip, this changes everything."

"Perhaps," Philip said. "If it is all true, it does indeed change everything."

He kissed her. One kiss led to two, and then to
her bed, where he made slow, deliberate love to her
and congratulated himself at having so deftly put the
matter to rest.

❧

Leaving Sukey's bed, Philip quickly dressed and went
to the writing desk where he scratched on a sheet of
foolscap. After signing and sanding the note, he rang
for a footman to dispatch it.

"What are you doing?" she asked sleepily.

"I think it would be prudent to seek legal counsel."
He returned to the desk and unlocked a drawer,
retrieving a silk purse from within. "Until I have all
the answers, I must also control the immediate damage
and buy some time to come about."

He absently weighed the gold, estimating it at no
more than one hundred guineas, and deposited it in
his waistcoat pocket.

Watching him, Sukey asked warily, "Just how do
you propose to do that? To come about?"

He answered with a grim smile. "My dearest love,
by any means at my disposal. By any means at all."

Thirty-Seven

A PERFECT REVENGE

AFTER DISPATCHING AN URGENT SUMMONS TO HIS solicitor, Philip secreted Lady Hastings's letter in his pocket and left his mistress. Hailing a sedan chair, he directed the bearers to Mayfair, where he discovered to his consternation that the gentleman he sought was not at home.

"Roberts should have arrived from Newmarket two days ago," Philip insisted, wondering if some new game might be afoot.

"Nevertheless, he is no longer in residence, my lord," the footman replied.

Philip pressed his booted foot against the closing door. "What do you mean, *no longer in residence*? You do not expect his return?"

"The gentleman was called away of a sudden. I am not at liberty to say more."

"That will be all, Henderson," a cool voice commanded from within.

Philip pressed harder, straining to see the man behind the voice. "Lee. It is you."

"Lord Hastings. An unexpected pleasure." Mr. Lee's

tone belied his delight. He came forward to admit his guest. "As always, your obedient." He sketched a bow. "Shall we, my lord?" He indicated that Philip should follow him inside.

Lee led Philip into a private chamber and closed the door. He gestured to the set of chairs, but Philip demurred.

"Do I understand correctly that Roberts has precipitately departed?"

"'Twas some very... personal business, my lord."

"One must suppose it a matter of some urgency for such extraordinary behavior from the *winner* of a monumental wager."

Philip's irony was not lost on Mr. Lee. "Nevertheless, Roberts sends his deepest regrets that once more I stand in his stead."

"Perhaps you might care to know the nature of *my business* before you volunteer to be his surrogate?" Lord Hastings retrieved the letter from his breast pocket. "Do you know the contents?"

Lee inclined his head. "I am in the gentleman's confidence."

"Then you are aware of our history and that the scoundrel has eloped with my wife?"

"A most unfortunate circumstance, my lord."

"Unfortunate? I don't believe so, Lee. This was purely premeditated. Malicious, unadulterated vengeance."

"It was a wager, my lord, nothing more. It was not forced upon you."

"I was intentionally baited!"

"As with any hardened gamester, your greed overcame your good sense."

The truth stung. Hubris, as much as greed, had led to this humiliation.

"That accounts for the wager, but what of my wife, Lee? She has run off with him."

"While none could have foreseen *that* consequence, the countess left of her own accord. It neither was abduction nor premeditated."

"Yet Roberts, *or should I say Devington*, refused to meet me man-to-man, but instead absconds with my wife like a thief in the night."

"I say he acted out of compassion for the lady's sake. She wished to depart swiftly and spare you what would have been a most uncomfortable and scandalously public confrontation."

"How considerate. Now I must ask, Lee, what reparation does Devington deem suitable for the loss of my countess as well as my reputation? I'll have satisfaction one way or another. Are you still so eager to stand as his proxy?"

Lee blanched. The American colonial had resided in London long enough to know how matters of honor were settled. Moreover, Lord Hastings was widely accounted a master swordsman. He chose his next words with the utmost care. "My Lord Hastings, it was the gentleman's belief that a compromise might be struck."

"Is that so?"

"By way of recompense, Roberts will grant clemency in settling the debt of honor. It was a fair wager that you lost, but he's agreed to save you from the public disgrace of bankruptcy... should this matter be quietly settled."

"And you are to negotiate?"

"Indeed, my lord. Your arrival was not entirely unanticipated."

"I would think not. What, precisely, are Roberts's terms?"

"He will allow ten years to repay the wager, provided you seek an immediate dissolution of the marriage."

"He expects me to just give him Charlotte? You know I must file a civil suit against him, don't you? It is my prerogative as the injured party to seek financial reparation."

"The terms are more than generous."

"Yet I must take this to the courts. I cannot legally seek a divorce without first obtaining a judgment of criminal conversation, not that I haven't legitimate grounds. Is not this very letter unquestionable evidence of Lady Hastings's willful and premeditated desertion?"

"There can be no denial of it."

"Then I must call upon you to act as a witness. I cannot move forward without witnesses."

"You expect me to act against Roberts? I would do no such thing!" said Lee.

"You would not be acting against *his interests*, if he indeed wishes to wed Charlotte. It is an impossibility until our marriage is legally severed. If you expedite the proceedings, you facilitate their union, don't you see?"

"But Roberts could face severe financial penalty."

"Would he rather sire bastards upon the woman he presumably loves? As you know, I cannot meet the legal fees to obtain a divorce. I intend to seek a judgment equal to the expense. If Roberts agrees, I am willing to forgo any further settlement."

Lee studied his friend's longtime nemesis before capitulating with a sigh. "I suppose it best we proceed as you wish."

A small triumph, Philip reasoned, but at least they'd come to an agreement of sorts. Although he'd been humiliated by this turn of events, deep down Philip knew he'd only reaped what he'd sown, though the harvest had taken some eight years. Charlotte and Robert, the victims of many an unscrupulous turn, had by fate's caprice prevailed in the end.

"Have you anything to drink, Lee? I am much inclined to celebrate." Ironically, though standing on the brink of ruin, Philip was elated at the prospect of liberation from the wretched and lingering purgatory that was his marriage. *Good God, to be free at last!*

Befuddled by the turn this encounter had taken, Lee frowned. "I fail to see the source of your good humor, my lord."

"I suppose you would not. You colonials are a singularly humorless lot."

Mr. Lee poured two glasses of claret. Philip downed the first and meditated his empty glass. "What am I to make of the rest, Lee?" He stabbed the letter with his index finger. "Am I to suppose some generosity of spirit led Lady Hastings to claim I have a son?"

Lee remained impassive. "There was mention of a young boy encountered at a Yorkshire tavern, but I know nothing further."

"A tavern in Yorkshire?" *When the deuce was he last in Yorkshire, outside of the races?* Philip had no recollection of the last time he'd swived a tavern wench. He'd abandoned those days long ago for Sukey, but if it were indeed true… "Damn it all, Lee, you must know something more!"

"Sadly, I had little curiosity in the matter."

"Answer me this, then—is there any reason Charlotte might have concocted the story?"

"I have no reason to believe so."

While part of him desired confirmation of the claim, the inclination was soon overpowered by the belief that if the boy indeed existed, he would do nothing but complicate an already impossible situation.

Thirty-Eight

A LEGAL TANGLE

ANY *SELF-RESPECTING* GENTLEMAN WOULD HAVE PUT A pistol in his mouth after his wife eloped with the very man who ruined him, thought Francis Willoughby, Esquire, as the chairmen conveyed him to his meeting with the Earl of Hastings.

The earnest, bespectacled young solicitor had responded promptly to the hastily scrawled summons, completely abandoning the documents and legal texts scattered about his cluttered Holborn Street apartments in Lincoln's Inn. At this stage in his career, Willoughby the younger could ill-afford to displease any of his clients, regardless of their notoriety.

His father, Phineas Willoughby, Esquire, had been the preeminent probate attorney of his time, and was the primary executor of the Hastings Estate until his recent demise. Now Francis had assumed that dubious honor.

The tersely worded brief had revealed little, but Mr. Willoughby had a fair preconception of what services he might be asked to render the Earl of Hastings. News traveled swiftly in London, and the coffee houses were already abuzz about the earl's calamitous wager.

Willoughby was not at first inclined to hire a sedan chair for the short transit across town, but decided the half shilling to the burly chairmen well worth the protection they afforded his shoes, his clothes, and his person from the filth and perils of the London streets. As the chair conveyed him to his appointment, Willoughby recalled what details he knew of the present Earl of Hastings.

As a scapegrace second son, Philip Drake had acceded to the earldom and its entailed estates upon the concurrent and accidental (though scandalmongers implied otherwise) deaths of his father and elder brother. Remarkably, although he'd gained the title, the family fortune was still held completely outside of his grasp.

The late earl, in his intense disapprobation of his second son, had taken extraordinary measures to circumvent traditional inheritance law in order to tie up the family fortune in trust. Although the entailment guaranteed Philip Drake the title and estates, the late earl's last will and testament firmly held all monies until the time Philip would produce a legitimate male heir.

Seven years of less-than-connubial bliss between Lord Hastings and his young countess had failed to produce any progeny, and the earl's holdings were known to be a shambles. Years of immoderate living had only worsened his circumstances and fueled him to more reckless and dissolute behavior, eventually leading to his most devastating and self-destructive act.

Word of the entire salacious affair had spread like a wildfire from coffee house to coffee house. He had accepted a racing wager and lost a fortune he could not touch. Now, with his wife's elopement, he would no doubt initiate proceedings for divorcement on grounds of desertion.

Truthfully, Willoughby couldn't quite decide if the Earl of Hastings was by now insensitive, impervious, or merely oblivious to obloquy.

❧

While the present Lord Hastings watched in ill-concealed edgy silence, the young lawyer furrowed his brow over the last will and testament of the late Anthony, Lord Hastings.

"Well? What do you make of it?" the present earl demanded.

"Ironclad. Truly a flawless document." Willoughby spoke the words with filial pride.

"What am I paying you for, if not to find a flaw?"

"But the will is immutable, my lord. You may not realize a farthing from the trust until you have... er... ensured the... ah... continuation... of the Hastings line."

"I am already painfully aware of this condition, Willoughby."

"Then I regret to disappoint you, my lord. The provisions of the will are very clear. Indeed, crystal."

"What if there were a child? A male of my blood? Could that satisfy the conditions to release the trust?"

"But you and *Lady Hastings* have no offspring."

Philip answered with a significant look.

The lawyer flushed. "You speak of a bar sinister?" The sanctimonious solicitor could not quite mouth the word "bastard."

"I understand there may be such a child. I care nothing of the social stigma, Willoughby; I would acknowledge the boy."

"If such a… child… exists, he still would not satisfy the requirements of the trust."

"Why not?"

"Because the will clearly states a *legitimate* male heir. In the eyes of the law, illegitimate shall *always be* illegitimate."

"Surely there is a loophole," the earl insisted.

"There is not."

"How can you say that? King Charles had a dozen or more bastard brats and ennobled them all."

"He had the power to create *new* titles, but not to confer existing ones. Even then, the eldest, Monmouth, was ineligible to accede to the throne."

Philip's gaze riveted to the Allan Ramsay portrait of the fourth Earl of Hastings over the mantel. "Damn your eyes, you sadistic old bastard, for leaving me in this impossible position!"

Willoughby nervously cleared his throat. "I fear that is not all, my lord."

"What do you mean?" Lord Hastings demanded.

The lawyer regarded Philip with an expression reminiscent of a frightened rabbit. "I may have discovered a further hindrance."

Philip's thick brows drew together in a frown. "Hindrance? What are you talking about?"

"Given your… er… circumstances, my lord, I

thought it appropriate to more closely examine the entailment as well as the trust. One can never be too thoroughgoing in these things, you know. Given you've no heir, the estate lies in a most precarious position. Should anything unforeseen happen—"

"Like my ending my misery with this interview by the end of a rope?"

Willoughby looked aghast. "God forbid such a thing, my lord! Accidents and illness are not prejudiced against the young and robust. If anything untoward were to befall you, with no declared heir the entire estate, as well as the fortune, would likely revert to the crown."

"If I am dead, Willoughby, I won't bloody well care who gets it," Philip retorted, but then reconsidered. "If it reverts to the crown, I would no doubt only shore up Prince Frederick's coffers, likely the last person I would wish to bless with my family's fortune. Of course fifty thousand would be nothing to our wastrel Prince of Wales."

"Fifty thousand?" repeated Willoughby. "That would only account for half of it."

"Half of what?"

"The trust, my lord."

"I don't follow you."

"The Hastings trust exceeds one hundred thousand pounds, my lord."

Philip started. "What did you say?"

"The initial sum left in trust seven years hence was indeed fifty thousand, but the returns on the funds have been extraordinarily well managed under Mr. Gideon's hand."

"I cannot bear the irony! How the cruel hand of fate mocks me!" Philip cried. "Here I live on the perpetual brink of insolvency while my family fortune continues to increase. Had I realized sooner, I may have been markedly less tolerant of my Lady Hastings's whim."

"Quite, but unless you wish to retrieve her…"

"Devil take you for suggesting it! I can only thank the hand of Providence for this whole twisted affair."

"Then we are back to the matter of the trust, the entailment, and the heir, my lord. As you are aware, Lord Anthony's will holds a substantial fortune for his eldest surviving son, at which time said son produces a male heir of his body. The conditions of Lord Anthony's will clearly adjure you not to continue in this state of intestacy."

"Pray tell me something I don't bloody well know," Philip snapped.

The solicitor stiffened in obvious affront. "As you are now apprised, the heir to an entailed estate cannot sell the land, nor bequeath it to an illegitimate child. Now then, under the *usual* circumstances, the titular property, according to fee tail, may only transfer to a legitimate male offspring, the purpose of which is to keep the land of a family intact and in the paternal line of succession."

"Enough of the legal tangrams. Get to the bloody point!"

"As you wish, my lord," Willoughby answered stiffly. "You are not the rightful heir to the Earldom of Hastings."

Philip froze. "The devil you say!"

"I assure you, my lord," the solicitor sniffed, "I would not have spoken so, had I not already substantiated my findings."

"You are mistaken," Philip ground through his teeth.

"I am not." Willoughby tilted his chin to meet the earl's incredulous stare.

"I am the sole surviving male of my line, Willoughby. How can I not be the Earl of Hastings?"

"That is what I was trying to explain previously."

"Then explain again! Damn your eyes!"

"My lord, I understand you are overwrought, but there is no need—"

"Answer before I throttle you, Willoughby!"

"Having traced the Hastings patent of nobility back to its original issuance, I have made the discovery that the language of the fee tail does not specify that the lands and title should devolve exclusively upon heirs male, but may be more generally conferred upon the first 'lineal descendant.'"

Philip regarded him blankly. "But I am the sole lineal descendant."

"I respectfully contend that you are not, my lord. Your elder brother, Edmund Viscount Uxeter, was next in the line. By the terms of the entail, you would accede in the event that he passed on *without issue*, but this is not the case. Lord Uxeter has a surviving daughter, does he not?"

What the hell had just happened? Philip fiercely shook his head, as if to clear it of the nonsense that was spewing forth from the solicitor's mouth. "Sophie? Anna Sophie is the heir? Why the devil has nothing been said of this before?"

"I fear certain assumptions were made according to the normal right of primogeniture but without close examination of the actual legal language of the fee tail itself. Indeed, my lord. Anna Sophia Drake, a legitimate daughter issued from Lord Uxeter's body as defined by law, meets the criteria of the entailed title and estates."

Philip was dumbstruck by this inexplicable chain of events. He crossed the room to pour himself a brandy and downed it in one long draught. He refilled the glass as he turned this revelation and its repercussions over in his mind, looking for some angle that would turn matters back to his advantage.

At length he ventured to ask, "What if, *theoretically speaking*, Edmund's daughter was not in truth his, but was in actuality sired by another?"

The solicitor turned his eyes to heaven and inhaled deeply, as if offering up a prayer for the forbearance to continue this interview. "Do you mean to imply that Lady Uxeter played her husband false?"

"I am only putting forth a hypothetical inquiry. What if it could be proven that Edmund's daughter by his wife was not of Edmund's blood? Would the trust then fall to me?"

"In the eyes of the law, it would not matter a jot or tittle, my lord. As long as Lord and Lady Uxeter were wed at time of birth, the child is legally his, even if it could be proven biologically to be otherwise."

Philip realized the hypocritical truth. Even Prime Minister Walpole was saddled with a son and heir that the world at large knew was sired by his wife's lover, Carr Hervey.

"Of course, having owned the title for six years, you would be in a position of strength to appeal to the chancery court, but this will no doubt prove a very drawn-out process."

"How long?" Philip asked in growing unease. "Are we talking weeks or months?"

"Oh no, my lord... in the usual case, this manner of litigation takes years to settle."

"Years?" As the urgency of his position began to set in, Philip once more emptied the contents of his glass. The initial burn had settled into welcoming warmth that infused his blood and fortified him enough to continue. "And in the interim?" he asked.

"In the interim, until the dispute can be resolved, I fear your patent of nobility and its associated privilege would be placed in abeyance."

"You mean suspended?"

"Indeed, my lord. Until the matter is settled by the Chancery."

"But the bloody title is all that protects me from the sponging house!"

"Then may I advise a complete liquidation of all viable assets."

"It's not enough! And once word of this circulates about London, my multifarious creditors will descend like a pack of hyenas to ravage whatever remains of my carcass."

His trepidation at spending the remainder of his days in the King's Bench was increasing by the minute, a place notorious for practicing every species of fraud, extortion, and torture, under the full protection of the law.

"Then I see no alternative but to appeal to your creditors to grant you some reprieve."

"I see you know nothing, Willoughby! No gentleman of honor would so demean himself."

"Then I would advise very careful consideration of the alternatives, my lord. The sacrifice of one's pride might be considered by many to be an immeasurably lesser evil than sacrificing one's freedom."

Philip dismissed Willoughby, far more rattled than when the lawyer had first arrived. He shuddered to think he was brought so low that he might be forced to choose between sacrificing his last vestige of honor and facing internment in debtors' prison. He considered another drink, but found the sobering effect of the lawyer's parting words was far stronger than the brandy's power to numb him.

Thirty-Nine

WAGERS AND WASTRELS

LORD HASTINGS ENTERED WHITE'S CHOCOLATE HOUSE with the sole purpose of dampening the furor before rumor became a raging inferno of ruin. He paused at the entrance, languidly surveying the room and nodding here or there to an acquaintance, noting that no one in this celebrated gentlemen's abode presented a more elegant or composed picture.

Determined that nothing in his demeanor, dress, or bearing could suggest the slightest disquiet about his circumstances, he wore an impeccably tailored coat of the finest velvet, cut to expose the rich crimson and gold silk brocade of the waistcoat beneath. French lace cascaded abundantly from his cravat and cuff, nearly concealing the hands that held his gold-laced hat and elaborately enameled snuffbox.

Nevertheless, upon his appearance, an astounding domino effect prevailed. The low drone of conversation virtually ceased. One by one, every pair of eyes peeked quizzically above the newsprint, or surreptitiously sneaked up from their cards, as if he was suddenly an apparition within their midst. Precisely as he had supposed, within four-and-twenty hours all of London was buzzing with his infamous defeat on the Rowley Mile.

The reigning silence was broken at last by Lord March who, seated at cards with George Selwyn, exclaimed, "Is it he, by God? Damn your eyes, Hastings! Unspeakably thoughtless to show your face after I laid a hundred guineas that by noon you'd have splattered your brains on the carpet!

"Capot," Lord March declared upon taking the final trick. "Selwyn, however, gave you until tomorrow forenoon to commit the unforgivable. By means of a rope, wasn't it, dear boy?" March asked his partner.

"Devil take you, March!" Selwyn cursed his defeat in the game.

"That's fifty-two guineas by my account," Lord March remarked.

"I trust you've no later engagement with a pistol?" George queried of the new arrival with affected hopefulness.

Philip's brow rose in a decidedly aristocratic fashion. "I so hate to disappoint you, George, but the tales of my misfortune appear greatly embellished."

"But my sources are most reliable," Lord March protested. "I seldom lose a prophetic wager."

"You are a veritable oracle, March," George Selwyn remarked dryly.

"You would gainsay me after the wager about old man Pigot?"

"*That* was nothing more than a freak of happenstance, March. I only pray you don't rain curses upon your head by continuing these morbid bets with the grim reaper."

March laughed. "The odds were decidedly in my favor, though I would never have guessed the gouty old worthy to be so very obliging as to die."

Lord Hastings looked his question.

"You may as well join us." George indicated a vacant chair at the baize-covered table. "It's a long story and I have tired of piquet."

Philip took the proffered seat and March continued his aborted narrative.

"George and I were congregated with a number of fine sporting fellows at Blackfriars following the match between the retired Broughton and Jack Slack, a Norwich butcher who proved no slacker but one hell of a bruiser."

"Took Broughton down with a hard right betwixt the eyes," George volunteered. "Some say Broughton threw the fight, but one don't dare speak of it in front of Cumberland, who lost ten thousand on the match."

"We digress, George," March said. "I was speaking of the Pigot wager. Now where was I?"

"At Blackfriars?" Philip prompted.

"Ah, yes. The lot of us had drunk liberally of arrack punch when Sir William Codrington claimed his seventy-year-old father could have fought a better match than Broughton. Then Mr. Pigot proposed to match his own gout-ridden sire against the former champion. Following half a case of Madeira, the match then was revised to pit the elder Pigot against the elder Codrington.

"I laid my money on Codrington the elder and we drank a bumper to these worthies' health. Then, lo and behold, Pigot received a message that Pigot senior had succumbed to gout in his head. Dead that very same day! Thus, I won the wager by default.

"Pigot, of course, protested vociferously, and even filed suit in the courts, but was eventually obliged to pay the five hundred guineas, no doubt heavily denting his inheritance." March laughed and regarded Philip appraisingly. "Judging by your coolness of manner after your travesty at Newmarket, one might suppose you also have some reasonable expectation? Death of a near kinsman, perhaps?"

George interjected, "I fear March suffers the erroneous belief that all men have such obliging relations as he, who pass from this earth at a precious early age just to leave him a handsome fortune."

"True enough!" March declared. "After burning through my first inheritance, courtesy of the Earldom of March, I was at *point non-plus* following an insufferable losing streak. I have since renounced basset for faro. Better odds," he added in an aside. "I was thought undone until my dear and sympathetic mother passed on and conferred my secondary Earldom of Ruglen, with a fortune of twenty thousand pounds."

"Confess, March. You never feared dunning for a moment," Selwyn protested. "Your inheritance prospects alone keep creditors at bay, though if ever there was a more undeserving sod, I know him not."

Lord March chuckled. "You don't know the half of it, my friend! I may live the most prodigal life without fear, now I have been counted among the possible heirs to the Earldom of Casellis and the Dukedom of Queensberry."

"Do you mean to say Lady Casellis is another relation of yours?" Selwyn asked. "Wasn't she involved with Lady Mordington in that fashionable gaming house in Covent Garden? As I recall, the Baroness of Mordington even had the audacity to claim a peeress's privilege to remain in operation, contrary to Parliament's Gaming Act. No doubt you remember the place, Drake."

"How could I ever forget?" Although he and Sukey agreed never to speak of it, choosing instead to bury all the mistakes of the past, the very mention of it brought the entire fateful night back to vivid life. He'd risked his life for her, and yet they'd parted. Sukey had never placed another wager after that, and he'd joined the King's Horse. They had come so very far since those early days, and over the years their mutual passion had seasoned and matured into what was now a profound and abiding love.

Lord March chuckled, snapping Philip abruptly out of his reverie. "My relations are quite an irreverent breed, are they not?"

"Are you heir to half the peers of the realm?" George asked.

March chuckled. "Not quite, though my connections are close enough to place me in several lines of succession, though a disobliging invalid cousin yet stands between me and the Dukedom of Queensberry. Happily, the fact does not keep the tradesmen from tripping over one another to offer me credit."

"If only we were all so blessed," said Selwyn.

Philip was no stranger, either, to getting by on credit. The existence of the considerable Hastings trust had allowed him to negotiate more than one loan to repair his tenants' properties and to sow the fallow fields of his Sussex estate.

The source of his greatest fear at present was that his loans would be called in once news of the lost wager reached his creditors' ears. That way lay absolute devastation. His only hope of holding his creditors at bay would be continued and timely interest payments until such time as he came about.

Although he'd eschewed the tables long ago, he saw no choice but returning in order to produce ready money to shore up his chief creditor's confidence. As chance would have it, the flush-pocketed Lord March had fallen neatly into his lap.

"If you have tired of piquet, shall it be hazard?" Philip asked, retrieving his dice box with a sly smile.

"With you? God no!" George retorted. "Hang me if I didn't learn better than that a decade ago at the Rose of Normandy."

"The Rose at Marylebone?" Lord March looked his astonishment. "What cause would either of you have to frequent that den of blacklegs, thieves, and cutthroats?"

George replied, "It was different in those days, March. Quite a fashionable place, frequented by a higher class of sharpers. Wouldn't you say, Hastings? Although I thought you and your bloody dice box would ultimately prove the death of us both. Remember that bruiser Knight?"

Philip chuckled. "Those were adventurous days, were they not, George?"

"I'd rather say infamous, and I daresay your life was much safer when you joined the army than when you frequented the gaming hells."

Lord March looked to his companion. "Selwyn, you don't possibly mean to imply…"

"Uphill throws? Nothing of the sort. Indeed, 'twas proven more than once with a hammer, but I warn you, March, never to engage in dice with this man. He is a magician, a veritable bone-setter with the ivories."

Lord March was intrigued. "Is he indeed? Then I proposed instead a rubber of lansquenet. You know the game?" he asked Philip.

"That goes without saying for an officer in His Majesty's army."

March signaled a lackey for a new pack of cards to replace those he'd swept off the table to join the mounds scattered about the floor.

"Deal or punt?" March offered Philip the cut.

Philip cut high. "Deal," he said, taking the pack and proceeding to shuffle them.

"Indeed, one can do very well on credit," March continued. "By way of example, I have no fewer than three carriage makers and four cartwrights currently engineering a contraption for my upcoming wager with Taaffe and Sprowle."

"Are you still about that madness, March?" Selwyn asked.

"What madness is this?" Philip asked, laying down fifty guineas and hoping his careless manner belied the near-emptiness of his pockets. March and Selwyn matched his stakes, and he absently dealt the first two cards face-up to his immediate left.

"A bloody chariot race," said George. "As a fellow turf man, you'll doubtless find the fellow's scheme most diverting."

Philip thoughtfully dealt a third card, placing it in front of him. Finally the fourth, the *rejouissance* card, the queen of hearts, he placed in the middle of the table.

"I daresay Hastings has had his fill of racing wagers." Lord March's jibe hit home.

"Not at all, my lord," Philip replied coolly. "When one plays, one must expect eventually to pay."

Lord March regarded Philip speculatively. "I never begrudge a man who wins from me fairly."

"Then I remind you 'tis now past noon, and our friend Hastings is alive, hale, and in present company," said George.

Lord March carelessly unfolded a fifty-pound bank note from a wad of bills in his pocket and handed it to George, whilst continuing his narrative.

"The chariot wager was made some six months past when Count Taaffe, that damnable upstart Irishman, boasted of having the fastest chaise and four in the country. When challenged to prove the claim, he asserted he'd clocked them at twelve miles in an hour. 'Twelve miles?' says I. 'Why, I'll lay you a thousand guineas I can produce a chaise and team half again as fast.' Believing me out of my head, Taaffe readily accepted my wager."

Philip replied with a chuckle, "You *are* out of your head, March! Eighteen miles in an hour? An impossible feat. The fastest coach pulled by a team of six doesn't exceed ten miles per hour."

"Nevertheless, I fully expect to achieve the so-called impossible, and break every chariot record known to man."

"How?" Philip asked, his interest piqued.

March broke into a slow, sly smile. "The wager was accepted without setting any particular restrictions on the vehicle, only that the vehicle has four wheels and the ability to carry a man. Thus, I have designed one to meet only those minimal specifications."

Philip turned over the next card from the deck. Good. A five to match the first hand card. No winner, but now fives were out of play.

"And finally," March continued, "after six different vehicles, Wright of Long Acre has produced such a chariot. It meets every letter of the law and its total weight does not exceed two-and-a-half hundredweight."

"For a carriage? How is this possible?" Philip asked in genuine amazement while turning over the next card, and matching the queen at last.

"I see the devil's luck is still with you," Selwyn remarked, doleful at his lost couch stakes.

Philip hoped it was true. The stakes were now three hundred pounds, and the pot would grow exponentially with each successive rubber.

Lord March frowned at his loss, and then with a shrug waived for a new deck. A lackey immediately appeared. The cards were shuffled. Play continued.

"A carriage is quite an ambiguous thing, is it not?" March said. "Since the terms of the wager did not specify a body be fitted to the carriage, our passenger will be slung on leather straps between the two hind wheels. While uniting the back carriage to the fore in the usual manner, to reduce weight we used cords and springs, and the pole and bars are of thin wood reinforced with supporting wire.

"As to the harness, an optimal lightness was achieved by constructing the traces from silk and the breechings of whalebone."

"Silk and whalebone? Do you wish to harness your horses or to corset them?" Philip chuckled. "And you think to drive this deathtrap at eighteen miles per hour?"

"A ridiculous notion, Hastings! You think *I'd* take such a risk when I employ any number of competent grooms to drive the contraption?"

"Dare I ask how many have perished in the trials?"

"Why, none have suffered worse than a few broken limbs," March replied indignantly, but then confessed that he had lost half a dozen horses, explaining, "They were only second-rate runners. For the true trials I require nothing less than four plate winners."

Philip was astounded. "You would risk four plate-winning horses for a thousand guineas? Four horses of this caliber are worth twice your wager. Mayhap your mind is disordered after all."

Lord March answered heatedly, "It's the principle of the thing, Hastings! Besides, the odds are posted at four to one against me, which means I stand to gain a huge sum in secondary wagers, but the money has become inconsequential. Hell, I'm seven hundred pounds invested already and as like to treble that amount before all is said and done. But I'll see it through, by God."

"That would answer," Philip replied. "My hat is off to you, March. You are truly one calculating devil. But if you lose any more horses in the training runs, how do you propose to win?"

"I only need four to race, Hastings. I propose to retain a stable of *six* plate winners as a contingency. I'm saving the best of the lot for last, and won't set the date until I deem the equipage fit, and the horses fitter." March's lips curved up at the corners. "I race only to win."

"That is very fortunate, my lord, given your luck at cards." Philip smirked and revealed his match once again, declaring, "The bank wins."

"So you do," March replied in resignation.

"Where do you propose to make this run?" Philip asked.

"Once I acquire the horses I seek, we'll begin training at the Beacon Course, Newmarket."

"You still seek your runners?" Philip asked, a plan now taking root in this wager. "As it happens I retain a number of exceptional blood horses. Notwithstanding one lamentable loss, there are several that would admirably suit your purpose."

"Your racing stud is at Cheveley, is it not?"

"With all the advantages of being a stone's throw from the exercise heath. March," Philip asked, "might I propose a partnership? If you can truly produce such a vehicle, I will venture half the couch stakes and half the horseflesh."

Philip swept the pile of gold he had won into his purse and with a renewed gleam, mentally began the calculations. At four to one odds, he would see this novel racing chaise.

Forty

A Time to Reap

Philip's measures to raise some instant capital had borne fruit, even without resorting to dice. He left White's with the added confidence that he'd bolstered his good credit—premeditated measures that he knew would serve him in good stead. He had two thousand from the sale of the mares, and was now still heavier in the pocket.

"Where to, my lord?" the hackney jarvey asked.

"East End. Stepney," said Lord Hastings.

"Ain't that the Jews quarter?"

"I trust you've no objection?" Lord Hastings's imperious look silenced the driver.

The hackney set out across the new Westminster Bridge, through London proper, toward Whitechapel. Continuing on Whitechapel Road, they passed King John's Gate and the fourteenth-century St. Dunstan's Church.

The street vendors' cries, in peculiar dialects of mixed Spanish and Portuguese, told Philip they'd arrived in the East End, a thriving community of merchants and shopkeepers dating back to the

Commonwealth when Cromwell had allowed sanctuary to the Sephardic Jews seeking refuge from the Spanish and Portuguese Inquisitions.

The hired carriage pulled up under the portico of the largest home on the street. It was, however, a modest abode for one of the wealthiest men in England when compared to the grand mansions of Mayfair and Grosvenor Square.

When Philip presented his card to the answering footman, he was led with especial deference to the master of the house, who sat at his desk nearly buried behind a mountain of papers. The grizzled gentleman frowned over his spectacles at the interruption, but his expression warmed with recognition. He came from behind the desk to offer a perfunctory bow.

He extended his hand to indicate a chair. Mr. Gideon beckoned to the manservant. "Would you care for refreshment?" When Philip declined, Gideon impatiently waved the servant away and then asked, "To what do I owe the honor, my Lord Hastings?"

Philip knew this man well enough to deliver a straightforward explanation. "I find myself in some difficulty. There was no question of evading you, so I came directly."

Gideon nodded. "I had indeed heard of your... misfortune. And given my knowledge of your finances, I could not help speculating that you would be tempted to leave the country. I am happy to see it is not so."

"How is it you come to be so swiftly appraised of my circumstances?" Philip asked. "It is scarce two days."

"I employ many eyes and ears, my lord. A man in

my position must maintain a most diligent watch over his investments."

"I should have known as much. Your so-called eyes and ears were better informed than the king's own generals during the Pretender's late invasion."

"I shan't deny it, and my diligence saved the Banks of England from complete collapse. Have you heard the story of old Thomas Snow?"

Philip shook his head with a quizzical look.

"Ah. I must then relate to you this tale. You will find it much diverting. Mr. Snow, a principal of the bank on the Strand, had loaned to me twenty thousand pounds for an agreed term of three months, but shortly thereafter the Pretender advanced on Derby. Panic ensued in the city, and Snow, with all the spirit of an old woman, demanded immediate repayment.

"By this time, however, I'd already been apprised of the Pretender's lack of reinforcements, but since my colleague was so near to hysteria I withdrew twenty one thousand pound notes and used them to wrap a bottle of hartshorn for his nerves." The gentleman chuckled.

"And by all accounts, the near-run invasion paid you very handsomely."

"I don't deny it. When the Exchange nearly went to pieces and everyone sold, sold, sold, I liquefied everything I owned to buy, buy, buy. When the country recovered, I had quadrupled my investment. Not to mention the political capital earned from our ministers for preventing economic collapse."

"A government's appreciation can be a priceless return," said Philip.

"Nevertheless, I am still denied the full rights of

English citizenship. Though I become the richest man in England, as a Jew I may never own a title, a landed estate, nor may my son attend university," Gideon lamented.

"When a man passes from this earth, posterity does not remember the numbers in his bank account. A sad state of affairs." Gideon sighed. "But it is not *my* state of affairs which brings you here." He leaned back in his chair, steepling his fingers in a listening posture.

"Regrettably not," Philip said. "As you are already aware, Mr. Gideon, a grave error in judgment has put me at a considerable pass. I come to seek renegotiation of the loan."

"But the terms were more than fair, with the interest half a percent below the customary rate, as you assured me the funds would be used to restore your estates and to sow your fields. Instead, you've hazarded my investment on a horse race." His expression was grim. "I am deeply aggrieved by this breach of trust."

Philip colored. "I have no intention of defaulting on the loan. I simply need more time." He retrieved his purse and placed it on the desk with a heavy clink.

"What is this?" Gideon reached for the bag and raised it, as if weighing the gold.

"Two thousand toward the principal, and another two hundred in interest due. There will be more upon full dispersal of the racing stud." Philip regarded Gideon intently.

"But what of the remaining principal?" the bespectacled gent asked. "The balance is well past due." He spoke gently, but his black gaze was penetrating. "While I appreciate the show of good faith, you, my lord, have proven a poor risk indeed. You are much prone to thoughtless risk-taking, and now your prospects of ever coming into your inheritance seem to have evaporated as well."

"Given time, you'll be repaid in full. Until then, you have my bond that I'll continue the interest payments."

Samson Gideon pulled the loan agreement from his desk and pointed. "Your signature is your bond, is it not? Now it appears worthless as well, my Lord Hastings."

Philip winced. The observation was salt in the wound of painful truth.

"I count myself a reasonable man, but I have not the patience of Job," said the older man.

"My circumstances are no secret to you." Gideon already knew all—the wager, the elopement, his full disgrace. "I can only appeal for your continued leniency." Philip's thumb worried the ring on the little finger of his right hand as he spoke.

The nervous gesture having attracted Gideon's attention, he regarded Philip with a perplexed expression. "How curious is that ring. Might I see it?"

Philip pulled the band from his finger and handed it to Gideon, who pushed up his spectacles and turned it slowly between his fingers in an attempt to decipher the worn inscription.

"Where did you come by this?" His question was almost a demand.

"It is a maternal heirloom."

"Impossible!" Gideon exclaimed. "The inscription, '*Ani L'Dodi V'Dodi Li*,' it is Hebrew. You can't mean your mother was a Jew?"

"My mother was an Englishwoman from Middlesex,

raised in the Anglican church. *Her mother*, however, was a Jewess married to a Dutch merchant who followed William and Mary to England at the beginning of the century."

"Then you carry Jewish blood." The statement emerged more as an accusation.

Philip shrugged. "While I don't embrace my maternal heritage in the spiritual sense, I don't deny it either."

Gideon considered the irony. While he had not denied his faith by adopting Christianity in the interest of furthering his ambitions, he had ensured his children were raised Anglican. Nevertheless, their Jewish roots would ever be a social stigma. Gideon handed the ring back and tapped his steepled fingers to his lips, studying Philip in thoughtful silence.

"This places matters in quite another light. Perhaps there is another solution, one in which both of our difficulties might be resolved."

Philip regarded the man intently. "I don't follow you."

"I have a daughter who will soon come of age to marry. My Elizabeth is a sweet and demure girl, raised in the Christian faith in your own Anglican Church."

"What has this to do with me?" Philip asked, his disquiet mounting by the second.

"I propose that you might wed my daughter."

"That's unfeasible," Philip said, his heart racing.

"Not at all, my lord. The church would fully sanction the union."

Gideon rang a bell. When the servant appeared, Gideon said, "Tell my son I wish to see him." He smiled at Philip. "I beg your indulgence."

A preadolescent boy entered the study, removing his tricorne and making his obeisance to his father and their guest with obvious trepidation.

"A good Christian boy is my son Samson. You'll see," Gideon said to Philip and then addressed his son. "Samson, who made thee?"

The boy's gaze flitted from his father to the stranger.

"God?" he answered.

"Indeed." Gideon nodded in encouragement. "Now, Samson, who redeemed thee?"

"Jesus Christ," the boy responded with growing confidence.

Gideon nodded to Philip again, and turning to the boy to answer the remaining catechism, his mind went blank. The boy regarded his father and clutched his hat in nervous expectation. Frustrated with the elusive question, Gideon finally blurted, "Who... who... gave you that hat?"

With a broad smile, the boy responded by rote. "The Holy Ghost."

His father's face lit with paternal pride. "You are dismissed my son, and may go to the cook for a sweetmeat."

The grinning lad departed.

"You see, my lord? A good Christian boy. And the same is my Elizabeth. There is no impediment to a marriage."

Philip was astounded. "No impediment? Are you not aware that I am already wed?"

"But your wife, she has abandoned you in an act of adultery and desertion. Such actions justify divorce in both of our faiths. I know that you have already

moved for such a petition. Given my influence
with the Ministry and your rank as a peer, neither
Parliament nor the church should have any compunction in granting your request."

Remembering the similar coercion that had led
to his unhappy marriage to Charlotte, Philip's palms
grew damp and his heart raced. It was as if the trap
were beginning to close about him all over again.

"As I said, my lord, the arrangement solves both
of our troubles. My Elizabeth will attain a title and
entry into a society that otherwise would hold her in
disdain, and the connection can only help to advance
my son."

"There must be other men," Philip protested. "And
I am twice her age."

Gideon's look challenged. "Age is of no consequence. As to the second issue, while another of your
station might be pleased to take her dowry, I fear he
might also hold her in contempt. Given your own
heritage, I have no reason to believe you would do so.
We have time," Gideon continued. "Elizabeth is yet
tender in years. We may defer the marriage until her
eighteenth birthday. For now we need only agree to
the betrothal."

Philip had indeed intended to press for divorce and
finally make his life with the only woman he'd ever
loved, but backed into a corner as he was by his own
actions, he was finding it difficult to demur.

"Why should I consent to this?" he asked. "Are
you saying you intend to forgive my debt if I wed
your daughter?"

"But I am remiss!" Gideon slapped his forehead.

"Pray forgive an old man. Did I not state that my Elizabeth's dowry is fifty thousand pounds?"

Philip's breathing stilled. His chest constricted. And the trap snapped shut.

∽∾

With Gideon beaming in pleasure and already writing instructions to his solicitor, Philip departed. Blind to his surrounds and deaf to the street hawkers' jumble of tongues, he set out on foot with no particular direction or destination.

In less than seventy-two hours, he had successively lost a wager and a wife. His title and estate had unexpectedly come into dispute. Compounding this, he'd just acquired a new betrothed before he was even divorced. The staggering chain of events threatened to addle his wits.

His head pounded, a dull incessant throb. Suffocating inside, he tore at his cravat as if it were a hangman's noose, but found no relief. His steps quickened in an echoing staccato and his eyes bulged wildly like a madman, causing people to scatter from his path. He broke into a run, shoving through the pedestrians and crashing through the vendor stalls as if the devil himself were on his heels.

Oblivious to the dangers of the squalid alleyways overrun with scurrying rats and fetid with the refuse of chamber pots emptied from the windows above, Philip ran as if to escape his own life—the distress, disappointments, duplicity, and disenchantments.

His estrangement from a cold and calculating father. His mother's broken heart and lonely death. The petty deceptions and selfish desires that drove him to betray his best friend. The coerced marriage to Charlotte, who would forever despise him for it. Two unacknowledged bastard children by two different women. His reckless wagering.

The resentment and regrets of his life threatened to crush him, but far worse was his remorse for the pain he would cause Sukey, and the brutal penalty he feared he might suffer for it.

When his chest felt like exploding from the exertion of breathing, he staggered to the nearest building, clutching the cold hard stone edifice for support. At length he looked up to recognize the thirteenth-century chapel of ease at St. Mary Matfelon.

Dropping to his knees on the stone steps, he cried out, "Dear Christ! Must I pay for all my sins at once?"

Forty-One

SHATTERED DREAMS

PHILIP ARRIVED VERY LATE AND COMPLETELY DISHEVELED, his clothes splattered with refuse from the streets, his wig and cravat discarded. He had a look of wild desperation in his eyes that was at once unfamiliar and unsettling.

He had woken Sukey from her bed, reminding her of his other times of crises when he'd arrived on her doorstep soaked to the skin with a tavern wench in tow, and years after that when he had come to her in the middle of the night disconsolate and the worse for drink. Both times, he'd only had to confess his need for her and she'd capitulated.

This night was no different. His look of wretched desolation spoke to her heart louder than if he'd shouted. With a hopeless groan, he pulled her into a crushing embrace, kissing her hard, jarring her teeth, and bruising her lips. They didn't exchange any more words, nor did they undress. Overcome with frantic need, they fumbled only as necessary to join.

His lovemaking was almost painful in its fervency, but sensing his deep distress Sukey endeavored to meet him body and soul. They came together with a furious urgency she'd never known from him, culminating in swift and intense completion in which they both cried out and then collapsed, exhausted and replete, into each other's arms.

❧

It was hours past morning when Philip finally stirred to the sensation of warm lips brushing his brow. When he opened his eyes, Sukey regarded him with an expression that was at once tender and tranquil.

"You must be famished, my love," she said. "Would you prefer tea or shall I ring for chocolate?"

"Nothing, thank you." He sat up abruptly in bed and scrubbed his face to discharge the somnolence from his brain. He studied her silently, with a peculiar, almost wistful expression. "Sukey," he began tentatively, as if feeling his way, "there's a matter standing between us of which I must speak."

Her pulse quickened. "If it's about the divorce, I know these matters take time. I've waited this long…"

"It's not precisely that." He guiltily averted his gaze.

"If you fret over the expense, I have a small investment," she offered. "And if need be, I would gladly sell my jewels." She regarded him expectantly, but something in his manner disturbed her.

"Sukey," he groaned her name. "My loving, giving Sukey." He pulled her beneath him and showered her face with heated kisses. She responded in kind, grinding against his body, but rather than capitulating to the invitation he captured her arms and pulled them over her head. "Must you make it so hard for me? We must talk *now*, before I lose my resolve to speak of it at all."

An alarm sounded in her head, transforming her anticipation to trepidation. "What is it? Whatever bedevils you—tell me, Philip!"

"You already know of the lost wager, but that is not the half of my foul turn of fortune. Yesterday I met with a man to whom I am greatly indebted. Knowing I have no means by which to pay him, he proposed a solution that would put an end to my ramshackle existence." His voice took on a passionate urgency. "I could be completely absolved, Sukey, and able to begin again. I could finally live without this crushing weight incessantly hovering over me."

The grip of his hands tightened on her wrists. Her eyes grew wider as he brought the full force of his will to bear. "Do you understand me, Sukey?" It was not a question. It was a demand.

"You're hurting me, Philip," she whispered. "And no, I do not understand. What are you trying to say?"

"That I have indeed petitioned for divorce, and that lack of money will never again be a hindrance to me… that I am betrothed to marry an heiress."

She stared at him for a beat, dumbfounded. When she gained her voice, it was raspy with disbelief. "I can't possibly have heard you properly."

"My dearest love. You must understand, this changes absolutely nothing between us."

"You think to marry another and believe it changes nothing?" She gasped and jerked her arms from his grasp. "How can you even say it!" She raised her hands to his chest and shoved with all her might, freeing herself from under him.

"How is anything different?" he demanded.

Her voice quivered with fury. "How? I'll bloody well tell you how! Charlotte never wanted you and never slept in your bed! Do you mean to tell me you would marry again and fail to consummate? Are you going to tell your new bride that you will take her money but will not sire an heir upon her?"

"It is not the same thing, damn it! Yes, I would need to consummate the union but that is all! We do not even have to maintain the same household."

"You think for one moment her dear Papa, who holds your purse strings, would countenance your living with your mistress? You errant cad!" She pitched herself across the bed. Flailing at him with fists and feet, she pummeled and kicked until she forced him bodily to the floor with an unceremonious thud.

"Sukey, please try to be reasonable," he pleaded.

"Be reasonable, you say? You may go to the devil with your reason, Philip Drake, if you think to wed and father children with another woman!" Her voice was a choked sob. "I have stood by you more faithfully than the best of wives these six years. I broke every vow I'd ever made to myself to never enter into such an arrangement as this, and you treat me with such contempt?"

"Be fair!"

"Fair? In a six-month I'll be nothing more than your cast-off whore!"

"Never! How can you think such a thing?"

"How can you deny it? But if I am now to be officially relegated to such a position, I'd far lief it be for the favors of a prince than to be bound to a deceitful, impoverished imposter to an earldom."

Snatching up his discarded clothing and throwing it at him piece by piece, she cried, "Get out! Out of my bed! Out of my home! Out of my life!"

He flinched as her poisonous words worked their venom. "You would court Frederick's favor to spite me?" he asked, incredulous.

"Would it pain you if I did, Philip?" Fire blazed from her eyes.

"More than you can ever know." His voice was pitched low, his expression grave.

"If it would grieve you half as much as you've wounded me, so be it." Shaking with rage, she grasped the mantel for support.

"Do you think this is what I want?" he shouted. "You've got to know this isn't how I intended it to be. Thrice—thrice!—I have asked to you marry me, Sukey, and thrice you refused. Now, when I find myself in a pit of ruin and despair, you suddenly take it into you head to change your mind?

"Sometimes, my love, we just can't have what we *want* and must settle for what we need; and at present, I *need* money! Lots of money!"

She looked up at him, her chest heaving from the exertions of their exchange. They stared at one another in stony silence. She was first to look away, blinking back her welling tears. "I thought you *needed* me." She looked desolate.

"Sukey." He spoke her name as a plea, and for the briefest instant he thought she would falter. He was mistaken.

Grabbing a candlestick from the mantel, she punctuated the request with an impromptu projectile toward his head. "Now for the last time, get out!"

Philip dodged behind the door, agonized beyond description by the botch he had made of it all.

Forty-Two

A POUND OF FLESH

"AH, JUST THE MAN I SEEK," SAID LORD MARCH, UPON remarking George Selwyn's entrance to White's. The three gentlemen with whom he played scarcely glanced up from their cards when March rose and beckoned him to their table.

George bowed in greeting. March offered him a pinch of snuff, which he declined before flipping his coat skirts aside to sit down at the table.

"George, you've a long-standing acquaintance with the devil of whom I speak. I've a curious bit of information about our friend Hastings I wish you to confirm or refute."

"I almost dread asking. What has he done now?"

March laughed. "I only inquire of a matter concerning the Hastings title and estate. I hear the whole is in dispute before the Chancery Court."

Lord Weston froze in the process of retrieving a card for his next play.

Remarking the presence of Philip's former nemesis at the table, George replied evasively, "Did you indeed? I've heard not a word of it, though to be candid, I've not shared Hastings's confidence for a number of years."

Pinning George with a piercing stare, Weston retrieved his card.

Lord March continued nonchalantly, "I have a petition of my own with the courts and quite by happenstance overheard some discussion of the particulars regarding our friend's misfortune. It is claimed a mere infant, and a female at that, may be the true heir to Hastings's title and estates."

"Curious indeed," Selwyn said. "It is true Philip's elder brother sired a daughter before his untimely death."

"Then the child is a considerable heiress," March remarked.

"Why such avid interest, March?" George asked, "Are you considering a match with a babe in arms to add the Hastings earldom to your collection of cornets?"

Lord March pulled at his lip. "In truth, I hadn't considered it... until now. Just how old is the child?"

"Hang you, March! It was said in jest! The infant can't be more than six or seven."

"Delayed gratification with a wait of ten years, but then again, I am a patient man." March smirked.

"An unscrupulous, poxy blighter more like," Selwyn retorted.

"I take exception to the poxy remark," said March. "But we digress. I'd like to propose a wager regarding the outcome of the Hastings estate. Care to take me up on it?"

"What do you mean?" George asked.

"I would wager on whether Hastings retains his title

or if it will be conferred upon the child. 'Twill be a matter of great debate after he has held it these—what? Six years or more? Poor sod, had it only been seven, he might have met the statute of limitations."

"You would wager on the fate of a friend?" George was taken aback at the notion.

"Why not? It's not as if it will affect the outcome in any way. Besides, it's nothing personal. One should never let friendships interfere with a good wager." He addressed the gentlemen sitting at cards. "I'll lay any of you fifty guineas that in less than a twelvemonth the Chancery will decide in favor of the child. Do you take the bet, George?"

"Without all of the facts at hand, I'll have to defer the matter."

Lord Weston slowly laid down his card, quoting softly, "*La vengeance est un plat qui se mange froid.*" He raked in his winnings with a meaningful look at George Selwyn. "I'll accept your wager, March, and I'll lay three to one odds that Chancery settles the matter within a six-month."

"Preposterous!" exclaimed Beau Colyear, Earl of Portmore. "The Chancery takes years to settle any case. I'll double your odds, both of you!"

"Very well, then. We'll make of it a general wager." March summoned a lackey to his side, commanding, "Bring the betting book."

His words caught the attention of another nearby group at cards, one of whom, the self-styled Count Taafe asked, "What is this new wager, March? We're still awaiting the appearance of your mythical chaise."

The group rumbled with laughter.

"The match is imminent, gentlemen, an event that will live forever in the annals of history."

"So you say!" Taafe was openly cynical. "And now what is this new madness for which you call the betting book?"

"Have you not heard? The Earldom of Hastings is in dispute."

A white bewigged head jerked up from his cards. "What did you say?"

"Hastings's estate is in Chancery," another replied. "It appears there is question of the entail."

By the arrival of the betting book, nearly every member of White's Chocolate House had placed a wager of some sort upon the outcome.

Waiting until the moment Lord Weston rose to enter his wager in the book, George Selwyn remarked, "I wouldn't have any dealings with Weston if I were you, March, especially where Hastings is concerned."

"And why is that, dear boy?"

"Didn't you note the look in his eye? And I doubt his revenge quote was over the game." George lowered his voice for Lord March's ears alone. "Have you never wondered how Weston acquired that peculiar list to his walk?"

"A list? As to one side? Can't say I've ever remarked it."

"Assuredly, he lists slightly to the right, as if that side were somewhat heavier than the left." George smirked. "And don't you wonder why he keeps so many mistresses?"

"Some men like variety."

"And others, to hide their inability to perform, pay

a mistress *or three* to merely ornament their arm and eat sweetmeats."

"What are you saying, George?"

"I'm amazed you never heard of it. But then again, you were yet in Scotland when the whole affair transpired."

"Do tell. You've teased me long enough."

"Some time ago, the Marquess of Weston dueled with a young rogue named Philip Drake and was, let us say... relieved of half his manhood."

Instinctively, March crossed his legs. "*Vindicta.*"

"Indeed. He has every reason for seeking vengeance, though he himself instigated the duel," George replied.

"It matters not in the land from whence I hail. *Nemo Me Impune Lacessit* is the motto of Scotland."

George reddened. "I confess my Latin is not what it should be."

"'None shall injure me with impunity,' George."

"Then you would sanction Weston's lust for revenge?"

"We Scots, dear boy, are known as a bloodthirsty breed. If Weston seeks vindication for an old injury, who am I to judge?"

&

At least the Jew enters with the proper air of deference, thought the Marquess of Weston, seated behind a massive Makassar ebony-wood desk.

When the footman departed the financier glanced at the nearby chair, but the marquess studied him in an oppressive silence before waving his lily-white bejeweled hand. "You are my guest, Mr. Gideon. Pray relieve your burden."

Gideon propped his cane against the chair and sat, but tension, as much as his tightly laced stays, served to maintain his rigid posture. "I am honored to have been summoned, but how might I be of service to you, my Lord Weston?"

"Ah, you misapprehend, my good man. My purpose is only to serve you a good turn."

Gideon look baffled. "I don't understand, my lord."

"There are few secrets in London. Word has come to my ear that your daughter is to be betrothed to a pretender."

"A pretender?" Gideon looked surprised.

"Indeed, a certain scoundrel who presumes to impersonate his betters, one who fraudulently calls himself the Earl of Hastings."

"Assuredly you are misinformed, my lord," Gideon protested. "I have known the present earl for a dozen years or more, and his father before him. The man is no imposter."

"The courts will soon deem him so, Mr. Gideon, and it would sicken me to see an honest man, who only desires the betterment of his family, be taken in by a charlatan."

"Why is it I've heard none of this?"

"Because Philip Drake has held the title for six years, the Chancery has kept the matter quiet to save embarrassment to all involved parties. The result, however, is that the title is in question. I pray you've not wholly committed to this fraud?"

"No, my lord." Gideon retrieved a handkerchief to mop his brow. "It is but a preliminary agreement, as the matter of Lord Hastings's divorce must first be settled. I am much in your debt for providing this information."

"Ah! Debt. That is the second matter I wish to discuss with you, Gideon. I understand the gentleman in question owes you a considerable sum."

"Indeed, my lord. A loan of ten thousand pounds, made in good faith, is yet to be repaid in full. It is not my habit to discuss such private business, but given the circumstances..."

"I would like to buy this debt." Lord Weston said. "I'll pay you all that is owed plus an additional ten percent."

Gideon sat back. "That is exceedingly generous, my lord."

"I have two conditions."

Gideon regarded him intently.

"The first—you must pledge to speak of this meeting and our subsequent transaction to no one."

"As you say, my Lord Weston. And the second?"

"Under no circumstances are you to communicate with Philip Drake without my prior knowledge."

Gideon's thick brows drew together. He wondered about this havey-cavey business between Lords Weston and Hastings, but then again a premium of ten percent interest was enough to dismiss his misgivings. "Very well, my lord," he agreed.

The Marquess of Weston inclined his head with a thin-lipped smile and rang for his footman. "Then I deem our business concluded."

With this abrupt pronouncement, Samson Gideon realized he was dismissed.

❧

Under normal circumstances a peer of the realm would be immune from civil prosecution, but with the Hastings title in dispute, opportunity had presented its lovely head. The Marquess of Weston had waited years for such a chance, and here it had dropped into his very lap.

Having purchased the debt, he only needed to call in a favor from an old family friend, Philip Yorke, Lord High Chancellor Hardwicke, the head of the Court of Chancery. Lord Weston sat back in his chair with a self-satisfied smile.

"I will have my pound of flesh at last."

Forty-Three

PRISONER OF DEBT

FOLLOWING THE BLOW-UP WITH SUKEY, AND THINKING what a delusional dolt he'd been to believe she would agree to carry on as before, Philip sought the first public house to lose himself in a bottle. The more he drank, the more morose he became. Though he sought oblivion, even drink could not free his mind of her anguished look of disbelief when he'd told her what he'd agreed to.

Deep down he'd known she would never accept a second woman who would bear his name... as well as his children. He had only seen the easy way out. Blind to all but the fifty thousand pound mountain of gold, he had convinced himself that he could convince her.

Bloody stupid jackass!

Though he still stood on the brink of losing it all—money, property, title, honor, none of it mattered when faced with the prospect of losing her forever. He resolved to end his agreement with Gideon, if it meant sacrificing Sukey.

After suffering a miserable night at the George

and Vulture, Philip returned to Stepney, knowing he could face a breach of promise suit for his actions, but consequences be damned.

In finding Gideon away from home, he'd left a note with the footman giving his present direction as the George and Vulture where, summarily evicted by Sukey, he had once more taken rooms. He dispatched a second message to Jonathan's Coffee House, Samson Gideon's well-known domain on Exchange Alley, and then returned to his lodgings.

He spent the rest of the evening lost in a bottle and self-rebuke while he alternately meditated his options of returning to military service or starting anew in America. While he'd come to no conclusions on either head, he *was* determined to make amends with Sukey. He had wronged her, taken for granted what she'd so freely given, and he couldn't fathom a life without her.

Philip had no more than snuffed the candle and closed his eyes when the heavy clomp of boots sounded outside his chamber, followed rapidly by a fist striking thrice in succession.

"Bailiff of Westminster," shouted a voice through the door.

"What the devil do you want here?"

"We've a warrant for the arrest of one Philip Drake, alias Lord Hastings."

"Arrest? There's obviously some mistake."

"I've a writ signed by the Westminster Magistrate Fielding hisself. There be no mistake. Now open the door afore we knock it from the hinges," the bailiff commanded.

Philip threw the bolt free to face his arrestors. "This is beyond the pale! What are the charges?"

"That of insolvent debtor," spoke the bailiff.

"You are assuredly misguided. I'm a peer of the realm. Privilege of peerage exempts me from such charges. Unless I have committed a criminal act, you have no right to arrest me."

"Beg pardon, *your worship*, but you are the misguided one."

Philip swore under his breath. "The devil you say!"

"The Chancery Court has suspended *your privilege*, and thus your immunity from arrest, *my lord*."

"How is that possible? Who has ordered it so?"

"The king's own Lord High Chancellor Hardwicke. Unless you have the ear of his Majesty hisself, there be no higher power."

Philip protested. "As a peer, I am guaranteed precisely such an audience."

"Ah, back to that again, are we?" said the bailiff. "According to the high chancellor, you are no longer amongst that august company." He turned in mocking empathy to his deputy. "'Tis a pity to see such a great man brought low as us commoners, eh?"

Philip looked from one to the other with deliberation. "Even if you deny me the privilege of my station, you can be hanged if you'll deny my full rights as an Englishman. The due process of insolvency precludes arrest before trial."

"You are arrested upon *mesne process* with a writ for *capias ad respondendum*," the Latin term rolled awkwardly over the bailiff's tongue. "That is to say, you must 'ave crossed a man greater than yerself, as you are to be bodily detained until called before the King's Bench to answer the charges."

"What of bail?"

"Let's see." The bailiff scratched his head as he examined the legal document. "Ah, here it be—bail." He smirked. "If your lordship has about his person the sum of fifty thousand quid, we'd be most delighted to release you on bail."

Philip was stunned. "'Tis five times what I owe!'"

"It seems you be deemed a flight risk, my lord."

"Whose hand is behind all this?" Philip demanded.

"There be more than enough time for questions at the King's Bench," the bailiff replied. With full awareness of his position, panic began to set in. Philip's gaze flicked from one potential jailer to the other, his every nerve poised to act.

"Ah, come now, my lord. Don't make it harder on yerself." The larger of the two men looked to his deputy, who produced and rattled a set of iron manacles. "For a guinea each, we can agree to forgo the shackles, or do we go about this the hard way?"

Realizing the futility of flight, Philip asked, "How long do you intend to detain me?"

"Now that is the question yet to be answered, isn't it, guvn'r?" The bailiff chuckled.

❧

When Philip finally heard from his solicitor, Willoughby informed him that his case would be petitioned by one of the lower clerks of the King's Bench.

"But you are my family's solicitor," Philip pointed out.

"I am the trustee of the Hastings estate," Willoughby

corrected him. "I can no longer represent your personal interests as they are in direct conflict with those of the estate."

"You would leave me here to rot?" Philip asked in alarm.

"Certainly not, my l... sir." The lawyer amended the honorific, to Philip's added chagrin. "But the process will take time, and the complication of your case in the Chancery does not help."

"How long will I be caged in this shit-hole?"

"You are interned under the *mesne* process, without the means to make bail. It could be months before you are brought before the Court of Insolvent Debtors."

"But what of my petition in the Chancery? If my title is restored..."

"If the matter of the estate were to be decided in your favor, this eventuality would secure your immediate release, but I would not pin too much hope upon it. The girl's mother is pressing the claim most fervently on her daughter's behalf."

"The social-climbing Beatrix? Of course she would, and no doubt her elderly country squire has all the money required for the legion of attorneys to back her, while I sit helplessly by watching it all slip away."

"Thus it would appear." Willoughby made no attempt to dispute Philip's grim assessment.

"Then what is to become of me, Willoughby? How long am I to languish here?"

"It is difficult to say," the lawyer dissembled. "From time to time Parliament passes acts of amnesty for insolvent debtors. Perhaps when the prisons become too overcrowded..."

"How long?" Philip demanded. "Weeks? Months? Years? Give me a straight answer, damn it!"

Willoughby had the grace to look apologetic. "I'm sorry to say, but without the means to pay the debt in full you could well be sentenced for life."

❧

The King's Bench, on the east side of High Street, was the largest of the debtors' prisons, and the most commodious, by penitentiary standards. The exterior walls, over twenty feet high, were built to enclose a very large common area, and the upper galleries overlooked the back of St. George's Fields, at least for those inmates flush enough to afford a window.

The lower prison gallery was comprised of the chapel, the tap, and coffee rooms, the latter two farmed out by the warden at exorbitant rents, with their prices reflecting that very extortion allowed under the full protection of the law.

For those wretches with no other means of support than begging for alms, the prison provided an iron grating encompassing a full exterior wall on the street-side for the express purpose of entreating charity from the passers-by.

The common prisoners, those too poor to afford private accommodations, were allotted twenty-five-square-foot rooms, appointed with seven or eight sleeping racks, where the less-fortunate slept two or three to a bed. The rest of the floors, or galleries, were comprised of private quarters, housing as many as were able to pay for the privilege.

Philip was, at least for the present, among the

lucky ones. Although he had no means of paying the debt and legal fees to achieve his release, he did have sufficient coin to secure a modicum of comfort, relative to the prison. He had procured a private though flea-infested bed and was the sole occupant of a third-flight, windowless chamber.

The greasy, black-toothed turnkey, receiving him from the bailiff, had offered the comparative luxury of complete bed and board for the paltry sum of twelve shillings per night. Fifteen if he desired clean bed linens. *Sodding extortionist*, thought Philip. The same price could have secured him a set of rooms for a week at one of the better public houses in London, but after surveying the chamber and finding no evidence of rat droppings, he placed the silver in the turnkey's extended palm.

"I knew ye was a fine gent when I first seen ye," he said, pocketing the coins. "There be a number of quality what resides wifin these walls."

"Is there indeed?" Philip voiced his skepticism.

"Aye, and ye'll be taking yer supper in the taproom wi' the rest," the jailer informed him. "Is there nuffin aught you require, guvn'r?"

"Only my personal effects. You will see they are brought to me?"

The turnkey scratched his head, picked out a louse, and pinched it between his fingernails. "You mean wifout incident?" he asked, rubbing his thumb and fingers together.

Growing all too familiar with the routine, Philip pulled another shilling from his purse. The man pocketed the money with a wink. "I knew ye was no rum cull."

In the first week of his internment, aside from his solicitor Philip had received only one visitor. Though they'd gone their separate ways years ago, George Selwyn's unexpected appearance had proven him a true friend to the last.

"My apologies for the appalling state of my person, George, but to my utter dismay this institution, housing over one thousand people, has not a single bath."

"From what I've seen of the place, it's the least of your concerns," George remarked with a shudder. "Now tell me, how the deuce am I to get you out?"

"I can't begin to answer that question until I understand how I got here to begin with," Philip said.

"Hang it all! I hold myself to blame!"

Philip's eyes narrowed. "What do you mean, George? How can you possibly have had anything to do with it?"

"It all began over cards at White's when March, damn his eyes, brought to light your case in the Chancery."

Philip frowned. "I understood it was not to become public knowledge until decided."

"Nevertheless, March got wind of it and you know how these things go. Before I knew it he'd proposed a wager."

"A wager? Over the outcome?"

"Aye."

"A friend indeed," Philip remarked cynically, "I'd expect no better from March, but I still don't comprehend."

"Did I not say Weston was one at the tables?"

"Ah, Weston was it? Now your convoluted tale begins to make sense."

"Apparently, he's close to the lord high chancellor."

"And used his personal connections to prejudice the court against me, thus suspending my privilege. He must have then gone to Gideon. The rest, as they say, is infamy." Philip laughed mirthlessly.

"The buggering bastard!" George exclaimed. "But what can be done?"

"Nothing. Absolutely nothing until the Chancery makes its decision. It's my only hope of release. In the meantime, I can only endeavor to survive this interminable state of purgatory."

"Here, ol' chap, I had some luck at the tables last night. I've no need of it." George reached into his pocket, but Philip stayed him.

"I'm not reduced to charity yet. Though coin disappears here at an alarming rate, I've yet a few resources to keep me from starvation. I do need assistance with some other matters, Bosky, someone to act as my agent before the bailiff discovers and confiscates my personal effects and what little remains of the Hastings Stud."

"Go on," George said. "Of course you can count on me."

"Firstly, you recall the wager with March? I was to have provided half the stakes and half the horses. I need you to transact the business on my behalf. Roderick Random, Chance, Tawny, and Little Dan are the best prospects. Among the lot, Little Dan is the only one who's not won a plate race, but tell March not to discount him. He has tremendous bottom.

"After settling with March, I need you to disperse what other horseflesh you can, and then find me a decent attorney. Put on retainer someone you trust."

"Surely. Is that all, old friend?"

"No," Philip said at length. "There is one last boon I beg of you. I've some items in a box at the Bank on the Strand. One is of particular value. You'll no doubt recognize it."

"You wish me to sell it?"

"No, George. You must give it to Sukey. She should understand what it signifies."

Forty-Four

BLACKLEGS, RASCALS, AND ROGUES

PHILIP SPENT THE NEXT FORTNIGHT AT THE KING'S Bench in self-imposed solitude, ordering via the turnkey what little food or drink he could tolerate, and refusing most. On top of that, he hadn't slept. The solid stone corridors of the prison echoed with the slightest sound. The nights were the worst, with the squeals of scampering rats, the ring of raucous, drunken laughter, the sobs and moans of abject despair. The grunts and groans were of another sort altogether, as the women who were able plied their only available trade to anyone who could afford the fleeting pleasure.

Those who were able to make an honest living within the prison walls did their best just to keep body and soul together, while the jailers raked their profits from every shoe re-soled and every clean-shaven face. Those with no trade to barter simply wasted their days in idleness, drunkenness, and assorted vice.

When Philip first arrived, he was keenly aware that a gentleman in such finery as he wore would present a tempting target to the rogues and footpads inhabiting the walls of such a purlieu, but safely calculated the sword at his side would serve to discourage any would-be assailants. Now the sword was sold and the price it had brought nearly gone.

He would have been surprised to know the wild look he had acquired in his weeks of confinement proved a much greater deterrent to the prison denizens than if he'd carried his weapon. His form was lean and hard, three weeks on the prison food having etched away any ounce of fat. His hair, long and lank, partially concealed his hard, hooded gaze, set now in a face chiseled almost to gauntness.

Weary of his own company, he was nevertheless more wary of the common taproom. Though strong drink was prohibited, the place swam in illicit gin; and no gaming hell in London boasted more sharps, black-legs, and rogues than the King's Bench Debtors' Prison.

Adopting his swagger of old, Philip entered the tap and slapped tuppence onto the bar. "A tankard of your best."

"Ye be tuppence short," said a mountain of a man devoid of front teeth and sporting a cauliflower ear.

Once Philip matched the coins, the tapster poured from the keg a tankard full to the brim of a cloudy, dark, amber brew. "The best in the house," remarked the mountain, spitting on the floor and setting it before him.

"Is it indeed?" Philip remarked with a curious look. "I'd say it more resembles piss from a poxy whore."

"Have you a death wish?" asked a man in shabby soldier's garb, appearing at Philip's elbow.

"I didn't say from *his* poxy whore," Philip amended

as the tapster, laying both hands on the bar, cast his massive menacing shadow over him.

"Ned," the shabby soldier addressed the barkeep. "Pay no heed to me friend 'ere. 'E's a foul-tempered fiend when in drink but will cause you no further trouble."

"Ye best see 'e don't at that!" growled Ned.

"Now my fine friend," the shabby soldier turned back to Philip with a smile, "since the house brew is not up to your exacting standards, would you care to join me and my comrades in the back? I've procured a case of mediocre Madeira I'd be honored to share with a gentleman of your obvious discernment." His gazed skimmed Philip's soiled and rumpled but still aristocratic accoutrements.

"Would you indeed? And just who the devil might you be?"

"Captain James McAfee, at your service." He swept a low bow.

McAfee reminded Philip of none more than MacHeath the highwayman from Gay's *Beggar's Opera*. Still, with a reckless disregard of the danger, he followed the captain to the back of the taproom, where cards, dice, and drink abounded amongst the ragtag occupants. While those few with sufficient coin shared in the smuggled fortified wines, those without tippled illicit gin, often adulterated with turpentine or sulfuric acid.

After drinking, supping, and drinking a great deal more, those who'd not already passed out formed rough circles around the tables, producing cards and dice, the drug of diversion for despairing souls.

The captain cleared a table with a forceful stroke of his arm and retrieved a greasy pack of cards from his pocket. "What say you to some friendly play, your lordship?" As Philip had in no way disclosed his rank, the honorific was more mocking than deferential. "Losers pay the reckoning?"

They had emptied several bottles of Madeira, not to mention the food. Philip doubted he had sufficient money remaining to cover it all, but then again he'd never played to lose.

"A gentleman's game between gentlemen?" The captain now spoke with a clipped and precise enunciation of every syllable. "Shall it be whist, dear boy?" His creditable aping of Philip's more cultured tones revealed much about the true nature of the self-styled captain's background.

"If you like." Philip shrugged acquiescence.

With a narrowed gaze, McAfee scanned the tap for likely prospects to complete a quartet for whist. "Sir Archie will no doubt join us." He nodded to an emaciated man in an old-fashioned wig wearing the tattered dress of a country gentleman. "The old squire loves nothing more than a game of chance. Lost a vast estate to his passion fifteen year since.

"And over there," McAfee jerked his head to indicate a shabby young man, "Willie Wills, the linen-draper's son. Squandered his entire patrimony on the dice, though his heartbroken papa still religiously sends him five shillings every Sunday fortnight. Being 'tis only Tuesday, he should still be ripe for the plucking," he added with a callous lack of shame.

McAfee only had to begin shuffling for both of

these worthies to express interest. Within moments they were seated at the table and dealing out the cards.

Philip's hardened gaze flitted from face to face, wondering how long before his own would be stamped with such wretched resignation. He shuddered to think himself brought so low that he would even consider fleecing the helpless and hopeless inmates. No, his conscience couldn't allow it, at least not yet.

He resolved to play an honest game unless McAfee evidenced an inclination to cheat, but soon learned to his consternation that it was actually *he* who had been accounted a pigeon for the plucking. Philip almost laughed at what was a truly remarkable set-up.

The play, commencing in a fast and furious manner, would have confused anyone inexperienced with the game or who may have overindulged in drink. It was almost comical as the players, to a man, employed every device of a cheat: signaling, mucking, culling, pegging, and palming the cards.

Although Philip's first impression of McAfee as a sharper of the lowest order was not mistaken, he had failed to anticipate that the captain would play in confederation with the other two hapless and benign-looking individuals. Even his partner, Sir Archie, conspiring with their opponents, was throwing good cards after bad and intentionally losing every possible trick. He would receive a cut from the winners after the game. It was an old and unoriginal ploy, but now he'd discovered the ruse the question remained— precisely how was he to counter their tactics?

At any gentleman's establishment, the rules of

conduct were clear. Call the cheat and call him out, but this was the King's Bench, not White's Chocolate House. Here such actions would be thought laughable, or worse might merit one a knife in the back.

Deciding discretion the better part of valor, upon completion of the play Philip threw down his cards and pushed back his chair.

"Surely you don't quit so soon, when we might take our revenge in the next rubber," baited Sir Archie.

"My friends, you are the worst assortment of blacklegs, rascals, and rogues, the likes of which I've not encountered for a goodly number of years. The worst of it is you're not even very good at it!" Philip tossed his purse onto the table with a snort. "I commend you all for a most diverting evening... that shan't be repeated."

❧

Dangerously low on coin after this experience, Philip failed to break his fast. Famished by noon, he inquired of the turnkey if he might take the midday meal alone in his chamber.

"Here ye be," said the jailer, picking his teeth. "We have a joint of mutton, some boiled cabbage, a loaf of white bread, and a pint of porter, all for the meager sum of two shillings."

"Bloody highway robbery," Philip remarked under his breath.

The jailer smiled. "Tell you what, guvn'r, I'll give ye double or nuffin' on the dice."

Philip had already taken up the two-pronged fork and knife to attack the first meat he'd had in two days. He paused, fork to his lips. "Double or nothing, you say?"

"Aye, guvn'r. Call your main. Best of three casts."

"All right, I accept your wager, Mr…" He realized belatedly that he had yet to learn his jailer's name.

"Cox. Allred Cox." Having made his introduction, Cox pulled a shaky wooden chair over to the narrow table and pulled a dice box from his pocket. He handed it to Philip, who laid his eating utensils aside. With a half smile, he called seven and threw, rolling up a pair of twos.

"Six be my lucky number," said Mr. Cox and took up the dice for his cast, turning up a pair of threes. "Nicked on the first roll, b' Jesus!"

Philip's second roll, called again at seven, turned up crabs, while the turnkey nicked again with twelve. "There appears no need for me to throw again," Philip said. "Unless you'd care to double once more?"

Cox grinned, a broad black-toothed grimace. "Didn't know you was such a sporting cove." He offered Philip the dice.

"No, no. You may cast first," said Philip and took up his fork.

Having studied the number of pips turning up that singularly defied the odds, a pattern had emerged in Philip's brain. One more "lucky" cast from the turnkey would either confirm or refute his theory.

As suspected, Cox rolled his second combination of sixes in as many turns. As he reached to retrieve the dice, he was startled by the awful crunch of cartilage and bone as Philip impaled his two-pronged fork straight through his jailor's right hand, effectively nailing the offending appendage to the table.

The primal howl that ensued was said to have rung clear through every one of the four prison galleries.

"A thousand pardons, my good fellow, if there are *not* two sixes on each of your dice and a set of low rollers in your left hand."

Some seconds passed before Cox could regain enough sense to remove the fork. Cradling his crippled right hand to his breast, Cox removed his dingy cravat with his left and fumbled to wrap it around the bloody and mutilated member. "You'll pay dearly for this, ye soddin' whoreson."

Philip smiled a humorless smile. "Then the joke is surely on you, Mr. Cox, for my money is already gone."

Forty-Five

A Woman Scorned

"You have a caller, my lady. Mr. George Selwyn requesting to see you."

Sukey paused in her packing and looked up in surprise. "George Selwyn, you say?" If Philip had sent him as an emissary, he was surely wasting the gentleman's time. "You may show him in, Bess, but pray be clear I've little time for social calls."

The maid promptly returned with the announced caller.

"My Lady Messingham." George doffed his hat and sketched a bow.

"It has been some time, Mr. Selwyn."

"A pleasure I have forgone for far too long," he replied gallantly.

She arched a brow. "Flattery is assuredly wasted if you are come on Philip's account. It is over between us." She punctuated the sentence by slamming the lid of her trunk.

"You are undertaking a journey, my lady?"

"Not a journey but removing to Leicester House. I have decided to accept a position offered to me long ago. I am to be a Woman of the Bedchamber to the Princess Augusta."

"Is that so? Then you have not yet heard?"

"Heard what?"

"The Prince of Wales is dead, my lady."

She froze in disbelief. "Dead?" She shook her head in vehement denial. "Death, especially of a future king, is no jesting matter, Mr. Selwyn."

"Why do you think I would make this up?"

"You can't be in earnest?"

"Dead earnest." He couldn't help the pun. "It happened early yesterday, though it was kept quiet until the cause of death could be determined."

"But the prince is only in his forties and in excellent health. The last I heard he only suffered from a chest cold."

"The king's physician pronounced it a burst abscess in his lungs."

She stared at him for a moment, dumbstruck. "Dear God! It's true? He would have been king, you know."

"And now, mercifully, he won't," said George.

"You should not speak ill of the dead, Mr. Selwyn," she chided.

"I am not the first, nor shall I be last," he replied. "Indeed the body had barely cooled before this irreverent verse began to turn up in every London coffee house." He pulled the page from his pocket, quoting:

> "Here lies poor Fred who was alive
>   and is dead,
> Had it been his father I had much
>   rather,

Had it been his sister nobody would
  have missed her,
Had it been his brother, still better
  than another,
Had it been the whole generation,
  so much better for the nation,
But since it is Fred who was alive
  and is dead,
There is no more to be said!"

"How callous!" she cried.

"Our dear departed Frederick was far from being the most shining example of his line," George said.

"I daresay you are right about that," Sukey agreed. "But one must still show the proper respect. I must call upon the princess and offer my condolences."

"You still intend to accept the position?"

"I don't know," she replied thoughtfully. "The princess and her entire household will observe an extended period of mourning, and I have no desire to play the hypocrite. Perhaps I will leave London instead. I have a great deal to ponder at the moment."

George remarked the hollow ring to her words. "Then I must suppose it truly is over between you and Philip."

"I said it was. I gave him all I had to give. There is nothing left."

"They have taken him to the King's Bench, you know."

She started at that, completely betraying herself. "How is that possible? He's an earl, for goodness' sake! What crime other than treason could cast *an earl* into prison?"

"Why, the crime of insolvency, my lady," George replied. "To a nation built on trade there can be no greater injury than of that to its commerce. Ergo, there is no higher law in Britain than protecting creditors from those who refuse to pay their debts. It is sacrosanct."

"But he is an earl!"

"And our dear friend Lord Weston perceived an opportunity to settle an old score." He eyed her intently, reminding her at once that she, herself, was the original cause of it. "The marquess has pulled some strings at the Court of Chancery, thereby suspending Philip's title and associated privileges."

"That is unconscionable!"

"Not surprising conduct from a worm like Weston, to kick a man who is already down."

"Yet, how can this be? Philip made a very *accommodating* arrangement to settle his accounts with the Jew."

"The unfortunate arrangement you speak of was based entirely upon Philip's rank and station, which is now under dispute. Moreover, it appears increasingly likely the Chancery will decide in favor of Edmund's daughter."

Once more she started. "So soon? I thought these questions took years to settle."

"One does wonder at the workings of justice," Selwyn said noncommittally. "But this unhappy turn of events has placed Philip in a most precarious position."

"I don't care, Mr. Selwyn. Philip Drake made his bed and he may now rot in it."

"If that is your wish, it may well be granted, but as his friend I cannot share your sentiments. Even if he could pay off the original debt, the attorney's fees, bailiff's fees, and other so-called 'taxed costs' will compound to double or treble the amount he owed. He is indeed in a hopeless position. This all brings me to my real point in coming here."

"If you have more to say, get on with it," she answered peevishly.

"I have come for any personal effects of his that might be sold for his maintenance. I can't bear the thought of him begging alms at passers-by through the iron grate of the Fleet."

"I thought you said he was at the King's Bench?"

"Indeed, but 'tis all the same, isn't it? Disgusting, filthy places, habited by the wretched, ragged, and half-starved, deprived of life, liberty, and any means of livelihood to repay the debts that interned them."

"Surely it is not so bad for *him*," she insisted.

"Not while he has any coin to buy food, bed, and coal, but his means are limited. Once all is depleted..." George gave a fatal shrug.

"What do you mean to do?" she asked, her urgency showing despite herself.

"There's not a damned thing I can do to release him, but I mean to sell what can be sold so at least the chap doesn't starve. Indeed, I've instructions to meet Lord March in Newmarket on a matter of some horses. I nigh forgot quite another charge I promised to perform on his behalf, against my better judgment I might add."

George retrieved an elongated, velvet-covered box from an inside coat pocket. He opened it slowly, revealing the almost blinding brilliance of diamonds. The necklace was still magnificent, and the shimmer of refracted light from the central pear-shaped stone, breathtaking. "Perhaps you recognize it?"

She gasped. "It can't be the one! It isn't real!"

"I assure you it is," said George.

"How did you come by this?"

"I was given a key to his safe deposit box containing certain items with instructions on how to dispose of each. Although the necklace might have kept him in comfort in that hellish place for years, he insisted I give it to you."

"I believed he had sold it years ago."

"So had I. I am certain he once intended to pay off your debts with it, but you took that matter into your own hands, if I remember. Even after that it seems he could never bring himself to part with it—the maudlin fool!"

"Why? Why would he have kept it all these years?" she asked in a voice choked with emotion.

"I believe he had hoped it might one day have been your bridal gift."

"No! I don't believe you!" she cried. "He never intended any such thing!"

"Did he not? Then pray reason for me why the man would have locked away such an item, if not solely out of a mawkish sentimentality?" George asked.

She stared at him in silence, clutching the necklace to her breast.

At times, a jolting revelation overtakes one in a crushing, incapacitating wave, and at others, it unsettles one in steady, subtle stages. It was in this manner, piece by wretched piece, in measured moments of increasing comprehension, that Sukey slowly came undone.

Forty-Six

CLAPPED IN IRONS

THE SO-CALLED CRYPT COMPARED TO NOTHING BETTER than its namesake, a place for interment of the dead. It was dark, dank, and fetid, redolent of offal. Its location, adjoining the dunghill where the bodily waste of hundreds of inmates was daily discarded, sent Philip retching toward the single tiny window where he gasped futilely for fresh air.

The room was no larger than five feet square and nine feet high, built of brick on all sides. A man of Philip's dimensions would be hard-pressed to lie down, but the irons applied to both his arms and legs already inhibited any posture more recumbent than squatting.

This was the price he paid for invoking the turnkey's wrath: beaten and now shackled. Philip had already known his tolerable treatment, dependent on money, would end when the money ran out, but by his actions he had hastened the inevitable.

He didn't know how long he'd already languished in the hellish crypt. His throat was so parched that swallowing was nigh impossible. He was weakened from lack of food and near delirium from want of sleep, but the crypt was infested with rats.

Squeaking, scurrying, stinking rats that only chain rattling and wakeful diligence kept at bay, but now he'd grown weak and his eyes heavy. So very, very heavy.

When Philip closed his eyes and dropped to his knees, he wondered vaguely if he would ever wake back up.

&

"Where is he? Damn your eyes!" a familiar voice demanded. "I'm a Member of Parliament, I'll have you know. I'll bring down an investigation the likes of which you've not seen since Oglethorpe's Fleet Committee!"

Philip awoke sputtering to a splash of foul water in his face.

"So you're not dead after all!" George grinned. "Get those infernal irons off him!" he shouted to the jailer.

"How commanding you sound, Bosky. Didn't know you had it in you." Philip's voice was a barely audible rasp. With the clink of the key releasing the irons, he fell to his hands and knees.

"Thank God I got here when I did, ol' chap. You are the image of impending death."

"Precisely how I feel," Philip croaked.

"Don't just stand there! Carry the man!" With George Selwyn taking command of the field, Philip was conveyed to a spacious, almost opulently appointed room on the fourth gallery. "Brought a few creature comforts," George explained, "but hang me if I'll let you infest the mattress with vermin."

Philip was shocked at his image in the pier glass.

"Here, old friend." George handed him a tankard of small beer that Philip gulped so desperately it ran down his face.

"Bring a barber and water for the hip bath," George instructed his newly recruited minions, while tossing shillings right and left. "We'll have to burn the clothes, of course," he said to Philip. "And shave your head as well as your face."

"I wouldn't care if you dragged me naked through the streets. But who is paying for all of this?"

George laughed. "Why, you are, of course!"

"Pox on you, George! How do you think I got into that pit to begin with?"

"Assault with a deadly fork is what I heard." He sobered at Philip's obvious distress. "You've had a considerable windfall, my friend."

"Dog's bollocks!" Philip exclaimed.

"No, dear boy. Roderick Random."

Philip looked his question.

"Remember my commission to take March to the Hastings stables? Well, you couldn't expect a man to buy a horse without seein' him run, could you? We took Roddy boy out to Newmarket, where Devonshire proposed a two hundred guinea match to trial a new runner of his, a chestnut colt got by Snip. When Roddy prevailed, March offered four hundred to buy him, and is considering Chance as well. Plans to make them his wheelers in his chaise match."

"George, advise March he would be best to place Roddy and Tawny as the leaders. Neither likes running behind the pack, and they are well

matched. Roddy would do well to regulate the speed
of the team as he won't quickly outrun himself as
others might. Tell March if he has not yet decided
on his wheelers that he might do well to consider
Little Dan."

"I will convey your recommendations. March is
well pleased with the progress of the cartwright and
anticipates setting the date very soon. And now you,
my boy, are three hundred guineas the richer."

"Three? I thought it was four hundred?"

"What, you think I took a cut?" George asked in
an injured tone. "Spent the first fifty to get a decent
Chancery lawyer on retainer and you can look about
you for the rest."

Philip looked contrite. "A thousand apologies. Not
quite myself, you know."

Ever amiable, George replied with forced cheer,
"Don't fret, my friend. We'll see this thing through yet."

"Is there any news from the Chancery?"

"I fear not, but no news is good news. At least
while the Chancery deliberates, there is hope."

While a favorable decision could assure his release,
Willoughby had called it an unlikely eventuality.
Payment of the debt in full was impossible, and
negotiation of terms unfeasible with Weston bent on
vengeance. If only he had means to raise the money.

He lived in daily torment knowing that one
hundred thousand pounds had once been within his
grasp. If only he had played out his life differently.
Perhaps if he had dealt differently with Charlotte? But
then again, he might have lost Sukey. *Sukey*. God,
how he missed her.

"And Sukey, George? You've not spoken of her. Did you give her the necklace?"

"I did."

"Did she say anything?" Philip prompted. "Is there any message? Is there any hope?"

George opened his palms in a helpless gesture.

"There's something you're not telling me. What is it? What did she say?" he demanded.

"She said it was over, that she had nothing left to give you."

"After you gave her the necklace?" Philip regarded him with a look of astonishment. He had tried to make amends with her in the only way he knew how. He was sure the necklace would have conveyed to her all he'd always meant to say, but now he feared it was too little, too late.

Philip flung himself into a chair with a helpless groan. Her silence meant she was lost to him, and without her he feared *he was lost* as well.

Forty-Seven

FRIENDS IN HIGH PLACES

LADY MESSINGHAM NEVER MADE IT TO LEICESTER House. Instead she thoughtfully composed a most humble and diffident letter to the princess, regretfully declining the position and expressing her heartfelt condolences for the prince's passing.

Although shadows clung to her eyes, she couldn't sleep. In helpless agitation, she tossed and turned, overcome by restless nerves. She barely ate, her appetite having waned to nothing between bouts of nausea.

While Philip's actions had injured her to the very quick, she still couldn't bear the thought of his imprisonment for what was only the thoughtless act of a man in desperate straits.

If only he could have had access to the trust, none of this would have happened. If only there was a way… But no heir, no trust. It always came back to what she could never give him—the heir, a legitimate male heir.

In her wistfulness, she could almost feel spasms in her empty womb. She unconsciously laid her hand upon her abdomen, only to be struck by the unthinkable. How long had it been since her last courses? Three months? More?

Given her age, she had paid little heed to the recent unpredictability of her cycle, but now she considered the undeniable signs; the tenderness and recent swelling of her breasts, the cramping in her lower belly, the lethargy and frequent bouts of vomiting. No. She must be deluding herself to think such a thing of a woman of forty.

Nevertheless, though her brain denied the possibility her heart secretly harbored hope, and as the days passed that hope sprouted and bloomed into conviction. Now, with much more to consider than just her injured pride, she deliberated her next move.

If only she was more knowledgeable of legal proceedings or had connections with the higher courts, but most of Nigel's former cronies had long passed on. She racked her brain for anyone in either the judicial or political spheres who might look upon her with a modicum of favor, anyone she might enlist to help Philip. One such name came to mind.

Taking to her desk, she feverishly wrote, grasping desperately at that solitary straw.

❧

The slender gentleman with arresting blue eyes entered her salon with an elegant bow. When she extended her hand, he raised it, kissing the air inches above her fingers. "My lady, I am truly your humble and obedient servant."

"Mr. Pitt," she said with her most disarming smile, "I cannot express my gratitude. I thought you might not remember me, given the brevity of our erstwhile acquaintance."

"On the contrary." He smiled. "You are a woman not easily forgotten. As I recall, it was only your timely and tactful intervention that saved a certain political dinner years ago. It's not often one meets a stateswoman of your caliber, let alone such a handsome one."

She laughed with true delight. "You are too kind, and soon to be disillusioned regarding my virtues. You will think me bold and importunate when you hear my purpose."

"Will I indeed?" he asked. "Perhaps you should let me be the judge?"

"Then pray take a dish of Hyson with me?" She rang for the tea cart, and then gestured for him to sit beside her on the settle.

"I confess I was mystified by your entreaty after all this time."

She appealed to him with a modestly averted gaze. "I find myself in rather dire straits, sir. And as a woman, I have few resources to call upon at such a time."

"Yet you thought of me? I am charmed to have entered your thoughts at all, but this begs another question altogether, if you will pardon my impertinence. Are you not under another gentleman's... protection?"

"I was," she answered vaguely. "Do you recall Philip, Lord Hastings?"

"Only remotely. Am I to presume he is...?"

"He was much more than that, sir." She turned her head with a sniff.

Mr. Pitt produced his handkerchief. "But no

more? Is this the source of your distress?" He looked perplexed. "Is the gentleman disobliging to you?"

"Not at all, sir. It is actually on his behalf that I act."

"He has not proven worthy of you, and no man is worth your tears," he said quietly.

She looked up into the vibrant blue of his gaze, taken aback at what she suddenly perceived. "Whatever do you mean, Mr. Pitt?"

"You may think me rash, but I am a politician, dear madam. In my vocation, a man must recognize and grasp advantage whenever it presents."

Her eyes grew wider with every word.

"I made mention of our first meeting, Lady Messingham, one in which you made an impression I have never forgotten. While at that time I was in no position to think of anything beyond my career, many things since have changed. I am now a man of three-and-forty, and an established politician. I maintain a seat in the House of Commons, the appointment of Paymaster-General, as well a position on the king's Privy Council. I have reasonable expectation of further promotion within the Ministry. As to my pecuniary state, you may have heard of a certain bequest from the late Duchess of Marlborough?"

"Indeed, sir. It is said she so admired your actions for the opposition in Parliament that she left you a considerable fortune."

"Ten thousand pounds, madam. Though it may have been as much an act of animadversion against Minister Walpole as approbation for me. Nevertheless, the gift has ensured my ability to provide reasonable comfort and security."

Her delicate brows drew together. "Why do you tell me this?"

He reached for her hand. "You and I are no longer young and naïve, but have both tasted the fruits of the world—the bitter and the sweet. As I stated, perceiving opportunity in plain sight, I am moved to act."

She snatched her hand away, the color high in her cheeks. "I have been one man's mistress. I do not seek another such post."

"My dear, dear lady! You assuredly misapprehend my purpose. I am proposing a partnership of like minds and abilities. I am asking that you consider my suit to become my wife."

Stunned by his declaration, she opened and closed her mouth soundlessly. When she replied her voice was a breathless whisper. "Mr. Pitt, you know so little of me…"

"What I do know sufficiently compelled me to speak."

"Then there is something I must tell you, something that will surely make you wish you had not declared yourself." She averted her face. "I believe I am carrying his child."

Silence stretched awkwardly between them.

"Does he know this?" he asked.

"No."

"Does anyone?"

"Not yet. I have not been certain myself and have not dared confess it aloud until this very moment."

"He will not wed you?" Mr. Pitt asked.

"He cannot. He is both imprisoned and still legally bound to another. So you see my predicament? If he is not freed in both events, I will be forced to pay the consequences, shunned from polite society with my bastard child."

Mr. Pitt once more offered his handkerchief, and this time she accepted.

"'Tis the reason I wrote you, sir, to enlist your aid. You have influence with the very men who could make his release possible. He has committed no crime. Privilege should have protected him from this wretched indignity! I humbly entreat you to exert your powers of persuasion to secure his freedom."

He knelt by her side as she dabbed her eyes. "My lady, your distress wounds me, but you may be over-estimating my power of persuasion."

"Am I?" She looked up plaintively. "Somehow I doubt that, Mr. Pitt."

Their gazes locked for a brief, intense moment.

"Nevertheless, I have offered an alternative I pray you will consider."

Her reply was arrested by the arrival of the footman with the tea cart.

"I shan't tarry any longer," Pitt said.

Her features crumpled when Pitt rose briskly to his feet. Realizing her mistaken impression, he quickly amended, "I depart in haste as I am moved to request a meeting with Lord Chancellor Hardwicke."

A tremulous smile broke over her face. "I don't know how I can ever thank you."

He took her hand once more in his, speaking earnestly. "As a man, you would have made a formidable politician... but as a woman, *you could yet be* a matchless mate for one."

Forty-Eight

MARCH'S MADNESS

King's Bench Debtors' Prison

"THEY INDEED WENT THE FULL NINETEEN MILES?" Philip asked.

"I never would have believed it had I not been a witness!" George replied. "I tell you, thousands turned out, lining the course in a frenzy, to see history made."

"One would expect so, given how long it took him to get around to it," Philip remarked.

"Ten months," said George. "According to March, six months just to engineer the contraption and another four spent in trials and training. It was like no driving vehicle you've ever seen, but more like a great long-legged spider on wheels."

When unveiled, March's racing chaise was indeed remarked upon as an object of singular fascination and universal awe.

"The strangest contraption I ever saw," George confessed. "Little more than an undercarriage, and the driver perched on nothing more substantial than a leather sling covered in velvet."

"He said it would be light as a feather when he finished with it," Philip said.

"They even installed oil tins in the wheel boxes to continuously lubricate the axle tree to prevent it taking fire."

"I can see how friction might be a concern, considering no vehicle has ever achieved a velocity nearing nineteen miles in an hour."

George continued his tale, "When I arrived at Newmarket they were mapping out the course with stakes and cord. They began at the Six-mile House, via the Warren and past the Rubbing House, and continued through the Devil's Ditch. In all, a four-mile loop. They had to run it three times and return back to the start, to get the total distance."

"So he did it? And under an hour's time?"

"In fifty-three minutes twenty-seven seconds!"

"The devil you say!"

"'Pon my word, Drake! But he never could have done it without Roderick Random, and he was infernally lucky to have had your Little Dan waiting in the wings. Thirty minutes prior to start, March's head groom appears in a state of agitation. 'My Lord March,' he says. 'There be sommat amiss w' Peeper. 'E come up sudden lame this morning.'

"'Hang you!' says March. 'Why wasn't I advised sooner? Get me another horse!' March then asks which ones are ready to run. The groom says Jack Slack and Little Dan were both ready to harness. Recalling what you've said of the horse, I suggested Little Dan."

"An intrepid little fellow with endless bottom," Philip said.

"Precisely what I conveyed to March, who commanded Little Dan be harnessed as the off-wheeler, and telling the groom to 'look smart about it!' Tugging a forelock, the groom dashes off to the rubbing house.

"At precisely seven o'clock comes Mr. Tuting, the 'course clearer,' fabulously well-mounted and garbed in crimson velvet like some self-proclaimed king of the turf. The chaise followed, pulled by the most impressive parade of racehorses in harness you've ever seen."

"I've never seen *any* racehorses in harness before."

"Beside the point!" George said. "The lot of 'em were jockeyed by postillions in matching blue satin waistcoats, buckskin breeches, white silk stockings, and black velvet caps."

"Blue and white? The Hastings racing colors, a nice touch," Philip remarked.

"The team was escorted on either side by the head grooms, but the horses were nervous. Jostling one another and pulling in their traces, they set the flimsy chaise to shake and rattle, and the odds to shift in one more last-minute wagering frenzy.

"With their ears pricked and nostrils flared in antici-pation, they danced and jigged their way to the start, while the three umpires calibrated their watches and positioned themselves along the course. The umpires looked up at March, who gives the nod.

"The flag dropped, and the horses bolted! Taking off at a frenzied pace, the whole herd of 'em tore over the track, wild-eyed and wide-open, as if chased by some equine-savaging monster! As the postillions fought for control, the contraption followed on their frantic heels, bucking and swaying with its passenger holding on for dear life. The wheels veered on and off the course, smashing stakes and hitting ruts along the way.

"March was pacing to and fro, cursing like a sailor and shouting to the grooms. 'Get hold of them, damn you! Before the bloody thing is rent to pieces!'

"Taafe calls out a new wager of one hundred guineas that the chaise won't make the first four miles, while Lord Portmore counters at two hundred that the horses will become entangled in their harness well before hand.

"I'd placed a hundred pounds on March and stayed the course with trepidation, while others continued to lay odds against his success. Miraculously, the chaise survived the first circuit fully intact, and by the second loop the horses were well in hand, with the vehicle traveling brisk and smooth behind. March consults his timepiece and declares the first four miles in less than nine minutes!

"After the first runaway miles, the pace slackened but March's racing vehicle indeed accomplished the impossible, upsetting the odds to win with six minutes thirty-three seconds to spare! They say two hundred thousand pounds exchanged hands on that wager, Drake!"

"Incredible, Bosky," Philip remarked. "Damn it all to hell that I couldn't have seen it."

"If it's any consolation, you came away with two thousand pounds! Surely more than enough to grease every palm needed to move your case along in the Chancery Court."

"So again, I sit and wait."

"I fear it's all you can do."

"But what of Sukey, George? You have not spoken of her. Have you seen her?"

"She is well enough," George answered evasively.

"Then you *have* seen her," Philip pressed.

"Aye," George sighed.

"And?"

"'Tis the very last thing you'll want to hear."

"What is it?" Philip demanded.

"I suppose you'd rather it come from me than from the infernal broadsheets." He took a breath, adding in a rush, "There's talk she entertains a marriage proposal."

"What! To whom? Who the blazes would be my rival? Tell me, George!"

"The Right Honorable William Pitt."

"That wooden windbag? She can't love him!"

"I'm sorry, old friend, but women are a fickle and faithless lot." George's attempt to soften the blow only further fed the flames of rage. Philip slammed his fist on the table. When that act failed to sufficiently vent his spleen, he upturned and smashed it against the stone wall.

"Damn her. And damn me to bloody hell!"

Forty-Nine

A DESPERATE DILEMMA

Ranelagh Pleasure Gardens, Chelsea

LADY MESSINGHAM WAS AWE-INSPIRED UPON ENTERING the Rotunda, the jewel of Ranelagh Pleasure Gardens. Hundreds of crystal chandeliers blazed with thousands of lights amidst the melodic echoes of a full orchestra, the brilliance and charm of which brought to mind an enchanted castle. So nearly overwhelmed by its magnificence was she that she didn't at first remark the gentleman's approach.

"It has the same effect upon me whenever I come here," said Mr. Pitt, offering his arm.

"It takes one's breath away."

"You should see it in the evening, my lady. I'd love nothing more than to show you its splendor."

"This is quite a public venue for our meeting," she remarked to his chuckle.

"You fear tongues will wag? I confess I am guilty for designing it so. I will resort to almost any means to sway you in my favor, even gossip."

"A shameless confession, Mr. Pitt! But it is after all only tea."

A liveried footman escorted them to one of the private boxes far above the orchestra. She gazed down into the pit and closed her eyes to the melodious strains of strings, harpsichord, and oboe in a Handel concerto. "Heavenly." She sighed and opened her eyes to find Pitt gazing at her. Discomfited, she looked away.

"You have something to tell me, sir?"

"Not so much to tell as to give to you, my dear lady."

He was briefly interrupted by the arrival of the footman with an enormously laden tea tray. A miniature of the Rotunda evoked in sugar provided the backdrop for the sumptuous selection of fresh and sugared fruits, trifle, lemon-cheese tarts, sponge cake, walnut cake, chocolate roll, pound cake, tea cakes, jams, jellies, creams, and various cheeses. It was an array of gastronomic delicacies to tempt even the most fickle palate.

After pouring their tea and taking a delicate bite of sponge cake, she dabbed her mouth with the fine linen and prompted, "You said you wanted to give me something?"

"Ah, my heart," he cried in mock dismay. "I confess to the selfish hope that I might have extended the fleeting pleasure of your company before tending to our business, but I would not prolong your unease to save my life." He reached into the deep pockets of his coat and retrieved two scrolled documents.

"The first of these is a writ signed and sealed by the Lord High Chancellor. As you may guess, some manner of compromise was required. Without tiring you with tedious details, the Chancery has restored all rights and privileges according to his station."

"Then the court decided in his favor?"

"Not quite, my lady. As I said, *compromise was required*. The courtesy title Viscount Uxeter is to be bestowed upon Philip Drake, thus restoring his privilege. The true title and entail, however, is to be conferred upon the minor child, Anna Sophia Drake, sole surviving issue of Edmund Drake. The child will become Countess of Hastings in her own right upon her twenty-first year. In the interim, she will be under her uncle's guardianship, who will also maintain control of her estate." He handed her the document.

She gaped at it in astonishment. "You said his privilege is restored. You mean he is free?"

"He should be released by the morrow."

"And the other document? What is that?"

"A judgment from the Court of Common Law that may be used to pursue a petition of divorce with the Ecclesiastical Court. As to the Act of Parliament, if the church grants the divorce *mensa et thoro* and you still wish to marry, I pledge my full support of the divorce *vinculo matromonii*."

"I can't believe you have done this for him."

His earnest gaze arrested her. "No, my lady. I have done this *for you*." He took her hand. "Are you certain this is the path you desire?"

"You refer to our prior conversation?"

"I do."

"But you know I don't love you. I've given my heart to another."

"Love, my dear, is irrelevant in a political marriage. I seek an equal partner. Affection would grow in time."

"And I need time to consider. But pray know this,

Mr. Pitt—whatever my decision, I'll ever hold you in
the very highest esteem."

❧

Lady Messingham entered the nave of Westminster
Abbey with a deep curtsey before kissing the
Bishop's ring. "My Lord Bishop, thank you for
granting my audience."

"'Tis a welcome distraction, my child," he replied.
"But we have met before, have we not?"

"It has been more than twenty years. I am
astounded by your memory, your Excellency. My
father, The Very Reverend Thomas Barnage, was the
rural Dean of Wiltshire."

"I knew him well, an excellent man and a credit to
the cloth."

"He always felt his calling was to shepherd his
beloved Wiltshire flock."

"Just as mine has been to restore this sacred House
of God," the bishop said.

Refusing promotion to the second-highest ecclesiastical position in the land, Bishop Wilcocks had
instead followed his passion to restore the dilapidated
Westminster Abbey. With over two decades spent on
his labor of love, the western face of the thirteenth-
century church was finally complete, its new towers
and windows remarked upon as objects of consummate beauty.

"Are you familiar with our abbey?" he asked.

"No, Your Excellency," she replied. "Although I
have long admired its beauty, I confess I have never
been inside its walls."

"Then pray walk with me, child, and I will show her to you."

"Her?"

"Of course. The word of God calls the church the bride of Christ, and if she is this bride, I have spent twenty years of my life on the bridal clothes!" He chuckled.

The frail octogenarian gallantly offered his arm, proudly describing the history and architecture of the breathtaking structure and singling out various *objets d'art* along their stroll within the church walls.

"It has consumed me, the restoration of this place. It has been my heart's desire to see it completed before my death, but it now appears a never-ending travail."

"I thought you were finished when the west towers were completed last year."

"So thought I, but now several rafters in the cloister are in such a state of decay as to threaten a portion of the roof. Moreover, our funds are depleted. There is no more money without an appeal to Parliament, which could take months. But enough of my troubles." The bishop sighed. "What moves you to seek out such an old clergyman?"

"I am in need of counsel," she said.

"Go on," he encouraged.

"I must beg your leave to speak plainly."

He gave a paternal nod.

She lowered her gaze. "I am with child and the father belongs to another."

"Adultery is a sin, my child." He spoke without judgment, stating the cold fact.

"While I do not deny my sin, Your Excellency, it is

not quite as you think. The man of whom I speak was never truly wed. That is, the marriage was performed in a highly irregular fashion. The bride was coerced by her guardian, and no license was procured."

"But was it sanctioned by the church?"

"It was a Fleet wedding."

"I see." The bishop frowned. "Although the church does not sanction such unions, the Common Law does recognize them."

"But there is more. The wife has now deserted her husband."

"Mayhap I should ask if you understand the lengthy process, and *the only way* by which by this man would ever be free to marry you."

"I do. A petition for divorce must be preceded by a civil suit for criminal conversation and a judgment awarded before any petition can be made to the Ecclesiastical Courts."

"But these requests are seldom granted," he said. The church is rightfully reluctant to sever what God hath joined, and even when granted it is little more than a legal separation. A private Act of Parliament is required to completely sever the marital bonds. Should you persist on this road, there is no guarantee of the outcome you wish. Have you sought God's guidance in the matter, child?"

"I have, and my time runs short."

They had arrived at the brass gates opening to Henry VII's Lady Chapel at the far eastern end of the abbey. When they entered the chapel, Sukey was struck by the colorful banners and heraldic arms displayed along all of the walls.

"This chapel was built to honor the Virgin Mary, and the ceiling is a work of art in itself," the bishop said with pride. "It is one of the loveliest known examples of a pendant fan vault ceiling. Do you love this man, the true father of your child?" he asked.

"Against my better judgment, I have loved him since the moment we met."

"Love is not often the basis of marriage, although it is unquestionably the strongest," he said. "I wed only once in my life, and it was indeed for love, but I lost my dear Jane twenty-six years ago. I could never think of loving another as I loved her, thus I gave the remainder of my heart to the abbey."

"You did love her deeply," she said in sympathy. A long moment of quiet ensued. "He has hurt me… deeply," she said, "but I also could never pledge my heart to another."

"Then, my dear, you must let that still, small voice be your guide."

"If I am to go with my heart, Your Excellency, I must beg your support. I have need of your influence, and you have a roof in need of repair. Perhaps there we might help one another?"

"Sadly, my dear, *that* would require a great deal of money."

She wondered which *that* he referred to—the influence or the roof. Nevertheless, she opened her cloak to finger the diamonds glittering about her throat. "What if I had in mind to make a gift to the abbey, a charitable donation, enough to fully replace the rafters?"

He regarded her for a long thoughtful moment before breaking into a conspiratorial smile. "Then, my dear," he patted her hand, "if it is truly as you say, that the union was never solemnized by the church nor consummated in the marriage bed, mayhap this process in the Ecclesiastical Court could be expedited after all."

Fifty

REDEEMED BY LOVE

SHE HAD WAITED IN RESTLESS AGITATION ALL THE DAY, one moment willing him to come to her, and the next fearing the very thing she wished. The last few hours she had tried to occupy herself with needlework, but had only managed to stain the cloth with drops of blood from every time she pricked her fingers.

When at last she glanced up from her embroidery, she thought she had conjured him, so startled was she to find his specter bracing the doorway. He was leaner than she'd ever seen him, his bones more prominent in his gaunt face, but his eyes were as dark and piercing as ever. She didn't know how long he'd stood there, watching her in stony silence.

He pushed himself from the door jamb and moved with slow purpose toward her. "Six months! Six months, Sukey," he said at last, "and not a single word from you?" His voice was low and hoarse with emotion.

Her hands shook as she brought the thread to her mouth, cutting it with her teeth. "It was over between us. There was no point." When she looked up into his afflicted stare, it required a herculean effort to regulate her breathing.

"You say it's over?" Three more strides and he was towering over her. "I don't believe you! Just as I don't believe you intend to marry Pitt."

"Why would you think I entertained such a thing?" she asked. Refusing to meet his gaze, she slowly and deliberately placed the needle in her box and laid down her hoop. When she looked up again, he accosted her with an accusing look.

"You deny you've kept his company?"

"I don't deny anything, but it's not what you think," she said quietly, willing herself to modulate her tone.

"I know you've been seen in his company. There's talk all over London. What the devil am I to think? But I won't have it, by God!" he thundered. "I won't let him have you!" His eyes were wild and his breathing ragged. He grasped her shoulders in a painful grip and jerked her to her feet.

When she thought he would haul her into an impassioned embrace, he froze. Philip's breath hitched and his fingers bit cruelly into her flesh. His expression grew blacker by the second as his burning stare traveled the length of her and back, finally coming to rest on her swollen belly.

What her voluminous skirts had concealed from him while she sat was suddenly and manifestly revealed.

The flame in his eyes went dead. He released her so abruptly she had to catch the chair arm to prevent falling.

When he looked to her again, his ardent display might never have happened, so blank was his expression.

"I now understand." His lips formed a bitter grimace. "Perhaps you should wed him, after all."

Shoving away from the chair, Sukey faced him squarely, quivering with righteous indignation. "You think I've played you false, Philip? Well, think again! You… you… great ass!" She beat against his chest, forcing him backward across the room, as she fiercely, intrepidly berated his lack of faith.

"There is no denying you are with child!" he accused.

"Thus you think me some faithless jade?" she asked, smoldering with fury.

"How else do you explain this!" he cried. "It's been six months since we were together!"

"Indeed six months! So take a good look at me, Philip, and work the sums, for I'm big as a house!" With breasts heaving as much from emotional as physical exertion, she awaited his reaction.

He opened his mouth again and then closed it again. When full comprehension dawned, it left him stunned and gaping.

When his voice finally came, it was little more than a hoarse whisper. "My God, Sukey! You can't mean to say—"

"Indeed I do mean to say! I'm nearly nine months heavy with *your child*."

His face lost all trace of color. "How? How can it be possible after all these years?"

She was rewarded by a display of utter shock as myriad conflicting emotions washed over his face, each in turn matching those inside her—confusion, fear, joy, anguish, befuddlement, and finally longing.

"I can only count it a blessed whim of Providence,"

she answered with a half smile. "Now, the question remains, what do *you* intend to do about it?" She regarded him intently, willing herself to remain calm and passive.

"Why didn't you tell me?" he asked with a look of desolation. "Didn't you think I had a right to know of this?"

"What good would it have done?" she asked, and looked away.

"It doesn't matter. I still had a right to know!"

"Perhaps that's true, but you were imprisoned and had enough on your shoulders without the added burden of worry. Thus, I chose to wait."

"When did you plan to tell me?"

"Now."

"But what if I had not been released?"

"Who do you think secured it?"

"You?" He was once more completely taken aback.

"With the aid of Mr. Pitt."

"Pitt?" Philip scowled.

"Hence all the talk."

"Once more—what is between you and Pitt, Sukey?"

"I needed help to free you, and he was there for me. He offered his aid and his friendship."

"There was nothing more?"

"No. I have no feelings for William Pitt, though he would no doubt have me."

"While you carry another man's bastard?" Philip was at first incredulous and then incensed.

"If I were to wed before this child's birth, there would be no bastardy, and any scandal would be very short-lived."

"So you *did* think to wed him? Is that what you want?"

Her gaze slid away from him in an evasive answer. "Do you think I wish to raise your bastard alone?"

"Damn it all! Do you really think I would do that to you? Leave you alone and unprotected?"

"Didn't you do just that?"

"Good God, Sukey!" He threw his hands in the air. "You think I would have chosen to leave you like this?"

"I don't know, Philip, but I have more than just myself to think of now. I won't raise a fatherless child."

"But what kind of father would I make? I have nothing to offer. I might be free again, but I am no better off than I was before. *I have nothing*, while he could offer you everything. Security, comfort, and eminent respectability." He added the last with a mirthless laugh.

"Yes, Philip, he could." She looked quickly away, but not before he caught the tremor of her lips.

He was upon her again in an instant, pulling her against him and searching her gaze. "Tell me, Sukey," he rasped. "Tell me what you want!"

"How can you be such a fool!" she cried. "I want what I've always wanted. I want *you*. Even after all this, heaven help me, I still do. But even now, you don't ask me!"

He pulled at his hair with a groan. "But how can I ask you and a child to live hand to mouth? I have lost my title. I have a fortune in trust that I can neither access nor borrow against. I have no lands, no home, and I am heavily indebted. I am nothing!" he shouted in anguish and then took her face roughly in his hands. "Look at me, Sukey. What do you see?"

She regarded him for a long, searching moment. "What I've always seen. The man I love."

"Do you think to live on air?"

"You still don't understand? None of the rest matters! Not the title, the trust, or the trappings! I'm going to have *your child*!" Her eyes glistened and she finished in a whisper. "That's all I ever really wanted. I still have a home and my widow's jointure. It's sufficient."

"And what kind of man would that make me?" he asked with a pained look. "One who lives off a woman's bounty?"

"Curse your damnable pride, Philip Drake! You will manage as you always have. You are strong, intelligent, capable, and *infinitely resourceful*. I could never doubt you. Why must you still doubt yourself?" she asked tenderly.

"Sukey, my dearest Sukey," he murmured her name helplessly. "I'm so unworthy of you. I've made such a mess of my life and have so very many regrets. I sought what I thought would yield happiness, but instead found emptiness. Only *you* have been my consolation, my only salvation. You were my only hope all the while in the King's Bench, and when I thought I'd lost you, I thought I'd lost my very life."

With this raw confession, he wrapped his arms around her trembling body, burying his face in her hair. Tears streamed down her face as he continued in a whisper.

"I told you years ago that you could be free of me whenever you choose, but I lied. *I can never let you go.* I know I don't deserve you, Sukey, but God only knows how much I need you. How much I love you."

He held her close for a long moment and then his fingers brushed her face and gently outlined her lips before meeting her in a tender kiss. He kissed along her jaw and her neck, his hands tracing her sides until moving up to cup and caress her swollen breasts with the most reverent touch.

His expression was awe-filled when he lowered his hands to her protruding belly. Slowly, gently, filled with fascination, he moved over her rounded form, exploring the contours of it, then dropping to his knees and locking her in a protective embrace. With a look of wonderment, he laid his cheek against her side. He closed his eyes, listening intently, his expression rapt with growing appreciation of the life inside her.

They held one another thus for long minutes before he looked up at her with glistening eyes and a convulsive swallow. When he spoke again his voice was hoarse with emotion, as if his words emanated from the very depths of his soul.

"You know I don't profess to be the best of men... but if you will take me... flawed as I am... I pledge my very life to cherish and protect you and this child, Sukey. Our child. You know I can't offer much more than that, but my heart and soul are yours. As they have always been. Only yours."

These words, so long in coming, played at her heartstrings and stirred her passion to life, breaking over her like a wave, cracking and disintegrating her reserve.

"Yes, Philip. Yes. I will have you," she cried and collapsed into his arms.

He held her to him, clutching her close, and when Philip kissed her again, it stole her breath away.

She was still amazed at the effect he had on her after twelve tumultuous years.

Epilogue

"*Ani L'Dodi V'Dodi Li*"
"I am my beloved's and my beloved is mine."

—Song of Songs

FROM *THE LONDON TATTLER*:

Philip Ian Drake, Viscount Uxeter, and Susannah Henrietta, Lady Messingham, were quietly wed in a private ceremony in the Lady's Chapel, Westminster Abbey, 12 November, A.D. 1751.

The sacrament was performed by Lord Bishop Wilcocks, Dean of Westminster.

The happy couple were delivered of twins within the fortnight.

∞

London, April 1752

Reclining on a divan, Sukey watched Philip cradling their infant son and daughter in each of his arms, her pulse quickening with his open and unaffected display of tenderness.

"My lady." George Selwyn entered, bowing to the viscountess. He then turned to Philip—"My lord"—and wrinkled a disapproving brow at Philip, Lord Uxeter's completely unabashed picture of domesticity. "At the risk of interfering with your nursemaid's duties, I am come to drag you off to Parliament. We are, after all, debating several important legislative acts today."

"Indeed?" Sukey asked.

"The first is Lord Uxeter's proposed Jewish Naturalization Bill to permit Jews the full benefit of citizenship without forswearing their religion. The second, nearer and dearer to my own heart, is the Murder Act."

"The Murder Act?" She looked bemused. "Don't we already have laws against that particular crime?"

Philip cast George a warning look that his friend shrugged off.

"Let us say it proposes a punishment more befitting the crime," George remarked with nonchalance.

Philip added, "It might have been better named *An Act to Decrease the Incidences of Grave Robbery in the Interest of Advancing Medical Science*, or even more aptly *George Selwyn's Act to Contribute to Vile and Base Public Entertainments*."

George laughed. "Rather a mouthful, but I'll keep it in mind."

Diverting the subject, Sukey asked Philip, "How long will you be gone, my love?"

"No longer than absolutely necessary." Philip reluctantly handed the children off to their respective nursemaids. "But after the session in Parliament, I am needed to meet with the estate factor on some matters of import pertaining to Hastings Park."

"Does that mean you'll be going to Sussex as well?"

"I hope not, my sweet, but if matters require my direct attention, *we* will repair to Sussex, nurses, baggage train and all. Actually," he considered, "I have had a mind to take you there eventually. Do you think you are up to the journey?"

"To your family estate?" She sat up eagerly. "I would love to see it."

"I would have been embarrassed to have taken you even six months ago, but great gains have been made in its restoration."

"Philip, have you ever considered raising our children away from town?"

He looked surprised. "You've never said anything of it."

"You've never asked." She smiled. "I was country-bred. I think it much healthier for a child. Don't you?"

"I confess to a pleasant enough childhood in Sussex while my mother lived. It would not be out of the question for us to take up residence there, if that is something you desire. The properties are all in my hands until Sophie comes of age."

"Philip, speaking of the child, you once implied that Sophie was not, in truth, Edmund's daughter…"

He frowned, scrambling for an answer that would appease without being a complete lie.

"My dearest, I was desperately grasping at straws when the subject arose, but I assure you there is no question of her bloodline. She is the rightful heir to the Hastings estate."

"What a burden for a little girl. She will assuredly be a target for fortune hunters when she comes of age. I truly wouldn't wish it on our own daughter, but at least she has you as her uncle to look after her interests."

"Indeed," Philip said. "It will be as if she were my own. Fatherhood has done much to bring out my protective instincts."

"You are the best of fathers, Philip," Sukey replied, eyes filled with love. "And the best of men. As I always knew you would be."

He leaned down to kiss her, and then murmured, with a fleeting glance to the recently re-hung portrait of his father, "Who but you, my dearest, would ever have thought so."

Bibliography

Besant, Walter. *South London*. London: Chatto & Windus, 1899. Print.

Boulton, William. *The Amusements of Old London*. London: John C. Nimmo, MDCCCI. Print.

"Captain John Godfrey: Eyewitness to Boxing History." *Boxing News and Views*. Web. 14 Dec. 2010. www.eastsideboxing.com/news.php?p=4924&more=1.

"Chronological Tables of Private Acts." *Office of Public Sector Information*. Web. 14 Dec. 2010. http.opsi.gov.uk/chron-tables/private/index.

"Court of Chancery." *Wikipedia, the Free Encyclopedia*. Web. 14 Dec. 2010. en.wikipedia.org/wiki/Court_of_Chancery.

"Duels with the Sword." *Classical Fencing: the Martial Art of Incurable Romantics*. Web. 14 Dec. 2010. www.classicalfencing.com/articles/DuelswiththeSword.php.

"Fencing Terminology." *Dragon Lords Domain*. Web. 14 Dec. 2010. www.dyasdesigns.com/roleplay/fencing.html.

"Gambling." *Gay History and Literature: Essays by Rictor Norton*. Web. 14 Dec. 2010. rictornorton.co.uk/grubstreet/gaming.htm.

Godfrey, John. *A Treatise upon the Useful Science of Defense*. London, 1747. Print.

Green, J. H. *An Exposure of the Arts and Miseries of Gambling*. Philadelphia: G. B. Zieber, 1847. Print.

"Hellfire Club." *Gothic Labyrinth*. Web. 14 Dec. 2010. omni.sytes.net/Monks.htm.

"Hellfire Club." *Wikipedia, the Free Encyclopedia*. Web. 14 Dec. 2010. en.wikipedia.org/wiki/Hellfire_Club.

Hoyle, Edmond. *Hoyle's Games: Containing the Rules for Playing Fashionable Games, with Copious Directions for Boaston… [et al]*. Philadelphia: Henry F. Anners, 1859. Print.

"James Figg & Jack Broughton—History of English Combat." *English Combat Is an English Fighting System for Self Defence & Competition*. Web. 14 Dec. 2010. english-combat.co.uk/figg.htm.

Jarman, Thomas, and J. C. Perkins. *A Treatise on Wills*. Boston: C.C. Little & J. Brown, 1849. Print.

Jesse, J. Heneage. *London: Its Celebrated Characters and Remarkable Places*. London: Richard Bentley, 1871. Web. 14 Dec. 2010. www.brynmawr.edu/library/speccoll/guides/london/history.shtml.

Jesse, John Heneage. *George Selwyn and His Contemporaries; with Memoirs and Notes*. New York: Scribner & Welford, 1882. Print.

The Linacre School of Defence. Web. 14 Dec. 2010.
www.sirwilliamhope.org/.

"List of Acts of the Parliament of Great Britain,
1740–1759." *Wikipedia, the Free Encyclopedia*.
Web. 14 Dec. 2010. en.wikipedia.org/wiki/
List_of_Acts_of_the_Parliament_of_Great_
Britain,_1740–1759#1750_.2824_Geo._II.29.

Lush, Robert. *The Act for the Abolition of Arrest on
Mesne Process, &c. (1 & 2 Vic. C. 110.)* London: C.
Reader; [etc., Et.], 1838. Print.

Maskelyne, John N. *Sharps and Flats: A Complete
Revelation of the Secrets of Cheating*. New York:
Longmans, Green and Co., 1894. Print.

May, Thomas Erskine, Reginald F. D. Palgrave,
Alfred Bonham Carter, William Edward Grey, and
Thomas Lonsdale Webster. *A Treatise on the Law,
Proceedings, and Usage of Parliament*. London: W.
Clowes and Sons, Limited, 1906. Print.

Mowbray, T. J. *Debtor's Manual*. London: Printed for
the Author, by E. Beckley, and Sold by J. Eedes;
Richardson; Chappel; and by All sellers in Town
and Country, 1825. Print.

"Office-Holders: Household of Princess Augusta
1736-72 | Institute of Historical Research." *Institute
of Historical Research | The National Centre for
History*. Web. 14 Dec. 2010. www.history.ac.uk/
publications/office/augusta.

O'Hara, Barratt. *From Figg to Johnson*. Chicago, IL:
Blossom Book Bourse, 1909. Print.

The Order of the Seven Hearts. Web. 14 Dec. 2010. www.salvatorfabris.com/Home.shtml.

"Pugilism–Georgian Index." *Georgian Index—Alphabetical Site Map.* Web. 14 Dec. 2010. www.georgianindex. net/Sport/Boxing/boxing.html.

Riley, Henry Thomas. *A Dictionary of Latin and Greek Quotations, Proverbs, Maxims and Mottos.* London: G. Bell, 1895. Print.

Robert-Houdin, Jean Eugène. *Card-Sharpers:Their Tricks Exposed.* London: Blackett, 1891. Print.

Roberts, Randy. "18th Century Boxing." *Journal of Sport History* 4.3 (1977). Print.

Robertson, John R. *Old Q: A Memoir of William Douglas Fourth Duke of Queensberry.* London: Samson Low, Marston and Co., 1895. *Internet Archive: Digital Library of Free Books, Movies, Music & Wayback Machine.* Web. 14 Dec. 2010.

Roscoe, E.S. *George Selwyn: His Letters and His Life.* London: T. Fisher Unwin, 1899. Print.

Rouge et Noir Henry Vizetelly. *The Gambling World: Anecdotic Memories and Stories of Personal Experience in the Temples of Hazard and Speculation…* New York: Dodd, Mead, 1898. Print.

Seymour, Richard. *The Compleat Gamester In Three Parts.* London: J. Hodges at the Looking Glass, 1754. Print.

Steinmetz, Andrew. *The Gaming Table: Its Votaries and Victims,: in All times and Countries, Especially in England and in France. In Two Volumes.* London: Tinsley Brothers, 1870. Print.

Sydney, William Connor. *England and the English in the 18th Century.* Vol. I. New York: Macmillan, 1892. Print.

"Tom King's Coffee House." *Wikipedia, the Free Encyclopedia.* Web. 14 Dec. 2010. en.wikipedia.org/wiki/Tom_King's_Coffee_House.

Thurston, Milo. "Compleat Sword-Man—Sir William Hope." *Association for Renaissance Martial Arts.* Web. 14 Dec. 2010. www.thearma.org/essays/hope.htm.

"War of Jenkins' Ear (1739–1742)." *War and Game.* Web. 14 Dec. 2010. warandgame.com/2008/02/17/war-of-jenkins'-ear-1739–1742/.

Wilson, John Lyde. *The Code of Honor, Or, Rules for the Government of Principals and Seconds in Duelling.* Charleston, SC: J. Phinney, 1858. Print.

Wroth, Warwick. *London Pleasure Gardens of the Eighteenth Century.* New York: Macmillan and Co., 1896. Web. 14 Dec. 2010.

Wycherley, William. *Drama Classics: The Country Wife.* London: Nick Hern, 2001. Print.

Acknowledgments

I would like to extend my heartfelt gratitude to the following individuals for their ongoing encouragement and support:

To Deb Werksman at Sourcebooks for your continued support and faith in *Fortune's Son,* based on only the first few chapters.

To my agent, Kelly Mortimer, my cheerleader and Rock of Gibraltar.

To Jill G., for your ongoing encouragement and help in critiquing this manuscript.

To my sons, Sean and Brandon, who actually read and enjoy my work!

To all the gang at Scott & White in Temple, Texas, for your friendship, support, and for putting up with me every day during this ten-month labor of love.

To Danielle, Shawna, Lacey, and Diana of the Austin Area Romantics Book Club for opening your arms and taking me into your fold.

And a very special thank you to Dr. Milo Thurston (http.sirwilliamhope.org) for helping me out of a pickle by sharing your invaluable expertise in the methodology of eighteenth-century swordplay.

About the Author

Combining meticulously researched historical settings and love of a great romantic tale, Emery Lee fictionally explores the Georgian era in her distinctly period voice.

She is a member of Romance Writers of America, Georgia Romance Writers, and The Historical Novel Society. Married with two children, she currently resides in northeast Georgia.

authoremerylee.com
emerylee.wordpress.com

New York Times and USA Today Bestseller

THE HEIR
GRACE BURROWES

AN EARL WHO CAN'T BE BRIBED...

Gayle Windham, Earl of Westhaven, is the first legitimate son and heir to the Duke of Moreland. To escape his father's inexorable pressure to marry, he decides to spend the summer at his townhouse in London, where he finds himself intrigued by the secretive ways of his beautiful housekeeper...

A LADY WHO CAN'T BE PROTECTED...

Anna Seaton is a beautiful, talented, educated woman, which is why it is so puzzling to Gayle Windham that she works as his housekeeper.

As the two draw closer and begin to lose their hearts to each other, Anna's secrets threaten to bring the earl's orderly life crashing down—and he doesn't know how he's going to protect her from the fallout...

A *PUBLISHERS WEEKLY* BEST BOOK OF THE YEAR

"A luminous and graceful erotic Regency...a captivating love story that will have readers eagerly awaiting the planned sequels."

— *Publishers Weekly* (starred review)

THE
MISTRESS' HOUSE

LEIGH MICHAELS

"A work of art... Deliciously decadent
from start to finish." — *Seriously Reviewed*

"Deft storytelling, abundant humor...and tenderness
in all the right places" — *Linda Banche Romance Author*

The rules are made to be broken...

When the handsome, rakish Earl of Hawthorne buys the
charming house across the back garden from his town home,
he never expects the lovely lady he installs there to ensnare him
completely...

Again...

After Lady Keighley marries the earl, it seems a shame to
leave the house empty, so she offers it to her childhood friend
Felicity Mercer, who discovers the earl's gorgeous cousin...

and again...

Finally, feisty Georgiana Baxter moves into the house to
escape an arranged marriage and encounters the earl's friend
Major Julian Hampton late one night in the back garden. The
handsome soldier is more than willing to give her the lessons
she asks for...

Plenty of gossip, scandal, and torrid speculations surround the
"mistress' house," but behind closed doors, passions blaze...

NEVER A BRIDE

BY AMELIA GREY

HER NAME IS ON EVERYONE'S LIPS...

When he left for America six years ago, the handsome Viscount Camden Brackley never suspected that he would return home to England to find his lovely fiancée embroiled in the scandal of the decade. The woman he planned on making his wife has been kissing every man in London...except him!

BUT SCANDAL DOESN'T MATTER IN SEARCH OF THE TRUTH...

Engaged and then abandoned, Lady Mirabella Wittingham is determined to find the man who drove her cousin to suicide, even if it means ruining her reputation and disgracing herself in the process...

When her plans go awry, Mirabella has no choice but to turn to her long-lost fiancé for help. But can she trust the man who deserted her so many years ago, or is he destined to fail her yet again?

"Witty dialogue and clever schemes... Grey's vivid characters will charm readers." —Booklist

"Readers will be quickly drawn in by the lively pace, the appealing protagonists, and the sexual chemistry that almost visibly shimmers between them in this charming, light-hearted, and well-done Regency." —Library Journal